PRAISE FOR

Bared to You

"Full of emotional angst, scorching love scenes, and a compelling story line."
                                                                    —*Dear Author*

"I love the writing, the sexual tension, and the intricate dance the characters do as they get together."
                                —Carly Phillips, *New York Times* bestselling author

"So hot it practically sizzles, *Bared to You* charts the life of Manhattan newbie Eva and her steamy romance with the unspeakably dashing Gideon. Move over Danielle Steel and Jackie Collins, this is the dawn of a new Day."
                                                                    —*Amuse*

"The secondary characters are just as flawed as Eva and Gideon, which makes *Bared to You* richer and more real to me than many of the contemporary books I've read in a while."   —*Romance Junkies*

"Day writes indulgent fantasy at its most enjoyable, in a story populated by high-society beauties and rakes, all of them hiding dark passions and darker secrets behind their glittering façades . . . Filled with catty socialite drama, dysfunctional personalities, and deliciously explicit love scenes, *Bared to You* takes a sensual look at a darker side of love."
                                                                    —*Shelf Awareness*

"*Bared to You* was getting tons of fanfare on *Goodreads*. People were going crazy over it! It didn't take long for me to understand why . . . This book was just incredible. I couldn't put it down! The sex was so hot and the relationship was so juicy that I just had to know what was coming next!"
                                                                    —*Read Our Lips*

continued . . .

"Filled with equal amounts of emotion and heat, *Bared to You* can easily be devoured in one evening. Day creates two multidimensional characters in heroine Eva and hero Gideon, whose successful and attractive exteriors hide traumatized pasts. These layers will help readers connect with the pair, and make this a story that sticks in the mind." —*RT Book Reviews* (4½ stars)

"I read this story over a sweltering weekend. And I was glad I had the air conditioner on full blast since this book cranked up the heat even more! Reaching the last page in this lusty, earthy book was sweet yet sad. I wanted more time with these fascinating characters." —*FIRST for Women*

"*Bared to You* obliterates the competition with its real, emotionally intense characters that deal with pain and pleasure with honesty. I felt these characters bare their hearts and souls in this story. Sometimes it was so intense it was painful to watch as they hurt themselves and each other with actions or words. Yet, this is what makes the story unique and unforgettable. I became so attached to Eva and Gideon that I actually hurt for them. I shared their pain and their joy as they fought to keep each other." —*Joyfully Reviewed*

"*Bared to You* is an intense novel full of hardships, heartbreak, overcoming obstacles, trust, and most of all . . . trying to find love in a relationship that may seem hopeless. I truly and wholeheartedly was amazed by this book. It literally blew my mind and after finishing it, I wasn't able to stop thinking about it!" —*Happily Ever After*

A Touch of Crimson

"Will rock readers with a stunning new world, a hot-blooded hero, and a strong, kick-ass heroine. This is Sylvia Day at the top of her game!" —Larissa Ione, *New York Times* bestselling author

"Angels and demons, vampires and lycans, all set against an inventive, intriguing story world that hooked me from the first page. Balancing action and romance, humor and hot sensuality, Sylvia Day's storytelling dazzles. I can't wait to read more about this league of sexy, dangerous guardian angels and the fascinating world they inhabit . . . A paranormal romance lover's feast!"

—Lara Adrian, *New York Times* bestselling author

"Explodes with passion and heat. A hot, sexy angel to die for and a gutsy heroine make for one exciting read."

—Cheyenne McCray, *New York Times* bestselling author

"Sylvia Day spins a gorgeous adventure in *A Touch of Crimson* that combines gritty, exciting storytelling with soaring lyricism. Adrian is my favorite kind of hero—an alpha-male angel determined to win the heart of his heroine . . . This is definitely a book for your keeper shelf."

—Angela Knight, *New York Times* bestselling author

"Absolutely perfect! There are so many levels to this book—plots, subplots, shades of gray—it was brilliantly constructed and written . . . Not only is the story magnificent, but it is truly one of the hottest books I've read this year."

—*Rage, Sex, and Teddy Bears*

"Catapults you headfirst into the action from the very first page . . . *A Touch of Crimson* had everything I could hope for in a book. Fantastic characters, a hunk of a leading man . . . a sympathetic and headstrong leading lady and an awesome story line . . . It is packed with action, killer one-liners, and gripping cliffhangers."

—*All About Me*

"A gripping, touching, and scintillating page-turner. [Day] skillfully blends a timeless tale of love lost and found. [This] is a perfect romance with excellent world building that's rich with angels, lycans, and vampires."

—*RT Book Reviews* (4½ stars)

REFLECTED
IN YOU

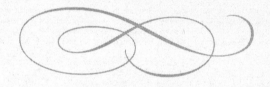

Sylvia Day

BERKLEY BOOKS, NEW YORK

THE BERKLEY PUBLISHING GROUP
Published by the Penguin Group
Penguin Group (USA) Inc.
375 Hudson Street, New York, New York 10014, USA

Penguin Group (Canada), 90 Eglinton Avenue East, Suite 700, Toronto, Ontario M4P 2Y3, Canada (a division of Pearson Penguin Canada Inc.) • Penguin Books Ltd, 80 Strand, London WC2R 0RL, England • Penguin Ireland, 25 St Stephen's Green, Dublin 2, Ireland (a division of Penguin Books Ltd) • Penguin Group (Australia), 707 Collins Street, Melbourne, Victoria 3008, Australia (a division of Pearson Australia Group Pty Ltd) • Penguin Books India Pvt Ltd, 11 Community Centre, Panchsheel Park, New Delhi–110 017, India • Penguin Group (NZ), 67 Apollo Drive, Rosedale, Auckland 0632, New Zealand (a division of Pearson New Zealand Ltd) • Penguin Books, Rosebank Office Park, 181 Jan Smuts Avenue, Parktown North 2193, South Africa • Penguin China, B7 Jiaming Center, 27 East Third Ring Road North, Chaoyang District, Beijing 100020, China

Penguin Books Ltd., Registered Offices: 80 Strand, London WC2R 0RL, England

This book is an original publication of The Berkley Publishing Group.

This is a work of fiction. Names, characters, places, and incidents either are the product of the author's imagination or are used fictitiously, and any resemblance to actual persons, living or dead, business establishments, events, or locales is entirely coincidental. The publisher does not have any control over and does not assume any responsibility for author or third-party websites or their content.

PUBLISHING HISTORY
Berkley trade paperback edition / October 2012

Library of Congress Cataloging-in-Publication Data

Day, Sylvia.
Reflected in you / Sylvia Day.—Berkley trade paperback ed.
p. cm.
ISBN 978-0-425-26391-4
1. Erotic fiction. 2. Love stories. I. Title.
PS3604.A9875R44 2012
813'.6—dc23
2012037035

PRINTED IN THE UNITED STATES OF AMERICA

10 9

This one is for Nora Roberts,
an inspiration and a true class act.

ACKNOWLEDGMENTS

I'm so grateful to Cindy Hwang and Leslie Gelbman for their support and encouragement, and most important, their love for Gideon and Eva's story. It takes passion to write a book and passion to sell it. I'm very thankful they have it.

I could write an entire book about everything I need to thank my agent Kimberly Whalen for. The Crossfire series is a massive multinational, multiformat endeavor, and she never misses a trick. Because she's always on the ball, I'm freed to focus on my part of our collaboration—the writing!—and I love her for it.

Behind Cindy, Leslie, Kim, Claire Pelly, and Tom Weldon are dynamic teams at Penguin and Trident Media Group. I wish I could mention everyone by name, but really, it takes a village. There are literally dozens of people to thank for their hard work and enthusiasm. The Crossfire series is being cared for and looked after by Trident and Penguin on a worldwide scale and I'm so grateful for the time you've all spent on my books.

My deepest gratitude to editor Hilary Sares, who is so instrumental in making the Crossfire series what it is. She keeps me straight.

Big thanks to my publicist, Gregg Sullivan, who makes my life easier in many ways.

I must also thank all of my international publishers (more than three dozen of you at the time I'm writing this) for welcoming Gideon and Eva into your countries and sharing them with your readers. You've all been so wonderful and I appreciate you.

And to all the readers around the world who've embraced Gideon and Eva's story—thank you! When I wrote *Bared to You* I was so sure I'd be the only person who loved it. I'm so thrilled that you do, too, and that we're following along on Eva and Gideon's journey together. Hot, bumpy roads are best traveled with friends!

1

I LOVED NEW York with the kind of mad passion I reserved for only one other thing in my life. The city was a microcosm of new world opportunities and old world traditions. Conservatives rubbed shoulders with bohemians. Oddities coexisted with priceless rarities. The pulsing energy of the city fueled international business bloodlines and drew people from all over the world.

And the embodiment of all that vibrancy, driving ambition, and world-renowned power had just screwed me to two toe-curlingly awesome orgasms.

As I padded over to his massive walk-in closet, I glanced at Gideon Cross's sex-rumpled bed and shivered with remembered pleasure. My hair was still damp from a shower, and the towel wrapped around me was my only article of clothing. I had an hour and a half before I had to be at work, which was cutting it a little too close for comfort. Obviously, I was going to have to allot time in my morning routine for sex, otherwise I'd always be scrambling. Gideon woke up ready to conquer the world, and he liked to start that domination with me.

How lucky was I?

Because it was sliding into July in New York and the temperature was heating up, I chose a slim pair of pressed natural-linen slacks and a sleeveless poplin shell in a soft gray that matched my eyes. Since I had no hairstyling talent, I pulled my long blond hair back in a simple ponytail, then made up my face. When I was presentable, I left the bedroom.

I heard Gideon's voice the moment I stepped into the hallway. A tiny shiver moved through me when I realized he was angry, his voice low and clipped. He didn't rile easily . . . unless he was ticked off with me. I could get him to raise his voice and curse, even shove his hands through his glorious shoulder-length mane of inky black hair.

For the most part, though, Gideon was a testament to leashed power. There was no need for him to shout when he could get people to quake in their shoes with just a look or a tersely spoken word.

I found him in his home office. He stood with his back to the door and a Bluetooth receiver in his ear. His arms were crossed and he was staring out the windows of his Fifth Avenue penthouse apartment, giving the impression of a very solitary man, an individual who was separate from the world around him, yet entirely capable of ruling it.

Leaning into the doorjamb, I drank him in. I was certain my view of the skyline was more awe-inspiring than his. My vantage point included him superimposed over those towering skyscrapers, an equally powerful and impressive presence. He'd finished his shower before I managed to crawl out of bed. His seriously addictive body was now dressed in two pieces of an expensively tailored three-piece suit—an admitted hot button of mine. The rear view of him showcased a perfect ass and a powerful back encased in a vest.

On the wall was a massive collage of photos of us as a couple and one very intimate one that he'd taken of me while I was sleeping. Most were pictures taken by the paparazzi who followed his every move. He was Gideon Cross, of Cross Industries, and at the ridiculous age of twenty-eight, he was one of the top twenty-five richest people in the world. I was pretty sure he owned a significant chunk of Manhattan; I was positive he was the hottest man on the planet. And he kept photos of me everywhere he worked, as if I could possibly be as fun to look at as he was.

He turned, pivoting gracefully to catch me with his icy blue gaze. Of course he'd known I was there, watching him. There was a crackling in the air when we were near each other, a sense of anticipation like the coiled silence before the boom of thunder. He'd probably deliberately waited a beat before facing me, giving me the opportunity to check him out because he knew I loved to look at him.

Dark and Dangerous. And all mine.

God . . . I never got used to the impact of that face. Those sculpted cheekbones and dark winged brows, the thickly lashed blue eyes, and those lips . . . perfectly etched to be both sensual and wicked. I loved when they smiled with sexual invitation, and I shivered when they thinned into a stern line. And when he pressed those lips to my body, I burned for him.

Jeez, listen to yourself. My mouth curved, remembering how annoyed I used to get at pals who waxed poetic about their boyfriends' good looks. But here I was, constantly awed by the gorgeousness of the complicated, frustrating, messed-up, sexy-as-sin man I was falling deeper in love with every day.

As we stared at each other, his scowl didn't lessen, nor did he cease speaking to the poor soul on the receiving end of his call, but his gaze warmed from its chilly irritation to scorching heat.

I should've become used to the change that came over him when he looked at me, but it still hit me with a force strong enough to rock me on my feet. That look conveyed how hard and deep he wanted to fuck me—which he did every chance he got—and it also afforded me a glimpse of his raw, unrelenting force of will. A core of strength and command marked everything Gideon did in life.

"See you at eight on Saturday," he finished, before yanking off the earpiece and tossing it on his desk. "Come here, Eva."

Another shiver slid through me at the way he said my name, with the same authoritative bite he used when he said *Come, Eva*, while I was beneath him . . . filled with him . . . desperate to climax for him . . .

"No time for that, ace." I backed into the hallway, because I was weak where he was concerned. The soft rasp in his smooth, cultured voice was nearly capable of making me orgasm just listening to it. And whenever he touched me, I caved.

I hurried to the kitchen to make us some coffee.

He muttered something under his breath and followed me out, his long stride easily gaining on mine. I found myself pinned to the hallway wall by six feet, two inches of hard, hot male.

"You know what happens when you run, angel." Gideon nipped my lower lip with his teeth and then soothed the sting with the caress of his tongue. "I catch you."

Inside me, something sighed with happy surrender and my body went lax with pleasure at being pressed so close to his. I craved him constantly, so deeply it was a physical ache. What I felt was lust, but it was also so much more. Something so precious and profound that Gideon's lust for me wasn't the trigger it would've been with another man. If anyone else had attempted to subdue me with the weight of his body, I would've freaked out. But it had never been an issue with Gideon. He knew what I needed and how much I could take.

The sudden flash of his grin stopped my heart.

Confronted with that breathtaking face framed by that lustrous dark hair, I felt my knees weaken just a little. He was so polished and urbane except for the decadent length of those silky strands.

He nuzzled his nose against mine. "You can't smile at me like that, then walk away. Tell me what you were thinking about when I was on the phone."

My lips twisted wryly. "How gorgeous you are. It's sickening how often I think about that. I need to get over it already."

He cupped the back of my thigh and urged me tighter against him, teasing me with an expert roll of his hips against mine. He was outrageously gifted in bed. And he knew it. "Damned if I'll let you."

"Oh?" Heat slid sinuously through my veins, my body too greedy for the feel of his. "You can't tell me you want another starry-eyed woman hanging on you, Mr. Hates-Exaggerated-Expectations."

"What I want," he purred, cupping my jaw and rubbing my bottom lip with the pad of his thumb, "is you being too busy thinking about me to think about anyone else."

I pulled in a slow and shaky breath. I was completely seduced by the smoldering look in his eyes, the provocative tone of his voice, the heat of his body, and the mouthwatering scent of his skin. He was my drug, and I had no desire to kick the habit.

"Gideon," I breathed, entranced.

With a soft groan, he sealed his chiseled mouth over mine, stealing away thoughts of what time it was with a lush, deep kiss . . . a kiss that almost succeeded in distracting me from seeing the insecurity he'd just revealed.

I pushed my fingers into his hair to hold him still and kissed him back, my tongue sliding along his, stroking. We'd been a couple for such a short period of time. Less than a month. Worse, neither of us knew how to have a relationship like the one we were attempting to build—a relationship in which we refused to pretend we weren't both seriously broken.

His arms banded around me and tightened possessively. "I wanted to spend the weekend with you down in the Florida Keys—naked."

"Umm, sounds nice." More than nice. As big of a kick as I got out of Gideon in a three-piece suit, I much preferred him stripped to the skin. I avoided pointing out that I wouldn't be available this weekend . . .

"Now I've got to spend the weekend taking care of business," he muttered, his lips moving against mine.

"Business you put off to be with me?" He'd been leaving work early to spend time with me, and I knew that had to be costing him. My mother was on her third marriage, and all of her spouses were successful, wealthy moguls of one kind or another. I knew the price for ambition was very late hours.

"I pay other people a generous salary so I can be with you."

Nice dodge, but noting the flash of irritation in his gaze, I distracted him. "Thank you. Let's get some coffee before we run out of time."

Gideon stroked his tongue along my bottom lip, then released me. "I'd like to get off the ground by eight tomorrow night. Pack cool and light. Arizona's got dry heat."

"What?" I blinked at his retreating back as it disappeared into his office. "Arizona is where your business is?"

"Unfortunately."

Uh . . . whoa. Instead of risking my shot at coffee, I postponed arguing and continued on to the kitchen. I passed through Gideon's spacious apartment with its stunning prewar architecture and slender arched windows, my heels alternately clicking over gleaming hardwood and muffled by Aubusson rugs. Decorated in dark woods and neutral fabrics, the luxurious space was brightened by jeweled accents. As much as his place screamed money, it managed to remain warm and welcoming, a comfortable place to relax and feel pampered.

When I reached the kitchen, I wasted no time in shoving a travel mug under the one-cup coffeemaker. Gideon joined me with his jacket draped over one arm and his cell phone in his hand. I put another portable mug under the spout for him before I went to the fridge for some half-and-half.

"It might be fortunate after all." I faced him and reminded him of my roommate issue. "I need to knock heads with Cary this weekend."

Gideon dropped his phone into the inner pocket of his jacket, then hung the garment off the back of one of the bar stools at the island. "You're coming with me, Eva."

Exhaling in a rush, I added half-and-half to my coffee. "To do what? Lie around naked, waiting for you to finish work and fuck me?"

His gaze held mine as he collected his mug and sipped his steaming coffee with too-calm deliberation. "Are we going to argue?"

"Are you going to be difficult? We talked about this. You know I can't leave Cary after what happened last night." The multibody tangle I'd found in my living room gave new meaning to the word *clusterfuck*.

I put the carton back in the fridge and absorbed the sensation of being drawn to him inexorably by the force of his will. It'd been that way from the beginning. When he chose to, Gideon could make me *feel* his demands. And it was very, very difficult to ignore the part of me that begged to give him whatever he wanted. "You're going to take care of business and I'm going to take care of my best friend, then we'll go back to taking care of each other."

"I won't be back until Sunday night, Eva."

Oh . . . I felt a sharp twinge in my belly at hearing we'd be apart that long. Most couples didn't spend every free moment together, but we weren't like most people. We both had hang-ups, insecurities, and an addiction to each other that required regular contact to keep us functioning properly. I hated being apart from him. I rarely went more than a couple of hours without thinking of him.

"You can't stand the thought, either," he said quietly, studying me in that way he had that saw everything. "By Sunday we'll both be worthless."

I blew on the surface of my coffee, then took a quick sip. I was unsettled at the thought of going the entire weekend without him. Worse, I hated the thought of him spending that amount of time away from me. He had a world of choices and possibilities out there, women who weren't so screwed up and difficult to be with.

Still, I managed to say, "We both know that's not exactly healthy, Gideon."

"Says who? No one else knows what it's like to be us."

Okay, I'd give him that.

"We need to get to work," I said, knowing this impasse was going to drive both of us crazy all day. We'd sort it out later, but for now we were stuck with it.

Resting his hip against the counter, he crossed his ankles and stubbornly settled in. "What we need is for you to come with me."

"Gideon." My foot began to tap against the travertine tile. "I can't just give up my life for you. If I turn into arm candy, you'll get bored real quick. Hell, I'd get sick of myself. It shouldn't kill us to

REFLECTED IN YOU · 9

spend a couple days straightening out other parts of our lives, even if we hate doing it."

His gaze captured mine. "You're too much trouble to be arm candy."

"Takes a troublemaker to know one."

Gideon straightened, shrugging off his brooding sensuality and instantly capturing me with his severe intensity. So mercurial—like me. "You've gotten a lot of press lately, Eva. It's no secret that you're in New York. I can't leave you here while I'm gone. Bring Cary with us if you have to. You can butt heads with him while you're waiting for me to finish work and fuck you."

"Ha." Even as I acknowledged his attempt to lighten the strain with humor, I realized what his real objection to being apart from me was—*Nathan*. My former stepbrother was a living nightmare from my past that Gideon seemed to fear might reappear in my present. It frightened me to concede that he wasn't totally wrong. The shield of anonymity that had protected me for years had been shattered by our highly public relationship.

God . . . we totally didn't have the time to get into *that* mess, but I knew it wasn't a point Gideon would concede on. He was a man who claimed his possessions utterly, fought off his competitors with ruthless precision, and would never allow any harm to come to me. I was his safe place, which made me rare and invaluable to him.

Gideon glanced at his watch. "Time to go, angel."

He fetched his jacket, then gestured for me to precede him through his luxurious living room, where I grabbed my purse and the bag holding my walking shoes and other necessities. A few moments later, we'd finished the descent to the ground floor in his private elevator and slid into the back of his black Bentley SUV.

"Hi, Angus," I greeted his driver, who touched the brim of his old-fashioned chauffeur's hat.

"Good morning, Miss Tramell," he replied, smiling. He was an older gentleman, with a liberal sprinkling of white in his red hair. I liked him for a lot of reasons, not the least of which was the fact that he'd been driving Gideon around since grade school and genuinely cared for him.

A quick glance at the Rolex my mother and stepfather had given me told me I'd make it to work on time . . . if we didn't get boxed in by traffic. Even as I thought this, Angus slid deftly into the sea of taxis and cars on the street. After the tense quiet of Gideon's apartment, the noise of Manhattan woke me as effectively as a jolt of caffeine. The blaring of horns and the thud of tires over a manhole cover invigorated me. Rapid-moving streams of pedestrians flanked both sides of the clogged street, while buildings stretched ambitiously toward the sky, keeping us in shadow even as the sun climbed.

God, I seriously loved New York. I took the time every day to absorb it, to try to draw it into me.

I settled into the leather seat back and reached for Gideon's hand, giving it a squeeze. "Would you feel better if Cary and I left town for the weekend? Maybe a quick trip to Vegas?"

Gideon's gaze narrowed. "Am I a threat to Cary? Is that why you won't consider Arizona?"

"What? No. I don't think so." Shifting in the seat, I faced him. "Sometimes it takes an all-nighter before I can get him to open up."

"You don't think so?" he repeated my answer, ignoring everything but the first words out of my mouth.

"He might feel like he can't reach out to me when he needs to talk because I'm always with you," I clarified, steadying my mug with two hands as we drove over a pothole. "Listen, you're going to have to get over any jealousy about Cary. When I say he's like a

REFLECTED IN YOU · 11

brother to me, Gideon, I'm not kidding. You don't have to like him, but you have to understand that he's a permanent part of my life."

"Do you tell him the same thing about me?"

"I don't have to. He knows. I'm trying to reach a compromise here—"

"I never compromise."

My brows rose. "In business, I'm sure you don't. But this is a relationship, Gideon. It requires give and—"

Gideon's growl cut me off. "My plane, my hotel, and if you leave the premises, you take a security team with you."

His sudden, reluctant capitulation surprised me silent for a long minute. Long enough for his brow to arch over those piercing blue eyes in a look that said *take it or leave it*.

"Don't you think that's a little extreme?" I prodded. "I'll have Cary with me."

"You'll forgive me if I don't trust him with your safety after last night." As he drank his coffee, his posture made it very clear that the conversation was done in his mind. He'd given me his acceptable options.

I might've gotten bitchy about that kind of high-handedness if I didn't understand that taking care of me was his motivation. My past had vicious skeletons, and dating Gideon had put me in a media spotlight that could bring Nathan Barker right to my door.

Plus, controlling everything around him was just part of who Gideon was. It came with the package and I had to make accommodations for that.

"Okay," I agreed. "Which hotel is yours?"

"I have a few. You can take your pick." He turned his head to look out the window. "Scott will e-mail you the list. When you've decided, let him know and he'll make the arrangements. We'll fly out together and return together."

Leaning my shoulder into the seat, I took a drink of my coffee and noted the way his hand was fisted on his thigh. In the tinted window's reflection, Gideon's face was impassive, but I could feel his moodiness.

"Thank you," I murmured.

"Don't. I'm not happy about this, Eva." A muscle in his jaw twitched. "Your roommate fucks up and I have to spend the weekend without you."

Hating that he was unhappy, I took his coffee from him and set our travel mugs in the backseat cup holders. Then I climbed into his lap, straddling him. I draped my arms around his shoulders. "I appreciate you bending on this, Gideon. It means a lot to me."

He caught me in his fierce blue gaze. "I knew you were going to drive me insane the moment I saw you."

I smiled, recalling how we'd met. "Sprawled on my ass on the lobby floor of the Crossfire Building?"

"Before. Outside."

Frowning, I asked, "Outside where?"

"On the sidewalk." Gideon gripped my hips, squeezing in that possessive, commanding way of his that made me ache for him. "I was leaving for a meeting. A minute later and I would've missed you. I'd just gotten into the car when you came around the corner."

I remembered the Bentley idling at the curb that day. I'd been too awed by the building to take note of the sleek vehicle when I arrived, but I had noticed it when I left.

"You hit me the instant I saw you," he said gruffly. "I couldn't look away. I wanted you immediately. Excessively. Almost violently."

How could I not have known that there'd been more to our first meeting than I'd realized? I thought we'd stumbled across each other by accident. But he'd been leaving for the day . . . which meant he had deliberately backtracked inside. For me.

"You stopped right next to the Bentley," he went on, "and your head tilted back. You were looking up at the building and I pictured you on your knees, looking up at me that same way."

The low growl in Gideon's voice had me squirming in his lap. "What way?" I whispered, mesmerized by the fire in his eyes.

"With excitement. A little awe . . . a little intimidation." Cupping my rear, he urged me tighter against him. "There was no way to stop myself from following you inside. And there you were, right where I'd wanted you, damn near kneeling in front of me. In that minute, I had a half dozen fantasies about what I was going to do to you when I got you naked."

I swallowed, remembering my similar reaction to him. "Looking at you for the first time made me think about sex. Screaming, sheet-clawing sex."

"I saw that." His hands slid up either side of my spine. "And I knew you saw *me*, too. Saw what I am . . . what I have inside me. You saw right through me."

And that was what had knocked me on my ass—literally. I'd looked into his eyes and realized how tightly reined he was, what a shadowed soul he had. I had seen power and hunger and control and demand. Somewhere inside me, I'd known he would take me over. It was a relief to know he'd felt the same upheaval over me.

Gideon's hands hugged my shoulder blades and pulled me closer, until our foreheads touched. "No one's ever seen before, Eva. You're the only one."

My throat tightened painfully. In so many ways, Gideon was a hard man, yet he could be so sweet to me. Almost childishly so, which I loved because it was pure and uncontrolled. If no one else bothered to look beyond his striking face and impressive bank account, they didn't deserve to know him. "I had no idea. You were so . . . cool. I didn't seem to affect you at all."

"Cool?" he scoffed. "I was on fire for you. I've been fucked up ever since."

"Gee. Thanks."

"You made me need you," he rasped. "Now I can't stand the thought of two days without you."

Holding his jaw in my hands, I kissed him tenderly, my lips coaxing and apologetic. "I love you, too," I whispered against his beautiful mouth. "I can't stand being away from you, either."

His returning kiss was greedy, devouring, and yet the way he held me close to him was gentle and reverent. As if I were precious. When he pulled back, we were both breathing hard.

"I'm not even your type," I teased, trying to lighten the mood before we went into work. Gideon's preference for brunettes was well known and well documented.

I felt the Bentley pull over and to a halt. Angus got out of the car to give us privacy, leaving the engine and air-conditioning running. I looked out the window and saw the Crossfire beside us.

"About the type thing—" Gideon's head fell back to rest against the seat. He took a deep breath. "Corinne was surprised by you. You weren't what she'd expected."

My jaw tightened at the mention of Gideon's former fiancée. Even knowing that their relationship had been about friendship and loneliness for him, not love, didn't stop the claws of envy from digging into me. Jealousy was one of my virulent flaws. "Because I'm blond?"

"Because . . . you don't look like her."

My breath caught. I hadn't considered that Corinne had set the standard for him. Even Magdalene Perez—one of Gideon's friends who wished she were more—had said she'd kept her dark hair long to emulate Corinne. But I hadn't grasped the complexity of that observation. My God . . . if it was true, Corinne had tremendous power over Gideon, way more than I could bear. My heart rate quickened and my stomach churned. I hated her irrationally. Hated that she'd had even a piece of him. Hated every woman who'd known his touch . . . his lust . . . his amazing body.

I started sliding off him.

"Eva." He stayed me by tightening his grip on my thighs. "I don't know if she's right."

I looked down at where he held me, and the sight of my promise ring on the finger of his right hand—my brand of ownership—calmed me. So did the look of confusion on his face when I met his gaze. "You don't?"

"If that's what it was, it wasn't conscious. I wasn't looking for her in other women. I didn't know I was looking for anything until I saw you."

My hands slid down his lapels as relief filled me. Maybe he hadn't been consciously looking for her, but even if he had, I couldn't be more different from Corinne in appearance and temperament. I was unique to him; a woman apart from his others in every way. I wished that could be enough to kill my jealousy.

"Maybe it wasn't a preference so much as a pattern." I smoothed his frown line with a fingertip. "You should ask Dr. Petersen when we see him tonight. I wish I had more answers after all my years of therapy, but I don't. There's a lot that's inexplicable between us, isn't there? I still have no idea what you see in me that's hooked you."

"It's what *you* see in *me*, angel," he said quietly, his features softening. "That you can know what I have in me and still want me as much as I want you. I go to sleep every night afraid I'll wake up and you'll be gone. Or that I scared you away . . . that I dreamed you—"

"No. Gideon." *Jesus.* He broke my heart every day. Shattered me.

"I know I don't tell you how I feel about you in the same way you tell me, but you have me. You know that."

"Yes, I know you love me, Gideon." Insanely. Outrageously. Obsessively. Just like my feelings for him.

"I'm caught up with you, Eva." With his head tilted back, Gideon pulled me down for the sweetest of kisses, his firm lips moving gently beneath mine. "I'd kill for you," he whispered, "give up everything I own for you . . . but I won't give *you* up. Two days is my limit. Don't ask for more than that; I can't give it to you."

I didn't take his words lightly. His wealth insulated him, gave him the power and control that had been stolen from him at some point in his life. He'd suffered brutality and violation, just as I had. That he would consider it worthwhile to lose his peace of mind just to keep me meant more than the words *I love you.*

"I just need the two days, ace, and I'll make them worth your while."

The starkness of his gaze bled away, replaced by sexual heat. "Oh? Planning on pacifying me with sex, angel?"

"Yes," I admitted shamelessly. "Lots of it. After all, the tactic seems to work well for you."

His mouth curved, but his gaze had a sharpness that quickened my breath. The dark look he gave me reminded me—as if I could forget—that Gideon wasn't a man who could be managed or tamed.

"Ah, Eva," he purred, sprawled against the seat with the predatory insouciance of a sleek panther who'd neatly trapped a mouse in his den.

A delicious shiver moved through me. When it came to Gideon, I was more than willing to be devoured.

2

JUST BEFORE I exited the elevator into the vestibule of Waters Field & Leaman, the advertising firm I worked for on the twentieth floor, Gideon whispered in my ear, "Think about me all day."

I squeezed his hand surreptitiously in the crowded car. "Always do."

He continued the ride up to the top floor, which housed the headquarters of Cross Industries. The Crossfire was his, one of many properties he owned throughout the city, including the apartment complex I lived in.

I tried not to pay attention to that. My mom was a career trophy wife. She'd given up my father's love for an affluent lifestyle, which I couldn't relate to at all. I'd prefer love over wealth any day, but I suppose that was easy for me to say because I had money—a sizable investment portfolio—of my own. Not that I ever touched it. I wouldn't. I'd paid too high a price and couldn't imagine anything worth the cost.

Megumi, the receptionist, buzzed me through the glass security door and greeted me with a big smile. She was a pretty woman, young like me, with a stylish bob of glossy black hair framing stunning Asian features.

"Hey," I said, stopping by her desk. "Got any plans for lunch?"

"I do now."

"Awesome." My grin was wide and genuine. As much as I loved Cary and enjoyed spending time with him, I needed girlfriends, too. Cary had already started building a network of acquaintances and friends in our adopted city, but I'd been sucked into the Gideon vortex almost from the outset. As much as I'd prefer to spend every moment with him, I knew it wasn't healthy. Female friends would give it to me straight when I needed it, and I was going to have to cultivate those friendships if I wanted them.

Setting off, I headed down the long hallway to my cubicle. When I reached my desk, I put my bag and purse in the bottom drawer, keeping my smartphone out so I could silence it. I found a text from Cary: I'm sorry, baby girl.

"Cary Taylor," I sighed. "I love you . . . even when you're pissing me off."

And he'd pissed me off royally. No woman wanted to come home to a sexual clusterfuck in progress on her living room floor. Especially not while in the middle of a fight with her new boyfriend.

I texted back, Block off the wknd 4 me if u can.

There was a long pause and I imagined him absorbing my request. Damn, he texted back finally. Must be some ass kicking u have planned.

"Maybe a little," I muttered, shuddering as I remembered the . . . orgy I'd walked in on. But mostly I thought Cary and I needed to spend some quality downtime together. We hadn't been living in Manhattan long. It was a new town for us, new apartment, new jobs and experiences, new boyfriends for both of us. We were out of our element and struggling, and since we both had barge loads of baggage from our pasts, we didn't handle struggling well. Usually we leaned on each other for balance, but we hadn't had much time for that lately. We really needed to make the time. Up for a trip to Vegas? Just u and me?

Fuck yeah!

K . . . more later. As I silenced my phone and put it away, my gaze passed briefly over the two collage photo frames next to my monitor—one filled with photos of both of my parents and one of Cary, and the other filled with photos of me and Gideon. Gideon had put the latter collection together himself, wanting me to have a reminder of him just like the reminder he had of me on his desk. As if I needed it . . .

I loved having those images of the people I loved close by: my mom with her golden cap of curls and her bombshell smile, her curvy body scarcely covered by a tiny bikini as she enjoyed the French Riviera on my stepdad's yacht; my stepfather, Richard Stanton, looking regal and distinguished, his silver hair oddly complementing the looks of his much younger wife; and Cary, who was captured in all his photogenic glory, with his lustrous brown hair and sparkling green eyes, his smile wide and mischievous. That million-dollar face was starting to pop up in magazines everywhere and soon would grace billboards and bus stops advertising Grey Isles clothing.

I looked across the strip of hallway and through the glass wall that encased Mark Garrity's very small office and saw his jacket hung over the back of his Aeron chair, even though the man himself wasn't in sight. I wasn't surprised to find him in the break room scowling into his coffee mug; he and I shared a java dependency.

"I thought you had the hang of it," I said, referring to his trouble with the one-cup coffeemaker.

"I do, thanks to you." Mark lifted his head and offered a charmingly crooked smile. He had gleaming dark skin, a trim goatee, and soft brown eyes. In addition to being easy on the eyes, he was a great boss—very open to educating me about the ad business and quick to trust that he didn't have to show me how to do something twice. We worked well together, and I hoped that would be the case for a long time to come.

"Try this," he said, reaching for a second steaming cup waiting on the counter. He handed it to me and I accepted it gratefully, appreciating that he'd been thoughtful about adding cream and sweetener, which was how I liked it.

I took a cautious sip, since it was hot, then coughed over the unexpected—and unwelcome—flavor. "What *is* this?"

"Blueberry-flavored coffee."

Abruptly, I was the one scowling. "Who the hell wants to drink that?"

"Ah, see . . . it's our job to figure out who, then sell this to them." He lifted his mug in a toast. "Here's to our latest account!"

Wincing, I straightened my spine and took another sip.

I was pretty sure the sickly sweet taste of artificial blueberries was still coating my tongue two hours later. Since it was time for my break, I started an Internet search for Dr. Terrence Lucas, a man who'd clearly rubbed Gideon the wrong way when I'd seen the two men together at dinner the night before. I hadn't gotten any further than typing the doctor's name in the search box when my desk phone rang.

"Mark Garrity's office," I answered. "Eva Tramell speaking."

"Are you serious about Vegas?" Cary asked without preamble.

"Totally."

There was a pause. "Is this when you tell me you're moving in with your billionaire boyfriend and I've got to go?"

"What? *No*. Are you nuts?" I squeezed my eyes shut, understanding how insecure Cary was but thinking we were too far along in our friendship for those kinds of doubts. "You're stuck with me for life, you know that."

"And you just up and decided we should go to Vegas?"

"Pretty much. Figured we could sip mojitos by the pool and live off room service for a couple days."

"I'm not sure how much I can pitch in for that."

"Don't worry, it's on Gideon. His plane, his hotel. We'll just cover our food and drinks." A lie, since I planned on covering everything except the airfare, but Cary didn't need to know that.

"And he's not coming with us?"

I leaned back in my chair and stared at one of the photos of Gideon. I missed him already and it'd been only a couple of hours since we'd been together. "He's got business in Arizona, so he'll share the flights back and forth, but it'll be just you and me in Vegas. I think we need it."

"Yeah." He exhaled harshly. "I could do with a change of scenery and some quality time with my best girl."

"Okay, then. He wants to fly out by eight tomorrow night."

"I'll start packing. Want me to put a bag together for you, too?"

"Would you? That'd be great!" Cary could've been a stylist or personal shopper. He had serious talent when it came to clothes.

"Eva?"

"Yeah?"

He sighed. "Thank you for putting up with my shit."

"Shut up."

After we hung up, I stared at the phone for a long minute, hating that Cary was so unhappy when everything in his life was going so well. He was an expert at self-sabotage, never truly believing he was worthy of happiness.

As I returned my attention to work, the Google search on my monitor reminded me of my interest in Dr. Terry Lucas. A few articles about him had been posted on the Web, complete with pictures that cemented the verification.

Pediatrician. Forty-five years of age. Married for twenty years. Nervously, I searched for "Dr. Terrence Lucas and wife," inwardly cringing at the thought of seeing a golden-skinned, long-haired brunette. I exhaled my relief when I saw that Mrs. Lucas was a pale-skinned woman with short, bright red hair.

But that left me with more questions. I'd figured it would be a woman who'd caused the trouble between the two men.

The fact was, Gideon and I really didn't know that much about each other. We knew the ugly stuff—at least he knew mine; I'd mostly guessed his from some pretty obvious clues. We knew some of the basic cohabitation stuff about each other after spending so many nights sleeping over at our respective apartments. He'd met half of my family and I'd met all of his. But we hadn't been together long enough to touch on a whole lot of the periphery stuff. And frankly, I think we weren't as forthcoming or inquisitive as we could've been, as if we were afraid to pile any more crap onto an already struggling relationship.

We were together because we were addicted to each other. I was never as intoxicated as I was when we were happy together, and I knew it was the same for him. We were putting ourselves through the wringer for those moments of perfection between us, but they were so tenuous that only our stubbornness, determination, and love kept us fighting for them.

Enough with making yourself crazy.

I checked my e-mail, and found my daily Google alert on "Gideon Cross." The day's digest of links led mostly to photos of Gideon, in black tie sans tie, and me at the charity dinner at the Waldorf Astoria the night before.

"God." I couldn't help but be reminded of my mother when looking at the pictures of me in a champagne Vera Wang cocktail dress. Not just because of how closely my looks mirrored my mom's—aside from my hair being long and straight—but also because of the megamogul whose arm I graced.

Monica Tramell Barker Mitchell Stanton was very, very good at being a trophy wife. She knew precisely what was expected of her and delivered without fail. Although she'd been divorced twice, both times had been by her choice and both divorces had left her exes despondent over losing her. I didn't think less of my mother, because she gave as good as she got and didn't take anyone for granted, but I'd grown up striving for independence. My right to say no was my most valued possession.

Minimizing my e-mail window, I pushed my personal life aside and went back to searching for market comparisons on fruity coffee. I coordinated some initial meetings between the strategists and Mark and helped Mark with brainstorming a campaign for a gluten-free restaurant. Noon approached and I was starting to feel seriously hungry when my phone rang. I answered with my usual greeting.

"Eva?" an accented female voice greeted me. "It's Magdalene. Do you have a minute?"

I leaned back in my chair, alert. Magdalene and I had once shared a moment of sympathy over Corinne's unexpected and unwanted reappearance in Gideon's life, but I'd never forget how vicious Magdalene had been to me the first time we'd met. "Just. What's up?"

She sighed, then spoke quickly, her words flowing in a rush. "I was sitting at the table behind Corinne last night. I could hear a bit of what was being said between her and Gideon during dinner."

My stomach tensed, preparing for an emotional blow. Magdalene knew just how to exploit my insecurities about Gideon. "Stirring up crap while I'm at work is a new low," I said coldly. "I don't—"

"He wasn't ignoring you."

My mouth hung open a second, and she quickly filled the silence.

"He was managing her, Eva. She was making suggestions for where to take you around New York since you're new in town, but she was doing it by playing the old remember-when-you-and-I-went-there game."

"A walk down memory lane," I muttered, grateful now that I hadn't been able to hear much of Gideon's low-voiced conversation with his ex.

"Yes." Magdalene took a deep breath. "You left because you thought he was ignoring you for her. I just want you to know that he seemed to be thinking about you, trying to keep Corinne from upsetting you."

"Why do you care?"

"Who says I do? I owe you one, Eva, for the way I introduced myself."

I thought about that. Yeah, she owed me for when she ambushed me in the bathroom with her catty jealous bullshit. Not that I bought it as her sole motivation. Maybe I was just the lesser of two evils. Maybe she was keeping her enemies close. "All right. Thank you."

No denying I felt better. A weight I hadn't realized I was carrying around was suddenly relieved.

"Something else," Magdalene went on. "He went after you."

REFLECTED IN YOU · 25

My grip tightened on the phone receiver. Gideon always came after me . . . because I was always running. My recovery was so fragile that I'd learned to protect it at all costs. When something threatened my stability, I ditched it.

"There have been other women in his life who've tried ultimatums like that, Eva. They got bored or they wanted his attention or some kind of grand gesture . . . So they walked away and expected him to come after them. You know what he did?"

"Nothing," I said softly, knowing my man. A man who never spent social time with women he slept with and never slept with women he associated with socially. Corinne and I were the sole exceptions to that rule, which was yet another reason why his ex sent me into fits of jealousy.

"Nothing more than making sure Angus dropped them off safely," she confirmed, making me think it'd been a tactic she'd tried at some point. "But when you left, he couldn't chase after you fast enough. And he wasn't himself when he said good-bye. He seemed . . . off."

Because he'd felt fear. My eyes closed as I mentally kicked myself. Hard.

Gideon had told me more than once that it terrified him when I ran, because he couldn't handle the thought that I might not come back. What good did it do to say that I couldn't imagine living without him when I so often showed him otherwise with my actions? Was it any wonder he hadn't opened up to me about his past?

I had to stop running. Gideon and I were both going to have to stand and fight for this, for *us*, if we were going to have any hope of making our relationship work.

"Do I owe you now?" I asked neutrally, returning Mark's wave as he left for lunch.

Magdalene exhaled in a rush. "Gideon and I have known each

other a long time. Our mothers are best friends. You and I will see each other around, Eva, and I'm hoping we can find a way to avoid any awkwardness."

The woman had come up to me and told me that the minute Gideon "shoved his dick" in me, I was "done." And she'd hit me with that at a moment when I was especially vulnerable.

"Listen, Magdalene, if you don't cause drama, we'll get by." And since she was being so forthright . . . "I can screw up my relationship with Gideon all by myself, trust me. I don't need any help."

She laughed softly. "That was my mistake, I think—I was too careful and too accommodating. He has to work at it with you. Anyway . . . I've taken up my minute. I'll let you go."

"Enjoy your weekend," I said, in lieu of thanks. I still couldn't trust her motivation.

"You, too."

As I returned the receiver to its cradle, my gaze went to the photos of me and Gideon. I was abruptly overwhelmed by feelings of greed and possession. He was mine, yet I couldn't be sure from one day to the next whether he'd stay mine. And the thought of any other woman having him made me insane.

I pulled open my bottom drawer and dug my smartphone out of my purse. Driven by the need to have him thinking as fiercely about me, I texted him about my sudden desperate hunger to devour him whole: I'd give anything to be sucking your cock right now.

Just thinking about how he looked when I took him in my mouth . . . the feral sounds he made when he was about to come . . .

Standing, I deleted the text the moment I saw it'd been delivered, then dropped my phone back in my purse. Since it was noon, I closed all the windows on my computer and headed out to reception to find Megumi.

"You hungry for anything in particular?" she asked, pushing to her feet and giving me a chance to admire her belted, sleeveless lavender dress.

I coughed because her question came so soon after my text. "No. Your choice. I'm not picky."

We pushed out through the glass doors to reach the elevators.

"I am *so* ready for the weekend," Megumi said with a groan as she stabbed the call button with an acrylic-tipped finger. "A day and a half left to go."

"Got something fun planned?"

"That remains to be seen." She sighed and tucked her hair behind her ear. "Blind date," she explained ruefully.

"Ah. Do you trust the person setting you up?"

"My roommate. I expect the guy will at least be physically attractive, because I know where she sleeps at night and paybacks are a bitch."

I was smiling as an elevator car reached our floor and we stepped inside. "Well, that ups your odds for a good time."

"Not really, since she found him by going on a blind date with him first. She swears he's great, just more my type than hers."

"Hmm."

"I know, right?" Megumi shook her head and looked up at the decorative, old-fashioned needle above the car doors that marked the passing floors.

"You'll have to let me know how it goes."

"Oh, yeah. Wish me luck."

"Absolutely." We'd just stepped out into the lobby when I felt my purse vibrate beneath my arm. As we passed through the turnstiles, I dug for my phone and felt my stomach tighten at the sight of Gideon's name. He was calling, not sexting me back.

"Excuse me," I said to Megumi before answering.

She waved it off nonchalantly. "Go for it."

"Hey," I greeted him playfully.

"*Eva.*"

I missed a step hearing the way he growled my name. There was a wealth of promise in the roughness of his voice.

Slowing, I found I was speechless, just from hearing him say my name with that edginess I craved—the sharp bite that told me he wanted to be inside me more than he wanted anything else in the world.

While people flowed around me, entering and exiting the building, I was halted by the weighted silence on my phone. The unspoken and nearly irresistible demand. He made no sound at all—I couldn't even hear him breathing—but I felt his hunger. If I didn't have Megumi waiting patiently for me, I'd be riding an elevator to the top floor to satisfy his unvoiced command to make good on my offer.

The memory of the time I'd sucked him off in his office simmered through me, making my mouth water. I swallowed. "Gideon . . ."

"You wanted my attention—now you have it. I want to hear you say those words."

I felt my face flush. "I can't. Not here. Let me call you later."

"Step over by the column and out of the way."

Startled, I looked around for him. Then I remembered that the Caller ID put him in his office. My gaze lifted, searching for the security cameras. Immediately, I felt his eyes on me, hot and wanting. Arousal surged through me, spurred by his desire.

"Hurry along, angel. Your friend's waiting."

I moved to the column, my breathing fast and audible.

"Now tell me. Your text made me hard, Eva. What are you going to do about it?"

My hand went to my throat, my gaze sliding helplessly to Megumi, who watched me with raised brows. I lifted one finger up, asking for another minute, then turned my back to her and whispered, "I want you in my mouth."

"Why? To play with me? To tease me like you're doing now?" There was no heat in his voice, just calm severity.

I knew to pay careful attention when Gideon got serious about sex.

"No." I lifted my face to the tinted dome in the ceiling that concealed the nearest security camera. "To make you come. I love making you come, Gideon."

He exhaled harshly. "A gift, then."

Only I knew what it meant for Gideon to view a sexual act as a gift. For him, sex had previously been about pain and degradation or lust and necessity. Now, with me, it was about pleasure and love.

"Always."

"Good. Because I treasure you, Eva, and what we have. Even our driving urge to fuck each other constantly is precious to me, because it matters."

I sagged into the column, admitting to myself that I'd fallen into an old destructive habit—I'd exploited sexual attraction to ease my insecurities. If Gideon was lusting after me, he couldn't be lusting after anyone else. How did he always know what was going on in my mind?

"Yes," I breathed, closing my eyes. "It matters."

There'd been a time when I'd turned to sex to feel affection, confusing momentary desire with genuine caring. Which was why I now insisted on having some sort of friendly framework in place before I went to bed with a man. I never again wanted to roll out of a lover's bed feeling worthless and dirty.

And I sure as hell didn't want to cheapen what I shared with Gideon just because I was irrationally scared of losing him.

It hit me then that I was off balance. I had this sick feeling in my gut, like something awful was going to happen.

"You can have what you want after work, angel." His voice deepened, grew raspier. "In the meantime, enjoy lunch with your co-
worker. I'll be thinking about you. And your mouth."

"I love you, Gideon."

It took a couple of deep breaths after I hung up to compose myself enough to join Megumi again. "I'm sorry about that."

"Everything all right?"

"Yes. Everything's fine."

"Things still hot and heavy with you and Gideon Cross?" She
glanced at me with a slight smile.

"Umm . . ." *Oh yes.* "Yes, that's fine, too." And I wished desperately that I could talk about it. I wished I could just open the valve
and gush about my overwhelming feelings for him. How thoughts
of him consumed me, how the feel of him beneath my hands drove
me wild, how the passion of his tortured soul cut into me like the
sharpest blade.

But I couldn't. Not ever. He was too visible, too well known.
Private tidbits about his life were worth a small fortune. I couldn't
risk it.

"He sure is," Megumi agreed. "Damn fine. Did you know him
before you started working here?"

"No. Although I suppose we would have met eventually." Because of our pasts. My mother gave generously to many abused children's charities, as did Gideon. It was inevitable that Gideon and I
would've crossed paths at some point. I wondered what that meeting
would have been like—him with a gorgeous brunette on his arm
and me with Cary. Would we have had the same visceral reaction to
each other from a distance as we'd had up close in the Crossfire
lobby?

He'd wanted me the moment he saw me on the street.

"I wondered." Megumi pushed through the revolving lobby door.

"I read that it was serious between you two," she went on when I joined her outside on the sidewalk. "So I thought maybe you'd known him before."

"Don't believe everything you read on those gossip blogs."

"So it's not serious?"

"I didn't say that." It was *too* serious at times. Painfully, brutally so.

She shook her head. "God . . . listen to me pry. Sorry. Gossip is one of my vices. So are extremely hot men like Gideon Cross. I can't help but wonder what it'd be like to hook up with a guy whose body screams *sex* like that. Tell me he's awesome in bed."

I smiled. It was good to hang out with another girl. Not that Cary couldn't also be appreciative of a hot guy, but nothing beat girl talk. "You won't hear me complaining."

"Lucky bitch." Bumping shoulders with me to show she was teasing, she said, "How about that roommate of yours? From the photos I saw, he's gorgeous, too. Is he single? Wanna hook me up?"

Turning my head quickly, I hid a wince. I'd learned the hard way never to set up an acquaintance or friend with Cary. He was so easy to love, which led to a lot of broken hearts because he couldn't love back the same way. The moment things started going too well, Cary sabotaged them. "I don't know if he's single or not. Things are . . . complicated in his life at the moment."

"Well, if the opportunity presents itself, I'm certainly not opposed. Just sayin'. You like tacos?"

"Love 'em."

"I know a great place a couple blocks up. Come on."

THINGS were going well in my world as Megumi and I headed back from lunch. Forty minutes of gossip, guy-ogling, and three awesome carne asada tacos later, I was feeling pretty good. And we were returning to work a little over ten minutes early, which I was glad for since I hadn't been the most punctual employee lately, even though Mark never complained.

The city was thrumming around us, taxis and people surging through the growing heat and humidity as they crammed what they could into the insufficient hours of the day. I people-watched shamelessly, my eyes skimming over everyone and everything.

Men in business suits walked alongside women in flowing skirts and flip-flops. Ladies in haute couture and five-hundred-dollar shoes teetered past steaming hot dog vendor carts and shouting hawkers. The eclectic mix of New York was heaven to me, stirring an excitement that made me feel more vibrant here than anyplace else I'd ever lived.

We were stopped by a traffic light directly across from the Crossfire, and my gaze was immediately drawn to the black Bentley sitting in front of it. Gideon must've just gotten back from lunch. I couldn't help but think about him sitting in his car on the day we'd met, watching me as I took in the imposing beauty of his Crossfire Building. It made me tingly just thinking about it—

Suddenly, I went cold.

Because a striking brunette breezed out of the revolving doors just then and paused, giving me a good, long look at her—Gideon's ideal, whether he'd been aware of it or not. A woman I'd witnessed him fixate on the moment he'd seen her in the Waldorf Astoria ballroom. A woman whose poise and hold over Gideon brought out all my worst insecurities.

Corinne Giroux looked like a breath of fresh air in a cream-colored sheath dress and cherry red heels. She ran a hand over her waist-length dark hair, which wasn't quite as sleek as it'd appeared last night when I'd met her. In fact, it looked a little disheveled. And her fingers were rubbing at her mouth, wiping along the outline of her lips.

I pulled my smartphone out, activated the camera, and snapped a picture. With the proximity of the zoom, I could see why she was fussing with her lipstick—it was smeared. No, more like *mashed*. As if from a passionate kiss.

The light changed. Megumi and I moved with the flow, closing the distance between me and the woman who'd once had Gideon's promise to marry her. Angus stepped out of the Bentley and came around, speaking to her briefly before opening the back door for her. The feeling of betrayal—Angus's and Gideon's—was so fierce, I couldn't catch my breath. I swayed on my feet.

"Hey." Megumi caught my arm to steady me. "And we only had virgin margaritas, lightweight!"

I watched Corinne's willowy body slide into the back of Gideon's car with practiced grace. My fists clenched as fury surged through me. Through the haze of my angry tears, the Bentley pulled away from the curb and disappeared.

3

WHEN MEGUMI AND I stepped into an elevator, I hit the button for the top floor.

"I'll be back in five minutes, if anyone asks," I told her, as she stepped off at Waters Field & Leaman.

"Give him a kiss for me, will you?" she said, playfully fanning herself. "Makes me hot just thinking about living vicariously through you."

I managed a smile before the doors closed and the car continued its ascent. When it reached the end of the line, I exited into a tastefully ornate and undeniably masculine entrance foyer. Smoky glass security doors were sandblasted with CROSS INDUSTRIES and softened by hanging baskets of ferns and lilies.

Gideon's redheaded receptionist was unusually cooperative and buzzed me in before I reached the door. Then she grinned at me in a way that got my back up. I'd always gotten the impression she didn't like me, so I didn't trust that smile for a minute. It made me twitchy. Still, I waved and said hello, because I wasn't a catty bitch— unless I was given good reason to be.

I took the long hallway that led to Gideon, stopping at a large secondary reception area where his secretary, Scott, manned the desk.

Scott stood as I approached. "Hello, Eva," he greeted me, reaching for his phone. "I'll let him know you're here."

The glass wall that separated Gideon's office from the rest of the floor was usually crystal clear but could be made opaque with the push of a button. It was frosted now, which increased my uneasiness. "Is he alone?"

"Yes, but—"

Whatever else he said was lost as I pushed through the glass door and into Gideon's domain. It was a massive space, with three distinct seating areas, each larger than my boss Mark's entire office. In contrast to the elegant warmth of Gideon's apartment, his office was decorated in a cool palette of black, gray, and white broken only by the jewel-toned crystal decanters that decorated the wall behind a bar.

Floor-to-ceiling windows overlooked the city on two sides. The one solid wall opposite the immense desk was covered in flat screens streaming news channels from around the world.

My gaze swept the room and caught on the throw pillow that had been carelessly knocked to the floor. Beside it were indents in the area rug that betrayed where the couch feet were usually planted. The piece of furniture had, apparently, been bumped askew by a few inches.

My heart rate sped up and my palms grew damp. That awful anxiety I'd felt earlier intensified.

I had just noticed the open door to the washroom when Gideon stepped into view, stealing my breath with the beauty of his exposed torso. His hair was damp, as if from a recent shower, and his neck and upper chest were still flushed, as they became when he exerted himself physically.

He froze when he saw me, his gaze darkening for an instant before his perfect, implacable mask slid effortlessly into place.

"It's not a good time, Eva," he said, shrugging into a dress shirt he'd had draped over the back of a bar stool . . . a different shirt from the one he'd been wearing earlier that morning. "I'm running late to an appointment."

I gripped my purse tightly. Seeing him so intimately brought home how badly I wanted him. I loved him insanely, needed him like I needed to breathe . . . which only made it easier for me to understand how Magdalene and Corinne felt, and to relate to any lengths they might go to in trying to lure him away from me. "Why are you half dressed?"

There was no help for it. My body responded instinctively to the sight of his, which made it even harder for me to rein in my rioting emotions. His open, neatly pressed dress shirt revealed golden skin stretched tightly over washboard abs and perfectly defined pectorals. A dusting of dark hair over his chest arrowed down and darkened into a thin line, leading to a cock presently encased in boxer briefs and slacks. Just thinking about how he felt inside me made me ache with longing.

"I got something on my shirt." He began buttoning up, his abs flexing with his movements as he crossed over to the bar, where I saw his cuff links waiting. "I have to run. If you need something, let Scott know and he'll see to it. Or I'll take care of it when I get back. I shouldn't be more than two hours."

"Why are you running late?"

He didn't look at me when he answered, "I had to squeeze in a last-minute meeting."

Did you now? "You showered this morning." *After making love to me for an hour.* "Why did you have to shower again?"

"Why the inquisition?" he snapped.

Needing answers, I went to the washroom. The lingering humidity was oppressive. Ignoring the voice in my head telling me not to look for trouble I couldn't bear to find, I dug his shirt out of the laundry basket . . . and saw red lipstick smeared like a bloodstain on one of the cuffs. Pain twisted through my chest.

Dropping the garment on the floor, I pivoted and left, needing to get as far away from Gideon as possible. Before I threw up or started sobbing.

"Eva!" he snapped as I hurried past him. "What the hell is the matter with you?"

"Fuck you, asswipe."

"Excuse me?"

My hand was on the door handle when he caught me, yanking me back by the elbow. Spinning, I slapped him with enough force to turn his head and set my palm on fire.

"Goddamn it," he growled, grabbing me by the arms and shaking me. "Don't fucking hit me!"

"Don't touch me!" The feel of his bare hands on the bare skin of my arms was too much.

He shoved back and away from me. "What the fuck's gotten into you?"

"I *saw* her, Gideon."

"Saw who?"

"Corinne!"

He scowled. "What are you talking about?"

Pulling my smartphone out, I thrust the photo in his face. "Busted."

Gideon's gaze narrowed on the screen, and then his scowl cleared. "Busted doing what, exactly?" he asked, too softly.

"Oh, screw you." I turned toward the door, shoving my phone in my purse. "I'm not spelling it out for you."

His palm slapped against the glass, holding the door closed. Caging me with his body, he leaned down and hissed in my ear, "Yes. Yes, you goddamn will spell it out."

I squeezed my eyes shut as our position at the door brought back a flood of heated memories from the first time I'd been in Gideon's office. He'd stopped me just like this, seducing me deftly, drawing us into a passionate embrace on the very couch that had recently seen some kind of action forceful enough to shove it out of position.

"Doesn't a picture say a thousand words?" I bit out through clenched teeth.

"So Corinne was manhandled. What does that have to do with me?"

"Are you kidding me? Let me out."

"I don't find anything even remotely funny about this. In fact, I don't think I've ever been this pissed off at a woman. You come in here with your half-assed accusations and self-righteous bullshit—"

"I *am* righteous!" I twisted around and ducked beneath his arm, putting some much-needed distance between us. Being close to him hurt too much. "I would never cheat on you! If I wanted to fuck around, I'd break it off with you first."

Leaning into the door, Gideon crossed his arms. His shirt remained untucked and open at the collar, a look I found hot and tempting, which only made me angrier.

"You think I cheated on you?" His tone was clipped and icy.

I sucked in a deep breath to get through the pain of imagining him with Corinne on the sofa behind me. "Explain to me why she was here at the Crossfire, looking like she did. Why your office looks like this. Why you look like that."

His gaze went to the couch, then to the cushion on the floor, then back to me. "I don't know why Corinne was here or why she looked like that. I haven't seen her since last night, when you were with me."

Last night seemed like it'd happened forever ago. I wished that it had never happened at all.

"But I wasn't with you," I pointed out. "She batted her eyelashes and said she wanted to introduce you to someone, and you left me standing there."

"Christ." His eyes blazed. "Not this again."

I swiped angrily at a tear that slid down my cheek.

He growled. "You think I went with her because I was overcome with the need to be with her and get away from you?"

"I don't know, Gideon. *You* ditched *me*. You're the one with the answers."

"You ditched me first."

My mouth fell open. "I did not!"

"The hell you didn't. Almost the second we arrived, you took off. I had to hunt you down and when I did, you were dancing with that prick."

"Martin is Stanton's nephew!" And since Richard Stanton was my stepdad, I thought of Martin as family.

"I don't care if he's a damned priest. He wants to nail you."

"Oh my God. That's absurd! Stop deflecting. You were talking business with your associates. It was awkward standing there. For them as well as me."

"That's your place, awkward or not!"

My head jerked back as if he'd slapped me. "Come again?"

"How would you feel if I walked away from you at a Waters Field and Leaman party because you started talking about a campaign? Then, when you found me, I was slow dancing with Magdalene?"

"I—" *God.* I hadn't thought of it like that.

Gideon appeared smooth and unruffled with his powerful frame lounging against the door, but I could sense the anger vibrating beneath that calm surface. He was riveting always, but most especially when he was seething with passion. "It's my place to stand beside you, and support you, and yes, just fucking look pretty on your arm sometimes. It's my right, my duty, and my privilege, Eva, just as it's yours in reverse."

"I thought I was doing you a favor by getting out of the way."

His arched brow was a silent, sarcastic comeback.

My arms crossed in front of me. "Is that why you walked off with Corinne? Were you punishing me?"

"If I wanted to punish you, Eva, I'd take you over my knee."

My gaze narrowed. *That* was never going to happen.

"I know how you get," he said curtly. "I didn't want you jealous over Corinne before I had a chance to explain. I needed a few minutes to make sure she understood how serious you and I are, and how important it was to me that you enjoy the evening. That's the only reason I walked away with her."

"You told her not to say anything about you two, didn't you? You told her to keep quiet about what she is to you. Too bad Magdalene screwed that up."

And maybe Corinne and Magdalene had planned it that way. Corinne knew Gideon well enough to anticipate his moves; it might've been easy for her to plan around his reaction to her unexpected appearance in New York.

Which shed a whole new light on why Magdalene had called

me today. She and Corinne had been talking at the Waldorf when Gideon and I spotted them. Two women who wanted a man who was with another woman. Nothing was going to happen for them while I was in the picture, and because of that, I couldn't rule out the possibility that they might be working together.

"I wanted you to hear it from me," he said tightly.

I waved that off, more concerned about what was happening now. "I saw Corinne get into the Bentley, Gideon. Right before I came up here."

His other brow rose to match the first. "Did you?"

"Yes, I did. Can you explain that?"

"I can't, no."

Injured fury burned through me. I suddenly couldn't bear to even look at him. "Then get out of my way, I have to get back to work."

He didn't move. "I just want to be clear on something before you go: Do you believe I fucked her?"

Hearing him say it aloud made me flinch. "I don't know what to believe. The evidence sure—"

"I wouldn't care if the 'evidence' included you finding me and her naked in a bed together." He uncoiled so swiftly, I stumbled back in surprise. He stalked closer. "I want to know if you think I fucked her. If you think I would. Or could. Do you?"

My foot began to tap, but I didn't retreat. "Explain the lipstick on your shirt, Gideon."

His jaw tightened. "No."

"What?" The flat-out refusal sent me into a tailspin.

"Answer my question."

I studied his face and saw the mask he wore around other people but had never worn with me. He reached his hand toward me as if to brush my cheek with his fingertips, then pulled back at the last minute. In that brief instant in which he pulled away, I heard his teeth grind, as if *not* touching me was a struggle. Agonized, I was grateful he hadn't.

"I *need* you to explain," I whispered, wondering if I imagined the wince that crossed his face. Sometimes I wanted to believe something so badly, I deliberately manufactured excuses and ignored painful reality.

"I've given you no reason to doubt me."

"You're giving me one now, Gideon." I exhaled in a rush, deflating. Withdrawing. He was standing in front of me, but he seemed miles away. "I understand you need time before you share secrets that are painful for you. I've been where you're at, knowing I needed to talk about what happened to me but just not ready. That's why I've tried very hard not to push you or rush you. But this secret is one that's hurting *me*, and that's different. Don't you see that?"

Cursing under his breath, he cupped my face with cool hands. "I go out of my way to make sure you don't have any reason to feel jealous, but when you do get possessive, I like it. I want you to fight for me. I want you to care that much. I want you crazy about me. But possessiveness without trust is hell. If you don't trust me, we've got nothing."

"Trust goes both ways, Gideon."

He sucked in a deep breath. "Damn it. Don't look at me like that."

"I'm trying to figure out who you are. Where's the man who came right out and said he wanted to fuck me? The man who didn't hesitate to tell me I tie him up in knots, even as I was breaking up with him? I believed you'd always be brutally honest like that. I counted on it. Now—" I shook my head, my throat too tight to say anything else.

Grimness thinned his lips, but they stayed stubbornly closed.

Catching his wrists, I pulled his hands away. I was cracking open inside, breaking. "I won't run this time, but you can push me away. You might want to think about that."

I left. Gideon didn't stop me.

I spent the rest of the afternoon focused on work. Mark loved to brainstorm out loud, which was an awesome learning exercise for me, and his confident and amiable way of dealing with his accounts was inspiring. I watched him breeze through two client meetings in which he conveyed an air of command that was both reassuring and nonthreatening.

Then we tackled a baby-toy company's needs analysis, zeroing in on poor return expenditures as well as untapped avenues, such as mom-blog advertising. I was grateful that my job was a distraction from my personal life, and I was looking forward to going to my Krav Maga class later, so I could burn off some of my edgy restlessness.

It was just past four when my desk phone rang. I answered briskly and felt my heart leap at the sound of Gideon's voice.

"We should leave at five," he said, "to get to Dr. Petersen's on time."

"Oh." I'd forgotten that our couples therapy sessions were on Thursdays at six P.M. It would be our first.

Abruptly, I wondered if it would also be our last.

"I'll come get you," he went on gruffly, "when it's time."

I sighed, feeling far from up to it. I was already raw and irritable from our fight earlier. "I'm sorry I hit you. I shouldn't have done that. I hate that I did."

"Angel." Gideon exhaled harshly. "You didn't ask the one question that matters."

My eyes closed. It was irritating how he read my mind. "Either way, it doesn't change the fact that you're keeping secrets."

"Secrets are something we can work through; cheating isn't."

I rubbed at the ache behind my forehead. "You're right about that."

"There's only you, Eva." His voice was clipped and hard.

A tremor moved through me at the fury underlying his words. He was still angry that I'd doubted him. Oh well. I was still angry, too. "I'll be ready at five."

He was prompt, as usual. While I put my computer to sleep and grabbed my belongings, he spoke with Mark about the ongoing work on the Kingsman Vodka account. I watched Gideon furtively. He cut an imposing figure with his tall, leanly muscular frame in his dark suit and carried himself in a way that projected impenetrability, yet I'd seen him terribly vulnerable.

I was in love with that tender, deeply emotional man. And I resented the façade and his attempts to hide himself from me.

Turning his head, he caught me staring. I saw a glimpse of my beloved Gideon in his wild blue gaze, which briefly exposed a helpless yearning. Then he was gone, replaced by the cool mask. "Ready?"

It was so obvious that he was holding something back, and it killed me to have that gulf between us. To know there were things he wouldn't trust me with.

As we exited through reception, Megumi rested her chin on her fist and gave a dramatic sigh.

"She's crushing on you, Cross," I murmured, as we made our way out and he hit the call button for the elevator.

"Whatever." He snorted. "What does she know about me?"

"I've been asking myself that same question all day," I said quietly.

That time, I was certain he winced.

DR. Lyle Petersen was tall, with neatly groomed gray hair and sharp yet kind denim blue eyes. His office was tastefully decorated in neutral shades and his furniture was extremely comfortable, something I noted on every one of my visits to him. It was a little weird for me to see him as *my* therapist now. In the past, he'd met with me only as my mother's daughter. He'd been my mom's shrink for the last couple of years.

I watched as he settled into the gray wingback chair across from the sofa Gideon and I sat on. His keen gaze shifted between us, clearly noting how we'd each taken seats on opposite ends of the sofa, our stiff postures revealing our defensiveness. We'd made the drive over in the same way.

Flipping open the cover of his tablet, Dr. Petersen gripped his stylus and said, "Shall we start with the cause of the tension between you?"

I waited a beat, to give Gideon a chance to speak first. I wasn't terribly surprised when he just sat there, silent. "Well . . . in the last twenty-four hours I've met the fiancée I didn't know Gideon had—"

"Ex-fiancée," Gideon growled.

"—I found out the reason he's dated brunettes exclusively is because of her—"

"It wasn't dating."

"—and I caught her leaving his office after lunch looking like this—" I dug out my phone.

"She was leaving the building," Gideon bit out, "not my office."

I pulled up the picture and passed my phone over to Dr. Petersen. "And getting into *your* car, Gideon!"

"Angus just told you before we got here that he saw her standing there, recognized her, and was being polite."

"Like he'd say anything different!" I shot back. "He's been your driver since you were a kid. Of course he'd cover your ass."

"Oh, it's a conspiracy now?"

"What was he doing there, then?" I challenged.

"Driving me to lunch."

"Where? I'll just verify you were there and she wasn't, and we'll get that part out of the way."

Gideon's jaw clenched. "I told you. I had an unexpected appointment. I didn't make it to lunch."

"Who was the appointment?"

"It wasn't Corinne."

"That's not an answer!" I turned back to Dr. Petersen, who calmly returned my phone to me. "When I went up to his office to ask him what the hell was going on, I discovered him half dressed and freshly showered, with one of his sofas bumped out of place, pillows strewn all over the floor—"

"One goddamned pillow!"

"—and red lipstick on his shirt."

"There are two dozen businesses in the Crossfire," Gideon said coldly. "She could have been visiting any one of them."

"Right," I drawled, my voice dripping sarcasm. "Of course."

"Wouldn't I have taken her to the hotel?"

I sucked in a sharp breath, reeling. "You still have that room?"

His mask slipped, revealing a flare of panic. The realization that he still had his sex pad—a hotel room he used exclusively for fucking and somewhere *I'd* never go again—hit me like a physical blow, sending a sharp pain through my chest. A low sound left me, a pained whimper that had me squeezing my eyes shut.

"Let's slow down," Dr. Petersen interrupted, scribbling rapidly. "I want to backtrack a bit. Gideon, why didn't you tell Eva about Corinne?"

"I had every intention of doing so," Gideon said tightly.

"He doesn't tell me anything," I whispered, digging for a tissue in my purse so I wouldn't have mascara running down my face. *Why would he keep that room?* The only explanation was that he intended to use it with someone other than me.

"What do you talk about?" Dr. Petersen asked, directing the question at both of us.

"I'm usually apologizing," Gideon muttered.

Dr. Petersen looked up. "For what?"

"Everything." He raked a hand through his hair.

"Do you feel that Eva's too demanding or expects too much from you?"

I felt Gideon's gaze on my profile. "No. She doesn't ask for anything."

"Except the truth," I corrected, turning toward him.

His eyes blazed, searing me with heat. "I've never lied to you."

"Do you want her to ask you for things, Gideon?" Dr. Petersen queried.

Gideon frowned.

"Think about that. We'll come back to it." Dr. Petersen turned his attention to me. "I'm intrigued by the photo you took, Eva. You were confronted with a situation that many women would find deeply upsetting—"

"There was no situation," Gideon reiterated coldly.

"Her perception of a situation," Dr. Petersen qualified.

"A patently ridiculous perception, considering the physical aspect of our relationship."

"All right. Let's talk about that. How many times a week do you have sex? On average."

My face heated. I looked at Gideon, who returned my look with a smirk.

"Umm . . ." My lips twisted ruefully. "A lot."

"Daily?" Dr. Petersen's brows rose when I uncrossed and re-crossed my legs, nodding. "Multiple times daily?"

Gideon stepped in, "On average."

Laying his tablet flat on his lap, Dr. Petersen met Gideon's gaze. "Is this level of sexual activity customary for you?"

"Nothing about my relationship with Eva is customary, Doctor."

"What was the frequency of your sexual encounters prior to Eva?"

Gideon's jaw tensed, and he glanced at me.

"It's okay," I told him, even as I conceded that I wouldn't want to answer that question in front of him.

He reached his hand out, spanning the distance between us. I placed mine in his and appreciated the reassuring squeeze he gave me. "Twice a week," he said tightly. "On average."

The number of women quickly added up in my mind. My free hand fisted in my lap.

Dr. Petersen sat back. "Eva has brought up concerns of infidelity and lack of communication in your relationship. How often is sex used to resolve disagreements?"

Gideon's brow arched. "Before you assume Eva's suffering under the demands of my overactive libido, you should know that she initiates sex at least as often as I do. If one of us were going to have concerns about keeping up, it'd be me just by virtue of possessing male anatomy."

Dr. Petersen looked at me for confirmation.

"Most interactions between us lead to sex," I conceded, "includ-ing fights."

"Before or after the conflict is considered resolved by both of you?"

I sighed. "Before."

He dropped the stylus and started typing. I thought he might end up with a novel's worth by the time all was said and done.

"Your relationship has been highly sexualized from the beginning?" he asked.

I nodded, even though he wasn't looking. "We're very attracted to each other."

"Obviously." He glanced up and offered a kind smile. "However, I'd like to discuss the possibility of abstinence while we—"

"There is no possibility," Gideon interjected. "That's a nonstarter. I suggest we focus on what's *not* working without eliminating one of the few things that is."

"I'm not sure it *is* working, Gideon," Dr. Petersen said evenly. "Not the way it should be."

"Doctor." Gideon set one ankle on the opposite knee and settled back, creating a picture of unyielding decisiveness. "The only way I'm keeping my hands off her is if I'm dead. Find another way to fix us."

"I'm new to this therapy thing," Gideon said later, after we'd gotten back into the Bentley and were heading home. "So I'm not sure. Was that the train wreck it felt like it was?"

"It could've gone better," I said wearily, leaning my head back and closing my eyes. I was bone tired. Too tired to even think about catching the eight o'clock Krav Maga class. "I'd kill for a quick shower and my bed."

"I have some things to take care of before I can call it a day."

"That's fine." I yawned. "Why don't we take the night off and see each other tomorrow?"

Thick silence greeted my suggestion. After a moment, it became so fraught with tension that I was motivated to lift both my head and my heavy eyelids to look at him.

His gaze was on my face, his lips thinned into a frustrated line. "You're cutting me off."

"No, I'm—"

"The hell you're not! You've tried and convicted me, and now you're shutting me out."

"I'm exhausted, Gideon! There's only so much bullshit I can take before I'm buried in it. I need sleep and—"

"*I* need *you*," he snapped. "What is it going to take to make you believe me?"

"I don't think you cheated. Okay? As suspicious as it all looks, I can't convince myself you'd do that. It's the secrets that are getting to be too much. I'm giving all I've got to this and you're—"

"You think I'm not?" He twisted in the seat, sliding one bent leg in between us so that he faced me directly. "I've never worked so hard for anything in my life as I have for you."

"You can't make the effort for me. You have to do it for you."

"Don't give me that crap! I wouldn't need to work on my relationship skills for anyone else."

With a low moan, I rested my cheek against the seat and closed my eyes again. "I'm tired of fighting, Gideon. I just want some peace and quiet for a night. I've been feeling off all day."

"Are you sick?" He shifted, cupping the back of my neck gently and pressing his lips to my forehead. "You don't feel hot. Is your stomach upset?"

I breathed him in, absorbing the delicious scent of his skin. The urge to press my face into the crook of his neck was nearly overwhelming.

"No." And then it hit me. I groaned.

"What is it?" He pulled me into his lap, cradling me close. "What's wrong? Do you need a doctor?"

"It's my period," I whispered, not wanting Angus to overhear. "It should start any day now. I don't know why I didn't realize it before. No wonder I'm so tired and cranky; I'm hormonal."

He stilled. After a heartbeat or two, I tilted my head back to search his face.

With his lips twisted ruefully, he admitted, "That's a new one for me. Not something that comes up in the course of a casual sex life."

"Lucky you. You get to experience the inconvenience reserved for men with girlfriends and wives."

"I *am* lucky." Gideon brushed loose strands of my hair away from my temples, his own luxuriant hair falling around that chiseled face. "And maybe, if I'm really lucky, you'll feel better tomorrow and like me again."

Ah, God. My heart ached in my chest. "I like you now, Gideon. I just don't like you keeping secrets. It's going to break us up."

"Don't let it," he murmured, tracing my brows with his fingertip. "Trust me."

"You have to trust me back."

Folding over me, he pressed his lips softly to mine. "Don't you know, angel?" he breathed. "There's no one I trust more."

Sliding my arms beneath his jacket, I hugged him, soaking up the warmth of his lean, hard body. I couldn't help but worry that we were beginning to drift from one another.

Gideon pressed the advantage, his tongue dipping into my mouth, lightly touching and teasing mine with velvet licks. Deceptively unhurried. I sought a deeper contact, needing more. Always more. Hating that aside from this, he gave me so little of himself.

He groaned into my mouth, an erotic sound of pleasure and need that vibrated through me. Tilting his head, he sealed those beauti-

fully sculpted lips over mine. The kiss deepened, our tongues stroking, our breaths quickening.

The arm he'd banded beneath my back tightened, pulling me
closer. His other hand slid beneath my shirt, cradling my spine in
his warm palm. His fingertips flexed, gentling me even as the kiss
grew wild. I arched into the caress, needing the reassurance of his
touch against my bare skin.

"Gideon . . ." For the first time, our physical closeness wasn't
enough to calm the desperate wanting inside me.

"Shh," he soothed. "I'm here. Not going anywhere."

Closing my eyes, I buried my face in his neck, wondering if we'd
both be too stubborn and stay, even if it turned out that it would be
best to let go.

4

I WOKE WITH a cry that was muffled by the sweaty palm mashed over my mouth. A crushing weight cut off my air as another hand shoved up beneath my nightgown, groping and bruising. Panic gripped me and I thrashed, my legs kicking frantically.

No . . . Please, no . . . No more. Not again.

Panting like a dog, Nathan yanked my legs apart. The hard thing between his legs poked blindly, ramming into my inner thigh. I fought, my lungs burning, but he was so strong. I couldn't buck him off. I couldn't get away.

Stop it! Get off me. Don't touch me. Oh, God . . . please don't do that to me . . . don't hurt me . . .

Ma-ma!

Nathan's hand pressed down on me, squashing my head into the pillow. The more I struggled, the more excited he became. Gasping horrible, nasty words in my ear, he found the tender spot between my legs and shoved into me, groaning. I froze, locking in a vise of horrendous pain.

"Yeah," he grunted, *". . . like it once it's in you . . . hot little slut . . . you like it . . ."*

I couldn't breathe, my lungs shuddering with sobs, my nostrils plugged by the heel of his palm. Spots danced before my eyes; my chest burned. I fought again . . . needing air . . . desperate for air—

"Eva! Wake up!"

My eyes snapped open at the barked command. I heaved myself away from the hands gripping my biceps, gaining my freedom. I clawed away . . . fighting the sheets that bound my legs . . . tumbling down . . .

The jolting impact of hitting the floor woke me fully, and an awful sound of pain and fear scraped up through my throat.

"Christ! Eva, damn it. Don't hurt yourself!"

I sucked in air with deep gulps and scrambled toward the bathroom on all fours.

Gideon scooped me up and gripped me to his chest. *"Eva."*

"Sick," I gasped, slapping a hand over my mouth as my stomach roiled.

"I've got you," he said grimly, carrying me with brisk, powerful strides. He took me to the toilet and tossed up the seat. Kneeling beside me, he held my hair back as I heaved, his warm hand stroking up and down my spine.

"Shh . . . angel," he murmured, over and over. "It's okay. You're safe."

When my stomach was empty, I flushed the toilet and rested my sweat-drenched face on my forearm, trying to focus on anything but the remnants of my dream.

"Baby girl."

REFLECTED IN YOU · 57

I turned my head to find Cary standing in the threshold of my bathroom, his handsome face marred by a frown. He was fully dressed in loose jeans and a henley, which made me aware that Gideon was fully dressed, too. He'd lost the suit earlier when we'd first come back to my apartment, but he wasn't wearing the sweats he had put on then. Instead he was in jeans and a black T-shirt.

Disoriented by their appearances, I glanced at my watch and saw it was just after midnight. "What are you guys doing?"

"I was just coming in," Cary said. "And caught up with Cross on his way up."

I looked at Gideon, whose concerned frown matched my roommate's. "You went out?"

Gideon helped me to my feet. "I told you I had some things to take care of."

Until midnight? "What things?"

"It's not important."

I shrugged out of his hold and went to the sink to brush my teeth. Another secret. How many did he have?

Cary appeared at my elbow, his gaze meeting mine in the reflection of my vanity mirror. "You haven't had a bad dream in a long time."

Looking into his worried green eyes, I let him see how worn down I was.

He gave my shoulder a reassuring squeeze. "We'll take it easy this weekend. Recharge. We both need it. You gonna be all right tonight?"

"I've got her." Gideon straightened from his perch on the lip of my bathtub, where he'd taken off his boots.

"That doesn't mean I'm not here." Cary pressed a quick kiss to my temple. "Holler if you need me."

The look he gave me before he left the room spoke volumes—he wasn't comfortable with Gideon sleeping over. Truth was, I had some reservations, too. I thought my lingering wariness over Gideon's sleep disorder was contributing a lot to my wild emotional state. As Cary had recently said, the man I loved was a ticking time bomb, and I shared a bed with him.

I rinsed out my mouth and dropped my toothbrush back into its holder. "I need a shower."

I'd taken one before I crashed, but now I felt dirty again. Cold sweat clung to my skin and when I closed my eyes, I could smell *him*—Nathan—on me.

Gideon turned on the water, then started stripping, blessedly distracting me with the sight of his gloriously tight body. His muscles were hard and well defined, his build lean yet powerful and elegant.

I left my clothes where they fell and stepped beneath the steamy spray with a groan. He entered the stall behind me, brushing my hair aside and pressing a kiss to my shoulder. "How are you?"

"Better." *Because you're near.*

His arms wrapped carefully around my waist and he released a shaky exhalation. "I . . . Jesus, Eva. Were you dreaming about Nathan?"

I took a deep breath. "Maybe one day we'll talk about our dreams, huh?"

He inhaled sharply, his fingertips flexing against my hip. "It's like that, is it?"

"Yeah," I muttered. "It's like that."

We stood there for a long moment, surrounded by steam and secrets, physically close yet emotionally distant. I hated it. The urge to cry was overwhelming and I didn't fight it. It felt good to get it out. All the pressure of the long day seemed to flow out of me as I sobbed.

"Angel . . ." Gideon pressed into my back, his arms tight around my waist, soothing me with the protective shield of his big body. "Don't cry . . . God. I can't take it. Tell me what you need, angel. Tell me what I can do."

"Wash it away," I whispered, leaning into him, needing the comfort of his tender possessiveness. My fingers laced with his against my stomach. "Make me clean."

"You are."

I sucked in a shuddering breath, shaking my head.

"Listen to me, Eva. No one can touch you," he said fiercely. "No one can get to you. Never again."

My fingers tightened on his.

"They'd have to get through me, Eva. And that will never happen."

I couldn't speak past the ache in my throat. The thought of Gideon facing my nightmare . . . seeing the man who'd done those things to me . . . tightened the cold knot that had been sitting in my gut all day.

Gideon reached for my shampoo and I closed my eyes, shutting it all out, everything but the man whose sole focus at that moment was me.

I waited, breathless, for the feel of his magic fingers. When it came, I reached out to the wall in front of me for balance. With both palms pressed flat against the cool tile, I savored the feel of his fingertips kneading into my scalp and moaned.

"Feel good?" he asked, his voice low and rough.

"Always."

I drifted in bliss as he washed and conditioned my hair, shivering lightly as he ran a wide-toothed comb through the soaked strands. I was disappointed when he finished and must have made some sound of regret, because he leaned forward and promised, "I'm not nearly done."

I smelled my body wash, then—

"*Gideon.*"

I arched into his soap-slick hands. His thumbs dug gently into the knots in my shoulders, melting them with the perfect amount of pressure. Then he worked his way down my spine . . . my buttocks . . . my legs . . .

"I'm going to fall," I slurred, drunk with pleasure.

"I'll catch you, angel. I'll always catch you."

The pain and degradation of my memories washed away beneath the selfless reverence of Gideon's patient caretaking. More than the soap and water, it was his touch that freed me from the nightmare. I turned around at his urging and looked at him crouched before me, his hands gliding up my calves, his body an amazing display of taut flexing muscle. Cupping his jaw, I tilted his head up.

"You can be so good for me, Gideon," I told him softly. "I don't know how I could ever forget that. Even for a minute."

His chest expanded on a quick, deep breath. He straightened, his hands gliding up my thighs, until he towered over me again. His lips touched mine, softly. Lightly. "I know today was all kinds of fucked up. Shit . . . the whole week. It's been hard for me, too."

"I know." I hugged him, pressing my cheek to his heart. He was so solid and strong. I loved the way I felt when I was in his arms.

He was already thick and hard between us, but he grew more so as I cuddled into him. "Eva . . ." He cleared his throat. "Let me finish, angel."

I nipped his jaw with my teeth and reached down to grip his perfect ass, tugging him tighter against me. "Why don't you get started instead?"

"That isn't where this was headed."

As if it could've ended any other way when we were both naked and running our hands all over each other. Gideon could put his

REFLECTED IN YOU · 61

hand to the small of my back while we were walking and make me as needy as if he'd put his hand between my legs. "Well . . . revisit and revise, ace."

Gideon's hands came up and gripped the sides of my throat, his thumbs beneath my chin to push it up. His frown gave him away, and before he could tell me why it wasn't a good idea to make love now, I caught his cock in my hands.

He growled, his hips jerking. "Eva . . ."

"It would be a shame to waste this."

"I can't screw this up with you." His eyes were dark as sapphires. "If you ever freaked out while I was touching you, I'd lose my mind."

"Gideon, please—"

"I say when." The command in his voice was unmistakable.

My grip loosened automatically.

He stepped back and away, his hand dropping to fist his cock.

I shifted restlessly, my attention riveted to that dexterous hand and its long, elegant fingers. As the distance between us widened, I began to ache, my body responding to the loss of his. The heated languidness he'd instilled with his touch turned into a slow burn, as if he'd banked a fire that had suddenly been stoked.

"See something you like?" he purred, pleasuring himself.

Astonished that he'd taunt me after denying me, I looked up . . . and my breath caught.

Gideon was smoldering, too. I couldn't think of another word to describe him. He was watching me with a heavy-lidded gaze like he wanted to eat me alive. His tongue slid leisurely along the seam of his lips, as if he tasted me. When he caught the full lower curve between his teeth, I could've sworn I felt it between my legs. I knew that look so well . . . knew what came after it . . . knew how ferocious he could be when he wanted me that badly.

It was a look that screamed SEX. Hard, deep, endless, mind-blowing sex. He stood on the far side of my shower, his feet planted wide, his ripped body flexing rhythmically as he caressed his beautiful cock with long, slow strokes.

I'd never seen anything so blatantly sexual or boldly masculine. "Oh my God," I breathed, riveted. "You are so fucking hot."

The gleam in his eyes told me he knew what he was doing to me. His free hand slid slowly up his ridged abdomen and squeezed his pectoral, making me jealous. "Could you come watching me?"

Realization struck me. He was afraid to touch me sexually so soon after my nightmare, afraid of what it might do to us if he triggered me. But he was willing to put on a show for me—*inspire* me—so I could touch myself. The surge of emotion I felt in that moment was devastating. Gratitude and affection, desire and tenderness.

"I love you, Gideon."

His eyes squeezed shut, as if the words were too much for him to take. When they opened again, the force of his will sent a shiver of need through me. "Show me."

The wide head of his cock was engulfed in his palm. He squeezed, bringing a flush to his face that had me pressing my thighs together. His thumb rubbed over the flat disk of his nipple. Once. Twice. He groaned a rough sound of delight that had me salivating.

The water pounding at my back and the billowing steam that plumed between us only added to the eroticism of the picture he presented. His hand quickened, sliding rhythmically up and down. He was so long and thick. Undeniably virile.

Unable to bear the ache of my tightened nipples, I cupped my breasts and squeezed.

"There you go, angel. Show me what I do to you."

There was a moment in which I wondered if I could. It hadn't been so long ago that I'd been embarrassed to talk about my vibrator with Gideon face-to-face.

"Look at me, Eva." He cupped his balls in one hand and his cock in the other. Shameless, which was such a turn-on. "I don't want to come without you. I need you with me."

I wanted to be as hot for him. I wanted him as aching and needy as I felt. I wanted my body—my *desire*—to be burned onto his brain the way this image of him would be burned onto mine.

With my eyes locked with his, my hands glided over my body. I watched his movements . . . listened for the catch of his breath . . . used his clues to know what drove him wild.

It was somehow as intimate as when he was inside me, maybe more so because we were wide open and on display. Totally bared. Our pleasure reflected in each other.

He started telling me what he wanted in that raspy sex god voice: *Tug your nipples, angel . . . Touch yourself—are you wet? Push your fingers inside you . . . Feel how tight you are? A hot, tight, plush little heaven for my dick . . . You're so fucking gorgeous . . . So sexy. I'm so damn stiff it hurts . . . See what you do to me? I'm going to come so hard for you . . .*

"Gideon." I gasped, my fingertips massaging my clit in rapid circles, my hips grinding into my touch.

"Right there with you," he said hoarsely, his hand jacking his cock with brutal speed and violence in his race to orgasm.

At the first jolting contraction of my core, I cried out, my legs quaking. My palm slapped against the glass enclosure for balance, the climax stealing the strength from my muscles. Gideon was on me in a second, gripping my hipbone in a way that conveyed greed and possession, his fingers flexing with restless agitation.

"Eva!" he growled, as the first thick, hot burst of semen hit my belly. "Fuck."

Hunching over me, his teeth sank into the tender spot between my shoulder and neck, a painless hold that conveyed the rawness of his pleasure. His groans vibrated against me and he came violently, spurting repeatedly against my stomach.

Iᴛ was a little after six o'clock in the morning when I slipped out of my bedroom. I'd been up for a while, watching Gideon sleep. It was a rare treat, because I hardly ever managed to wake up before he did. I could stare at him without any worries that he'd be weirded out.

I padded down the hallway until it emptied into the expansive open floor plan of the main living area. It was ridiculous that Cary and I lived on the Upper West Side in an apartment large enough for a family, but I'd long ago learned to pick my battles when it came to arguing with my mother and stepfather over my safety. There was no way they were budging on location or security features like a doorman and front desk, but I could exploit my cooperation on my living arrangements to get them to ease up on other points.

I was in the kitchen waiting for the coffee to finish brewing when Cary joined me. He strolled in looking amazing in a pair of gray San Diego State University sweats, sleep-mussed chocolate brown hair, and a day's worth of stubble along his square jaw.

"Morning, baby girl," he murmured, pressing a kiss to my temple as he passed me.

"You're up early."

"Look who's talking." He grabbed two mugs out of the cupboard, then the half-and-half out of the fridge. He brought them over and studied me. "How are you doing?"

"I'm good. Really," I insisted, when he shot me a skeptical look. "Gideon took care of me."

"Okay, but is that really so great if he's the reason you were stressed enough to have the nightmare to begin with?"

I filled mugs for both of us, adding sugar to mine and cream to both. As I did, I told him about Corinne and the Waldorf dinner, then the argument I'd had with Gideon over her appearance at the Crossfire.

Cary stood with his hip cocked into the counter, his legs crossed at the ankle, and one arm banding his chest. He sipped his coffee. "No explanation, huh?"

I shook my head, feeling the weight of Gideon's silence. "How about you? How are you doing?"

"You just gonna change the subject?"

"What else is there to say? It's a one-sided story."

"You ever stop to think that he might always have secrets?"

Frowning, I lowered my mug. "What do you mean?"

"I mean he's the twenty-eight-year-old son of a suicidal Ponzi scheme swindler, and he just happens to own a large chunk of Manhattan." One brow arched upward in challenge. "Think about it. Can they really be mutually exclusive things?"

Lowering my gaze to my mug, I took a drink and didn't confess that I'd wondered the same thing once or twice. The extent of Gideon's fortune and empire was staggering, especially considering his age. "I can't see Gideon bilking people, not when it's more of a challenge to accomplish what he has legitimately."

"With all the secrets he's got, can you be sure you know him well enough to make that judgment call?"

I thought of the man who'd spent the night with me and felt relief at how sure I was about my answer—at least at that moment. "Yes."

"All right, then." Cary shrugged. "I talked to Dr. Travis yesterday."

My thoughts immediately veered in another direction at the mention of our therapist in San Diego. "You did?"

"Yeah. I really fucked up the other night."

From the agitated way he scooped his long bangs back from his face, I knew he was referring to the orgy I'd walked in on.

"Cross broke Ian's nose and split his lip," he said, reminding me of how violently Gideon had responded to Cary's . . . *friend* rudely propositioning me to join them. "I saw Ian yesterday and he looks like he was hit in the face with a brick. He was asking who clocked him, so he could press charges."

"Oh." My lungs seized for the length of two heartbeats. "Oh, crap."

"I know. Billionaire plus lawsuit equals beaucoup bucks. What the fuck was I thinking?" Cary closed his eyes and rubbed them. "I told him I didn't know who your date was, that it was some guy you picked up and dragged home. Cross blindsided him, so Ian didn't see shit."

"The two girls with you got a real good look at Gideon," I said grimly.

"They took off out that door"—Cary pointed across the living room as if our door were still reverberating with the slam—"like she-bats out of hell. They didn't go to the urgent care with us, and neither of us knows who they are. If Ian doesn't run into them again, we're okay."

I rubbed at the quiver in my tummy, feeling unsettled again.

"I'll keep an eye on the situation," he assured me. "The whole night was a major wake-up call, and talking it out in therapy gave me some perspective. Afterward, I went to see Trey. To apologize."

Hearing Trey's name made me sad. I'd hoped Cary's budding relationship with the veterinary student would work out, but Cary had sabotaged that. As usual. "How'd that go?"

REFLECTED IN YOU · 67

He shrugged again, but the movement was awkward. "I hurt him the other night because I'm an asshole. Then I hurt him again yesterday trying to do the right thing."

"Did you break it off?" I held my hand out to him and squeezed his when he placed it in mine.

"It's seriously cooled off. Like on ice. He wants me to be gay, and I'm not."

It was painful to hear that someone wanted Cary to be anything other than who he was, because it'd always been that way for him. I couldn't understand why. To me, he was wonderful as is. "I'm so sorry, Cary."

"So am I, because he's a great guy. I'm just not ready for the stress and demands of a complicated relationship right now. I'm working a lot. I'm not stable enough yet to be fucked up in the head." His lips pursed. "You might want to think about that, too. We just moved out here. We've both still got some settling in to do."

I nodded, understanding where he was coming from and not disagreeing, but unwavering in my decision to see my relationship with Gideon through. "Did you talk to Tatiana, too?"

"No need." His thumb brushed over my knuckles before he released me. "She's easy."

Snorting, I took a large gulp of my cooling coffee.

"Not just *that* way," he chided, giving me a wicked grin. "I mean she doesn't expect anything or make any demands. As long as I suit up and she orgasms at least as many times as I do, she's good. I'm actually okay with her, and not just because she could suck chrome off a bumper. It's relaxing being with someone who just wants to have fun and causes no stress."

"Gideon knows me. He understands and tries to work around my issues. He's working for this, too, Cary. It's not easy for him, either."

"Do you think Cross had a nooner with his ex?" he asked bluntly.

"No."

"Are you sure?"

Sucking in a deep breath, I took a fortifying gulp and admitted, "Mostly. I think I'm the one doing it for him now. It's pretty hot with us, you know? But his ex has some kind of hold on him. He says it's guilt, but that doesn't explain his brunette fascination."

"It explains why you lost it and hit him—her being around again is eating at you. And he still won't tell you what's going on. Does that sound healthy to you?"

It wasn't. I knew that. I hated it. "We saw Dr. Petersen last night."

His brows rose. "How'd that go?"

"He didn't tell us to run far, far away from each other as fast as we can."

"And if he does? Will you listen?"

"I'm not bailing when things get rough this time. Seriously, Cary"—I held his gaze—"am I really all that far ahead if I can't take any waves?"

"Baby girl, Cross is a tsunami."

"Ha!" I smiled, unable to help it. Cary could get me to smile through tears. "To tell you the truth, if I don't work this out with Gideon, I have doubts I'll work it out with anyone."

"That's your shitty self-esteem talking."

"He knows what I'm carrying around in me."

"All right."

My brows shot up. "All right?" *That was too easy.*

"I'm not sold. But I'll deal." He grabbed my hand. "Come on. Let's get your hair done."

I smiled, grateful. "You're the best."

He bumped his hip into mine. "And I won't let you forget it."

5

"AS FAR AS death traps go," Cary said, "this one's pretty swank." I shook my head as I preceded him into the main cabin of Gideon's private jet. "You are *not* going to die. Flying is safer than driving."

"And you don't think the airline industry paid for the compilation of those statistics?"

Pausing to smack him in the shoulder with a laugh, I glanced at the amazingly opulent interior and felt more than a little awe. I'd seen my share of private planes over the years, but as usual, Gideon went to lengths to which few could afford to go.

The cabin was spacious, with a wide center aisle. The underlying palette was neutral with accents of chocolate brown and ice blue. Deep, swiveling bucket seats with tables were positioned on the left, while a sectional sofa sat on the right. Each chair had a private entertainment console beside it. I knew a bedroom would be found at the back of the plane and a luxurious bathroom or two.

A male flight attendant took my duffel bag and Cary's, then gestured for us to take a seat at one of the groupings of chairs that had a table. "Mr. Cross is expected within the next ten minutes," he said. "In the meantime, can I serve you something to drink?"

"Water for me, please." I glanced at my watch. It was just past seven thirty.

"Bloody Mary," Cary ordered, "if you've got it."

The steward smiled. "We've got everything."

Cary caught my look. "What? I haven't had dinner. The tomato juice will hold me over until we eat, and the alcohol will help the Dramamine kick in faster."

"I didn't say anything," I protested.

I turned to look out the window at the evening sky, and my thoughts settled on Gideon, as usual. He'd been quiet all day, starting with when he'd woken up. The ride to work had been made in silence, and when my day ended at five, he'd called just long enough to tell me that Angus would take me home alone, then drive me and Cary to the airport, where he'd meet us.

I opted to walk home instead, since I hadn't hit the gym the night before and didn't have time to work out prior to the flight. Angus had cautioned that Gideon wouldn't like me refusing the ride, even though I'd done it politely and with good reason. I think Angus thought I was still upset with him for giving Corinne a ride, which I kind of was. I was sorry to say that a tiny part of me hoped he'd feel bad about it. A bigger part of me hated that I could be that petty.

As I'd walked through Central Park, taking a meandering path through tall trees, I had determined that I wasn't going to be small over a guy. Not even Gideon. I wasn't going to let my frustration

REFLECTED IN YOU · 71

with him get in the way of having a good time in Vegas with my best friend.

Halfway home, I'd stopped and turned, picking out Gideon's penthouse high above Fifth Avenue. I wondered if he was there, packing and planning for a weekend without me. Or if he was still at work, wrapping up the week's pressing business.

"Uh-oh," Cary singsonged, as the flight attendant returned with a tray laden with our drinks. "You've got that look."

"What look?"

"The hell-on-wheels look." He clinked his tall, slender glass against the side of my squat tumbler. "Wanna talk about it?"

I was about to reply when Gideon stepped onto the plane. He looked grim and carried a briefcase in one hand and a duffel in the other. After passing his bag over to the attendant, he paused by me and Cary, giving my roommate a cursory nod before brushing the backs of his fingers across my cheek. The simple touch shot through me like a surge of electricity. Then he was gone, slipping into a cabin in the back and shutting the door.

I scowled. "He's so damn moody."

"And seriously hot. What he does for that suit . . ."

Most suits made the man. Gideon did things to a three-piece suit that should've been illegal.

"Don't distract me with his looks," I groused.

"Give him a blowjob. That's a guaranteed mood improver."

"Spoken like a man."

"You expected something different?" Cary grabbed the frosty glass bottle holding the excess water that wouldn't fit in my crystal tumbler. "Check this out."

He showed me the label, which was branded to the Cross Towers and Casino. "Now *that's* swank."

My lips twisted wryly. "For the whales."

"What?"

"Casino high rollers. Gamblers who don't blink an eye at dropping a hundred grand or more on the turn of a card. They get a lot of comps to lure them in—food, suites, and travel to and fro. My mom's second husband was a whale. It's one of the reasons why she left him."

He shook his head at me. "The shit you know. So this is a company jet?"

"One of five," the attendant said, returning with a tray of fruit and cheese.

"Jesus," Cary muttered. "That's a damned fleet."

I watched as he dug a travel packet of Dramamine out of his pocket and washed the pills down with his Bloody Mary.

"Want some?" he asked, tapping at the wrapper on the table.

"Nope. Thanks."

"You gonna deal with Mr. Hot and Moody?"

"Not sure. I may just pull out my e-reader."

He nodded. "Probably safer for your sanity."

Thirty minutes later, Cary was snoring lightly in his fully reclined seat, his ears covered with noise-canceling headphones. I watched him for a long minute, appreciating the sight of him looking restful and relaxed, the shallow grooves around his mouth softening in slumber.

Then I got up and went to the cabin I'd seen Gideon disappear into earlier. I debated knocking, then thought against it. He was shutting me out elsewhere; I wasn't going to give him the opportunity to do so now.

He glanced up when I walked in, his face showing no surprise at my abrupt appearance. He sat at a desk, listening to a woman who was speaking to him via satellite video. His coat was hung on the

REFLECTED IN YOU · 73

back of his chair and his tie was loosened. After that one brief glance at me, he resumed his conversation.

I started stripping.

My tank top came off first, followed by my sandals and jeans. The woman continued talking, mentioning "concerns" and "discrepancies," but Gideon's eyes were on me—hot and avid.

"We'll pick this up in the morning, Allison," he interjected, hitting a button on the keyboard that darkened the screen just before my bra landed on his head.

"I'm the one with PMS," I said, "but you're the one having mood swings."

He pulled my bra into his lap and leaned back in his chair, setting his elbows on the armrests and steepling his fingers together. "And you're putting on a striptease to improve my mood?"

"Ha! Men are so predictable. Cary suggested I blow you to make you happy. No . . . don't get excited. That's not going to happen." I hooked my thumbs in the waistband of my panties and rocked back on my heels. I had to give him points for keeping his eyes on mine and not on my breasts. "I think you owe me, ace. Big-time. I've been an exceptionally understanding girlfriend under the circumstances, don't you think?"

His brow arched.

"I mean, I'd like to see what you would do," I went on, "if you came over to my place and caught an ex-boyfriend stepping outside still tucking his shirt in his pants. Then, when you came upstairs, you found my couch messed up and me fresh from a shower."

Gideon's jaw tightened. "Neither of us wants to see what I'd do."

"So we're both agreed that I've been pretty damn awesome under extraordinary circumstances." I crossed my arms, knowing how that would showcase the assets he loved. "You've made it very clear how you'd choose to punish me. How would you choose to reward me?"

"Is it my choice?" he drawled, his eyes heavy-lidded.

I smiled. "No."

He set my bra on his keyboard and unfolded from the chair in a leisurely, graceful rise. "Then that's your reward, angel. What do you want?"

"I want you to stop being grumpy, for starters."

"Grumpy?" His lips twitched with a suppressed smile. "Well, I woke up without you, and now I face two more mornings of the same."

I dropped my arms to my sides and went to him, placing my palms flat to his broad chest. "Is that really all it is?"

"Eva." He was such a strong, physically powerful man, and yet he could touch me with such reverence.

I ducked my head, knowing something in my voice had given me away. He was too perceptive.

Cupping my jaw in his hands, Gideon tipped my head back and searched my face. "Talk to me."

"I feel like you're pulling away."

A low growl rumbled through the air between us. "I've got a lot on my mind. That doesn't mean I'm not thinking about you."

"I *feel* it, Gideon. There's distance between us that wasn't there before."

His hands slid down to my neck, wrapping around it. "There's no distance. You've got me by the throat, Eva." His grip tightened fractionally. "Can't you feel *that*?"

I sucked in a quick, tight breath. Agitation spurred my heartbeat, a physical response to fear that came entirely from within and not from Gideon, who I knew absolutely would never physically harm me or put me in danger.

"Sometimes," he said huskily, watching me with searing intensity, "I can hardly breathe."

I might've broken free if not for his eyes, which revealed such yearning and turmoil. He was making me feel the same loss of power, the same sense of being dependent on someone else for every breath I took.

So I did the opposite of running. Tilting my head back, I surrendered, and the tingles of fear left me in a rush. I was learning that Gideon was right about my desire to give up control to him. Doing so soothed something inside me, some need I hadn't realized I possessed.

There was a long pause, filled only by his breathing. I sensed him warring with his emotions and wondered what they were, wondered why he was so conflicted.

He released the tension with a deep exhalation. "What do you need, Eva?"

"You—a mile high."

His hands slid over my shoulders and squeezed, then caressed the length of my arms. His fingers linked with mine and he nuzzled our temples together. "What is it with you, sex, and modes of transportation?"

"I'll take you any way I can get you," I told him, repeating the sentiment he'd once said to me. "It'll probably be next weekend before I'm good to go again, thanks to my period."

"Fuck."

"That's the idea."

Reaching for his coat, he wrapped it around me and ushered me out of the cabin.

"Oh, God." My hands fisted the sheets beneath me, my back arching as Gideon pinned my hips to the bed and fluttered his tongue across

my clit. My skin was coated in a fine sheen of sweat, my vision blurring as my core tightened viciously in preparation for orgasm. My pulse was thrumming, racing in unison with the steady hum of the jet's engines.

I'd come twice already, as much from the sight of his dark head between my legs as from his wickedly gifted mouth. My panties were ruined, literally shredded by his grip, and he was still fully dressed.

"I'm ready." I pushed my fingers into his hair, feeling the dampness at the roots. His restraint was costing him. He was always so careful with me, taking the time to make sure I was soft and wet before filling me too full with his long, thick cock.

"I'll decide when you're ready."

"I want you inside—" The plane shook suddenly, then dropped, leaving me weightless but for the suction of Gideon's mouth. *"Gideon!"*

I trembled through another climax, my body arching with the need to feel him in me. Through the roaring of blood in my ears, I heard a voice making an announcement over the comm system, but I couldn't register the words.

"You're so sensitive now." Lifting his head, he licked his lips. "You're coming like crazy."

I gasped. "I'd come harder if you were inside me."

"I'll keep that in mind."

"It doesn't matter if I get a little sore now," I argued. "I'll have days to recover."

Something sparked in the depths of his gaze. He rose. "No, Eva."

My postorgasmic haze faded at the harshness of his voice. I levered up onto my elbows and watched him begin to strip, his moves quick and economically graceful.

"My choice," I reminded.

In short order he removed his vest, tie, and cuff links. His voice was too even when he asked, "You really want to play that card, angel?"

"If that's what it takes."

"It'll take more than that for me to hurt you deliberately." His shirt and slacks followed more slowly, a striptease that was far more seductive than mine had been. "For us, pain and pleasure are mutually exclusive."

"I didn't mean—"

"I know what you meant." He straightened from shoving his boxer briefs down, then knelt on the foot of the bed and crawled toward me like a sleek panther on the prowl. "You ache without my cock inside you. You'll say anything to have me there."

"Yes."

He hovered over me, his hair falling in a dark curtain around his face, his big body casting a shadow over mine. Tilting his head, he lowered his mouth and lightly traced the seam of my lips with the tip of his tongue. "You crave it. You feel empty without it."

"Yes, damn you." I gripped his lean hips, arching upward to try to feel his body against mine. I never felt closer to him than when we were making love, and I needed that closeness now, needed to feel like we were okay before we spent the weekend without each other.

He settled between my legs, his erection lying hard and hot between the lips of my sex. "It hurts you a little when I push all the way in, and there's no help for that—you have a tight little cunt and I cram you full. Sometimes I lose control and get rough, and there's no help for that, either. But don't *ever* ask me to hurt you deliberately. I can't."

"I want you," I breathed, rubbing my wet cleft shamelessly along the heated length of his cock.

"Not yet." He moved, rolling his hips to find me with the broad head of his penis. He pushed gently against me, parting me, spreading me open as he slipped just the tip inside. I writhed against the tight fit, my body resisting. "You're not ready yet."

"Fuck me. God . . . just fuck me!"

He reached down with one hand and grabbed my hip, stemming my frenzied attempts to push up and take more of him. "You're swollen."

I fought his hold. My nails dug into the tight curves of his ass and I tugged him against me. I didn't care that it might hurt. If I didn't get him in me I thought I'd lose my mind. "Give it to me."

Gideon slid his hand into my hair, fisting it to hold me where he wanted me. "Look at me."

"Gideon!"

"Look at me."

I stilled at the command in his voice. I stared up at him, my frustration melting as I watched a slow, gradual transformation sweep over his handsome face.

His features tightened first, as if he were pained. A wince knit his brow. His lips parted with a gasp, his chest beginning to heave with labored breaths. A tic began in his jaw, the muscle spasming violently. His skin grew hot, searing me. But what mesmerized me most was his piercing blue eyes and the unmistakable vulnerability that sifted through them like smoke.

My pulse quickened in response to the change in him. The mattress shifted as he dug his feet in, his body bracing—

"Eva." He jerked, then started coming, spurting hotly into me. His pleasured groan vibrated against me, his cock sinking through the sudden flood of semen to bottom out inside me. "Ah . . . Christ."

All the while he looked at me, showing me his face when he usually hid in the crook of my neck. I saw what he'd wanted me to see . . . the point he'd wanted to make—

There was nothing between us.

Rolling his hips, he rubbed out the rest of his orgasm, emptying himself inside me, lubricating me so there would be no pain or resistance. He released my hip and let me rock upward; let me seek the perfect pressure on my clit to set me off. With his eyes still on mine, he reached behind him to claim my wrists. One at a time, he lifted my arms over my head, restraining me.

Pinned to the mattress by his grip, his weight, and his unflagging erection, I was completely at his mercy. He began to thrust, stroking through the trembling walls of my sex with the thickly veined length of his big cock. Claiming me. Possessing me.

"Crossfire," he whispered, reminding me of my safe word.

I moaned as my sex rippled in climax, tightening and squeezing, milking him greedily.

"Feel that?" Gideon's tongue traced the shell of my ear, his breath gusting in humid pants. "You've got me by the throat and the balls. Where's the distance, angel?"

For the next three hours, there was none.

THE hotel manager threw open the double doors to our suite and Cary gave a long, low whistle.

"Hell yeah," he said, hustling me into the room with a hand on my elbow. "Look at the size of this place. You could do cartwheels in here."

He was right, but I'd have to wait until the morning to prove it. My legs were still shaky from my induction into the Mile-High Club.

Directly in front of us was a dazzling view of the Vegas Strip at night. The windows were floor to ceiling, wrapping around a corner that was filled with a piano.

"Why are there always pianos in high-roller suites?" Cary asked, flipping up the cover and tapping out a quick tune on the keys.

I shrugged and looked toward the manager, but she'd already moved off, her stilettos moving silently over the thick white carpet. The suite was decorated in what I'd call fifties Hollywood chic. The double-sided fireplace was faced with rough gray stone and decorated with a piece of art that resembled a hubcap with spacey spokes protruding from the center. The sofas were seafoam green with wooden legs as slender as the manager's heels. Everything had a retro vibe that was at once glamorous and inviting.

It was way too much. I'd expected a nice room, but not the presidential suite. I was about to refuse it when Cary gifted me with a big grin and two thumbs up. Having no willpower to refuse his joy, I gave in and hoped we weren't putting Gideon out of a more profitable reservation.

"Still want a cheeseburger?" I asked him, reaching for the room service menu on the console table behind the sofa.

"And a beer. Make that two."

Cary followed the manager into a bedroom on the left side of the living area, and I picked up the vintage rotary phone to place our order.

Thirty minutes later, I was fresh from a quick shower and dressed in my pajamas, eating chicken Alfredo cross-legged on the area rug. Cary was plowing through his burger and looking at me with happy eyes from his position on the opposite side of the coffee table.

"You never eat a massive pile of carbs this late," he noted between bites.

"My period's coming."

"I'm sure the workout you got on the way here helped, too."

I narrowed my eyes at him. "How would you know? You were passed out."

"Deductive reasoning, baby girl. When I went to sleep, you looked irritated. When I woke up, you looked like you'd just smoked a fat joint."

"How did Gideon look?"

"He looked the same—tight-assed and hot as hell."

I stabbed my fork into my noodles. "That's not fair."

"Who cares?" He gestured around us. "Look how he puts you up."

"I don't need a sugar daddy, Cary."

He munched on a French fry. "Have you thought any more about what you *do* need? You've got his time, his rockin' bod, and access to everything he owns. That's not bad."

"No," I agreed, twirling my fork. I knew from my mom's many marriages to powerful men that getting their time was the most important thing of all, because for them, it was truly the most valuable thing in their lives. "It's not bad. It's just not enough."

"This is the life," Cary pronounced, while lying like a god on a lounger by the pool. He wore pale green trunks and dark shades and caused an unusually large volume of women to walk on our side of the pool. "The only thing missing is a mojito. Gotta have alcohol to celebrate."

My mouth curved. I was sunbathing on the lounger beside him, enjoying the dry heat and occasional splashes of water. Celebrating was habitual for Cary, something I'd always considered quite charming. "What are we celebrating?"

"Summer."

"Okay, then." I sat up and slid my legs off the lounger, tying my sarong around my hips before I stood. My hair was still damp from an earlier dip in the pool and pinned atop my head with a lobster clip. The scorching sun felt good on my skin, a sensual kiss that was nearly enough to make me less self-conscious about the water I was retaining—thanks to my period starting.

I headed over to the pool bar, my gaze raking the other loungers and cabanas through the purple tint of my sunglasses. The area was packed with guests, many of whom were attractive enough to warrant second and third looks. One couple in particular caught my eye, because they reminded me of myself and Gideon. The blonde lay on her stomach, her torso propped up on her arms and her legs kicking playfully. Her very yummy dark-haired man stretched out on the chair beside her, his head propped on one hand while the fingers of the other hand stroked up and down her spine.

She caught me staring and her smile instantly faded. I couldn't see her eyes behind her Jackie O shades, but I knew she was glaring at me. With a smile, I looked away, knowing just how she felt about finding another woman checking out her man.

I found an empty space at the bar and gestured at the bartender to let him know I was ready to order when he was. Misters attached to the ceiling cooled my skin and lured me to slide onto a suddenly vacated bar stool while I waited.

"What are you drinking?"

Turning my head, I looked at the man who'd talked to me. "Nothing yet, but I'm considering a mojito."

"Let me buy you one." He smiled, revealing perfectly white but slightly crooked teeth. He extended his hand to me, a movement that brought my attention to his nicely defined arms. "Daniel."

I placed my hand in his. "Eva. Nice to meet you."

He crossed his arms on the bar and leaned over it. "What brings you to Vegas? Business or pleasure?"

"R and R. You?" Daniel had an interesting tattoo written in a foreign language on his right biceps, and I admired it. He wasn't traditionally good-looking, but he had confidence and poise, two things I found more attractive in a man than just his physical features.

"Work."

I shot a look at his swimming trunks. "I've got the wrong job."

"I sell—"

"Excuse me."

We both turned to face the woman who had intruded on our conversation. She was a compact brunette dressed in a dark polo shirt embroidered with both her name—*Sheila*—and *Cross Towers and Casino*. The earpiece in her ear and the utility belt around her waist gave her away as security.

"Miss Tramell." She greeted me with a nod.

My brows rose. "Yes?"

"There's a server who can take your order by your cabana."

"Cool, thanks. But I don't mind waiting here."

When I didn't move, Sheila turned her attention to Daniel. "If you'll move to the other end of the bar, sir, the bartender will see that your next drinks are on the house."

He gave a cursory nod, then smiled winningly at me. "I'm good here, too, thanks."

"I'm afraid I'll have to insist."

"What?" His smile turned into a scowl. "Why?"

I blinked at Sheila as realization sank in. *Gideon had me under watch.* And he thought he could control what I did from a distance.

Sheila returned my look, her face impassive. "I'll escort you back to your cabana, Miss Tramell."

For a minute, I considered making her day hell, maybe grabbing Daniel and kissing him senseless just to send a message to my overbearing boyfriend, but I managed to restrain my temper. She was only doing what she was paid to do. It was her boss who needed the kick in the ass.

"Sorry, Daniel," I said, flushing with embarrassment. I felt like a scolded kid and that *really* irked me. "It was nice meeting you."

He shrugged. "If you change your mind . . ."

I felt Sheila's gaze on my back as I preceded her to my lounger. Abruptly, I faced her. "So, is getting hit on the only time you're instructed to step in? Or do you have a list of situations?"

She hesitated a moment, then sighed. I could only imagine what she must think of me, the pretty blond piece of ass who couldn't be trusted to be out mingling in public. "There's a list."

"Of course there is." Gideon wouldn't leave anything to chance. I wondered when he'd worked on the list, if he'd compiled it just since I mentioned Vegas or if he'd had it on hand. Maybe it was a list he had formed while he was with other women. Maybe he'd written it for Corinne.

The more I thought about it, the angrier I got.

"Un-fucking-believable," I complained to Cary when she'd stepped a discreet distance away, as if that action alone would be enough to make me forget she was hovering. "I've got a babysitter."

"What?"

I told him what happened and watched his jaw tighten.

"That's crazy, Eva," he snapped.

"No shit. And I'm not putting up with it. He's got to learn that relationships don't work that way. And after all the crap he gave me about trust." I collapsed on my lounger. "How much does he trust me, if he's got to have someone shadowing me to chase strangers away?"

"I'm not down with this, Eva." He sat up and swung his legs over the side of his chair. "This isn't okay."

"You think I don't know that? And what's with her being a woman? Nothing against my gender and tough jobs. I'm just wondering if he expects her to follow me into ladies' rooms or just doesn't trust a guy to watch me."

"Are you serious? Why the hell are you sunbathing instead of chewing him a new one?"

The idea I'd been toying with fully formed in my mind. "I'm plotting."

"Oh?" His mouth curved in a wicked grin. "Do tell."

I picked my smartphone up from the little mosaic-topped table between us and scrolled through my contacts until I found *Benjamin Clancy*—my stepfather's personal bodyguard.

"Hey, Clancy. It's Eva," I greeted him when he answered after the first ring.

Cary's eyes widened behind his shades. "Ooh . . ."

Pushing to my feet, I mouthed, *I'm going upstairs.*

He nodded. "Everything's fine," I said, in answer to Clancy's query. I waited until I'd ducked indoors and knew Sheila was several paces behind me and still outside. "Listen, I have a favor to ask you."

I'D just ended my call with Clancy when another call came in. I grinned when I saw the Caller ID and answered with an exuberant, "Hi, Daddy!"

He laughed. "How's my girl?"

"Causing trouble and enjoying it." I spread my sarong out on a dining room chair and took a seat. "How are you?"

"Stopping trouble from happening and occasionally enjoying it."

Victor Reyes was an Oceanside, California, street cop, which was why I'd chosen to attend SDSU. My mom had been going through a rough patch with husband number two and I'd been in a rebellious phase, making my own life hell as I tried to forget what Nathan had done to me for so long.

Moving out of my mom's suffocating orbit had been one of the best decisions I'd ever made. My dad's quietly unshakeable love for me, his only child, had changed my life. He gave me much-needed freedom—within clearly defined limits—and arranged for me to see Dr. Travis, which led to the start of my long journey of recovery and my friendship with Cary.

"I miss you," I told him. I loved my mom dearly and knew she loved me back, but my relationship with her was a rocky one and it was just so easy with my dad.

"You might be happy about my news, then. I can come out and see you in about two weeks—the week after this upcoming one—if that works for you. I don't want to put you out."

"Oh my God, Dad. You could never put me out. I'd love to see you!"

"It'll be a short trip. I'd come in on the red-eye Thursday night and fly out again Sunday evening."

"I'm stoked! Yay! I'll make plans. We'll have a blast."

My dad's soft chuckle sent warmth flowing through me. "I'm coming to see *you*, not New York. Don't go crazy with any sightseeing or anything."

"Don't worry. I'll make sure we have lots of downtime. And you'll get to meet Gideon." Just the thought of the two of them together made my tummy flutter.

"Gideon Cross? You said nothing was going on there."

"Yeah." I wrinkled my nose. "We'd hit a rough spot at the time. I thought we were over."

There was a pause. "Is it serious?"

I paused, too, shifting restlessly. My dad was a trained observer;

he'd see right away that Gideon and I had tension between us—sexual and otherwise. "Yes. It's not always easy. It's a lot of work—*I'm* a lot of work—but we're both making the effort."

"Does he appreciate you, Eva?" My dad's voice was gruff and far too serious. "I don't care how much money he has; you don't have anything to prove to him."

"It's not like that!" I stared at my wriggling pedicured toes and realized the meeting would be more complicated than just a protective father being introduced to his daughter's new boyfriend. My dad had issues with rich men, thanks to my mom. "You'll see how it is when you meet him."

"All right." Skepticism colored his voice.

"Really, Dad." I couldn't begrudge him his concern, since it'd been my self-destructive run with not-so-good-for-me guys that had led him to finding Dr. Travis. He'd especially had trouble with a lead singer for whom I'd been little more than a groupie and a tattoo artist whom my dad had pulled over to find him getting a blowjob while driving—and not from me. "Gideon's good for me. He gets me."

"I'll keep an open mind, okay? And I'll e-mail you a copy of my itinerary when I book the flight. How's everything else going?"

"We just started working on a campaign for blueberry-flavored coffee."

Another pause. "You're kidding."

I laughed. "If only. Wish us luck trying to sell that! I'll be sure to stock some up for you to try."

"I thought you loved me."

"With all my heart. How's your love life going? Did your date go well?"

"Yeah . . . it wasn't bad."

Snorting, I asked, "Are you going to see her again?"

"That's the plan so far."

"You're a font of information, Dad."

He chuckled again and I heard his favorite chair creak as he shifted. "You don't really want to know about your old man's love life."

"True." Although I did sometimes wonder what his relationship had been like with my mom. He'd been the Latino boy from the wrong side of the tracks and she'd been the golden debutante with dollar signs in her blue eyes. I figured it must've been pretty hot between them.

We talked for a few more minutes, both of us excited to see each other again. I'd hoped we wouldn't drift apart after I moved away after college, which was why I'd made it a necessity to have a weekly catch-up call on Saturdays. Having him visit so soon helped to ease that worry.

I'd just hung up when Cary strolled in, looking every bit like the model he was.

"Still plotting?" he asked.

I stood. "All done. That was my dad. He's coming out to New York next week."

"Really? Rock on. Victor's cool."

We both moved into the kitchen, and he grabbed two beers out of the refrigerator. I'd noticed earlier that a number of items and products I used at home had been stocked in the suite. I wondered if Gideon was just that observant or if he'd found the information another way—like from looking at my receipts. I couldn't put it past him. Recognizing the boundaries between us was very difficult for him, as evidenced by his siccing his guards on me.

"When's the last time your parents were in the same state together?" Cary asked, prying the caps off the bottles with a bottle opener. "Let alone the same city."

Ah, God . . . "I'm not sure. Before I was born?" I took a long pull on the beer he handed me. "I'm not planning on putting them together."

"Here's to best-laid plans." He clinked the necks of our beers together. "Speaking of which, I was considering a quick bang with a chick I met at the pool, but I came up here instead. Figured you and I'd both go without today and just spend the time together."

"I'm honored," I said dryly. "I was going to come back down."

"Too hot out. That sun is brutal."

"Same sun we have in New York, isn't it?"

"Smart-ass." His green eyes sparkled. "How about we clean up and go out to lunch somewhere? My treat."

"Sure. But I can't say Sheila won't insist on tagging along."

"Fuck her and her boss. What is it with rich people and control issues?"

"They get rich because they take control."

"Whatever. I prefer our kind of crazy—we pretty much only screw with ourselves." He crossed one arm over his chest and leaned into the counter. "You gonna put up with his bullshit?"

"Depends."

"On what?"

I grinned and started backing out toward my bedroom. "Get ready. I'll tell you about it over lunch."

6

I'D JUST BARELY finished repacking my bag for the trip home when I heard the unmistakable sound of Gideon's voice in the living room. A rush of adrenaline pumped through my veins. Gideon had yet to say a word to me about what I'd done, even though we'd talked the night before after Cary and I had gotten back from clubbing and again this morning when I'd woken up.

Feigning ignorance was slightly nerve-racking. I'd wondered if Clancy had even managed to do what I had asked of him, but when I double-checked with my stepdad's bodyguard, he assured me that all was going as I'd planned.

On bare feet, I padded over to the open door of my bedroom just in time to see Cary walk out the door of our suite. Gideon stood alone in the small foyer, his inscrutable gaze on me as if he'd expected me to appear at any moment. He wore loose-fitting jeans and a black T-shirt, and I'd missed the sight of him so much my eyes stung.

"Hi, angel."

The fingers of my right hand toyed restlessly with the material of my black yoga pants. "Hi, ace."

His beautifully etched lips thinned for a moment. "Is there a particular meaning behind that endearment?"

"Well . . . you ace everything you do. And it's the nickname of a fictional character I have a crush on. You remind me of him sometimes."

"I'm not sure I like you having a crush on anyone but me, fictional or not."

"You'll get over it."

Shaking his head, he started toward me. "Like I'll get over the sumo wrestler you have shadowing me?"

I bit the inside of my cheek to keep from laughing. I hadn't been specific about appearance when I'd asked Clancy to arrange for someone he knew in the Phoenix area to guard Gideon the way Sheila was guarding me. I'd just asked for a man and provided a relatively small list of things to intercede with. "Where's Cary going?"

"Downstairs to play with the credit I arranged for him."

"We're not leaving right away?"

He slowly closed the distance between us. There was no mistaking the danger inherent in the way he stalked me. It was visible in the set of his shoulders and the gleam in his eyes. I might've been more worried if the sinuousness of his stride hadn't been so blatantly sexual. "You on your period?"

I nodded.

"Then I'll just have to come in your mouth."

My brows rose. "Is that right?"

"Oh, yeah." His mouth curved. "Don't worry, angel. I'll take care of you first."

He lunged and caught me up, surging into the bedroom and toppling us onto the bed. I gasped and his mouth was on mine, the kiss deep and ravenous. I was swept away by his passion and the beloved feel of his weight pressing me into the mattress. He smelled so good. His skin was so warm.

"I missed you," I moaned, wrapping my arms and legs around him. "Even though you're seriously irritating sometimes."

Gideon growled. "You're the most exasperating, infuriating woman I've ever met."

"Yeah, well, you pissed me off. I'm not a possession. You can't—"

"Yes, you are." He nipped my earlobe with his teeth, causing a sharp sting that made me cry out. "And yes, I can."

"Then you are, too. And I can, too."

"So you demonstrated. Have any idea how difficult it is to do business with someone when they can't get within three feet of you?"

I froze, because I'd made the three-feet rule applicable only to women. "Why would someone need to be that close to you?"

"To point out areas of interest on design schematics spread out in front of me and to fit alongside me within camera range for a teleconference—two things you made very difficult." Lifting his head, he looked down at me. "I was working. You were playing."

"I don't care. If it's good for me, it's good for you." But I was secretly pleased that Gideon had put up with the inconvenience, just as I had.

Reaching down, he caught me by the back of the thigh and yanked my legs wider apart. "You're not going to get a hundred percent equality in this relationship."

"The hell I'm not."

His hips settled into the opening he'd made. He rocked against me, rubbing the thick ridge of his erection against my sex. "You're not," he repeated, his hands pushing into my hair to grip my scalp and hold me in place.

Rolling his hips, he massaged my hypersensitive clit. The seam of his jeans was in the perfect place to stir my ever-simmering lust for him. Arousal spiked in my blood. "Stop it. I can't think when you do that."

"Don't think. Just listen, Eva. Who I am and what I've built makes me a target. You know the score, because you know what it's like to live with wealth and the attention it attracts."

"The guy at the bar wasn't a threat."

"That's debatable."

Irritation burned through me. It was the perceived lack of trust that bugged me, mostly because he didn't trust me with whatever secrets he was keeping, and I was dealing with that. "Get off me."

"I'm comfortable right here." He hitched his hips, rubbing against me.

"I'm pissed at you."

"I can tell." He didn't stop moving. "That won't stop you from coming."

I shoved at his hips, but he was too heavy to budge. "I can't when I'm mad!"

"Prove it."

He was way too smug, which made my anger swell. Since I couldn't turn my head, I closed my eyes, shutting him out. He didn't care. He kept on flexing against me. The clothes between us and the lack of penetration made me even more aware of the elegant fluidity of his body.

The man knew how to fuck.

Gideon didn't just shove his big dick in and out of a woman. He worked her with it, exploiting friction, changing angles and depth of penetration. The nuances of his skill were lost when I was writhing beneath him and focused only on the sensations he stoked in my body. But I felt them all now.

I fought against the pleasure, but I couldn't stifle a moan.

"That's it, angel," he coaxed. "Feel how hard I am for you? Feel what you do to me?"

"Don't use sex to punish me," I complained, my heels digging into the mattress.

He stilled for a moment, and then his mouth was suckling at my throat, his body undulating as if he were fucking me through our clothes. "I'm not mad, angel."

"Whatever. You're pushing me around."

"And you're driving me insane. You know what happened when I realized what you'd done?"

I glared at him through slitted eyes. "What?"

"I got hard."

My eyes opened wide.

"Inconveniently and publicly." He cupped my breast in his hand, his thumb stroking over the hardened point of my nipple. "I had to drag out a finished discussion while I waited for it to go down. It turns me on when you challenge me, Eva." His voice lowered and became raspier, dripping with sex and sin. "It makes me want to fuck you. For a very, very long time."

"God." My hips pumped upward, my core tightening with the need to come.

"And since I can't," he purred, "I'm going to get you off like this, then watch you return the favor with your mouth."

A whimper escaped me, my mouth watering at the promise of pleasing him that way. He was always so attuned to me when we made love. The only time he really let go and focused on his own pleasure was when I went down on him.

"That's it," he murmured, "keep rubbing your cunt against me like that. Christ, you're so damn hot."

"Gideon." My hands were gliding all over his flexing back and buttocks, my body arching and grinding into his. I came with a long and drawn-out moan, the tension breaking in a rush of relief.

His mouth covered mine, drinking in the sounds I made as I shivered beneath him. I clutched his hair, kissing him back.

He rolled us so that he was beneath me, his hands going to his button fly and ripping it open. "Now, Eva."

I scrambled down the bed, as eager to taste him as he was to have me do so. The moment he shoved his boxer briefs down, I had his penis in my hands, my lips flowing over the wide crest.

Groaning, Gideon grabbed a pillow and shoved it under his head. My gaze met his and I pulled him deeper.

"Yes," he hissed, the fingers of his right hand tangling in my hair. "Suck it hard and fast; I want to come."

I breathed in the scent of him, feeling the satiny softness of his heated flesh on my tongue. Then I took him at his word.

Hollowing my cheeks, I took him to the back of my throat, then pulled up to the crown. Over and over. Focusing on suction and speed, as greedy for his orgasm as he was, spurred by the abandoned sounds he made and the sight of his fingers clawing restlessly at the comforter. His hips churned, his hand in my hair guiding my pace.

"Ah, God." He watched me with dark, hot eyes. "I love the way you suck me off. Like you can't get enough."

I couldn't. I didn't think I ever could. His pleasure meant so much to me, because it was real and raw. For him, sex had always been staged and methodical. He couldn't hold back with me because he wanted me beyond reason. Two days without me and he was . . . undone.

I pumped him with my fist, feeling the thick veins throbbing beneath the smooth skin. A ragged sound tore from his throat and salty warmth spurted on my tongue. He was close, his face flushed and his lips parted with gasping breaths. Sweat misted my brow. My excitement mounted along with his. He was completely at my mercy, near mindless with the need to climax, muttering filthy sexy things about what he was going to do to me the next time he fucked me.

"That's it, angel. Milk it . . . make me come for you." His neck arched, his breath exploding from his lungs. *"Fuck."*

He came as I had—hard and brutal. Semen burst from the tip of his cock in a thick, hot rush that I struggled to swallow. He growled my name, his hips pumping upward into my working mouth, taking what he needed from me, giving me all he had until he was emptied.

Then he curled toward me, pulling me into a strangling embrace that pinned me to his heaving chest. For long moments, he just held me. I listened as his raging heartbeat slowed and his breathing returned to normal.

Finally, he spoke with his lips in my hair. "Needed that. Thank you."

I smiled and snuggled into him. "My pleasure, ace."

"I missed you," he said softly, his lips pressing to my brow. "So damn much. And not just for this."

"I know." We needed this—the physical closeness, the frenzied touching, the rush of orgasm—to release some of the wild, overwhelming emotions that affected us when we were together. "My dad's coming out to visit next week."

He stilled. Lifting his head, he looked at me wryly. "You have to tell me that while my dick's still hanging out?"

I laughed. "Caught you with your pants down?"

"Hell." He pressed his lips to my forehead, then rolled to his back and righted his clothes. "You have an idea of how you want the first meeting to go? Dinner out or in? Your place or mine?"

"I'll cook at my place." I stretched, then tugged the wrinkles out of my shirt.

He nodded, but his vibe changed. My sated, grateful lover of a moment before was replaced by the grim-faced man who'd been around more frequently lately.

"Would you prefer something different?" I asked.

"No. It's a good plan and what I would've suggested. He'll feel comfortable there."

"Will you?"

"Yes." He propped his head on one hand and looked down at me, brushing my hair back from my forehead. "I'd rather not hit him in the face with my money if we can help it."

I took a deep breath. "I hadn't considered that. I just thought I'd be less anxious about making a mess in my own kitchen than in yours. But you're right. It'll be okay, though, Gideon. Once he sees how you feel about me, he'll be good with us being together."

"I only care what he thinks if it affects how *you* feel. If he doesn't like me and that changes something between us—"

"You're the only one who can do that."

He gave a curt nod, which didn't help me feel better about what he was feeling. A lot of men got nervous meeting their girlfriend's parents, but Gideon wasn't like other men. He didn't rattle. Usually. I wanted him and my dad to be loose and easy around each other, not tense and defensive.

I changed the subject. "Did you get everything worked out in Phoenix?"

"Yes. One of the project managers noted some anomalies in accounting, and she was right to push me to look deeper into it. Embezzling isn't something I tolerate."

I winced, thinking of Gideon's father, who'd bilked investors out of millions before killing himself. "What's the project?"

"A golf resort."

"Nightclubs, resorts, luxury living, vodka, casinos . . . with a chain of gyms thrown in to keep fit for the high life?" I knew from checking out the Cross Industries website that Gideon also had software and games divisions, and a growing social media platform for young urban professionals. "You're a pleasure god in more ways than one."

"Pleasure god?" His eyes sparkled with humor. "I spend all my energy worshipping you."

"How did you get to be so rich?" I blurted out, pricked by the memory of Cary's insinuations about how Gideon could've amassed so much at such a young age.

"People like to have fun, and they'll pay for the privilege."

"That's not what I meant. How did you get Cross Industries started? Where did you get the capital to get things going?"

His eyes took on a speculative gleam. "Where do you think I got it?"

"I have no idea," I told him honestly.

"Blackjack."

I blinked. "Gambling? Are you kidding?"

"No." He laughed and tightened his arms around me.

But I couldn't see Gideon as a gambler. I'd learned, thanks to my mom's third husband, that gambling could become a very nasty and insidious disease that caused total lack of control. I just couldn't see someone as rigidly controlled as Gideon finding anything appealing about something so dependent on luck and chance.

Then it hit me. "You count cards."

"When I played," he agreed. "I don't anymore. And the contacts I made over card tables were as instrumental as the money I made."

I tried to absorb that information, struggled with it, then let it go for the moment. "Remind me not to play cards with you."

"Strip poker could be fun."

"For you."

He reached down and squeezed my ass. "And for you. You know how I get when you're naked."

I shot a pointed glance down at my fully dressed body. "And when I'm not naked."

Gideon's grin flashed, dazzling and entirely unapologetic.

"Do you still gamble?"

"Every day. But only in business and with you."

"With me? With our relationship?"

His gaze was soft on my face, filled with a sudden tenderness that made my throat tight. "You're the greatest risk I've ever taken." His pressed his lips gently to mine. "And the greatest reward."

WHEN I got to work Monday morning, I felt like things were finally settling back into their natural pre-Corinne rhythm. Gideon and I were dealing with adjusting to my period, which had never been an issue for either of us in any previous relationship we'd had, but was in ours because sex was how he showed me what he was feeling. He could say with his body what he couldn't with words, and my lust for him was how I proved my faith in us, something he needed to feel connected to me.

I could tell him I loved him over and over again, and I know it affected him when I did, but he needed the total surrender of my body—a display of trust he knew meant a great deal because of my past—to really believe it.

As he'd told me once, he had been the recipient of many *I love yous* over the years, but he'd never believed them because they hadn't been backed up with truth, trust, and honesty. The words meant little to him, which was why he refused to say them to me. I tried not to let him see how it hurt me that he wouldn't say them. I figured that was an adjustment I'd have to make to be with him.

"Good morning, Eva."

I glanced up from my desk and found Mark standing by my cubicle. His slightly crooked smile was always a winner. "Hey. I'm ready to roll when you are."

"Coffee first. You up for a refill?"

Grabbing my empty mug off my desk, I stood. "You bet."

We headed toward the break room.

"You look like you got a tan," Mark said, glancing over at me.

"Yeah, I did a little sun lounging over the weekend. It was good to be lazy and do nothing. Actually, that's probably one of my favorite things to do, period."

"I'm envious. Steven can't sit still for too long. He always wants to drag me somewhere for something."

"My roommate's the same way. It's exhausting how he runs around."

"Oh, before I forget." He gestured for me to enter the break room first. "Shawna wants you to get in touch. She's got concert tickets for some new rock band. I think she wants to see if you'd want them."

I thought of the attractive red-haired waitress I'd met the week before. She was Steven's sister, and Steven was Mark's longtime partner. The two men had met in college and had been together ever since. I really liked Steven. I was pretty sure I'd really like Shawna, too.

"Are you okay with me reaching out to her?" I had to ask, because she was—for all intents and purposes—Mark's sister-in-law and Mark was my boss.

"Of course. Don't worry. It won't be weird."

"All right." I smiled and hoped to add another girlfriend to my new life in New York. "Thanks."

"Thank me with a cup of coffee," he said, pulling out a mug from the cupboard and handing it to me. "You make it taste better than I do."

I shot him a look. "My dad uses that line."

"Must be true, then."

"Must be a standard guy finagle," I shot back. "How do you and Steven divvy up coffee making?"

"We don't." He grinned. "There's a Starbucks on the corner by our place."

"I'm sure there's a way to call that cheating, but I haven't had enough caffeine to think of it yet." I passed over his filled mug to him. "Which probably means I shouldn't share the idea that just came to me."

"Go for it. If it really sucks, I can hold it against you forever."

"Gee. Thanks." I held my mug between both hands. "Would it work to market the blueberry coffee like tea instead? You know, the coffee in a chintz teacup and saucer with maybe a scone and some clotted cream in the background? Give it a high-end, midafternoon snack sort of treatment? Throw in a fabulously handsome Englishman to sip it with?"

Mark's lips pursed as he thought about it. "I think I like it. Let's go run it by the creatives."

"WHY didn't you tell me you were going to Las Vegas?"

I sighed inwardly at the high note of irritated anxiety in my mother's voice and adjusted my grip on the receiver of my desk phone. I'd barely returned my butt to my chair when the phone had rung. I suspected if I checked my voice mail, I'd find a message or two from her. When she got worked up about something, she couldn't let it go. "Hi, Mom. I'm sorry. I planned on calling you at lunch and catching up."

"I love Vegas."

"You do?" I thought she hated anything remotely related to gambling. "I didn't know that."

"You would've if you'd asked."

There was a hurt note in my mother's breathy voice that made me wince. "I'm sorry, Mom," I said again, having learned as a child that repeated apologies went a long way with her. "I needed to spend some downtime with Cary. We can talk about a future trip to Vegas, though, if you'd like to go sometime."

"Wouldn't that be fun? I'd like to do fun things with you, Eva."

"I'd like that, too." My eyes went to the picture of my mother and Stanton. She was a beautiful woman, one who radiated a vulnerable sensuality to which men responded helplessly. The vulnerability was real—my mom was fragile in many ways—but she was a man-eater, too. Men didn't take advantage of my mom; she walked all over them.

"Do you have plans for lunch? I could make a reservation and come get you."

"Can I bring a co-worker?" Megumi had hit me up with a lunch invitation when I'd come in, promising to regale me with the tale of her blind date.

"Oh, I'd love to meet the people you work with!"

My mouth curved with genuine affection. My mom drove me nuts a lot, but at the end of the day, her biggest fault was that she loved me too much. Combined with her neurosis, it was a maddening flaw, but one motivated by the best of intentions. "Okay. Pick us up at noon. And remember, we only get an hour, so it'll have to be close by and quick."

"I'll take care of it. I'm excited! See you soon."

MEGUMI and my mother took to each other right away. I recognized the familiar starry-eyed look on Megumi's face when they met, because I'd seen it so often over the years. Monica Stanton was a stunning woman, the kind of classic beauty you couldn't help but stare at because you couldn't believe anyone could be that perfect. Plus, the royal purple hue of the wingback she'd elected to sit in was an amazing backdrop for her golden hair and blue eyes.

For her part, my mom was delighted by Megumi's fashion sense. While my wardrobe choices leaned more toward traditional and ready-to-wear, Megumi favored unique combinations and color, much like the décor of the trendy café near Rockefeller Center my mom had taken us to.

The place reminded me of *Alice in Wonderland*, with its gilt and jewel-toned velvets used on uniquely shaped furniture. The chaise Megumi was perched on had an exaggerated curved back, while my mother's wingback had gargoyles for feet.

"I'm still trying to figure out what's wrong with him," Megumi went on. "I was looking, let me tell you. I mean a guy that great shouldn't be slumming it with blind dates."

"Hardly slumming it," my mom protested. "I'm sure he's wondering how he lucked out with you."

"Thanks!" Megumi grinned at me. "He was seriously hot. Not Gideon Cross hot, but hot all the same."

"How is Gideon, by the way?"

I didn't take my mom's question lightly. She was aware that

Gideon knew about the abuse I'd suffered as a child, and she'd taken the news hard. It was her greatest shame that she hadn't known what was going on under her own roof, and her guilt was enormous, as well as entirely undeserved. She hadn't known because I'd hidden it. Nathan had made me fear what he'd do if I ever told anyone. Still, my mother was anxious about Gideon's knowing. I hoped that she'd soon come to realize that Gideon didn't hold it against her any more than I did.

"He's working hard," I answered. "You know how it is. I've taken up a lot of his time since we hooked up, and I think he's paying for it now."

"You're worth it."

I took a large gulp of my water when I felt the nearly overwhelming urge to tell her that my dad was coming to visit. She'd be an ally in convincing him of Gideon's affection for me, but that was a self-ish reason to say anything. I had no idea how she would react to Victor's being in New York, but it was highly possible she'd be distressed, and that would make everyone's life hell. Whatever her reasons, she preferred to have no contact with him whatsoever. I couldn't ignore how she'd managed to avoid seeing or talking to him since I'd become old enough to communicate with him directly.

"I saw a picture of Cary on the side of a bus yesterday," she said.

"Really?" I sat up straighter. "Where?"

"On Broadway. A jeans ad, I think it was."

"I saw one, too," Megumi said. "Not that I paid any attention to what he was wearing. That man is *fine*."

The conversation made me smile. My mother was adept at admiring men. It was one of the many reasons they adored her—she made them feel good. Megumi was more than her match in the guy-appreciation department.

"He's been getting recognized on the street," I said, glad that in this case we were talking about an ad and not a tabloid candid with me. The gossips thought it was so juicy that Gideon Cross's girlfriend lived with a sexy male model.

"Of course," my mom said, with a slight note of chastisement. "You didn't doubt he would eventually?"

"I'd hoped," I qualified. "For his sake. It's a sad fact that male models don't make as much or work as often as the women do." Although I'd expected Cary would break through somehow. Emotionally, he couldn't afford not to. He'd learned to put so much value on his looks that I didn't think he could allow himself to fail. It was one of my deepest fears that his career choice would come back to haunt him in ways neither of us could bear.

My mother took a delicate sip of her Pellegrino. The café specialized in cacao-laced menu items, but she was careful not to waste her daily calorie allotment on one meal. I was less cautious. I'd ordered a soup and sandwich combination plus a dessert that was going to cost me at least an extra hour on the treadmill later. I excused the indulgence with a mental reminder that I was on my period, which was a carte blanche chocolate zone in my opinion.

"So," Monica smiled at Megumi, "will you be seeing your blind date again?"

"I hope so."

"Darling, don't leave it to chance!"

As my mom started doling out her wisdom in regard to managing men, I sat back and enjoyed the show. She was of the firm belief that every woman deserved to have a wealthy man to dote on her, and for the first time in forever, she wasn't concentrating her matchmaking efforts on me. While I was worried about how my dad and Gideon would hit it off, I had no concerns about my mom's feelings on the matter. We both thought I was with the right guy for me, although for different reasons.

"Your mom rocks," Megumi said, when Monica ducked into the ladies' room to freshen up before we left. "And you look just like her, lucky you. How bad would it suck to have a mom who's hotter than you are?"

Laughing, I told her, "I'll have to drag you along with us again. This worked out great."

"I'd like that."

When it was time to go, I looked at Clancy and the town car waiting at the curb for us and realized I wanted to walk off some of my lunch before I got back to work. "I think I'm going to hoof it back," I told them. "I ate too much. You two go on without me."

"I'll go with you," Megumi said. "I could use the air, hot as it is. That canned air in the office makes my skin dry."

"I'll come, too," my mom offered.

I eyed her delicate heels skeptically, but then again, my mom wore nothing but heels. For her, walking in those was probably the same as walking in flats was to me.

We headed back to the Crossfire at the standard stride rate for Manhattan, which was something of a steady, purposeful clip. While weaving around human obstacles was usually part of the process, it was far less of an issue with my mom in the lead. Men moved reverently off to the side for her, then followed her with their eyes. In her simple, sexy wrap dress of ice blue, she looked cool and refreshing in the humid heat.

We'd just turned the corner to reach the Crossfire when she came to an abrupt halt that caused Megumi and me to crash into the back of her. She stumbled forward, wobbling, and I barely caught her by the elbow before she teetered over.

I looked at the ground to see what had held her up, but when I didn't see anything I looked at her. She was staring at the Crossfire in a daze.

"Jesus, Mom." I urged her out of the flow of pedestrians. "You're white as a sheet. Is the heat getting to you? Do you feel dizzy?"

"What?" Her hand went to her throat. Her dilated gaze remained fixed on the Crossfire.

Turning my head, I followed her line of sight, trying to see whatever it was that she did.

"What are you two looking at?" Megumi asked, frowning down the street.

"Mrs. Stanton." Clancy approached, having abandoned the town car he'd been driving at a safe but discreet distance behind us. "Is everything all right?"

"Did you see—?" she began, looking to him with her question.

"See what?" I demanded, as his head snapped up and his trained gaze raked the length of the street. The absoluteness of his focus sent a shiver down my spine.

"Let me drive you three the rest of the way," he said quietly.

The entrance to the Crossfire was literally across the street, but something in Clancy's tone brooked no argument. We all climbed in, with my mother taking the front seat.

"What was that about?" Megumi asked after we'd been dropped off and had moved into the cool interior of the building. "Your mom looked like she'd seen a ghost."

"I have no idea." But I felt ill.

Something had frightened my mother. It was going to drive me crazy until I found out what it was.

7

M Y BACK HIT the mat with enough force to knock the air from my lungs. Stunned, I blinked up at the ceiling, trying to catch my breath.

Parker Smith's face came into view. "You're wasting my time. If you're going to be here, be *here*. One hundred percent. Not a million miles away in your head somewhere."

I grabbed the hand he extended to me, and he yanked me to my feet. Around us, a dozen more of Parker's Krav Maga students were hard at work. The Brooklyn-based studio was alive with noise and activity.

He was right. My thoughts were still stuck on my mom and the bizarre way she'd reacted when we returned to the Crossfire after lunch.

"Sorry," I muttered. "I've got something on my mind."

He moved like lightning, tagging me first on one knee, then my shoulder with rapid-fire slaps. "Do you think an attacker is going to wait until you're alert and ready before he comes after you?"

I crouched, forcing myself to focus. Parker crouched as well, his brown eyes hard and watchful. His shaved head and café au lait skin gleamed beneath the overhead fluorescent lighting. The studio was in a converted warehouse, which had been left rough for both economic reasons and atmosphere. My mother and stepfather were paranoid enough to have Clancy accompany me to my classes. The neighborhood was presently undergoing revitalization, which I thought was encouraging but they thought was troubling.

When Parker came at me again, I blocked him. The tagging came fast and furious then, and I pushed all other thoughts aside until later, when I was home.

When Gideon came over about an hour later, he found me in the bath surrounded by vanilla-scented candles. He undressed to join me, even though his damp hair told me he'd already showered after spending time with his own personal trainer. I watched him strip, riveted. The play of muscles beneath his skin and the inherent gracefulness in the way he moved sent a delicious sense of contentment sliding through me.

He climbed into the deep oval tub behind me, his long legs sliding in on either side of mine. His arms wrapped around me, and then he surprised me by lifting me up and back, so that I was sitting on his lap and my legs were draped over his.

"Lean into me, angel," he murmured. "I need to feel you."

I sighed with pleasure, sinking into the hardness of his powerful body as he cradled me. My aching muscles softened in surrender, eager as always to become completely pliable to his touch. I loved moments like this, when the world and our emotional triggers were far away. Moments when I *felt* the love he wouldn't profess for me.

"Soaking more bruises?" he asked with his cheek pressed to mine.

"My fault. My head wasn't in the game."

"Thinking about me?" he purred, nuzzling against my ear.

"I wish."

He paused, then switched gears. "Tell me what's bugging you."

I loved how easily he could read me, then revise and revisit his approach on the fly. I tried to be as adaptable for him. Really, flexibility was a requirement in a relationship between two high-maintenance people.

Linking my fingers with his, I told him about my mother's weird reaction after lunch.

"I almost expected to turn around and see my dad or something. I was wondering . . . You have security cameras that cover the front of the building, don't you?"

"Of course. I'll look into it."

"It's a ten-minute window of time, max. I just want to see if I can figure out what went on."

"Consider it done."

I tilted my head back and kissed his jaw. "Thank you."

His lips pressed to the top of my shoulder. "Angel, there's nothing I wouldn't do for you."

"Including talking about your past?" I felt him tense and mentally kicked myself. "Not right this second," I hastened to add, "but sometime. Just tell me we'll get there."

"Have lunch with me tomorrow. In my office."

"Are you going to talk about it then?"

Gideon exhaled harshly. "Eva."

I turned my face away and released him, disappointed with his evasion. Reaching for the edges of the tub, I prepared to get out and away from the man who somehow made me feel more connected to another human being than I'd ever been, yet was impossibly distant as well. Being with him fucked with my head, made me doubt the very things I'd been sure of just moments before. Rinse and repeat.

"I'm done," I muttered, blowing out the nearest candle. Smoke curled up and away, as intangible as my grasp on the man I loved. "I'm getting out."

"No." He cupped my breasts, restraining me. Water lapped around us, as agitated as I was.

"Let go, Gideon." I caught his wrists to pull his hands away.

He buried his face in my neck, obstinately holding on. "We'll get there. Okay? Just— We'll get there."

I deflated, feeling little of the triumph I had hoped to feel when I'd first asked and anticipated his answer.

"Can we give it a rest tonight?" he asked gruffly, still clinging tight. "Give it all a rest? I just want to be with you, all right? Order something in for dinner, watch TV, hold you when I sleep. Can we do that?"

Realizing something was seriously off, I twisted to face him. "What's wrong?"

"I just want some time with you."

My eyes stung with tears. There was more he wasn't telling me, so much more. Our relationship was swiftly becoming a minefield of words left unsaid and secrets not shared. "Okay."

"I need it, Eva. You and me with no drama." His wet fingertips brushed across my cheek. "Give me that. Please. Then give me a kiss."

Turning around, I straddled his hips and cupped his face in my hands. I angled my head to find the perfect approach and pressed my lips to his. I started out soft and slow, licking and suckling. I tugged on his bottom lip, then coaxed him to forget our problems with teasing strokes of my tongue along his.

"Kiss me, damn it," he growled, his hands bracketing my spine and kneading restlessly. "Kiss me like you love me."

"I do," I promised, breathing the words into him. "I can't help it."

"Angel." Pushing his hands into my damp hair, he held me how he wanted me and kissed me senseless.

AFTER dinner, Gideon worked in bed, propping his back against my headboard and his laptop on a lap desk. I sprawled on the bed on my belly, facing the TV and kicking my feet in the air.

"Do you know every line in this movie?" he asked, luring me to turn my attention away from *Ghostbusters* to look at him. He wore black boxer briefs and nothing else.

I loved that I got to see him that way—relaxed, comfortable, intimate. I wondered if Corinne had ever seen this view. If so, I could imagine her desperation to see it again, because I was desperate to never lose the privilege.

"Maybe," I conceded.

"And you have to say them all aloud?"

"Got a problem with that, ace?"

"No." Amusement lit his eyes and curved his mouth. "How many times have you seen it?"

"A gazillion times." I curled around and rose up on my hands and knees. "Want more?"

A dark winged brow rose.

"Are you the keymaster?" I purred, crawling forward.

"Angel, when you're looking at me like that, I'm whatever you want me to be."

I looked at him beneath lowered eyelids and breathed, "Do you want this body?"

Grinning, he set his lap desk aside. "All the damn time."

Straddling his legs, I climbed his torso. I wrapped my arms around his shoulders and growled, "Kiss me, subcreature."

"That's not how that line goes. And what happened to me being a pleasure god? Now I'm a subcreature?"

I pressed my cleft against the hard ridge of his cock and rolled my hips. "You're whatever I want you to be, remember?"

Gideon gripped my rib cage and tipped his head back. "And what's that?"

"Mine." I nipped his throat with my teeth. "All mine."

I couldn't breathe. I tried to scream, but something blocked my nose . . . covered my mouth. A high-pitched moan was the only sound to escape, my frantic calls for help trapped inside my mind.

Get off me. Stop it! Don't touch me. Oh, God . . . please don't do that to me.

Where was Mama? *Ma-ma!*

Nathan's hand covered my mouth, mashing my lips. The weight of his body pressed down on me, squashing my head into the pillow. The more I fought, the more excited he became. Panting like the animal he was, he lunged into me, over and over . . . trying to shove himself inside me. My panties were in the way, protecting me from the tearing pain I'd lived through too many times to count.

As if he'd read my mind, he growled in my ear, "You haven't felt pain yet. But you will."

I froze. Awareness hit me like a bucket of ice water. I *knew* that voice.

Gideon. No!

My blood roared in my ears. Sickness spread through my gut. Bile flooded my mouth.

It was worse, so much worse, when the person trying to rape you was someone you trusted with everything you had.

Fear and fury blended in a potent rush. In a moment of clarity, I heard Parker's barked commands. I remembered the basics.

I attacked the man I loved, the man whose nightmares blended with mine in the most horrific way. We were both sexual-abuse survivors, but in my dreams I was still a victim. In his, he'd become the aggressor, viciously determined to inflict the same agony and humiliation on his attacker as he himself had suffered.

My stiffened fingers rammed into Gideon's throat. He reared back with a curse and shifted, and I slammed my knee between his legs. Doubled over, he fell away from me. I rolled out of bed and hit the floor with a thud. Scrambling to my feet, I threw myself toward the door to the hallway.

"Eva!" he gasped, awake and aware of what he'd almost done to me in his sleep. "God. *Eva*. Wait!"

I bolted out the door and ran into the living room.

Finding a darkened corner, I curled into a ball and struggled to breathe, my sobs echoing through the apartment. I pressed my lips to my knee when the light came on in my bedroom and didn't move or make a sound when Gideon stepped into the living room an eternity later.

"Eva? Jesus. Are you okay? Did I . . . hurt you?"

Atypical sexual parasomnia was what Dr. Petersen called it, a manifestation of Gideon's deep psychological trauma. I called it hell. And we were both trapped in it.

His body language broke my heart. His normally proud bearing was weighted with defeat, his shoulders slumped and his head bowed. He was dressed and carrying his overnight bag. He stopped by the breakfast bar. I opened my mouth to speak; then I heard a metallic *clink* against the stone countertop.

I'd stopped him the last time; I'd made him stay. This time, I didn't have it in me.

This time, I wanted him to go.

The barely audible latching of the front door lock reverberated through me. Something inside me died. Panic welled. I missed him the moment he was gone. I didn't want him to stay. I didn't want him to go.

I don't know how long I sat there in the corner before I found the strength to stand and move to the couch. I vaguely registered that dawn was lighting the night sky when I heard the distant sound of Cary's cell phone ringing. Shortly after that, he came running into the living room.

"Eva!" He was on me in a minute, crouching in front of me with his hands on my knees. "How far did he go?"

I blinked down at him. "What?"

"Cross called. Said he'd had another nightmare."

"Nothing happened." I felt a hot tear roll down my cheek.

"You look like something happened. You look . . ."

I caught his wrists when he surged to his feet with a curse. "I'm okay."

"Shit, Eva. I've never seen you look like this. I can't stand it." He took a seat beside me and pulled me into his shoulder. "Enough is enough. Cut him off."

"I can't make that decision now."

"What are you waiting for?" He forced me back to glare at me. "You're going to wait too long and then this won't be just another bad relationship, it'll be one that permanently fucks you up."

"If I give up on him, he'll have no one. I can't—"

"That's not your problem. Eva . . . Goddamn it. It's not your responsibility to save him."

"It's— You don't understand." I wrapped my arms around him. Burying my face in his shoulder, I cried. "He's saving me."

I threw up when I found Gideon's key to my apartment lying on the breakfast bar. I barely made it to the sink.

When my stomach was empty, I was left with pain so agonizing it was crippling. I clung to the edge of the counter, gasping and sweating, crying so hard I wondered how I'd make it through another five minutes, let alone the rest of the day. The rest of my life.

The last time Gideon had returned my keys to me, we'd broken up for four days. It was impossible not to think that repeating the gesture signified a more permanent break. What had I done? Why hadn't I stopped him? Talked to him? Made him stay?

My smartphone signaled an incoming text. I stumbled to my purse and dug it out, praying it was Gideon. He'd talked to Cary three times already, but he'd yet to contact me.

When I saw his name on the screen, a sweet, sharp ache pierced my chest.

I'm working from home today, his message read. Angus will be waiting out front to give you a ride to work.

My stomach cramped again with dread. It had been a tremendously difficult week for both of us. I could understand why he'd just given up. But that understanding was wrapped in a gut-gnawing fear so cold and insidious that goose bumps swept up my arms.

My fingers shook as I texted him back: Will I see you tonight?

There was a long pause, long enough that I was about to demand a yes or no answer when he sent: Don't count on it. I have my appt with Dr. Petersen and a lot of work to do.

My grip tightened on my phone. It took me three attempts before I was able to type: I want to see you.

For the longest time, my phone sat silently. I was reaching for my landline in a near panic when he replied: I'll see what I can do.

Oh God . . . Tears made it hard for me to see the letters. He was done. I knew it deep down in my heart. Don't run. I'm not.

It seemed like forever before he replied: You should.

I debated calling in sick after that, but I didn't. I couldn't. I had been down that road too many times. I knew I could so easily fall back into old self-destructive habits to dull pain. It would kill me to lose Gideon, but I'd be dead anyway if I lost myself.

I had to hang on. Get through. Get by. One step at a time.

And so I climbed into the back of the Bentley when I was supposed to, and while Angus's grim face only made me worry more, I locked it down and slid into the autopilot mode of self-preservation that would get me through the hours ahead.

My day passed in a blur. I worked hard and focused on my job, using it to keep me from going crazy, but my heart wasn't in it. I spent my lunch hour running an errand, unable to tolerate the thought of eating or making small talk. After my shift was over, I almost blew off going to my Krav Maga class, but I stuck it out and gave a similar amount of focus to the drills as I'd given to my work. I had to keep moving forward, even if I was heading in a direction I couldn't bear to go.

"Better," Parker said, during a break. "You're still off, but you're better than last night."

I nodded and wiped the sweat from my face with a towel. I'd started Parker's classes solely as a more intense alternative to my usual gym visits, but last night had shown me that personal safety was more than just a convenient side benefit.

The tribal tattoos that banded his biceps flexed as he lifted a water bottle to his lips. Because he was left-handed, his simple gold wedding band caught the light and my eye. I was reminded of the promise ring on my right hand and I looked down at it. I remembered when Gideon had given it to me and how he'd said that the diamond-crusted Xs wrapping around the roped gold were representative of him "holding on" to me. I wondered if he still thought that way; if he still thought it was worth it to try. God knew I did.

"Ready?" Parker asked, tossing his empty bottle in the recycle bin.

"Bring it."

He grinned. "There she is."

Parker still worked me over, but it wasn't from lack of trying on my part. I was in it every step of the way, venting my frustration with good, healthy exercise. The few victories I managed to earn spurred my determination to fight for my rocky relationship, too. I was willing to put in the time and effort to be there for Gideon, to be a better and stronger person so we could get through our issues. And I was going to tell him that, whether he wanted to hear it or not.

When my hour was over, I cleaned up and waved good-bye to my classmates and then shoved at the push bar of the exit door and stepped out into the still-warm evening air. Clancy had already brought the car around to the door and was leaning against the fender in a pose that only a moron would think was casual. Despite the heat, he wore a jacket, which concealed his sidearm.

"Things moving along?" He straightened to open the door for me. As long as I'd known him, he'd kept his dark blond hair in a military crew cut. It added to the impression of his being a very somber man.

"Working on it." Sliding into the backseat, I told Clancy to drop me off at Gideon's. I had my own key and I was prepared to use it.

On the drive over, I wondered if Gideon had gone to see Dr. Petersen for his appointment or if he'd blown it off. He'd agreed to individual therapy only because of me. If I wasn't part of the equation anymore, he might not see any reason to make the effort.

I entered the understated and elegant lobby of Gideon's apartment building and checked in with the front desk. It wasn't until I was alone in his private elevator that the nerves really hit me. He'd placed me on his approved list weeks before, a gesture that meant so much more to him and me than it would to others because Gideon's home was his sanctuary, a place he allowed few visitors to see. I was the only lover he'd ever entertained there and the only person, aside from his household staff, who had a key. Yesterday I wouldn't have doubted my welcome, but now . . .

I exited into a small foyer decorated with checkerboard marble tiles and an antique console bearing a massive arrangement of white calla lilies. Before I unlocked his front door, I took a deep breath, steeling myself for however I might find him. The one previous time he'd attacked me in his sleep, it had shattered him. I couldn't help but fear what the second time had done to him. I was terrified that his parasomnia might be the wedge that drove us apart.

But the moment I entered his apartment, I knew he wasn't home. The energy that thrummed through a space when he occupied it was markedly absent.

Lights that were activated by my movements came on when I entered the expansive living room, and I forced myself to settle in as if I belonged there. My room was down the hall and I went to it, pausing on the threshold to absorb the weirdness of seeing my bedroom replicated in Gideon's place. The duplication was uncanny, from the color on the walls to the furniture and fabrics, but its existence was more than a little unnerving.

Gideon had created it as my safe room, a place for me to run to when I needed some space. I supposed I was running to it now, in a way, by using it instead of his.

Leaving my workout bag and purse on the bed, I showered and changed into one of the Cross Industries T-shirts Gideon had set aside for me. I tried not to think about why he still wasn't home. I'd just poured a glass of wine and turned on the living room television when my smartphone rang.

"Hello?" I answered, unfamiliar with the number on the nameless Caller ID.

"Eva? It's Shawna."

"Oh, hey, Shawna." I tried not to sound disappointed.

"I hope it's not too late to call."

I looked at the screen of my phone, noting that it was almost nine o'clock. Jealousy mingled with my concern. Where was he? "No worries. I'm just watching TV."

"Sorry I missed your call last night. I know it's short notice, but I wanted to see if you'd be up for going to a Six-Ninths concert on Friday."

"A what concert?"

"Six-Ninths. You haven't heard of 'em? They were indie until late last year. I've been following them for a while and they gave their e-mail list first dibs, so I scored tickets. Thing is, everyone I know likes hip-hop and dance pop. Not to say you're my last hope, but . . . well, you're my last hope. Tell me you like alt rock."

"I like alt rock." My phone beeped. Incoming call. When I saw it was Cary, I let it go to voice mail. I didn't think I'd be on the phone with Shawna too long and I could call him back.

"How did I know that?" She laughed. "I've got four tickets if you've got someone you'd like to bring along. Meet up at six? Grab something to eat first? The show starts at nine."

Gideon walked in just as I answered, "You've got a date."

He stood just inside the door with his jacket slung over one arm, the top button of his dress shirt undone, and a briefcase in his hand. His mask was in place, showing no emotion whatsoever at finding me sprawled on his couch in his T-shirt with a glass of his wine on his table and his television on. He raked me with a head-to-toe glance, but nothing flickered in those beautiful eyes. I suddenly felt awkward and unwanted.

"I'll get back to you about the other ticket," I told Shawna, sitting up slowly so I didn't flash him. "Thanks for thinking of me."

"I'm just glad you're coming! We're going to have a great time."

We agreed to talk the next day and hung up. In the interim, Gideon set his briefcase down and tossed his jacket over the arm of one of the gilded chairs flanking the ends of the glass coffee table.

"How long have you been here?" he asked, yanking the knot of his tie loose.

I stood. My palms grew damp at the thought that he might kick me out. "Not long."

"Have you eaten?"

I shook my head. I hadn't been able to eat much all day. I'd gotten through the session with Parker courtesy of a protein drink I'd picked up during my lunch hour.

"Order something." He walked past me toward the hallway. "Menus are in the kitchen drawer by the fridge. I'm going to grab a quick shower."

"Do you want something?" I asked his retreating back.

He didn't stop or look at me. "Yes. I haven't eaten, either."

I'd finally settled upon a local deli boasting organic tomato soup and fresh baguettes—figuring my stomach could maybe handle that—when my phone rang again.

"Hey, Cary," I answered, wishing I were home with him and not about to face a painful breakup.

"Hey, Cross was just here looking for you. I told him to go to hell and stay there."

"Cary." I sighed. I couldn't blame him; I'd do the same thing for him. "Thanks for letting me know."

"Where are you?"

"At his place, waiting for him. He just showed. I'll probably be home sooner rather than later."

"You kicking him to the curb?"

"I think that's on his agenda."

He exhaled audibly. "I know it's not what you're ready for, but it's for the best. You should call Dr. Travis ASAP. Talk it out with him. He'll help you put things in perspective."

I had to swallow past the lump in my throat. "I'm— Yeah. Maybe."

"You okay?"

"Ending it face-to-face has dignity, at least. That's something."

My phone was pulled from my hand.

Gideon held my gaze as he said, "Good-bye, Cary," then powered off my phone and set it on the counter. His hair was damp and he wore black pajama bottoms that hung low on his hips. The sight of him hit me hard, reminding me of all that I stood to lose when I lost him—the breathless anticipation and desire, the comfort and intimacy, the ephemeral sense of *rightness* that made everything worthwhile.

"Who's the date?" he asked.

"Huh? Oh. Shawna—Mark's sister-in-law—has concert tickets for Friday."

"Have you figured out what you want to eat?"

I nodded, tugging at the thigh-length hem of my shirt because I felt self-conscious.

"Get me a glass of whatever you're drinking." He reached around me and picked up the menu I'd set out on the counter. "I'll order. What do you want?"

It was a relief to move over to the cabinet that held the wine-glasses. "Soup. Crusty bread."

As I tugged the cork out of the bottle of merlot I had left on the counter, I heard him call the deli and speak in that firm, raspy voice of his that I loved from the moment I'd first heard it. He ordered tomato soup and chicken noodle, which caused a painful tightness in my chest. Without being told, he'd ordered what I wanted. It was another of the many serendipitous things that always made me feel like we were destined to end up in the same place, together, if only we could make it that far.

I passed him the glass I'd poured for him and watched as he took a drink. He looked tired, and I wondered if he'd stayed up all night like I had.

Lowering the glass, he licked the lingering trace of wine off his lips. "I went to your place looking for you. I expect Cary told you."

I rubbed at the painful ache in my chest. "I'm sorry . . . about this and—" I gestured at what I was wearing. "Damn it. I didn't plan this well."

He leaned back into the counter and crossed one ankle over the other. "Go on."

"I figured you'd be home. I should've called first. When you weren't here, I should have just waited for another time instead of making myself at home." I rubbed at my stinging eyes. "I'm . . . confused about what's going on. I'm not thinking straight."

His chest expanded on a deep breath. "If you're waiting for me to break up with you, you can stop waiting."

I grabbed on to the kitchen island to steady myself. *That's it? That's the end?*

"I can't do it," he said flatly. "I can't even say I'll let you walk, if that's why you're here."

What? I frowned in confusion. "You left your key at my place."

"I want it back."

"Gideon." My eyes closed and tears tracked down my cheeks. "You're an ass."

I walked away, moving toward my bedroom with a quick and slightly weaving stride that had nothing to do with the small amount of wine I'd sipped.

I had scarcely cleared the doorway of my room when he grabbed my elbow.

"I won't follow you inside," he said gruffly, his head bent to reach my ear. "I promised you that. But I'm asking you to stay and talk to me. At least listen. You came all this way—"

"I have something for you." It was hard for me to get the words past my tight throat.

He released me and I hurried to my purse. When I faced him, I asked, "Were you breaking up with me when you left the key on my counter?"

He filled the doorway. His hands were extended above his shoulders, his knuckles white from the force with which he gripped the frame, as if he were physically restraining himself from following me. The pose displayed his body beautifully, defining every muscle, allowing the drawstring waistband of his pants to cling to his hip bones. I wanted him with every breath I took.

"I wasn't thinking that far ahead," he admitted. "I just wanted you to feel safe."

My grip tightened around the object in my hand. "You ripped my heart out, Gideon. You have no idea what seeing that key lying there did to me. How bad it hurt me. No idea."

His eyes squeezed shut and his head bowed. "I wasn't thinking clearly. I thought I was doing the right thing—"

"Fuck that. Fuck your damn chivalry or whatever the hell you think that was. Don't do it again." My voice took on an edge. "I'm telling you right now and I mean it like I've never meant anything before—you ever give me my keys back again, we're done. There's no coming back from that. Do you understand?"

"I do, yes. I'm not sure you do."

My breath left me in a shaky exhalation. I approached him. "Give me your hand."

His left hand stayed on the doorjamb, but his right lowered and extended toward me.

"I never gave you the key to my place; you just took it." I cupped his hand between both of mine, placing my gift in his palm. "I'm giving it to you now."

Stepping back, I released him, watching as he looked down at the gleaming monogrammed fob with my apartment key on it. It was the best way I could think of to show him that it belonged to him and that it was given freely.

His hand fisted, closing tightly around my gift. After a long minute, he looked up at me and I saw the tears that wet his face.

"No," I whispered, my heart breaking further. I cupped his face in my hands, my thumbs brushing over his cheekbones. "Please . . . don't."

Gideon caught me up, his lips pressing to mine. "I don't know how to walk away."

"Shh."

"I'll hurt you. I already am. You deserve better—"

"Shut up, Gideon." I climbed him and wrapped my legs around his waist, holding on.

"Cary told me how you looked . . ." He began to shake violently. "You don't see what I'm doing to you. I'm breaking you, Eva—"

"That's not true."

He sank to his knees on the floor, clasping me tightly. "I've trapped you in this. You don't see it now, but you knew from the beginning— You knew what I would do to you, but I wouldn't let you run."

"I'm not running anymore. You've made me stronger. You gave me a reason to try harder."

"God." His eyes were haunted. He sat, stretching his legs out, pulling me closer. "We're so fucked up, and I've handled everything all wrong. We're going to kill each other with this. We'll tear each other apart until there's nothing left."

"Shut up. I don't want to hear any more of that shit. Did you go to Dr. Petersen?"

His head fell back against the wall and his eyes closed. "Yes, damn it."

"Did you tell him about last night?"

"Yes." His jaw clenched. "And he said the same thing he started on last week. That we're in too deep. We're drowning each other. He thinks we need to pull back, date platonically, sleep separately, spend more time together with others and less time alone."

It would be better, I thought. Better for our sanity, better for our chances. "I hope he's got a Plan B."

Gideon opened his eyes and looked at my scowling face. "That's what I said. Again."

"So we're fucked up. Every relationship has issues."

He snorted.

"Seriously," I insisted.

"We *are* going to sleep separately. That's something I let go too far."

"Separate beds or separate apartments?"

"Beds. That's all I can stand."

"All right." I sighed and rested my head on his shoulder, so grateful that he was in my arms again and that we were together. "I can deal. For now."

His throat worked on a hard swallow. "When I came home and found you here—" His arms tightened around me. "God, Eva. I thought Cary was lying about you not being home, that you just didn't want to see me. Then I thought you might be out . . . moving on."

"You're not that easy to get over, Gideon." I didn't think I'd ever get over him. He was in my blood. I straightened so he could see my face.

He placed his hand over his heart, the hand with the key. "Thank you for this."

"Don't let that go," I warned again.

"Don't regret giving it to me." He pressed his forehead to mine. I felt the warmth of his breath on my skin and thought he might have whispered something, but I didn't catch it if he did.

It didn't matter. We were together. After the long awful day, nothing else was important.

8

THE SOUND OF my bedroom door opening ended my forgettable dream, but it was the mouthwatering aroma of coffee that really woke me up. I stretched but kept my eyes closed, allowing the anticipation to build.

Gideon took a seat on the edge of the mattress, and a moment later his fingers drifted across my cheek. "How did you sleep?"

"I missed you. Is that coffee I smell for me?"

"If you're good."

My eyes popped open. "But you like me bad."

His smile did crazy things to me. He'd dressed already in one of his amazingly sexy suits and looked much better this morning than he had the night before. "I like you bad *with me*. Tell me about this concert on Friday."

"It's a band called Six-Ninths. That's all I know. Wanna go?"

"It's not a question of whether I want to go. If you're going, so am I."

My brows rose. "Is that right? And what if I hadn't asked you?"

He reached for my hand and gently twirled my promise ring around my finger. "Then you wouldn't be going, either."

"Excuse me?" I shoved my hair back. Noting the set look on his gorgeous face, I sat up. "Gimme that coffee. I want to be caffeinated when I kick your ass."

Gideon grinned and handed the mug over.

"Don't look at me like that," I warned. "I'm seriously not happy with you telling me I can't go somewhere."

"We're talking specifically about a rock concert, and I didn't say you couldn't go, just that you can't go without me. I'm sorry you don't like it, but it is what it is."

"Who says it's rock? Maybe it's classical. Or Celtic. Or pop."

"Six-Ninths signed with Vidal Records."

"Oh." Vidal Records was run by Gideon's stepfather, Christopher Vidal Sr., but Gideon had controlling interest. I wondered how a boy grew up to take over his stepfather's family business. I figured whatever the reason was, it was also why Gideon's half brother, Christopher Jr., hated him to the extreme.

"I've seen videos of their indie shows," he said dryly. "I'm not risking you to a crowd like that."

I sucked down a big gulp of coffee. "I get it, but you can't order me around."

"Can't I? Shh." He placed his fingers over my lips. "Don't argue. I'm not a tyrant. I may occasionally have concerns, and you'll be sensible about acknowledging them."

I shoved his hand away. "'Sensible' being whatever you've decided is best?"

"Of course."

"That's bullshit."

He stood. "We're not going to fight over a hypothetical situation. You asked me to go to the concert with you on Friday and I said yes. There's nothing to argue about."

Setting my coffee on the nightstand, I kicked off the covers and slid out of bed. "I have to be able to live my life, Gideon. I still have to be *me* or this won't work."

"And I have to be me. I'm not the only one who needs to compromise."

That hit me hard. He wasn't wrong—I had a right to expect him to give me my space, but he had a right to be understood as the man he was. I had to make accommodations for the fact that he had triggers, too. "What if I want a girls' night out clubbing with my friends?"

He caught my jaw in both hands and kissed my forehead. "You can take the limo and stick to clubs I own."

"So you can have your security people spy on me?"

"Keep an eye on you," he corrected, his lips sliding over my brow. "Is that so terrible, angel? Is it so unforgivable that I hate taking my eyes off you?"

"Don't twist this around."

He tilted my head back and looked down at me with hard, determined eyes. "You need to understand that even if you take the limo and stick to my clubs, I'm still going to go crazy until you get home. If that means you're driven a little crazy with my safety precautions, isn't that part of the give-and-take?"

I growled. "How do you make something unreasonable sound reasonable?"

"It's a gift."

Grabbing his very fine, very taut ass in my hands, I squeezed. "I need more coffee to deal with your gift, ace."

∽

It had become somewhat of a Wednesday tradition for Mark, his partner Steven, and me to go out to lunch. When Mark and I arrived at the little Italian restaurant he'd chosen and found Shawna waiting with Steven, I was really touched. Mark and I had a very professional relationship, but somehow we'd managed to make that personal and it meant a lot to me.

"I'm so jealous of your tan," Shawna said, looking casual and cute in jeans, embellished tank top, and filmy scarf. "The sun just makes me red and gives me more freckles."

"But you've got that beautiful hair to show for it," I pointed out, admiring the deep red hue.

Steven ran a hand through his hair, which was the exact same color as his sister's, and grinned. "The things one sacrifices to be hot."

"How would you know?" Shawna shoved at his shoulder with a laugh, an effort that didn't budge her brother even an inch. Where she was slender as a reed, Steven was big and strapping. I knew from talking to Mark that his partner was very hands-on with his construction business, which explained both his size and the rugged condition of his hands.

We entered the restaurant and were seated right away, thanks to the reservation I'd made when Mark had invited me to lunch. It was a small establishment, but it had great charm. Sunlight poured in through the floor-to-ceiling windows and the aroma of the food was so tantalizing it made my mouth water.

"I am so excited about Friday." Shawna's soft blue eyes were lit with anticipation.

"Yeah, she'll take *you*," Steven told me dryly, "and not her big brother."

"Sooo not your scene," she shot back. "You hate crowds."

"Just gotta establish some personal space, that's all."

Shawna rolled her eyes. "You can't be a bruiser everywhere."

The talk about crowds had me thinking of Gideon and his protective streak. "Mind if I bring the guy I'm seeing?" I asked. "Or is that a buzzkill?"

"Not at all. Does he have a friend who'd like to come?"

"Shawna." Mark was clearly shocked. And disapproving. "What about Doug?"

"What about him? You didn't let me finish." She looked at me and explained, "Doug's my boyfriend. He's in Sicily for the summer taking a culinary course. He's a chef."

"Nice," I said. "I dig guys who can cook."

"Oh, yeah." She grinned, then aimed a glare at Mark. "He's a keeper and I know it, so if your guy has a friend who's fine with filling the empty seat with no possibility of a hookup, bring him along."

I immediately thought of Cary and grinned.

But later that day, after Gideon and I had spent quality time with our personal trainers and had returned to his apartment for the night, I changed my mind. I got up from the couch where I'd been trying unsuccessfully to read a book and padded down the hall to his home office.

I found him frowning at whatever he was working on, his fingers flying over the keyboard. The glow of the monitor and the spotlight aimed at the photo collage on the wall were the only sources of illumination in the room, which left much of the large space in shadow. He sat in the semidark, bare-chested and beautiful, alone and powerfully self-contained. As he always did while working, he looked solitary and unreachable. I felt lonely just looking at him.

The combination of the physical distance caused by my period and Gideon's understandable decision to sleep separately stirred my deepest insecurities, made me want to cling tighter and try harder to keep his attention focused on me.

That he was working instead of spending time with me shouldn't have rankled—I knew how busy he was—but it did. I felt abandoned and needy, which told me I was regressing into familiar bad patterns. The simple fact was, Gideon and I were the best and worst things that had ever happened to each other.

He looked up and pinned me with his gaze. I watched his focus shift from work to me.

"Am I neglecting you, angel?" he asked, leaning back in his chair.

I flushed, wishing he couldn't read me so well. "I'm sorry to interrupt."

"You should always come to me when you need something." Pushing his keyboard drawer in, he patted the empty space on the desk in front of him and wheeled his chair back. "Come sit."

A thrill rushed through me. I hurried over, making no effort to hide my eagerness. I hopped onto the desk in front of him and smiled wide when he rolled his chair forward to fill the space between my legs.

Draping his arms over my thighs, he hugged me around the hips and said, "I should've explained that I'm trying to clear my schedule so we can take off this weekend."

"Really?" I pushed my fingers through his hair.

"I want you all to myself for a while. And I really, really need to fuck you for a very long time. Maybe the whole time." His eyes closed as I touched him. "I miss being inside you."

"You're always inside me," I whispered.

His mouth curved in a slow, wicked smile and his eyes opened. "You're making me hard."

"What's new?"

"Everything."

I frowned.

"We'll get to that," he said. "For now, tell me what you came in here for."

I hesitated, still stuck on his cryptic comment.

"Eva." His firm tone focused me. "What do you need?"

"A date for Shawna. Uh . . . not really a date. Shawna's got a man, but he's out of the country. It'd just be better if we made it an even party of four."

"You don't want to ask Cary?"

"I thought of him first, but Shawna's *my* friend. I thought you might want someone *you* know to come. You know, keep the dynamic even."

"All right. I'll see who's free."

I realized then that I hadn't really expected him to take me up on my offer.

Some of my thoughts must have shown on my face, because he asked, "Is there more?"

"I . . ." How did I say what I was thinking without making an ass of myself? I shook my head. "No. Nothing."

"Eva." His voice was stern. "Tell me."

"It's stupid."

"That wasn't a request."

An electric tingle coursed through me, as it always did when he took on that commanding tone. "I just thought you socialized for business and screwed random women occasionally."

Saying that last part was hard. As lame as it was to be jealous of women in his past, I couldn't help it.

"You didn't think I had friends?" he asked, clearly amused.

"You've never introduced me to any," I said sullenly, picking at the hem of my T-shirt.

"Ah . . ." His amusement deepened, his eyes sparkling with laughter. "You're my sexy little secret. Have to wonder what I was thinking when I made sure we were photographed kissing in public."

"Well." My gaze moved to the collage on the wall where that very picture could be found, a picture that had been plastered all over gossip blogs for days. "When you put it like that . . ."

Gideon laughed, and the sound spread through me in a heated rush of pleasure. "I've introduced you to a few of my friends when we've been out."

"Oh." I'd assumed everyone I had met at the events we'd attended were business associates.

"But keeping you all to myself isn't a bad idea."

I shot him a look and revisited the point I'd made when we argued about my going to Vegas instead of Phoenix. "Why can't *you* be the one lying around naked waiting to be fucked?"

"Where's the fun in that?"

I shoved at his shoulders and he hauled me into his lap, laughing.

I couldn't believe how good his mood was and wondered what had set it off. When I glanced at his monitor, all I saw was a spreadsheet that made my eyes cross and a half-written e-mail. But something was different about him. And I liked it.

"It'd be a pleasure," he murmured, with his lips to my throat, "to lie around with a hard-on that you rode whenever the mood struck you."

My sex clenched at the visual in my mind. "You're making me horny."

"Good. I like you that way."

"So," I mused, "if my fantasy is you providing around-the-clock stud servicing—"

"Sounds like reality to me."

I nipped him on the jaw with my teeth.

He growled. "Want to play rough, angel?"

"I want to know what your fantasy is."

Gideon adjusted me so that I was draped across his lap. "You."

"It better be."

He grinned. "In a swing."

"Huh?"

"A sex swing, Eva. Your gorgeous ass in a seat, feet in stirrups, legs spread wide, your perfect cunt wet and waiting." He rubbed seductive circles into the small of my back. "Totally at my mercy and unable to do anything but take all the cum I can give you. You'd love it."

I pictured him standing between my legs, naked and glistening with sweat, his biceps and pecs flexing as he rocked me back and forth, sliding me on and off his beautiful cock. "You want me helpless."

"I want you bound. And not on the outside. I'm working my way in."

"Gideon—"

"I won't ever take it further than you can handle," he promised, his eyes glittering hotly in the muted lighting. "But I'll take you to the edge."

I squirmed, both aroused and disturbed by the thought of giving up that much control. "Why?"

"Because you want to be mine and I want to possess you. We'll get there." His hand slid under my shirt and cupped my breast, his fingers rolling and tugging my nipple, igniting my body.

"Have you done that before?" I asked breathlessly. "The swing?"

His face shuttered. "Don't ask questions like that."

Oh God. "I just—"

His mouth sealed over mine. He nipped my lower lip, then thrust his tongue into my mouth, holding me where he wanted me with his fist in my hair. The dominance of the act was undeniable. Hunger surged through me, a need for him I couldn't control or fight. I whimpered, my chest aching at the thought of him putting that much time and effort into gaining pleasure from someone else.

Gideon's hand shoved between my legs and cupped my sex. I jerked, surprised at his aggression. He made a low sound of reassurance and massaged me, rubbing my tender flesh with the consummate skill I'd grown so addicted to.

He broke the kiss, moving his arm to arch my back and lift my breast to his mouth. He bit my nipple through the cotton, then wrapped his lips around the aching peak, sucking so strongly I felt the echo in my core.

I was under siege, my brain short-circuiting as desire pumped through me. His fingers slid beneath the edge of my panties to touch my clit, the feel of flesh on flesh just what I needed. *"Gideon."*

He lifted his head and watched with dark eyes as he made me come for him. I cried out when the tremors rippled through me, the release of tension after days of deprivation almost too much to bear. But he didn't let up. He stroked my sex until I came again, until violent shivers racked my body and I squeezed my legs shut to stop the onslaught.

When he pulled his hand away, I sagged, boneless and breathing heavily. I curled into him, my face pressed into his throat, my arms wrapping around his neck. My heart felt as if it had swelled in my chest. Everything I felt for him, all the torment and love, overwhelmed me. I clawed at him, trying to get closer.

"Shh." He held me tighter, squeezing me until it was hard to breathe. "You're questioning everything and driving yourself crazy."

"I hate this," I whispered. "I shouldn't need you this much. It's not healthy."

"That's where you're wrong." His heart beat strongly beneath my ear. "And I take responsibility for that. I've taken the lead with some things and given it to you with others. That's left you confused and worried. I'm sorry about that, angel. It'll be easier moving forward."

I leaned back so I could search his face. My breath caught when our eyes met and he stared back at me unflinchingly. I comprehended the difference then—there was a calm, solid serenity about him. Seeing that settled something inside me, too. My breathing slowed and evened; my anxiety lessened.

"That's better." He kissed my forehead. "I was going to wait until the weekend to talk about this, but now works. We're going to come to an agreement. Once it's met, there's no turning back. Understand?"

I swallowed hard. "I'm trying."

"You know the way I am. You've seen me at my worst. Last night, you said you want me anyway." He waited for my nod. "That's where I fucked up. I didn't trust you to make that decision for yourself and I should have. Because I didn't, I've been too cautious. Your past scares me, Eva."

The thought of Nathan indirectly taking Gideon away from me was so painful, my knees drew even closer into my chest. "Don't give him that power."

"I won't. And you have to realize there's more than one answer for everything. Who says you need me too much? Who says it's not healthy? Not you. You're unhappy because you're holding yourself back."

"Men don't—"

"Fuck that. Neither of us is typical. *And that's okay.* Turn off that voice in your head that's screwing you up. Trust me to know what you need, even when you think I'm wrong. And I'll trust your decision to be with me despite my faults. Got it?"

I bit my lower lip to hide its trembling and nodded.

"You don't look convinced," he said softly.

"I'm afraid I'll lose myself in you, Gideon. I'm scared I'll lose the part of me I worked so hard to get back."

"I'd never let that happen," he promised fiercely. "What I want is for us both to feel safe. What you and I have together shouldn't be draining us like this. It should be the one rock-solid thing we both count on."

My eyes stung with tears at the thought. "I want that," I whispered. "So much."

"I'm going to give it to you, angel." Gideon bent his dark head and brushed his lips over mine. "I'm going to give it to both of us. And you're going to let me."

"THINGS seem to be looking better this week," Dr. Petersen said when Gideon and I arrived for our Thursday night therapy appointment.

We sat near each other this time, with our hands clasped together. Gideon's thumb caressed my knuckles, and I looked at him and smiled, feeling settled by the contact.

Dr. Petersen flipped open the protective case of his tablet and settled more comfortably in his seat. "Is there anything in particular you'd like to discuss?"

"Tuesday was tough," I said quietly.

"I imagine so. Let's talk about Monday night. Can you tell me what happened, Eva?"

I told him about waking up from my own nightmare to find myself trapped in Gideon's. I walked him through that night and the following day.

"So you're sleeping separately now?" Dr. Petersen asked.

"Yes."

"Your nightmares"—he looked up at me—"how often do you have them?"

"Rarely. Prior to dating Gideon, it'd been almost two years since my last one." I watched him set the stylus down and start typing quickly. Something about his somberness made me anxious. "I love him," I blurted.

Gideon stiffened beside me.

Dr. Petersen's head came up, and he studied me. He glanced at Gideon, then back to me. "I don't doubt it. What made you say that, Eva?"

I shrugged awkwardly, hyperaware of Gideon's gaze on my profile.

"She wants your approval," Gideon said grimly.

His words rubbed over me like sandpaper.

"Is that true?" Dr. Petersen asked me.

"No."

"The hell it isn't." The rasp in Gideon's voice was pronounced.

"It's not," I argued, although I'd needed him to say it aloud for me to understand that. "I just . . . It's just the truth. That's the way I feel."

I looked at Dr. Petersen. "We have to make this work. We're *going* to make this work," I stressed. "I just want to know that you're on the same page. I need to know that you understand that failure isn't an option."

"Eva." He smiled kindly. "You and Gideon have a lot to work through, but it's certainly not insurmountable."

My breath left me in a rush of relief. "I love him," I said again, with a decisive nod.

Gideon surged to his feet, his grip crushingly tight on my hand. "If you'll excuse us a minute, Doctor."

Confused and a little worried, I stood and followed him out to the empty reception area. Dr. Petersen's receptionist had already gone home, and we were his last appointment of the day. I knew from my mother that these evening appointments came at a premium. I was grateful that Gideon was willing to pay for them not once but twice a week.

The door shut behind us, and I faced him. "Gideon, I swear it's not—"

"Hush." He cupped my face in both hands and kissed me, his mouth moving softly but urgently over mine.

Startled, it took me the length of two heartbeats to slide my hands beneath his jacket and grip his lean waist. When his tongue stroked deep into my mouth, a low moan escaped me.

He pulled back and I looked up at him, seeing the same gorgeous businessman in a dark suit that I'd first met, but the look in his eyes . . .

My throat burned.

The power and scorching intensity, the hunger and need. His fingertips brushed over my temples, across my cheeks, down to my throat. He tilted my jaw up and his lips pressed gently against mine. He didn't say anything, but he didn't have to. I got it.

He linked our fingers and led me back inside.

I HURRIED THROUGH the security turnstiles of the Crossfire and grinned when I saw Cary waiting for me in the lobby.

"Hey, you," I greeted him, admiring how he managed to make worn jeans and a V-neck T-shirt look expensive.

"Hey, stranger." He held out his hand to me and we stepped out of the building through the side door hand-in-hand. "You're looking happy."

The noonday heat hit me like a physical barrier. "Ugh. It's hot as hell. Let's pick somewhere close. You up for tacos?"

"Hell yeah."

I took him to the little Mexican place Megumi had introduced me to and tried not to let him see how guilty his greeting made me feel. I hadn't been home in a couple days and Gideon was planning a weekend trip away, which meant it would be another few days before I hung out with Cary again. It had been a relief when he'd agreed to meet me for lunch. I didn't want to go too long without checking in with him and making sure he was all right.

"Got any plans tonight?" I asked, after ordering for both of us.

"One of the photographers I've worked with is having a birthday bash tonight. I figured I'd pop in for a bit and see how it goes." He rocked back on his heels as we waited for our tacos and blended virgin margaritas. "You still planning on hanging with your boss's sister? You guys wanna come with?"

"Sister-in-law," I corrected. "And she's got concert tickets. I'm her last hope, she said, but even if I wasn't, I think it'll be fun. At least I hope so. I've never heard of the band, so I'm just hoping they don't suck."

"Who is it?"

"Six-Ninths. Know 'em?"

His eyes widened. "Six-Ninths? Really? They're good. You'll like them."

I grabbed our drinks off the counter and left the tray with our plates for him to carry. "You've heard of them and Shawna's a big fan. Where have I been?"

"Under Cross and his hard place. You taking him with you?"

"Yes." I hurried to grab a table as two businessmen stood to leave. I didn't tell Cary about Gideon's assertion that I couldn't go without him. I knew that wouldn't go over well with Cary, which made me wonder why I'd let it go as easily as I did. Usually Cary and I agreed about stuff like that.

"Can't see Cross liking alt rock." Cary sank fluidly into the chair across from me. "Does he know how much *you* like it? Especially the musicians who play it?"

I stuck my tongue out at him. "I can't believe you brought that up. Ancient history."

REFLECTED IN YOU · 145

"So? Brett was hot. Ever think about him?"

"With shame." I picked up one of the carne asada tacos. "So I try not to."

"He was a decent guy," Cary said, before slurping up a hefty swallow of margarita-flavored slush.

"I'm not saying he wasn't. He just wasn't good for me." Just thinking about that time in my life made me want to squirm in embarrassment. Brett Kline was hot and he had a voice that made me wet just hearing it, but he was also one of the prime examples of an unfortunate choice in my previously sordid love life. "Moving on . . . You talk to Trey lately?"

Cary's smile faded. "This morning."

I waited patiently.

Finally, he sighed. "I miss him. Miss talking to him. He's so fucking smart, you know? Like you. He's going to that party with me tonight."

"As friends? Or as a date?"

"These are really good." He chewed a bite of one of his tacos before replying. "We're supposed to be going as friends, but you know I'll probably screw that up and fuck him. I asked him to meet me there and to head home from there so we're not alone, but I can always bang him in the bathroom or a goddamn maintenance closet. I have no willpower and he can't say no to me."

My heart hurt at his dejected tone.

"I know what that's like," I reminded him softly. That'd been me once. I'd been so desperate to feel connected with somebody. "Why don't you . . . you know . . . take care of it beforehand. Maybe that'll help."

A slow, mischievous smile spread across his handsome face. "Can I get you to record that for my voice mail message?"

I threw my wadded-up napkin at him.

He caught it with a laugh. "You can be such a prude sometimes. I love it."

"I love *you*. And I want you to be happy."

Lifting my hand to his lips, he kissed the back. "I'm working on it, baby girl."

"I'm here if you need me, even if I'm not home."

"I know." He squeezed my hand before releasing it.

"I'll be around a lot next week. Gotta get ready for my dad's visit." I bit into a taco and my feet did a little happy tap dance at how delicious it was. "I wanted to ask you about Friday. I've got to work, so if you're around, would you keep an eye on him? I'll stock up on the food he likes and leave him some city maps, but—"

"No problem." Cary winked at a pretty blonde as she walked by. "He'll be in good hands."

"Want to see a show with us while he's in town?"

"Eva honey, I'm always game to hang with you. Just let me know where and when, and I'll keep things clear as much as possible."

"Oh!" I quickly chewed and swallowed. "Mom told me she saw your pretty mug on the side of a bus the other day."

He grinned. "I know. She forwarded a pic she'd taken with her phone. Awesome, right?"

"Beyond. We'll need to celebrate," I said, stealing his signature line.

"Hell yeah."

"WHOA!" Shawna paused on the sidewalk outside her Brooklyn apartment complex and gaped at the limousine idling in the street. "You went all out."

"Not me," I said dryly, checking out her tight red shorts and strategically slashed Six-Ninths screened T-shirt. Her bright hair had been pulled up and teased, and her lips were painted to match her shorts. She looked hot and ready to party, and I felt vindicated in my clothing choice of ultra-short black leather pleated skirt, fitted white ribbed tank top, and cherry red sixteen-eye Doc Martens.

Gideon, who'd had his back to us while talking to Angus, turned to face us, and I found myself as dumbstruck now as I'd been when I first saw him after he had showered and changed. He wore loose-fitting black jeans and a plain black T-shirt with heavy black boots and somehow made the severely casual combination look so fuck-ing sexy, I wanted to jump his bones. As Dark and Dangerous as he was in a suit, he was even more so when ready to rock. He looked younger and every bit as mouthwateringly gorgeous.

"Holy shit, tell me that's for me," Shawna whispered, gripping my wrist like a vise.

"Hey, you've got your own. That one's mine." And it gave me a huge thrill to say so. Mine to claim, to touch, to kiss. And later on, to fuck to exhaustion. *Oh yeah* . . .

She laughed when I rocked onto my tiptoes in anticipation. "All right. I'll settle for an introduction."

I did the honors, then waited for her to hop into the limo first. I was about to climb in after her when I felt Gideon's hand slide up beneath my skirt to squeeze my butt.

He pressed against my back and whispered in my ear, "Make sure I'm standing behind you when you bend over, angel, or I'll be spanking this pretty ass."

Turning my head, I leaned my cheek against his. "My period's over."

He growled, his fingertips biting into the flesh of my hip. "Why didn't you tell me that earlier?"

"Delayed gratification, ace," I told him, using a phrase he'd once tormented me with. I was laughing at his curse when I dropped onto the bench seat beside Shawna.

Angus slid behind the wheel and we headed out, breaking into a bottle of Armand de Brignac on the way. By the time we pulled up to Tableau One, a hot new fusion bistro that had a healthy line out front and energetic music pouring out onto the street, the combination of the champagne and Gideon's hot gaze on the nearly indecent hemline of my skirt had me feeling giddy.

Shawna slid forward on the seat and stared wide-eyed through the tinted windows. "Doug tried to get us in here before he left, but the waiting list is two months long. You can walk up, but the wait can be hours and there's no guarantee you'll be seated."

The limo door opened and Angus helped her out, then me. Gideon joined us, taking my arm as if we were dressed for a gala and not a rock concert. We were escorted inside so quickly, with the manager being so gushy and welcoming, that I looked at Gideon and mouthed, *One of yours?*

"Yes, in partnership."

I just sighed, reconciled to the inevitable. "Is your friend going to meet us for dinner?"

Gideon gestured with an easy nod of his chin. "He's already here."

I followed his gaze to an attractive man sporting blue jeans and a Six-Ninths T-shirt. The gentleman was acting as the focal point in a photo op with two pretty women on each side. He smiled wide for the person wielding a smartphone camera, then waved at Gideon and excused himself.

"Oh my God." Shawna bounced on her feet. "That's Arnoldo Ricci! He owns this place. And he's got a show on the Food Network!"

Gideon released me to clasp hands with Arnoldo and engage in the backslapping ritual of close male friends. "Arnoldo, my girl-friend, Eva Tramell."

I extended my hand and Arnoldo grabbed it, pulled me closer, and kissed me straight on the mouth.

"Back off," Gideon snapped, tugging me behind him.

Arnoldo grinned, his dark eyes flashing with humor. "And who's this vision?" he asked, turning to Shawna and lifting her hand to his lips.

"Shawna, this will be your escort, Arnoldo Ricci, *if* he manages to survive dinner." Gideon shot his friend a warning look. "Arnoldo, Shawna Ellison."

She practically glowed. "My boyfriend's a huge fan of yours. I am, too. He made your lasagna recipe once and it was. To. Die. For."

"Gideon told me your man is in Sicily now." Arnoldo's voice was flavored with a delicious accent. "I hope you can make the time to visit with him there."

My gaze darted to Gideon, knowing damn well I'd never given him that much information about Shawna's boyfriend. He glanced down at me with a look of mock innocence and an almost impercep-tible smirk.

I shook my head, exasperated, but I couldn't deny that this would be a night Shawna would never forget.

The next hour passed in a blur of excellent food and fine wine. I was polishing off an extraordinary zabaione with raspberries when I caught Arnoldo watching me with a wide smile.

"*Bellissima,*" he praised. "Always a joy to see a woman with a healthy appetite."

I flushed, slightly embarrassed. I couldn't help it; I loved food.

Gideon draped his arm along the back of my chair and toyed with the hair at my nape. His other hand lifted a glass of red wine to his mouth and when he licked his lips, I *knew* he was thinking about tasting me instead. His desire was charging the air between us. I had been falling under its spell all through dinner.

Reaching beneath the tablecloth, I cupped his cock through his jeans and squeezed. He went from semihard to stone instantly but gave no other outward indication of his arousal.

I couldn't help but see that as a challenge.

I began to stroke the rigid length of him with my fingers, careful to keep my movements slow and easy to prevent detection. To my delight, Gideon continued his conversation without a hitch in his voice or change of expression. His control excited me, made me bolder. I reached for his button fly, turned on by the thought of releasing him and stroking him skin on skin.

Gideon took another leisurely sip, then set his wineglass down.

"Only you, Arnoldo," he said dryly in response to something his friend had said.

My wrist was caught just as I tugged at the top button of his jeans. He lifted my hand to his lips, the gesture appearing to be an absentminded show of affection. The quick nip of his teeth into the pad of my finger caught me by surprise and made me gasp.

Arnoldo smiled; it was the knowing and slightly mocking smile one bachelor gave to another who'd been caught by a woman. He said something in Italian. Gideon replied, his pronunciation sounding fluid and sexy, his tone wry. Arnoldo threw his dark head back and laughed.

I squirmed in my seat. I loved seeing Gideon like this, relaxed and enjoying himself.

He looked at my empty dessert plate, then at me. "Ready to go?"

"Oh, yes." I was dying to see how the rest of the night would go, how many more sides of Gideon I'd get to discover. Because I loved this side of the man as much as I loved the powerful businessman in the suit and the dominant lover in my bed and the broken child who couldn't hide his tears and the tender partner who held me when I cried.

He was so complex and still a huge mystery to me. I'd barely scratched the surface of who he was. Which didn't stop me from being in too deep.

"THESE guys are good!" Shawna yelled as the opening act barreled headlong into their fifth song.

We'd left our seats after the third, working our way through a writhing crowd to the railing that divided the seating area from the mosh pit in front of the stage. Gideon surrounded me, his arms caging me on both sides, his hands gripping the rail. The audience pressed in around us, collectively pushing forward, but I was cushioned from it by his body, just as Shawna was by Arnoldo beside us.

I was sure Gideon could have gotten us way better seats, but I didn't have to tell him that the way Shawna had scored her fan-only tickets and the fact that *she'd* invited *us* meant her seats were our only option. I loved him for understanding that and for going with the flow.

Turning my head, I looked at him. "Is this band with Vidal, too?"

"No. But I like them."

I was stoked that he was enjoying the show. Lifting my arms in the air, I screamed, feeling pumped by the energy of the crowd and the driving beat. I danced within the circle of Gideon's arms, my body drenched in sweat, my blood raging.

When the act was done, the stagehands quickly set to work breaking down the equipment and setting up for Six-Ninths. Grateful for the evening, for the joy, for the awesomeness of going wild with the man I loved, I turned and threw my arms around Gideon's neck, mashing my lips to his.

He lifted me and urged my legs around his waist, kissing me violently. He was hard and pressing against me, luring me to grind into him. Around us people whistled and catcalled things that ranged from "Get a room" to "Fuck her, man!" but I didn't care and neither did Gideon, who seemed as swept away by the sensual craziness as I was. His hand on my buttocks rocked me into his erection while the other fisted in my hair, holding me where he wanted me as he kissed me as if he couldn't stop, as if he were starving for the taste of me.

Our open mouths slid desperately across each other. He tongued me deep and fast, fucking my mouth, making love to it. I drank him in, licking and tasting, moaning at his insatiable need. He sucked on my tongue, the circle of his lips sliding along it. It was too much. I was slick and aching for his cock, nearly frantic with the need to feel him filling me.

"You're going to make me come," he growled, before tugging on my bottom lip with his teeth.

I was so into him and the ferocity of his passion for me that I barely registered when Six-Ninths started. It wasn't until the vocals kicked in that I was jolted back to where I was.

I stiffened, my mind clawing its way up through the fog of desire to process what I was hearing. I knew the song. My eyes opened as Gideon pulled back. Over his shoulder I saw handwritten signs held up in the air.

BRETT KLINE IS MINE! And BANG ME, BRETT! And my personal favorite, BRETT, I'D HIT IT WITH YOU LIKE THE WRATH OF GOD!!!

Hell. What were the chances?

And Cary had known, of course. He'd known and hadn't warned

me. Probably thought it'd be hysterical for me to find out by accident instead.

My legs loosened from around Gideon's hips and he set me down, protecting me from the frenzied fans with the shield of his body. I turned to face the stage, feeling a mad fluttering in my belly. Sure enough, it was Brett Kline at the mic, his deep, powerful, sexy-as-hell voice pouring over the thousands who'd come to see him in action. His short hair was spiked and tipped with platinum, his lean body clothed in olive cargo pants and a black tank top. It was impossible to see from where I was, but I knew his eyes were a brilliant emerald green, his face was ruggedly handsome, and his killer smile revealed a dimple that drove women crazy.

Tearing my eyes away from him, I looked at the other band members, recognizing all of them. They hadn't been called Six-Ninths back in San Diego, though. They'd been called Captive Soul then, and I wondered what had led to the name change.

"Good, aren't they?" Gideon asked with his mouth to my ear so I could hear him. He had one hand on the railing and the other around my waist, keeping me pulled up tight against him as he moved to the music. The combination of his body and Brett's voice did insane things to my already raging sex drive.

I closed my eyes, focusing on the man behind me and the unique rush I'd always felt while listening to Brett sing. The music throbbed through my veins, bringing back memories—some good and some bad. I swayed in Gideon's arms, desire pounding through me. I was achingly aware of his hunger. It poured off him like heat waves, sinking into me, making me crave him until the physical distance between us was painful.

Grabbing the hand he had pressed flat against my stomach, I urged it downward.

"Eva." His voice was harsh with lust. I'd been pushing him all.

night, from the moment I told him my period was over, to the hand job beneath the restaurant table, to the scorching kiss during intermission.

He gripped my bare thigh and squeezed. "Open."

I set my left foot on the bottom of the railing. My head fell back against his shoulder and a heartbeat later, his hand was under my skirt. His tongue traced the shell of my ear, his breathing hard and fast. I felt him groan as much as heard it when he discovered how wet I was.

One song blended into another. Gideon rubbed me through the crotch of my boyshorts, moving in circles, then vertically through my cleft. My hips rolled into his touch, my core clenching, my ass grinding into the hard ridge of his erection. I was going to come right there, inches away from dozens of people, because that was what Gideon did to me. That was how insanely he turned me on. Nothing mattered when his hands were on me, his attention completely riveted to me.

"That's it, angel." His fingers pushed my underwear aside and two sank into me. "I'm going to fuck this gorgeous cunt for days."

With bodies pressing in all around us, music pounding over us, and privacy granted only by distraction, Gideon slid his fingers deep into my soaked sex and stayed there. The solid, unmoving penetration drove me wild. I ground my hips into his hand, working toward the orgasm I needed so desperately.

The song ended and the lights went out. Drenched in darkness, the crowd roared. Anticipation weighted the audience, building until the strum of guitar strings broke the heavy expectation. Shouts rang out, then lighters flickered to life, turning the sea of people into thousands of fireflies.

A spotlight hit the stage, revealing Brett sitting on a bar stool, shirtless and glistening with sweat. His chest was hard and defined,

REFLECTED IN YOU · 155

his abs ridged with muscle. He lowered the height of the microphone stand and the piercings in his nipples glittered with his movements. The women in the audience screamed, including Shawna, who jumped in place and gave an earsplitting whistle.

I totally got it. Sitting there as he was, with his feet propped on the rungs of the stool and his muscular arms covered in sleeves of black and gray tattoos, Brett looked insanely sexy and extremely fuckable. For six months nearly four years ago I'd debased myself to get him naked every chance I could, so infatuated with him and desperate to be loved that I took whatever scraps he threw me.

Gideon's fingers began to slide in and out of me. The bass kicked in. Brett began to sing a song I'd never heard before, his voice low and soulful, the words crystal clear. He had the voice of a fallen angel. Mesmerizing. Seductive. And the face and body to enhance the temptation.

Golden girl, there you are.
I'm singing for the crowd, the music's loud.
I'm living my dream, riding the high,
But I see you there, sunlight in your hair,
And I'm ready to go, desperate to fly.

Golden girl, there you are.
Dancing for the crowd, the music's loud.
I want you so bad. I can't look away.
Later, you'll drop to your knees. You'll beg me please.
And then you'll go, it's only your body I know.

Golden girl, where'd you go?
You're not there, with sunlight in your hair.
I could have you in the bar or the back of my car,

But never your heart. I'm falling apart.
I'll drop to my knees, I'll beg you. Please.

Please don't go. There's so much more I want to know.
Eva, please. I'm on my knees.

Golden girl, where'd you go?
I'm singing for the crowd, the music's loud.
And you're not there, with sunlight in your hair.
Eva, please. I'm on my knees.

The spotlight went dark. A long moment passed as the music faded. Then the lights came back on and the drums exploded with sound. The flames winked out and the crowd went crazy.

But I was lost to the roaring in my ears, the tightness in my chest, and a confusion that had me reeling.

"That song," Gideon growled in my ear, his fingers fucking me forcefully, "makes me think of you."

His palm pressed into my clit and massaged, and I climaxed in a rush that took me by storm. Tears came to my eyes. I cried out, shaking in his arms. Gripping the railing in front of me, I held on and let the unstoppable pleasure pulse through me.

WHEN the show was over, all I could think about was getting to a phone and calling Cary. While we waited for the crowd to thin, I leaned heavily into Gideon, drawing support from the strength of his arms around me.

"You okay?" he asked, running his hands up and down my back.

"I'm fine," I lied. Honestly, I didn't know how I was feeling. It shouldn't matter that Brett wrote a song about me that painted a

different light on our fuck-buddy history. I was in love with someone else.

"I want to go, too," he murmured. "I'm dying to get inside you,
angel. I can barely think straight."

I pushed my hands into the back pockets of his jeans. "So let's
get out of here."

"I've got backstage access." He kissed the tip of my nose when I
leaned back to look up at him. "We don't have to tell them, if you'd
rather get out of here."

I seriously debated it for a moment. After all, the night had been
great as it was, thanks to Gideon. But I knew it'd bother me later if
I denied Shawna and Arnoldo—who was also a Six-Ninths fan—
something they'd remember for the rest of their lives. And I'd be
lying if I didn't admit to myself that I wanted to catch a glimpse of
Brett up close. I didn't want him to see me, but I wanted to see him.
"No. Let's take them back there."

Gideon grabbed my hand and spoke to our friends, whose excitement over the news gave me the excuse to say I'd done it solely for
them. We headed down toward the stage, then off to the side of it,
where Gideon spoke to the massive man acting as security. When
the guy spoke into the mic of his headset, Gideon pulled out his cell
and told Angus to bring the limo around to the back. While he
spoke, his eyes met mine. The heat in them and the promise of pleasure took my breath away.

"Your man is the ultimate," Shawna said, eyeing Gideon with a
look of near reverence. It wasn't a predatory look, just an appreciative one. "I can't believe this night. I owe you big-time for this."

She pulled me in for a quick, hard hug. "Thank you."

I hugged her back. "Thank you for inviting me."

A tall, rangy man with blue streaks in his hair and stylish black-framed glasses approached us. "Mr. Cross," he greeted Gideon, extending his hand. "I didn't know you'd be coming tonight."

Gideon shook the man's hand. "I didn't tell you," he replied smoothly, reaching his other hand out to me.

I caught it and he pulled me forward, introducing me to Robert Phillips, Six-Ninths' manager. Shawna and Arnoldo were introduced next; then we were led back through the wings, where activity was high and groupies loitered.

I suddenly didn't want to catch even a glimpse of Brett. It was so easy to forget how it'd been between us while I was listening to him sing. It was so easy to *want* to forget after listening to the song he'd written. But that time in my past was something I was far from proud of.

"The band's right in here," Robert was saying, gesturing to an open door from which music and raucous laughter poured out. "They'll be excited to meet you."

My feet dug in suddenly and Gideon paused, glancing at me with a frown.

I pushed up onto my toes and whispered, "I'm not all that interested in meeting them. If you don't mind, I'm going to hit the backstage bathroom and head out to the limo."

"Can you wait a few minutes and I'll go with you?"

"I'll be okay. Don't worry about me."

He touched my forehead. "Are you feeling all right? You look flushed."

"I'm feeling great. I'll show you exactly how great as soon as we get home."

That did the trick. His frown faded and his mouth curved. "I'll hurry this along, then." He looked at Robert Phillips and gestured at Arnoldo and Shawna. "Can you take them in? I need a minute."

"Gideon, really . . ." I protested.

"I'm walking you over there."

I knew that tone. I let him walk me the twenty feet to the bathroom. "I can take it from here, ace."

"I'll wait."

"Then we'll never get out of here. Go do your thing. I'll be fine."

He gave me a very patient look. "Eva, I'm not leaving you alone."

"I can manage. Seriously. The exit is right there." I pointed down the hall to the open double doors beneath a lighted exit sign. Roadies were already transporting equipment out. "Angus is right out there, isn't he?"

Gideon leaned his shoulder into the wall and crossed his arms.

I threw up my hands. "Okay. Fine. Have it your way."

"You're learning, angel," he said with a smile.

Muttering under my breath, I went into the bathroom and took care of business. As I washed up at the sink, I looked into the mirror and winced. I had raccoon eyes from sweating so damn much and my pupils were dark and dilated.

"What does he see in you?" I asked myself derisively, thinking of how awesome he still looked. As hot and sweaty as he'd been, he looked none the worse for wear, while I looked damp and limp. But more so than my exterior, it was my personal failings I was thinking of. I couldn't get away from them. Not while Brett was in the same building with us.

I rubbed a dampened square of paper towel under my eyes to get rid of the black smudges, then headed back out to the hall. Gideon waited a few feet away, talking with Robert, or more accurately, listening to him. The band's manager was clearly excited about something.

Gideon spotted me and held up a hand to get me to wait a minute, but I didn't want to take the risk. I gestured down the hall at the exit, then turned and headed that way before he could stall me. I hurried past the greenroom door, chancing a quick glance inside to see Shawna laughing with a beer in her hand. The room was packed and boisterous, and she looked like she was having a great time.

I made my escape with a sigh of relief, feeling ten times lighter the moment I left. Spotting Angus standing next to Gideon's limo on the far side of the line of buses, I waved and set off toward him.

Looking back on the night, I was tantalized by how uninhibited Gideon had been. He sure as hell hadn't been the man who'd used mergers and acquisitions as parlance for getting me into bed.

I couldn't wait to get him naked.

A burst of flame in the darkness to my right startled me. I jolted to a halt and watched Brett Kline lift a match to the clove cigarette hanging from his lips. As he stood in the shadows to the side of the exit, the flickering light of the flame caressed his face and threw me back in time for a long minute.

He glanced up, caught me in his gaze, and froze. We stared at each other. My heart kicked into a mad beat, a combination of excitement and apprehension. He cursed suddenly, shaking out the match as it burned his fingers.

I took off, struggling to maintain a casual pace as I made a beeline for Angus and the limo.

"Hey! Hold up," Brett shouted. I heard his footsteps approaching at a jog, and adrenaline surged through me. A roadie was pushing a flat hand truck loaded with heavy gear and I darted around him, using him as cover to duck between two buses. I pressed my back flat against the side of one, standing between two open cargo compartments. I cringed into the shadows, feeling like a coward, but knowing I had nothing to say to Brett. I wasn't the girl he knew anymore.

I watched him rush by. I decided to wait, give him time to look and give up. I was hyperaware of the time passing, of the fact that Gideon would be looking for me soon.

"Eva."

I flinched at the sound of my name. Turning my head, I found Brett approaching from the other side. While I'd been looking to the right, he'd come up on the left.

"It *is* you," he said roughly. He dropped his clove smoke on the ground and crushed it beneath his boot.

I heard myself saying something familiar. "You should quit."

"So you keep telling me." He approached cautiously. "You saw the show?"

I nodded and stepped away from the bus, backing up. "It was awesome. You guys sound really great. I'm happy for you."

He took a step forward for every one of mine backward. "I was hoping I'd find you like this, at one of the shows. I had a hundred different ideas about how it might go if I saw you at one."

I didn't know what to say to that. The tension between us was so thick it was hard to breathe.

The attraction was still there.

It was nothing like what I felt with Gideon. Nothing more than a shadow of that, but it was there nonetheless.

I retreated back out into the open, where the activity was high and there were lots of people milling around.

"Why are you running?" he asked. In the pool of light from a parking lot lamp, I saw him clearly. He was even better looking than before.

"I can't . . ." I swallowed. "There's nothing to say."

"Bullshit." The intensity of his glare burned through me. "You stopped coming around. Didn't say a word, just stopped showing up. Why?"

I rubbed at the knot in my stomach. What was I going to say? *I finally grew a pair and decided I deserved better than to be one of the many chicks you fucked in a bathroom stall between sets?*

"Why, Eva? We had something going and you just fucking disappeared."

Turning my head, I looked for Gideon or Angus. Neither was anywhere in sight. The limo waited alone. "It was a long time ago."

Brett lunged forward and caught me by the arms, startling me, briefly frightening me with the sudden aggressive movement. If we hadn't been so near other people, it might have triggered panic.

"You owe me an explanation," he bit out.

"It's not—"

He kissed me. He had the softest lips, and he sealed them over mine and kissed me. By the time I registered what was happening, he'd tightened his grip on my arms and I couldn't move away. Couldn't push him away.

And for a brief span of time I didn't want to.

I even kissed him back, because the attraction was still there and it soothed something hurting inside me to think I might've been more than a convenient piece of ass. He tasted like cloves, smelled seductively like hardworking male, and he took my mouth with all the passion of a creative soul. He was familiar, in very intimate ways.

But in the end, it didn't matter that he got to me still. It didn't matter that we had a history, painful as it was for me. It didn't matter that I was flattered and affected by the lyrics he'd written, that after six months of watching him enjoy other women while nailing me anywhere with a door that locked, it was *me* he was thinking about when he seduced screaming-for-it women from the stage.

None of that mattered because I was madly in love with Gideon Cross, and he was what I needed.

I wrenched away with a gasp—

—and faced Gideon charging at a dead run, his speed unchecked as he rammed into Brett and took him down.

10

I STUMBLED BACK from the impact, nearly falling. The two men hit the asphalt with a sickening thud. Someone yelled. A woman screamed. I could do nothing. I stood frozen and silent, emotions twisting through me in a frenzied tangle.

Gideon pinned Brett by the throat and pummeled his ribs with a relentless series of blows. He was like a machine, silent and unstoppable. Brett grunted with each brutal impact and struggled to break free.

"Cross! *Dio mio.*"

I wept when Arnoldo appeared. He leaped forward, reaching for Gideon, only to scramble back as Brett wrenched to the side and the two men rolled.

Brett's bandmates pushed in through the growing crowd around the front of the buses, prepared to brawl . . . until they saw *who* Brett was fighting with—the man with the money behind their record label.

"Kline, you fuckhead!" Darrin, the drummer, gripped his own hair in both fists. "What the hell are you doing?"

Brett broke free, lurched to his feet, and tackled Gideon into the side of a bus. Gideon linked his hands and hammered Brett's back like a club, forcing Brett to lurch away. Pressing the advantage, Gideon lashed out with a roundhouse kick and followed with a lightning-quick jab to the gut. Brett swung, his powerful biceps bunching with his fist, but Gideon ducked fluidly and retaliated with an uppercut that snapped Brett's head back.

Jesus.

Gideon didn't make a sound, not when he struck out and not when Brett landed a direct hit to his jaw. The quiet intensity of his fury was chilling. I could feel the rage pumping off him, saw it in his eyes, but he remained controlled and eerily methodical. He'd disconnected in some way, retreated to a place where he could objectively observe his body doing serious damage to someone else.

I'd caused that. I had turned the warm, wickedly playful man who'd enchanted me all evening into the cold, murderous fighter in front of me.

"Miss Tramell." Angus grabbed my elbow.

I looked at him desperately. "You have to stop him."

"Please, return to the limousine."

"What?" I looked over and saw blood dripping from Brett's nose. No one was intervening. "Are you crazy?"

"We need to take Miss Ellison home. She's your guest; you need to see to her."

Brett swung and when Gideon feinted to the side, Brett rammed his other fist forward, nailing Gideon in the shoulder and sending him backward a few steps.

I grabbed Angus by the arms. "What's the matter with you?! Stop them!"

His pale blue eyes softened. "He knows when to stop, Eva."

"Are you *shitting* me?!"

He looked over my shoulder. "Mr. Ricci, if you would, please."

The next thing I knew, I was slung over Arnoldo's shoulder and en route to the limo. Lifting my head, I saw the circle of bystanders close in with my absence, blocking my view. I screamed my frustration and pounded at Arnoldo's back, but it didn't faze him. He climbed right into the back of the limo with me, and when Shawna hopped in a moment later, Angus shut the door as if everything was totally fucking normal.

"What the hell are you doing?" I snapped at Arnoldo, scrambling for the door handle as the limo rolled smoothly into motion. It wouldn't open and no matter what I did, I couldn't get it to unlock. "He's your friend! You're just going to leave him like that?"

"He's your boyfriend." The calm neutrality in Arnoldo's voice cut me deep. "And *you* are the one who left him like that."

I slumped back into the seat, my stomach churning and my palms damp. *Gideon . . .*

"You're the Eva in the song 'Golden,' aren't you?" Shawna asked quietly, from her position on the opposite bench seat.

Arnoldo started, obviously surprised by the connection. "I wonder if Gideon—" He sighed. "Of course he knows."

"That was a long time ago!" I said defensively.

"Not long enough, apparently," he pointed out.

Desperate to get to Gideon, I couldn't sit still. My feet tapped, my body battling against restlessness so intense I felt like crawling out of my skin.

I'd hurt the man I loved and through him, another man who'd done nothing more than be himself. And I had no good explanation for it. Looking back, I had no idea what had come over me. Why hadn't I pulled away sooner? Why had I kissed Brett back?

And what was Gideon going to do about it?

The thought that he might break up with me triggered overwhelming panic. I was sick with worry. Was he hurt? God . . . the thought of Gideon in pain ate at me like acid. Was he in trouble? He'd assaulted Brett. My palms went damp when I remembered Cary's news that his clusterfuck buddy also wanted to press assault charges.

Gideon's life was spiraling out of control—because of me. At some point he was going to realize I wasn't worth the trouble.

I glanced at Shawna. She was looking out the window pensively. I'd blown her awesome night. And Arnoldo's, too. "I'm sorry." I sighed miserably. "I screwed up everything."

She looked at me and shrugged, then offered a sympathetic smile that made my throat burn. "No big. I had a great time. I hope you work things out for the best."

The best thing for me was Gideon. Had I blown that? Had I thrown away the most important thing in my life over some weird, inexplicable head trip?

I still felt Brett's mouth on mine. I scrubbed at my lips, wishing I could erase the last half hour of my life as easily.

My anxiety made it feel like it took an eternity to drive Shawna home. I got out and gave her a hug on the sidewalk in front of her apartment building.

"I'm sorry," I said again, for both earlier and then, because I was dying to get to Gideon—wherever he was—and I was afraid my impatience showed. I wasn't sure I'd ever forgive Angus or Arnoldo for taking me away when and how they did.

Arnoldo hugged Shawna and told her that she and Doug had a

standing reservation for Tableau One anytime. I softened a little toward him. He'd taken good care of her all night.

We climbed back into the limo and set off for the restaurant. I curled into a darkened corner of the seat and cried silently, unable to contain the flood of despair overwhelming me. When we arrived at the restaurant, I used my tank top to dry my face. Arnoldo stopped me from getting out.

"Be gentle with him," he scolded, staring hard at my face. "I have never seen him the way he is with you. I can't say you are worthy of him, but you can make him happy. I saw that myself. Do it or walk. Don't fuck with his head."

I couldn't speak past the lump in my throat, so I nodded, hoping he could see in my eyes how much Gideon meant to me. *Everything.*

Arnoldo disappeared into the restaurant. Before Angus shut the door, I slid forward on the seat. "Where is he? I need to see him. Please."

"He called." Angus's face was kind, which made me start crying again. "I'm taking you to him now."

"Is he okay?"

"I don't know."

I pushed back into the seat, feeling physically ill. I barely paid attention to where we were headed, my only thought being that I needed to explain. I needed to tell Gideon that I loved him, that I'd never leave him if he'd still have me, that he was the only man I wanted, the only man who set my blood on fire.

Eventually, the car slowed and I looked out, realizing we'd returned to the amphitheater. As I peered out the window, searching for him, the door behind me opened, startling me, and I shifted around to see Gideon duck inside and settle on the opposite bench from me.

168 · SYLVIA DAY

I lurched toward him. "Gideon—"

"Don't." His voice whipped with anger, sending me recoiling and falling on my rear. The limo set into motion, jostling me.

Crying, I watched him pour a glass of amber liquor at the bar and toss it back. I waited on the floorboards, my stomach churning with fear and grief. He refilled his glass before shutting the bar and dropping back in his seat. I wanted to ask him if Brett was okay or badly hurt. I wanted to ask how Gideon was, if he was injured or fine. But I couldn't. I didn't know if he would take the questions the wrong way and assume my concern for Brett meant more than it did.

His face was impassive, his eyes hard as sapphires. "What is he to you?"

I swiped at the tears streaming down my face. "A mistake."

"Then? Or now?"

"Both."

His lip curled in a sneer. "You always kiss your mistakes like that?"

My chest heaved as I tried to stem the need to sob. I shook my head violently.

"You want him?" he asked tightly, before taking another drink.

"No," I whispered. "I only want you. I love *you*, Gideon. So much it hurts."

His eyes closed and his head fell back. I took the opportunity to crawl closer, needing to bridge the physical distance between us, at least.

"Did you come for me when I had my fingers inside you, Eva? Or because of his goddamn song?"

Oh my God . . . How he could doubt—?

I made him doubt. I did that. "You. You're the only one who can get to me like that. Make me forget where I am. Make it so I don't care who's around or what's happening as long as you're touching me."

"Isn't that what happened when he kissed you?" Gideon's eyes opened and focused on me. "He's had his dick in you. He's fucked you . . . blown his load inside you."

I cringed away from the horrible bitterness in his tone, the vicious nastiness. I knew just how he felt. How badly the mental images could sting and claw until you felt like you were going mad. In my mind, he and Corinne had fucked dozens of times while I watched in sick, jealous fury.

He straightened suddenly, leaning forward to rub his thumb roughly across my lips. "He's had your mouth."

I grabbed his glass and drank what was left in it, hating the harsh taste and searing burn. I swallowed by force of will alone. My stomach roiled, protesting. The heat of the alcohol spread outward from my gut.

Gideon sagged back into the seat, his arm thrown across his face. I knew he was still seeing me kissing Brett. Knew it was eating a hole in his mind.

Dropping the glass on the floor, I surged between his legs and fumbled with his button fly.

He caught my fingers in an iron grip but kept his eyes covered with his forearm. "What the fuck are you doing?"

"Come in my mouth," I begged. "Wash it away."

There was a long pause. He sat there, utterly still except for the heavy lift and fall of his chest.

"Please, Gideon."

With muttered curse, he released me, his hand falling limply to his side. "Do it."

I rushed to get to him, my pulse pounding at the thought that he might change his mind and deny me . . . that he might decide he was done with me. The only help he gave me was a momentary lift of his hips, so I could yank his jeans and boxer briefs out of the way.

Then his big, beautiful cock was in my hands. My mouth. I moaned at the taste of him, at the warmth and satiny softness of his skin, at the smell of him. I nuzzled my cheek against his groin and balls, wanting his scent all over me, marking me as his. My tongue followed the thick veins coursing the length of him, licking him up and down.

I heard his teeth grind when I sucked him with long drawing pulls, moans of apology and bliss vibrating in my throat. It broke my heart that he was so silent, my vocal lover who always talked dirty to me. Always told me what he wanted and needed . . . how good he felt when I made love to him. He was holding himself back, denying me the satisfaction of knowing I pleased him.

Pumping the thick root with my fist, I milked him, sucking on the plush crown, luring his pre-cum to the tip where I could lick it up with rapid flutters of my tongue. His thighs bunched, his breath came in fierce pants. I felt him coil tight and I went wild, double-fisting him, my mouth working so hard that my jaw ached. His spine straightened, his head lifting from the seat only to slam backward as the first thick spurt exploded in my mouth.

I whimpered, his flavor igniting my senses, making me crave more. I swallowed convulsively, my hands pulling and rubbing on his throbbing penis to lure more of his rich, creamy semen onto my tongue. His body quaked as he came for long minutes, filling my mouth until he spilled out of the sides of my lips. He made no sound, as unnaturally silent as he'd been during the fight.

I would've sucked him off for hours. I wanted to, but he put both hands on my shoulders and urged me away. I looked up into his heartrendingly gorgeous face, saw his eyes glittering in the semi-darkness. He touched my lips with his thumb, smearing his semen over and around the swollen curves.

"Slide your tight cunt around me," he ordered hoarsely. "I've got more to give you."

Shaky and frightened by his harsh remoteness, I wriggled out of my boy shorts.

"Take it all off. Everything except the boots."

I did as he said, my body quickening at his command. I'd do anything he wanted. I would prove to him that I was his and only his. I would atone however he needed me to so he'd know I loved him. I unzipped my skirt and pushed it off, then whipped my tank top over my head and threw it on the opposite bench. My bra followed.

When I straddled him, Gideon caught my hips and looked up at me. "Are you wet?"

"Yes."

"It turns you on to suck my cock."

My nipples hardened further. The blunt, crude way he talked about sex turned me on, too. "Always."

"Why did you kiss him?"

The abrupt change in topic knocked me askew. My lower lip trembled. "I don't know."

He released me, reaching up and over his shoulders with both hands to grip the sides of the headrest. His biceps bulged with the pose. I was aroused by the sight, as I was by everything about him. I wanted to see his bare chest glistening with sweat, his abs tightening and flexing as he pumped his cock into me.

I licked my lips, tasting him. "Take your shirt off."

His gaze narrowed. "This isn't for you."

I stilled, my heart racing in my chest. He was using sex against me. In the limo where we'd first made love, in the same position I'd first taken him . . . "You're punishing me."

"You've earned it."

It didn't matter that he was right. If I'd earned it, so had he.

I gripped the top of the seat back for balance and wrapped the fingers of my other hand around his cock. He was still hard, still throbbing. A muscle in his neck twitched as I stroked him in my fist, priming him. I placed the wide crest between the lips of my cleft, rubbing him back and forth, coating him with the slickness of my desire.

My gaze never left his. I watched him as I teased us both, looking for any sign of the passionate lover I adored. He wasn't there. A furious stranger glared back at me, daring me, taunting me with his detachment.

I let the first thick inch push inside me, spreading me open. Then I slammed my hips down, crying out as he pierced me deep and stretched me almost unbearably.

"Jesus. Fuck," he bit out, shuddering. "Goddamn it."

His uncontrolled outburst spurred me. Digging my knees into the seat, I set my hands on either side of his and lifted, pulling off him, my trembling sex clinging tightly. I pushed back down, the glide easier now that he was wet from me. When my buttocks hit his thighs I found his muscles hard as stone, his body giving away the lie—he wasn't indifferent.

I lifted again, slowly, making us both feel every nuance of the delicious friction. When I pushed back down, I tried to be as stoic as he was, but the sensation of fullness, the heated connection, was too exquisite to contain. I moaned, and he shifted restlessly, his hips moving in a delicious little circle before he could stop himself.

"You feel so good," I whispered, stroking his raging cock with my eager, aching sex. Sliding up and down. "You're all I need, Gideon. All I want. You were made for me."

"You forgot that," he bit out, his knuckles white from his grip on the seat back.

I wondered if he was just holding on or physically restraining himself from reaching for me. "Never. I could never forget. You're a part of me."

"Tell me why you kissed him."

"I don't know." I rested my damp forehead against his, feeling the tears burning behind my eyes. "God, Gideon. I swear I don't know."

"Then shut up and make me come."

If he'd slapped my face, it couldn't have shocked me more. I straightened and leaned away from him. "Fuck you."

"Now you're getting the idea."

Hot tears slid down my face. "Don't treat me like a whore."

"Eva." His voice was low and raspy, filled with warning, but his eyes were dark and desolate. Filled with pain that matched my own. "You want to stop, you know what to say."

Crossfire. With one word I could unmistakably, irrefutably put an end to this agony. But I couldn't use it now. Just the fact that he brought up my safe word told me he was testing me. Pushing me. He had an agenda, and if I gave up now, I'd never know what it was.

Reaching behind me, I set my hands on his knees. I arched my back and dragged my soaked sex along the rigid length of his cock, then slammed back down. I adjusted the angle, lifted and fell again, gasping at the feel of him. Mad as hell or not, my body worshipped his. Loved the feel of him, the sense of *rightness* that was there despite the anger and hurt.

His breath was powering out of his lungs with every plunge of my hips. His body was hot, so hot, radiating heat like a blast furnace. I pumped my hips. Up. Down. Taking the pleasure he refused to give me. My thighs, buttocks, stomach, and core tightened with every lift, fisting him from root to tip. They relaxed when I dropped, letting him sink deep.

I fucked him with everything I had, pounding myself onto his cock. His breath hissed out between his clenched teeth. Then he was coming hard, jetting inside me so fiercely I felt each scorching burst of semen like a separate thrust. I cried out, loving the feel of it, chasing an orgasm that would shatter me. I was wound so tightly, my body desperate for release after pleasing him twice.

But he moved, grabbing me by the waist and restraining my movements, holding himself deep as he pumped me full. I choked off a scream when I realized he was deliberately preventing me from coming.

"Tell me why, Eva," he growled. *"Why?"*

"I don't know!" I yelled, trying to grind my hips onto him, pounding his shoulders with my fists when his grip tightened.

Holding me pinned to his pelvis and filled with his cock, Gideon pushed to his feet and everything shifted. He pulled out of me, flipped me to face away from him, then bent me over the edge of the seat with my knees on the floorboard. With one hand at the small of my back, holding me down, he cupped my sex and rubbed, massaging his semen into my cleft. He spread it around, coating me with it. My hips circled, seeking that perfect bit of pressure to get me off . . .

He kept it from me. Deliberately.

The pounding in my clit and the needy clenching of my empty core was driving me mad, my body hungry for release. He pushed two fingers into me and my nails dug into the black leather seat. He finger-fucked me leisurely, sliding lazily in and out, keeping me on the edge.

"Gideon," I sobbed, the sensitive tissues inside me rippling greedily around him. I was coated in sweat, barely able to breathe. I began to pray for the car to stop, for us to reach our destination, holding my breath in desperate anticipation of escape. But the limo never pulled over. It kept driving and driving, and I was restrained so completely that I couldn't rise up enough to see where we were.

He folded over my back, his cock lying within the seam of my ass. "Tell me why, Eva," he crooned in my ear. "You knew I'd be coming after you . . . that I'd find you . . ."

My eyes squeezed shut, my hands clenching into fists. "I. Don't. Know. Damn you! I don't fucking know!"

His fingers pulled free and then his cock was pushing into me. My sex spasmed around the delicious hardness, sucking him deeper. I heard his breath catch on a muffled groan, and then he was taking me.

I cried with the pleasure of it, my entire body shivering with delight as he fucked me thoroughly, the wide head of his gorgeous penis rubbing and tugging at tender, hyperstimulated nerves. The pressure built and built, brewing like a storm . . .

"*Yes,*" I gasped, stretched tight with anticipation.

He pulled out at the first grasp of my sex and left me hanging on the precipice again. I screamed with frustration, fighting to get up and away from the lover who'd become the source of unbearable torment.

He whispered in my ear like the devil himself. "Tell me why, Eva. Are you thinking of him now? Are you wishing it were his cock inside you? Wishing it were his cock fucking your perfect little cunt?"

I screamed again. "I hate you! You're a sadistic, selfish son of a—"

He was in me again, filling me, stroking rhythmically into my quivering core.

Unable to stand it a minute longer, I struggled to reach my clit with my fingers, knowing a single stroke would have me coming violently.

"No." Gideon caught my wrists and held my hands down on the seat, his thighs between my own, keeping my legs spread wide so he could sink deep. Over and over. The tempo of his thrusts unfaltering and relentless.

I was thrashing, screaming, losing my mind. He could make me come with just his cock, giving me an intense vaginal orgasm just from riding me at the right angle, rubbing his thick crest over and over whatever spot I needed him to, a random place inside me he knew instinctively every time he had me.

"I hate you," I sobbed, tears of frustration wetting my face and the seat beneath my cheek.

Bending over me, he gasped in my ear, "Tell me why, Eva."

Fury boiled up inside me and spewed out. "Because you deserved it! Because you should know what it feels like! How bad it hurts, you self-centered asshole!"

He stilled. I felt his breath heave out of him. My blood was roaring in my ears, so loudly that at first I thought I was deliriously imagining his voice softening with tenderness.

"Angel." His lips brushed over my shoulder blade, his hands releasing my wrists to slide beneath me and cup my full, heavy breasts. "My stubborn, beautiful angel. Finally, we get to the truth."

Gideon lifted me up, straightening me. Exhausted, my head lolled against his shoulder, my tears dripping onto my chest. I had nothing left to fight with, barely able to whimper when he rolled an aching nipple between his fingertips and reached between my splayed legs. His hips began to lunge, his cock pumping upward into me as he pinched the lips of my sex around my throbbing clit and rubbed.

I came with a hoarse cry of his name, my entire body convulsing in fierce tremors as the relief exploded through me. The orgasm lasted forever and Gideon was tireless, extending my pleasure with the perfect thrusts I'd been so frantic for earlier.

When I finally collapsed in his arms, panting and soaked with sweat, he lifted me carefully off him and placed me lengthwise on the bench seat. Shattered, I covered my face with my hands, incapable of stopping him when he pushed my thighs apart and put his mouth on me. I was soaked with his semen and he didn't care, tonguing and suckling my clit until I came again. And again.

My back arched with each orgasm, my breath soughing from my lungs. I lost track of how many times I climaxed after they began rolling into each other, cresting and waning like the tide. I tried to curl away from him, but he just straightened and yanked his shirt off, climbing over me with one knee on the seat and the other leg extended to the floor. He placed his hands on the window above my head, putting his body on display as he'd refused to do before.

I shoved at him. "No more! I can't take any more."

"I know." His abs tightened as he slid into me, his eyes on my face as he pushed carefully through swollen tissues. "I just want to be inside you."

My neck arched as he slid deeper, a low sound escaping me because it felt *sooo* good. As worn out and overstimulated as I was, I still craved to possess him and to be possessed by him. I knew I always would.

Bending his head, he pressed his lips to my forehead. "You're all I want, Eva. There's no one else. There will never be anyone else."

"Gideon." He understood, as I hadn't, that the night had fallen apart because of *my* jealousy and the deep-seated need I had to make him feel it for himself.

He kissed me softly, reverently, erasing every memory of anyone else's lips on mine.

⟨◦⟩

"ANGEL." Gideon's voice was a warm rasp in my ear. "Wake up."

I moaned, squeezing my eyes shut tighter and burying my face deeper in his neck. "Leave me alone, you sex fiend."

His silent laughter shook me. He pressed a hard kiss to my forehead and wiggled out from under me. "We're here."

Cracking one eye open, I watched him put his shirt back on. He'd never gotten out of his jeans. I realized the sun was out. I sat up and looked out the windows, gasping when I saw the ocean. We'd stopped for gas once but I hadn't been able to get my bearings or figure out where we were. Gideon had declined to tell me when I asked, saying only that it was a surprise.

"Where are we?" I breathed, thrilled by the sight of the sun climbing over the water. It had to be solidly into morning. Maybe even midmorning.

"North Carolina. Lift your arms."

I obeyed automatically, and he slid my tank top over my head. "I need my bra," I muttered, when I could see him again.

"No one's here to see you but me and we're going straight into the bathtub."

I looked again at the weathered shingle-covered building we'd parked beside. It was at least three stories, with wraparound decks and balconies on the front and sides, and a quaint single-door entrance off the back. It stood on stilts at the shoreline, so close to the water that I knew the tide must come up right beneath it. "How long have we been driving?"

"Almost ten hours." Gideon slid my skirt up my legs and I stood, allowing him to twist it straight and pull up the zipper. "Let's go."

He got out first, then held his hand out for me. The bracing, salty breeze hit my face, waking me. The rhythmic surge of the ocean grounded me to the moment and where we were. Angus was no-where to be seen, which was a relief, since I was very aware of my lack of underwear. "Angus drove all night?"

"We switched drivers when we stopped for gas."

I looked at Gideon and my pulse stuttered at the tender, haunted way he was looking at me. A shadow of a bruise marred his jaw and I reached up to touch it, my chest aching when he nuzzled into my palm.

"Are you hurt anywhere else?" I asked, feeling so emotionally raw after the long night we'd had.

He caught my wrist and pulled my hand down to press flat over his heart. "Here."

My love . . . It had been hard on him, too. "I'm so sorry."

"So am I." He kissed my fingertips, then linked our hands and led me up to the house.

The door was unlocked and he walked right in. A wire mesh bas-ket sat on a console just inside the door, holding a bottle of wine and two glasses tied with ribbon. As Gideon turned the dead bolt with a firm click, I plucked the *Welcome* envelope out and opened it. A key fell into my palm.

"We won't be needing that." He took the key from me and set it on the console. "For the next two days, we're going to be hermits together."

A hum of pleasure warmed me from the inside, followed by more than a little awe that a man like Gideon Cross could enjoy my com-pany so much he didn't need anyone else.

"Come on," he said, tugging me toward the stairs. "We'll break into that wine later."

"Yeah. Coffee first."

I took in the décor of the house. It was rustic on the outside and modern contemporary on the inside. The wainscoted walls were painted a bright white and decorated with massive black-and-white photos of seashells. The furniture was all white, and most of the accessory pieces were glass and metal. It would have been stark if not for the gorgeous view of the ocean and the color introduced in the area rugs covering the hardwood floors and the collection of hardcover books filling built-in bookcases.

When we reached the top floor, I felt a flutter of happiness. The master suite was a totally open space, with only two support columns to break it up. Bouquets of white roses, white tulips, and white calla lilies covered nearly every flat surface, and some even sat on the floor in strategic areas. The bed was massive and covered in white satin, which made me think of a bridal suite, an impression reinforced by the black-and-white photo of a filmy scarf or veil blowing in the breeze hanging over the headboard.

I looked at Gideon. "Have you been here before?"

He reached up and freed my now-lopsided ponytail. "No. What reason would I have to come here?"

Right. He didn't take women anywhere but his hotel fuck pad— that he apparently still had. My eyes closed wearily as he ran his fingers through the loosened tresses of my hair. I didn't have the energy to get riled up about that.

"Take your clothes off, angel. I'll start the bath."

He backed up. I opened my eyes and caught him by the shirt. I didn't know what to say; I just didn't want him to go.

He understood, because he got me.

"I'm not going anywhere, Eva." Gideon cupped my jaw in his hands and stared into my eyes, showing me the intensity and laser focus that had snared me from the first. "If you wanted him, it wouldn't be enough for me to let you go. I want you too much. I want you with me, in my life, in my bed. If I can have that, nothing else matters. I'm not too proud to take what I can get."

I swayed into him, drawn to his obsessive and insatiable raw need for me, which reflected the depth of my need for him. My hand fisted in the cotton of his T-shirt.

"Angel," he breathed, lowering his head to press his cheek to mine. "You can't let me go, either."

He swept me up in his arms and carried me into the bathroom with him.

11

I RECLINED WITH my eyes closed, my back cradled against Gideon's chest, listening to the sound of lapping water as his hands glided lazily over me in the claw-foot tub.

He'd washed my hair and then my body, pampering me, spoiling me. I knew he was making up for last night and the method he'd used to get me to face the truth—a truth he'd clearly known but needed me to see as well.

How did he know me so well . . . better than I knew myself?

"Tell me about him," he murmured, his arms wrapping around my waist.

I took a deep breath. I'd been waiting for him to ask about Brett. I knew Gideon well, too. "First, tell me if he's okay."

There was a pause before he answered. "There's no permanent damage. Would you care if there was?"

"Of course I'd care." I heard his teeth grind.

"I want to know about you two," he demanded tightly.

"No."

"Eva . . ."

"Don't take that tone with me, Gideon. I'm tired of being an open book for you while you hoard all your secrets." My head rolled to the side so that my cheek was pressed against his damp chest. "If all I get of you is your body, I'll take it. But I can't give you more in return."

"You mean you *won't.* Let's be—"

"I *can't.*" I pulled away from him, twisting so that I faced him. "Look what it's doing to me! I *hurt* you last night. On purpose. Without even realizing it, because the resentment is eating at me even while I'm convincing myself that I can live with everything you're not telling me."

Sitting up, he spread his arms. "I'm wide open for you, Eva! You're making it sound like you don't know me . . . that all we have is sex . . . when you know me better than anyone else."

"Let's talk about what I *don't* know. Why do you own so much of Vidal Records? Why do you hate your family home? Why are you estranged from your parents? What's between you and Dr. Terrence Lucas? Where'd you go the other night when I had that nightmare? What's behind *your* nightmares? Why—"

"Enough!" he snapped, shoving his hands through his wet hair.

I settled back, watching and waiting as he clearly struggled with himself. "You should know you can tell me anything," I said softly.

"Can I?" He pierced me with his gaze. "Don't you have enough to look past as it is? How much shit can I pile on you before you run like hell?"

Laying my arms along the rim of the tub, I leaned my head back and closed my eyes. "Okay, then. We'll just be fuck buddies who bitch to a therapist once a week. Good to know."

"I screwed her," he spat. "There. Do you feel better?"

I shot up so fast, water surged over the edge of the tub. My stomach cramped. "You screwed Corinne?"

"No, damn it." His face was flushed. "Lucas's wife."

"Oh . . ." I remembered the photo I'd found of her through my Google search. "She's a redhead," I said lamely.

"My attraction to Anne was based entirely on her relationship to Lucas."

I frowned, confused. "So things were off between you and Dr. Lucas *before* you slept with his wife? Or because of it?"

Gideon set his elbow on the side of the tub and scrubbed at his face. "He alienated me from my family. I returned the favor."

"You broke them up?"

"I broke *her*." He exhaled harshly. "She came on to me at a fundraiser. I brushed her off until I learned who she was. I knew it'd kill Lucas to know I'd banged her, and the opening was there so I took it. It was just supposed to be that once, but Anne contacted me the next day. Because it would hurt him more to know she couldn't get enough, I let it go on. When she was ready to leave him for me, I sent her back to her husband."

I stared at him, noting his defiant embarrassment. He would do it again, but he was ashamed of what he'd done.

"Say something!" he snapped.

"Did she think you loved her?"

"No. Fuck. I'm an asshole for nailing another man's wife, but I didn't promise her anything. I was screwing Lucas through her—I didn't expect for her to become collateral damage. I wouldn't have let it get that far, if I had."

"Gideon." I sighed and shook my head.

"What?" He was practically bristling with restless, anxious energy. "Why did you say my name like that?"

"Because you're ridiculously dense for such a smart guy. You were sleeping with her regularly and didn't expect her to fall in love with you?"

"Jesus." His head fell back with a groan. "Not this again."

Then he straightened abruptly. "Actually, you know what? You keep on thinking I'm God's gift to women, angel. It's better for me if you believe I'm the best you can get."

I splashed him. The ease with which he dismissed his appeal was another way he mirrored me. We knew our strengths and played up our assets. But we couldn't see what made us unique enough for someone to really love us.

Gideon lunged forward and caught my hands. "Now, tell me what the fuck you had with Brett Kline."

"You didn't tell me what Dr. Lucas did to piss you off."

"Yes, I did."

"Not the details," I argued.

"It's your turn to spill. Out with it."

It took me a long time to get the words out. No guy wanted a recovering slut for his girlfriend. But Gideon waited patiently. Obstinately. I knew he wasn't going to let me get out of the tub until I told him about Brett.

"I was nothing but a convenient fuck for Brett," I confessed in a rush, wanting to get it over with, "and I put up with it—went out of my way for it—because in that period of my life, sex was the only way I knew how to feel loved."

"He wrote a love song about you, Eva."

I looked away. "The truth wouldn't make much of a ballad, would it?"

"Did you love him?"

"I— No." I looked at Gideon when he exhaled audibly, as if he'd been holding his breath. "I had a crush on him and the way he sings, but it was totally superficial. I never got to really know him."

His entire body visibly relaxed. "He was part of a . . . phase? That's it?"

I nodded and tried to pull my hands free of his, wishing I could get past my feelings of shame. I didn't blame Brett or any of the guys who'd drifted through my life then. I had no one to blame but myself.

"Come here." Gideon caught me by the waist and pulled me closer, tucking me against his chest again. His embrace was the most wonderful feeling in the world. His hands stroked the length of my spine, gentling me. "I won't lie. I want to beat the hell out of any man who's had you—you'd be smart to keep them the hell away from me—but nothing in your past can change how I feel about you. And God knows I'm no saint."

"I wish I could make it go away," I whispered. "I don't like remembering the girl I was then."

He rested his chin atop the crown of my head. "I get it. It didn't matter how long I showered after I'd been with Anne, it was never long enough to feel clean."

I tightened my arms around his waist, giving comfort and acceptance. And gratefully accepting both in return.

THE white silk robe I found hanging in the closet was gorgeous. It was lined with the softest terry cloth and embroidered with silver thread at the cuffs. I loved it, which was a good thing since it was, apparently, the only article of clothing for me in the entire house.

I watched Gideon pull on a pair of black silk pajama pants and tie the drawstring. "Why do you get clothes and I get a robe?"

He glanced up at me through a lock of inky hair that draped over his brow. "Because I'm the one who arranged everything?"

"Fiend."

"Just makes it easier for me to keep up with your insatiable sexual demands."

"*My* insatiable demands?" I headed into the bathroom to take the towel off my head. "I clearly remember begging to be left alone last night. Or was it this morning, after an all-nighter?"

He filled the doorway behind me. "You'll be begging again tonight, too. I'll go make some coffee."

In the mirror, I watched him turn away and saw the darkening bruise on his side. It was low on his back, where I hadn't had a chance to see it before. I spun around. "Gideon! You're hurt. Let me see."

"I'm fine." He was partway down the stairs before I could stop him. "Don't take too long."

Guilt swamped me, and a terrible urge to cry. My hand shook as I ran a wide-toothed comb through my damp hair. The bathroom had been stocked with my usual toiletries, demonstrating once again how thoughtful and attentive Gideon was, which only emphasized my deficits. I was making his life hell. After all he'd already suffered, my issues were the last thing he needed to deal with.

I took the stairs down to the first floor and found myself unable to join Gideon in the kitchen. I needed a minute to pull myself together and put on a happy face. I didn't want to ruin the weekend for him, too.

I stepped out through the French doors that led to the deck. The roar of the surf and the biting salt spray hit me at once. The hem of my robe whipped gently in the ocean breeze, cooling me in a way I found invigorating.

Taking a deep breath, I gripped the railing and closed my eyes, trying to find the peace I needed to keep Gideon from worrying. My problem was *me*, and I didn't want to concern him with something he couldn't change. Only *I* could make myself a stronger person, and I needed to, if I wanted to make him happy and offer him the security he so desperately wanted from me.

The door opened behind me, and I took a deep breath before turning to face him with a smile. Gideon came out with two steaming mugs gripped in one hand—one filled with black coffee and the other lightened with half-and-half. I knew it would be made perfectly to my tastes and delicious, because Gideon knew exactly what I liked. Not because I'd told him, but because he paid attention to everything about me.

"Stop beating yourself up," he ordered sternly, setting the mugs on the railing.

I sighed. Of course I couldn't hide my mood from him with just a smile. He saw right through me.

He caught my face in his hands and glared down at me. "It's over and done with. Forget it."

I reached out and ran my fingertips over the place where I'd seen the bruise.

"It needed to happen," he said curtly. "No. Shut up and listen to me. I thought I understood your feelings about Corinne, and, frankly, I thought you just weren't dealing with it well. But I had no clue. I was a self-centered idiot."

"I'm *not* dealing with it well. I hate her fucking guts. I can't think about her without feeling violent."

"I get it now. I didn't before." His mouth twisted ruefully. "Sometimes it takes something drastic to shake me up. Luckily, you've always been very good at getting my attention."

"Don't try to tease this away, Gideon. You could've been seriously hurt because of me."

He caught me by the waist when I would've turned away. "I *was* seriously hurt because of you. Seeing you in another guy's arms, kissing him . . ." His eyes grew hot and dark. "It shredded me, Eva. Cut me open and left me bleeding. I kicked his ass in self-defense."

"Oh, God," I breathed, devastated by his brutal honesty. "Gideon."

"I'm disgusted with myself for not being more understanding about Corinne. If a kiss could make me feel like that . . ." He wrapped his arms tight around me, one arm banding my hips while the other crossed my back so he could grip the back of my head. Capturing me.

"If you ever cheated on me," he said hoarsely, "it would kill me."

Turning my head, I pressed my lips to his throat. "That stupid kiss meant nothing. Less than nothing."

His hand gripped my hair and tilted my head back. "You don't understand what your kisses mean to me, Eva. For you to just give one away and call it stupid—"

Gideon dipped his head and sealed his mouth over mine. It started softly, sweet and teasing, his tongue stroking across my bottom lip. I opened my mouth, my tongue flicking out to touch his. He tilted his head and licked into my mouth. Fast, shallow licks that stirred a simmering desire.

I reached up and slid my fingers into his damp hair, pushing up onto my tiptoes to deepen the kiss. I moaned when he sucked on my tongue, leaning heavily against him. His lips moved against mine, growing wetter and hotter. We ate at each other, growing wilder by the second until we were fucking each other's mouths, passionately mating with lips and tongues and tiny bites. I was panting with my hunger for him, my lips slanting over his, needy sounds spilling from my throat.

His kisses were gifts. He kissed with everything he had, with power and passion and hunger and love. He held nothing back, giving everything, exposing everything.

Tension gripped his powerful frame, his rough satin skin growing feverishly hot. His tongue was plunging into my mouth, tangling with mine, his quickened breaths mingling with my own and filling my lungs. My senses were drenched in him, in his flavor and scent, my mind spinning as I angled my head, seeking a deeper taste. Wanting to lick deeper, suck harder. Devour.

I wanted him so much.

His hands ran up and down my spine, trembling and restless. He groaned and my sex tightened in answer. Tugging at the belt of my robe, he loosened it, spreading open the halves to grip my bare hips in his hands. He tugged on my lower lip, sinking his teeth into it, his tongue caressing it. I whimpered, wanting more, my mouth feeling swollen and sensitive.

No matter how close we were, it was never close enough.

Gideon gripped both cheeks of my ass and pulled me up hard against him, his erection like hot steel burning my belly through the thin silk of his pants. He released my lip and took my mouth again, filling me with the taste of his desire and need, his tongue a velvet lash of tormenting pleasure.

A hard shudder shook him and he growled, his hips circling. His fingers bit into my rear and his groan vibrated against my lips. I felt his cock jerk between us, then scorching warmth spread over my skin. He came with a tormented groan, soaking the silk between us.

I cried out, melting and aching, so insanely aroused by the knowledge that I could make him lose control with just a kiss.

His grip loosened, his lungs heaving. "Your kisses are *mine.*"

"Yes. *Gideon* . . ." I was shaken, left emotionally raw and open by the most erotic moment of my life.

He sank to his knees and tongued me to a shattering climax.

$\backsim$

WE showered and napped the morning away. It felt so good to sleep beside him again, with my head pillowed on his chest, my arm draped over his rock-hard stomach, and my legs tangled with his.

When we woke shortly after one in the afternoon, I was starving. We headed down to the kitchen together and I found that I liked the ultra-stark modern look in that space. The watered-glass cabinet doors and granite paired beautifully with the dark hardwood. Better yet, the pantry was fully stocked. There was no need to leave the house for anything.

We went the easy route and made sandwiches, which we took into the living room and ate cross-legged on the couch facing each other.

I was halfway through when I caught Gideon watching me with a grin.

"What?" I asked, around a bite.

"Arnoldo's right. It's fun watching you eat."

"Shut up."

His grin widened. He looked so carefree and happy it made my heart hurt.

"How did you find this place?" I asked him. "Or how did Scott find it?"

"I found it." He shoved a potato chip in his mouth and licked the salt from his lips, which I found sexy as hell. "I wanted to take you away to an island, where no one could bother us. This is pretty close to that, without the travel time. I planned for us to fly down originally."

I ate thoughtfully, remembering the long drive. As insanity-inducing as the trip had been, there was something exciting about the idea of him rearranging our schedule just to fuck me senseless over hours, using my need for him to face a truth I'd blocked. Imagining all the frustration and fury that must have driven his plans . . . his thoughts focused on unleashing all of that seething passion on my helpless, willing body . . .

"You're getting that fuck-me look on your face," he observed. "And you call me a sex fiend."

"Sorry."

"Not complaining."

I rewound my thoughts to earlier in the evening. "Arnoldo doesn't like me anymore."

One dark brow arched. "You're getting the fuck-me look and thinking about Arnoldo? Do I have to kick *his* ass now, too?"

"No. Jeez. I threw that out there to distract us from sex and because it needs to be addressed."

He shrugged. "I'll talk to him."

"I think *I* should do it, for what it's worth."

Gideon studied me with those amazing blue eyes. "What would you say?"

"That he's right. I don't deserve you and I fucked up bad. But I'm crazy in love with you and I'd like a chance to prove to you both that I can be what you need."

"Angel, if I needed you more, I couldn't function." He lifted my hand to his lips to kiss my fingertips. "And I don't care what anyone else thinks. We've got our own rhythm and it works for us."

"*Does* it work for you?" I grabbed my bottle of iced tea off the coffee table and took a drink. "I know it drains you. Do you ever think it's just too hard or too painful?"

"You do realize how suggestive that sounds, right?"

"Oh my God." I laughed. "You're terrible."

His eyes sparkled with amusement. "That's not what you usually say."

Shaking my head, I went back to eating.

"I'd rather argue with you, angel, than laugh with anyone else."

Jesus. It took me a minute to be able to swallow the last bite in my mouth. "You know . . . I love you madly."

He smiled. "Yes, I know."

AFTER we'd cleaned up the mess from lunch, I tossed the sponge into the sink and said, "I need to make my Saturday phone call to my dad."

Gideon shook his head. "Not possible. You'll have to wait 'til Monday."

"Huh? Why?"

He caged me to the counter by gripping the edge on either side of me. "No phones."

"Are you serious? What about your cell phone?" I'd left mine at home before we went to the concert, knowing I had no place to carry it and having no intention of using it anyway.

"It's heading back to New York with the limo. No Internet, either. I had the modem and phones taken out before we got here."

I was speechless. With all the responsibilities and commitments he had, cutting himself off for the weekend was . . . unbelievable. "Wow. When's the last time you fell off the face of the earth like this?"

"Hmm . . . that would be never."

"There have to be at least a half dozen people freaking out because they can't run something by you."

He lifted one shoulder in a careless shrug. "They'll deal with it."

Pleasure surged through me. "I have you all to myself?"

"Completely." His mouth curved in a wicked smile. "What will you do with me, angel?"

I smiled back, ecstatically happy. "I'm sure I'll think of something."

WE went for a walk on the beach.

I rolled up a pair of Gideon's pajama bottoms and put on my white tank top, which was indecent since my bra was heading back to New York along with Gideon's cell phone.

"I have died and gone to heaven," he pronounced, checking out my chest as we strolled along the shore, "where the embodiment of every wet-dream, spank-bank fantasy of my adolescence is real and totally mine."

I bumped my shoulder into his. "How do you go from devastatingly romantic to crude in the space of an hour?"

"It's another one of my many talents." His gaze dropped again to the prominent points of my nipples, which were hard from exposure to the ocean breeze. He squeezed my hand and gave an exaggerated happy sigh. "Heaven with my angel. It doesn't get any better than this."

I had to agree. The beach was beautiful in a moody, untamed way that reminded me a lot of the man whose hand I held. The sounds of the surf and the crying of the gulls filled me with a unique sense of contentment. The water was cold on my bare feet, and the wind whipped my hair across my face. It had been a long time since I'd felt so good, and I was grateful to Gideon for giving us this time away to enjoy each other. We were perfect together when we were alone.

"You like it here," he noted.

"I've always loved being close to the water. My mother's second husband had a lake house. I remember walking along the shore like this with her and thinking I'd buy something on the water for myself one day."

He released my hand and draped his arm around my shoulders instead. "So let's do it. How about this place? You like it?"

I glanced up at him, loving the sight of the wind sifting through his hair. "Is it for sale?"

He looked down the stretch of beach in front of us. "Everything's for sale at the right price."

"Do *you* like it?"

"The interior's a little cold with all that white, although I like the master bedroom the way it is. We could change all the rest. Make it more us."

"Us," I repeated, wondering what that would be. I loved his apartment with its old world elegance. I think he felt comfortable at my place, which was more modern traditional. Combining the two . . . "Big step, buying a property together."

"Inevitable step," he corrected. "You told Dr. Petersen failure isn't an option."

"Yep, I did." We walked a little farther in silence. I tried to figure out how I felt about Gideon wanting to have a more tangible tie between us. I also wondered why he'd choose joint property ownership as the way to achieve it. "So I take it you like it here, too?"

"I like the beach." He brushed his hair back from his face. "There's a picture of me and my father building a sand castle on a beach."

It was a miracle my steps didn't falter. Gideon volunteered so little information about his past that when he did, it was nearly an earthshaking event. "I'd like to see it."

"My mother has it." We took a few more steps before he said, "I'll get it for you."

"I'll go with you." He hadn't told me why yet, but he'd told me once that the Vidal home was a nightmare for him. I suspected that whatever was at the root of his parasomnia had taken place there.

Gideon's chest expanded on a deep breath. "I can have it couriered."

"All right." I turned my head to kiss his bruised knuckles where they rested on my shoulder. "But my offer stands."

"What did you think of my mother?" he asked suddenly.

"She's very beautiful. Very elegant. She seemed gracious." I studied him, seeing Elizabeth Vidal's inky black hair and stunning blue eyes. "She also seems to love you a lot. It was in her eyes when she looked at you."

He kept looking straight ahead. "She didn't love me enough."

My breath left me in a rush. Because I didn't know what had given him such tormenting nightmares, I'd wondered if maybe she'd loved him too much. It was a relief to know that wasn't the case. It was awful enough that his father committed suicide. To be betrayed by his mother, too, might be more than he could ever recover from.

"How much is enough, Gideon?"

His jaw tightened. His chest expanded on a deep breath. "She didn't believe me."

I came to a dead stop and pivoted to face him. "You told her what happened to you? You told her and she didn't believe you?"

His gaze was trained over my head. "It doesn't matter now. It's long done."

"Bullshit. It matters. It matters a lot." I was furious for him. Furious that a mother hadn't done her job and stood by her child. Furious that the child had been Gideon. "I bet it hurts like fucking hell, too."

His gaze lowered to my face. "Look at you, so pissed off and upset. I shouldn't have said anything."

"You should've said something earlier."

The tension in his shoulders eased and his mouth curved ruefully. "I haven't told you anything."

"Gideon—"

"And of course you believe me, angel. You've had to sleep in a bed with me."

I grabbed his face in my hands and stared hard up into his eyes. "I. Believe. You."

His face contorted with pain for a split second before he picked me up in a bear hug. "Eva."

I slung my legs around his waist and wrapped my arms around his shoulders. "I believe you."

WHEN we got back to the house, Gideon went into the kitchen to open a bottle of wine and I perused the bookshelves in the living room, smiling when I came across the first book in the series I'd told him about, the one where'd I'd picked up his nickname, *ace*.

We sprawled on the couch and I read to him while he played absently with my hair. He was in a pensive mood after our walk, his mind seemingly far from me. I didn't resent that. We'd given each other a lot to think about over the last couple of days.

When the tide came in, it did indeed rush up under the house, which sounded amazing and looked even more so. We stepped out onto the deck and watched it ebb and flow, turning the house into an island in the surf.

"Let's make s'mores," I said, while leaning over the railing with Gideon wrapped around my back. "On that portable patio fireplace."

His teeth caught my earlobe and he whispered, "I want to lick melted chocolate off your body."

Yes, please . . . I teased him, "Wouldn't that burn?"

"Not if I do it right."

I turned to face him, and he picked me up and sat me on the wide handrail. Then he stepped between my legs and hugged me around the hips. There was a wonderful peace that accompanied the twilight and we both sank into it. I ran my hands through his hair, just as the night breeze did.

"Have you talked to Ireland at all?" I asked, thinking of his half sister, who was as beautiful as their mother. I'd met her at a Vidal Records party, and it became evident pretty quickly that she was hungry for any word or news about her eldest brother.

"No."

"What do you think about bringing her over for dinner when my dad's in town?"

Gideon's head tilted to the side as he observed me. "You want to invite a seventeen-year-old to dinner with me and your dad."

"No, I want your family to meet my family."

"She'll be bored."

"How would you know?" I challenged. "In any case, I think your sister hero-worships you. As long as you pay attention to her, I'm sure she'll be thrilled."

"Eva." He sighed, clearly exasperated. "Be real. I haven't the slightest idea how to entertain a teenage girl."

"Ireland's not some random kid, she's—"

"She might as well be!" He scowled at me.

It struck me then. "You're afraid of her."

"Come on," he scoffed.

"You are. She scares you." And I doubted it had anything to do with his sister's age or that she was a girl.

"What's gotten into you?" he complained. "You're stuck on Ireland. Leave her alone."

"She's the only family you've got, Gideon." And I was willing to support that choice. His half brother, Christopher, was an asshole, and his mother didn't deserve to have him in her life.

"I have *you*!"

"Baby." I sighed and wrapped my legs around him. "Yes, you've got me. But there's room for more people who love you in your life."

"She doesn't love me," he muttered. "She doesn't know me."

"I think you're wrong about that, but if not, she'd love you if she knew you. So let her know you."

"Enough. Let's go back to talking about s'mores."

I tried to stare him down, but it was impossible. When he considered a subject exhausted, there was no continuing it. So I'd have to go around it instead.

"You wanna talk about s'mores, ace?" I traced my lower lip with my tongue. "All that melty gooey chocolate on our fingers."

Gideon's gaze narrowed.

I ran my splayed fingers over his shoulders and down his chest. "I could be persuaded to let you smear that chocolate all over me. I could also be persuaded to smear some all over you."

His brow arched. "Are you trying to bribe me with sex again?"

"Did I say that?" I blinked innocently. "I don't think I said that."

"It was implied. So let's be clear." His voice was dangerously low, his eyes dark as his hand slid up under the hem of my tank top and cupped my bare breast. "I'll invite Ireland to dinner with your father because it'll make you happy and that makes me happy."

"Thank you," I said breathlessly, because he'd begun to tug rhythmically on my nipple, making me whimper in delight.

"I'm going to do whatever the hell I want with melted chocolate and your body because it'll please me and that will please you. I say when, I say how. Repeat that."

"You say—" I gasped as his mouth wrapped around my other nipple through the ribbed cotton. "Oh, God."

He nipped me with his teeth. "Finish."

My entire body tightened, so quick to respond to that authoritative tone. "You say when. You say how."

"There are things you can bargain with, angel, but your body and sex aren't negotiable."

My hands clutched his hair, an instinctive response to his relentless, delicious milking of my sensitive nipple. I gave up trying to understand why I wanted him in control. I just did. "What else can I bargain with? You have everything."

"Your time and attention are the two things you can leverage. I'll do anything for them."

A shiver moved through me. "I'm wet for you," I whispered.

Gideon stepped away from the railing, carrying me with him. "Because that's how I want you."

12

Gideon and I arrived back in Manhattan just before midnight on Sunday. We'd spent the previous night sleeping apart, but most of the day together in the master bed. Kissing and touching. Laughing and whispering.

By silent agreement we didn't talk about painful things during the rest of our time away. We didn't turn on the television or radio, because it seemed wrong to share our time with anyone. We walked on the beach again. We made long, slow, lazy love on the third-story deck. We played cards and he won every hand. We recharged and reminded ourselves that what we'd found with each other was worth fighting for.

It was the most perfect day of my life.

We returned to my apartment when we got back into the city. Gideon unlocked the door for us with the key I'd given him, and we entered the darkened space as quietly as possible so that we didn't wake Cary. Gideon gave me one of his soul-melting kisses good night and headed to the guest room, and I crawled into my lonely bed without him. Missing him. I wondered how long we'd be sleeping apart from each other. Months? Years?

Hating to think of it, I closed my eyes and started to drift.

The light flicked on.

"Eva. Get up." Gideon strode into the room and straight to my dresser, digging through my clothes.

I blinked at him, noting that he'd changed into slacks and a button-down dress shirt. "What's wrong?"

"It's Cary," he said grimly. "He's in the hospital."

A cab was waiting for us at the curb when we left my apartment building. Gideon ushered me in, then slid in beside me.

The cab seemed to pull away very slowly. Everything seemed to be moving slowly.

I clutched at Gideon's sleeve. "What happened?"

"He was attacked Friday night."

"How do you know?"

"Your mother and Stanton both left messages on my cell phone."

"My mother . . . ?" I looked at him blankly. "Why didn't she . . . ?"

No, she *couldn't* call me. I hadn't had my phone. Guilt and worry drowned me, making it hard to breathe.

"Eva." He put his arm around my shoulders, urging me to rest my head against him. "Don't worry until we know more."

"It's been *days*, Gideon. And I wasn't here."

Tears poured down my face and wouldn't stop, even after we arrived at the hospital. I barely registered the exterior of the building, my attention dulled by the hard-driving anxiety pounding through me. I thanked God for Gideon, who was so calm and in control. A staff member provided the number of Cary's room, but his helpfulness ended there. Gideon made a few middle-of-the-night phone calls that got me access to see Cary, even though it was well outside visiting hours. Gideon had been a very generous benefactor at times and that wasn't easily dismissed or forgotten.

When I stepped into Cary's private room and saw him, my heart shattered so completely, my knees went weak. Only Gideon kept me from falling. The man I thought of as my brother, the best friend I'd ever had or ever would have, lay silent and unmoving in the bed. His head was bandaged and his eyes blackened. One of his arms was stuck with intravenous lines, while the other was in a cast. I wouldn't have recognized him, if I hadn't known who he was.

Flowers covered every flat surface, cheerful and colorful bouquets. There were balloons, too, and a few cards. I knew some would be from my mother and Stanton, who were certainly paying for Cary's care as well.

We were his family. And everyone had been there for him but me.

Gideon led me closer, his arm tight around my waist to hold me up. I was sobbing, the tears flowing thick and hot. It was everything I could do to remain silent.

Still, Cary must have heard me or sensed me. His eyelids fluttered, then opened. His beautiful green eyes were bloodshot and unfocused. It took him a minute to find me. When he did, he blinked a few times, and then tears started rolling down his temples.

"Cary." I rushed to him and slipped my hand in his. "I'm here."

He gripped me so tightly, it was painful. "Eva."

"I'm sorry I took so long. I didn't have my phone. I had no idea. I would've been here if I'd known."

"S'okay. You're here now." His throat worked on a swallow. "God . . . everything hurts."

"I'll get a nurse," Gideon said, running his hand down my back before slipping silently out of the room.

I saw a small pitcher and cup with straw on the rolling tray table. "Are you thirsty?"

"Very."

"Can I sit you up? Or no?" I was afraid to do anything to cause him pain.

"Yeah."

Using the remote lying near his hand, I raised the top part of the bed so that he was reclined. Then I brought the straw to his lips and watched him drink greedily.

He relaxed with a sigh. "You're a sight for sore eyes, baby girl."

"What the hell happened?" I set the empty cup down and grabbed his hand again.

"Fuck if I know." His voice was weak, almost a whisper. "Got jumped. With a bat."

"With *a bat*?" Just the thought made me physically ill. The brutality of it. The violence . . . "Was he insane?"

"Of course," he snapped, a deep line of pain between his brows.

I backed up a half step. "I'm sorry."

"No, don't. Shit. I'm—" His eyes closed. "I'm exhausted."

Just then the nurse came in wearing scrubs decorated with cartoon tongue depressors and animated stethoscopes. She was young and pretty, with dark hair and sloe eyes. She checked Cary over, took his blood pressure, then pressed the button on a remote wrapped around the guardrail.

"You can self-administer every thirty minutes for pain," she told him. "Just press this button. It won't dispense a dose if it's not time, so you don't have to worry about pressing it too often."

"Once is too often," he muttered, looking at me.

I understood his reluctance; he had an addictive personality. He'd traveled a short ways down the junkie road before I kicked some sense into him.

But it was a relief to see the lines of pain on his forehead smooth out and his breathing settle into a deeper rhythm.

The nurse looked at me. "He needs his rest. You should come back during visiting hours."

Cary looked at me desperately. "Don't go."

"She's not going anywhere," Gideon said, reentering the room. "I've arranged to have a cot brought in tonight."

I didn't think it was possible to love Gideon more than I already did, but he somehow kept finding ways to prove me wrong.

The nurse smiled shyly at Gideon.

"Cary could use more water," I told her, watching her pull her gaze reluctantly away from my boyfriend to look at me.

She grabbed the pitcher and left the room.

Gideon stepped closer to the bed and spoke to Cary. "Tell me what happened."

Cary sighed. "Trey and I went out Friday, but he had to bail early. I walked him out to grab a cab, but it was nuts right in front of the club, so we went around the corner. He'd just taken off when I got nailed in the back of the head. Took me straight down and whaled on me a few times. Never got a chance to defend myself."

My hands began to shake, and Cary's thumb rubbed soothingly over the back.

"Hey," he murmured. "Teaches me. Don't stick my dick in the wrong chick."

"What?"

I watched Cary's eyes drift shut, and a moment later it was clear he was sleeping. I glanced helplessly across the bed at Gideon.

"I'll look into it," he said. "Step out with me for a minute."

I followed him, my gaze repeatedly turning back to Cary. When the door closed behind us, I said, "God, Gideon. He looks terrible."

"He got knocked around good," he said grimly. "He's got a skull fracture, a nasty concussion, three cracked ribs, and a broken arm."

The list of injuries was horribly painful to listen to. "I don't understand why someone would do this."

He pulled me close and pressed his lips to my forehead. "The doctor said it's possible Cary will be allowed to leave in a day or two, so I'll make arrangements for home care. I'll also let your work know you won't be coming in."

"Cary's agency needs to know."

"I'll see to it."

"Thank you." I hugged him hard. "What would I do without you?"

"You're never going to find out."

My mother woke me at nine the next morning, gliding fretfully into Cary's room as soon as visiting hours began. She pulled me out to the hallway, drawing the attention of everyone in the immediate area. It was early, but she looked amazing in eye-catching red-soled Louboutins and an ivory sleeveless sheath dress.

"Eva. I can't believe you went the entire weekend without your cell phone! What were you thinking? What if there had been an emergency?"

"There *was* an emergency."

"Exactly!" She threw up one hand, since the other arm had her clutch tucked beneath it. "No one could get hold of you or Gideon. He left a message saying that he was taking you away for the weekend, but no one knew where you were. I can't believe he was so irresponsible! What was he thinking?"

"Thank you," I interjected, because she was getting wound up and repeating herself, "for taking care of Cary. It means a lot to me."

"Well, of course." My mother took it down a notch. "We love him, too, you know. I'm devastated this happened."

Her lower lip trembled and she dug in her bag for her ever-ready handkerchief.

"Are the police investigating?" I asked.

"Yes, of course, but I don't how much good it will do." She dabbed at the corners of her eyes. "I love Cary dearly, but he's a tramp. I doubt he can recall all the women and men he's been with. Remember the charity auction you attended with Gideon? When I bought you that stunning red dress?"

"Yes." I'd never forget it. It was the night Gideon and I first made love.

"I'm certain Cary slept with a blonde he danced with that night—while they were there! They disappeared and when they came back . . . Well, I know what a satisfied man looks like. I would be surprised if he knew her name."

I remembered what Cary had said before he fell asleep. "You think this attack has something to do with someone he slept with?"

My mother blinked at me, seeming to remember that I didn't know anything. "Cary was told to keep his hands off 'her'—whoever 'her' is. The detectives will be coming back later today to try to pull some names out of him."

"Jesus." I scrubbed at my eyes, needing my face wash badly and a cup of coffee even more. "They need to talk to Tatiana Cherlin."

"Who's that?"

"Someone Cary's been seeing. I think she'd get a kick out of something like this. Cary's boyfriend caught them together and she ate it up with a spoon. She loved being the cause of the drama."

I rubbed at the back of my neck, then realized the tingle I felt was for another reason entirely. I looked over my shoulder and saw Gideon approaching, his long legs closing the distance between us with that measured stride. Dressed for work in a suit, with a large cup of coffee in one hand and a small black bag in the other, he was exactly what I needed at just the moment I needed him.

"Excuse me." I walked toward Gideon and straight into his arms.

"Hey," he greeted me, with his lips in my hair. "How are you holding up?"

"It's awful. And senseless." My eyes burned. "He didn't need another disaster in his life. He's had more than his share."

"So have you, and you're suffering along with him."

"And you're doing the same with me." I pushed up onto my tiptoes and kissed his jaw, then stepped back. "Thank you."

He handed me the coffee. "I brought some things for you—a change of clothes, your cell and tablet, bathroom stuff."

I knew his thoughtfulness had to come at a price—literally. After a weekend away, he should be digging his way out of a small mountain of work worth millions, not running around taking care of me. "God. I love you."

"Eva!" My mother's startled exclamation made me wince. She advocated withholding the words *I love you* until the wedding night.

"Sorry, Mom. Can't help it."

Gideon brushed coffee-warmed fingertips down my cheek.

"Gideon," my mother began, coming up right beside us, "you should know better than to take Eva away without any means of calling for help. You do *know* better."

She was clearly referring to my past. I wasn't sure why she thought

I was so delicate that I couldn't function on my own. She was far more fragile.

I shot a sympathetic glance Gideon's way.

He held out the bag he'd brought for me, the calm and confident look on his face conveying his total comfort in dealing with my mother. So I left him to it. I didn't have it in me to deal with her until I'd caffeinated myself.

I slipped back into Cary's room and found him awake. Just the sight of him made the tears well and my throat close up tight. He was such a strong and vibrant man, so full of life and mischief. It was the worst pain to see him looking so broken.

"Hey," he muttered. "Quit the waterworks every time you see me. Makes me feel like I'm gonna die or something."

Hell. He was right. My tears didn't do him any good. Instead, what little relief they gave me just put more of the burden on him. I needed to be a better friend than that.

"I can't help it," I said, sniffling. "It sucks. Someone beat me to it and kicked your ass before I could."

"Is that right?" His scowl faded. "What'd I do now?"

"You didn't tell me about Brett and Six-Ninths."

"Oh yeah . . ." A bit of his old sparkle came back into his eyes. "How'd he look?"

"Good. Really good." Very hot, but I kept that thought to myself. "Although right now, he might not look much better than you."

I told him about the kiss and the resulting fight.

"Cross threw down, huh?" Cary shook his head, then winced and stopped. "Taking on Brett took guts—he's a barroom brawler who loves a good fight."

"And Gideon is a trained mixed martial artist." I began digging through the bag Gideon had brought. "Why didn't you tell me Captive Soul had signed with a major label?"

"Because you didn't need to fall into that hole again. There are girls who can date rock stars; you're not one of them. All that time on the road, all those groupies . . . You'd drive yourself and him insane."

I shot him a look. "I'm in total agreement with you. But I'm insulted that you'd think I'd run back to him just because he made it big."

"That's not why. I didn't want you to hear their first single if it could be helped."

"'Golden'?"

"Yeah . . ." He studied me as I headed toward the bathroom. "What'd you think of it?"

"It's better than a song titled 'Tapped That.'"

"Ha!" He waited until I came out again with my face washed and hair brushed. "So . . . you kissed him."

"That's the beginning and end of that story," I said dryly. "Have you talked to Trey since Friday?"

"No. They've got my phone somewhere. My wallet, too, I'm guessing. When I came to, I was here, wearing this"—he pinched at his hospital gown—"freakin' thing."

"I'll get your stuff for you." I dumped my toiletries back in the bag, then went to sit in the chair beside him with my coffee in hand. "Gideon's making arrangements to get you home with a private nurse."

"Ooh . . . that's a fantasy of mine. Can you make sure the nurse is hot? And single?"

My brows rose. Inside, though, I was so relieved to see him looking and sounding more like himself. "You're obviously feeling better, if you're feeling frisky. How did things go with Trey?"

"Good." He sighed. "I'd worried that the party wouldn't be his scene. I forgot that he knew a lot of the people already."

Cary and Trey had met at a photo shoot, with Cary modeling and Trey assisting the photographer behind the camera. "I'm glad you had a good time."

"Yeah. He was totally set on *not* getting laid."

"So you tried . . . after you said you wouldn't."

"This is *me* we're talking about." He rolled his eyes. "Hell yeah, I tried. He's hot and great in bed—"

"—and in love with you."

He released his pent-up breath in a rush, wincing as his chest expanded. "No one's perfect."

I had to bite back a laugh. "Cary Taylor. Loving you isn't a character defect."

"Well, it's not very smart. I was such an asshole to him," he muttered, looking disgruntled. "He could do so much better."

"That isn't your decision to make for him."

"Someone needs to make it."

"And you're volunteering because you love him, too." My mouth curved. "Don't you think that sounds ass-backwards?"

"I don't love him enough." All traces of levity were wiped from his face, leaving behind the wounded and lonely man I knew all too well. "I can't be faithful like he wants. Just him and me. I like women. Love them, actually. I'd be cutting off half of who I am. Just thinking about it makes me resent him."

"You fought too hard to accept yourself," I said softly, remembering that time with more than a little twinge of sadness. "I totally understand and don't disagree, but have you tried talking to Trey about it?"

"Yes, I talked to him about it. He listened." He rubbed his fingers over his brow. "I get it, I do. If he told me he wanted to bang some other guy while seeing me, it'd bother the fuck out of me."

"But not if it were a woman?"

"No. I don't know. Shit." His bloodshot green eyes pleaded with me. "Would it make a difference to you if Cross were banging another man? Or just another woman?"

The door opened and Gideon walked in. I held his gaze when I said, "If Gideon's dick touched anything but his hand or me, we'd be over."

His brows rose. "Well, then."

I smiled sweetly and winked. "Hi, ace."

"Angel." He looked at Cary. "How are you feeling this morning?"

Cary's lips twisted wryly. "Like I got hit by a bus . . . or a bat."

"We're working on getting you set up at home. It looks like we can make that happen by Wednesday."

"Big tits, please," Cary said. "Or bulging muscles. Either will do."

Gideon looked at me.

I grinned. "The private nurse."

"Ah."

"If it's a woman," Cary went on, "can you get her to wear one of those white nurse dresses with the zipper down the front."

"I can only imagine the media frenzy over that sexual-harassment lawsuit," Gideon said dryly. "How about a collection of naughty-nurse porn instead?"

"Dude." Cary smiled wide and looked, for a moment, like his old self. "You're the man."

Gideon looked at me. "Eva."

I stood and bent over to kiss Cary on the cheek. "I'll be right back."

We stepped out of the room and I saw my mother in conversation with the doctor, who looked dazzled by her.

"I talked to Garrity this morning," Gideon said, referring to Mark, my boss. "So don't worry about that."

I hadn't been, because he said he'd handle it. "Thank you. I'll need to go in tomorrow. I'm going to see if I can get hold of Trey, Cary's boyfriend. Maybe he can stop in while I'm at work."

"Let me know if you need any help with that." Gideon glanced at his watch. "You'll want to stay here again tonight?"

"Yes, if that's possible. Until Cary comes home."

He took my face in his hands and pressed his lips to mine. "All right. I have a lot of work to catch up on. Charge your cell so I can reach you."

I heard a faint buzzing. Gideon backed away and reached into an inner jacket pocket to withdraw his phone. He read the screen, then said, "I have to get this. I'll talk to you later."

Then he was gone, striding down the hallway as quickly as he'd arrived.

"He's going to marry you," my mother said, coming up to stand beside me. "You know that, don't you?"

I didn't, no. I still felt a little flare of gratitude every morning when I woke up and realized that we were still together. "What makes you say that?"

My mother looked at me with her baby blue eyes. It was one of the rare physical traits we didn't share. "He's completely taken you over and assumed control of everything."

"That's just his nature."

"That's the nature of all powerful men," she said, reaching up to fuss with my no-nonsense ponytail. "And he'll indulge you, because he's making an investment in you. You're an asset to him. You're beautiful, well bred and well connected, and independently wealthy. You're also in love with him and he can't take his eyes off you. I bet he can't keep his hands off you, either."

"Mother, please." I was so *not* in the mood for one of her lectures on the fine points of catching and marrying a rich man.

"Eva Lauren," she scolded, facing me directly. "I don't care if you listen to me because I'm your mother and you have to—or because you love him and don't want to lose him, but you *will* listen."

"Like I have a choice," I muttered.

"You're an asset now," she repeated. "See that your life choices don't make you a liability."

"Are you talking about Cary?" Anger sharpened my voice.

"I'm talking about the bruise on Gideon's jaw! Tell me that has nothing to do with you."

I flushed.

She *tsk*ed. "I knew it. Yes, he's your lover and you see an intimate side to him that few see, but don't ever forget that he's also Gideon Cross. You've got everything you need to be the perfect wife for a man of his stature, but you're still replaceable, Eva. What he's built is not. You jeopardize his empire and he'll leave you."

My jaw tightened. "Are you done?"

She ran her fingertips over my brows, her gaze shrewd and assessing. I knew she was giving me a mini-makeover in her mind, thinking of ways to improve what she'd given me from birth. "You think I'm a coldhearted gold digger, but my concern is maternal, believe it or not. I want very desperately for you to be with a man who has the money and wherewithal to guard you with everything he has, so I'll know you're safe. And I want you to be with a man you love."

"I've found him."

"And I can't tell you how thrilled I am. I'm thrilled he's young and still open to taking risks, so he's more forgiving and understanding of your . . . quirks. And he *knows*," she whispered, her gaze softening and growing liquid. "Just be careful. That's all I'm trying to say. Don't give him any reason to turn away from you."

"If he did, that wouldn't be love."

Her lips curved wryly and she pressed a kiss to my forehead. "Come now. You're my daughter. You can't be that naïve."

"Eva!"

I turned at the sound of my name and felt a rush of relief to see Trey hurrying toward me. He was of average height and nicely muscular, with unruly blond hair, hazel eyes, and a slight angle to his nose that told me it'd been broken at some point. He was dressed in faded, frayed jeans and a T-shirt, and I was struck by the fact that he wasn't Cary's usual flashy type. For once, it seemed, the attraction had been more than skin deep.

"I just found out," he said when he reached me. "Detectives came by my work this morning and questioned me. I can't believe this happened Friday night and I'm only just finding out about it."

I couldn't hold his slightly accusatory tone against him. "I just found out early this morning myself. I was out of town."

After a quick introduction between my mother and Trey, she excused herself to go sit with Cary, leaving me to elaborate on the information Trey had gleaned from the detectives.

Trey shoved his hands through his hair, making it look even messier. "This wouldn't have happened if I'd taken him with me when I left."

"You can't blame yourself for this."

"Who else do I blame for the fact that he's screwing around with another guy's girl?" He gripped the back of his neck. "I'm the one who's not enough for him. He's got the drive of a hormonal teenager and I'm working or in school all the damn time."

Ugh. Total TMI. It was a struggle not to wince. But I understood that Trey likely didn't have anyone else he felt comfortable discussing Cary with.

"He's bisexual, Trey," I said softly, reaching out to run a comforting hand down his biceps. "That doesn't mean you're lacking."

"I don't know how to live with this."

"Would you consider counseling? With both of you, I mean."

He looked at me with haunted eyes for a long minute; then his shoulders slumped. "I don't know. I think I have to decide if I can live with him cheating. Could you do it, Eva? Could you sit at home waiting for your man, knowing he was sticking it somewhere else?"

"No." An icy shiver coursed through me at the mere words. "No, I couldn't."

"And I don't even know if Cary would agree to counseling. He keeps pushing me away. He wants me, and then he doesn't. He's committed, and then he isn't. I want in, Eva, like he's let you in, but he keeps shutting me out."

"It took me a long time to break through to him. He tried pushing me away with sex, always coming on to me, taunting me. I think you made the right decision keeping it platonic on Friday. Cary puts his value on his looks and sex appeal. You need to show him that it's not just his body you want."

Trey sighed and crossed his arms. "Is that how you two got close? Because you wouldn't sleep with him?"

"Partly. Mostly it's because I'm a mess. It's not as obvious now as it was when we met, but he knows I'm not perfect."

"Neither am I! Who is?"

"He believes you're better than he is, that you deserve better." I grinned. "Me . . . well, I bet part of him thinks I deserve him. That we deserve each other."

"Crazy fucker," he muttered.

"He is that," I agreed. "That's why we love him, isn't it? Do you want to go in and see him? Or do you want to go home and think about it?"

"No, I want to see him." Trey's shoulders rolled back and his chin lifted. "I don't care what put him here. I want to be with him while he's going through this."

"I'm glad to hear that." I linked my arm with his and led him to Cary's room.

We entered to the sound of my mother's trilling, girlish laughter. She sat on the edge of the bed, with Cary smiling adoringly at her. She was as much a mother to him as she was to me, and he loved her so much for that. His own mother had hated him, abused him, and allowed others to abuse him.

He looked over and saw us, and the emotions that swept across his face in that moment caused a tightness in my chest. I heard Trey's breath catch as he got his first sight of Cary's condition. I kicked myself for not telling him in advance not to make the mistake of getting weepy like I had.

Trey cleared his throat. "Drama queen," he said with gruff affection. "If you wanted flowers, you should've just asked for them. This is extreme."

"And ineffective, apparently," Cary rejoined hoarsely, clearly trying to pull himself together. "I don't see any flowers."

"I see a ton." Trey's gaze did a brief slide across the room, then went back to Cary. "Just wanted to see what I was up against, so I could beat out my competition."

There was no way to miss the double meaning in that statement.

My mom rose from the bed. She leaned over and kissed Cary's cheek. "I'll take Eva out to breakfast. We'll see you in about an hour or so."

"Gimme a sec," I said, passing the bed quickly, "and I'll get out of your hair, guys."

I grabbed my phone and charger out of my bag and plugged it into an outlet by the window.

As soon as the screen flickered to life, I sent a quick group text message to Shawna and my dad, saying simply: I'll call later. Then I made sure my phone was silenced and left it on the window ledge.

"Ready?" my mom asked.

"As I'll ever be."

13

I HAD TO get up before dawn Tuesday morning. I left a note for Cary where he'd see it as soon as he woke up, then headed out to grab a cab back to our place. I showered, dressed, made coffee, and tried to talk myself out of feeling like something was off. I was stressed and suffering from lack of sleep, which always led to tiny bouts of depression.

I told myself that it had nothing to do with Gideon, but the knot in my stomach said differently.

Looking at the clock, I saw it was a little after eight. I'd have to leave soon, because Gideon hadn't called or texted to say that he'd be giving me a ride. It had been almost twenty-four hours since I'd last seen him or even really talked to him. The call I'd made to him at nine the night before had been less than brief. He'd been in the middle of something and barely said hello and good-bye.

I knew he had a lot of work to do. I knew I shouldn't resent him for having to pay for the time away with extra hours of work getting caught up. He'd done a lot to help me deal with Cary's situation, more than anyone could've expected. It was up to me to deal with how I was feeling about it.

Finishing my coffee, I rinsed out my mug, then grabbed my purse and bag on the way out. My tree-lined street was quiet, but the rest of New York was wide awake, its ceaseless energy thrumming with a tangible force. Women in chic office wear and men in suits tried to hail taxis that streaked by, before settling for packed buses or the subway instead. Flower stands exploded with brilliant color, the sight of them always capable of cheering me up in the morning, as did the sight and smell of the neighborhood bakery, which was doing a brisk business at that hour.

I was a little ways down Broadway before my phone rang.

The little thrill that shot through me at the sight of Gideon's name quickened my steps. "Hey, stranger."

"Where the hell are you?" he snapped.

A frisson of unease dampened my excitement. "I'm on my way to work."

"Why?" He spoke to someone offline, then, "Are you in a cab?"

"I'm walking. Jeez. Did you wake up on the wrong side of the bed or what?"

"You should have waited to be picked up."

"I didn't hear from you, and I didn't want to be late after missing work yesterday."

"You could've called me instead of just taking off." His voice was low and angry.

I became angry, too. "The last time I called, you were too busy to give me more than a minute of your time."

"I've got things to take care of, Eva. Give me a break."

REFLECTED IN YOU · 223

"Sure thing. How about now?" I hung up and dropped my phone back into my bag.

It began ringing again immediately and I ignored it, my blood simmering. When the Bentley pulled up beside me a few minutes later, I kept walking. It followed, the front passenger window sliding down.

Angus leaned over. "Miss Tramell, please."

I paused, looking at him. "Are you alone?"

"Yes."

With a sigh, I got in the car. My phone was still ringing nonstop, so I reached in and shut the ringer off. One block later, I heard Gideon's voice coming through the car's speakers.

"Do you have her?"

"Yes, sir," Angus replied.

The line cut out.

"What the hell crawled up his ass and died?" I asked, looking at Angus in the rearview mirror.

"He's got a lot on his mind."

Whatever it was, it sure wasn't me. I couldn't believe what a jerk he was being. He'd been curt on the phone the night before, too, but not rude.

Within a few minutes after I arrived at work, Mark came up to my cubicle. "I'm sorry to hear about your roommate," he said, setting a fresh cup of coffee on my desk. "Is he going to be all right?"

"Eventually. Cary's tough; he'll pull through." I dropped my stuff in the bottom drawer of my desk and picked up the steaming mug with gratitude. "Thank you. And thanks for yesterday, too."

His dark eyes were warm with concern. "I'm surprised you're here today."

"I need to work." I managed a smile, despite feeling all twisted up and achy inside. Nothing was right in my world when things weren't right between me and Gideon. "Catch me up on what I missed."

THE morning passed swiftly. I had a checklist of follow-ups waiting from the week before, and Mark had an eleven thirty deadline to turn around a request for proposal for a promotional items manufacturer. By the time we sent the RFP off, I was back in the groove and willing to just forget Gideon's mood that morning. I wondered if he'd had another nightmare and hadn't slept well. I decided to call him when lunchtime rolled around, just in case.

And then I checked my inbox.

The Google alert I'd set up for Gideon's name was waiting for me. I opened the e-mail hoping to get an idea of what he might be working on. The words *former fiancée* in some of the headlines leaped out at me. The knot I'd had in my gut earlier returned, tighter than before.

I clicked on the first link, and it took me to a gossip blog sporting pictures of Gideon and Corinne having dinner at Tableau One. They sat close together in the front window, her hand resting intimately on his forearm. He was wearing the suit he'd worn to the hospital the day before, but I checked the date anyway, desperately hoping the photos were old. They weren't.

My palms began to sweat. I tortured myself by clicking through all the links and studying every photo I found. He was smiling in a few of them, looking remarkably content for a man whose girlfriend was at a hospital with her beaten-half-to-death best friend. I felt like throwing up. Or screaming. Or storming up to Gideon's office and asking him what the hell was going on.

He'd blown me off when I'd called him the night before—to go to dinner with his ex.

I jumped when my desk phone rang. I picked it up and woodenly recited, "Mark Garrity's office, Eva Tramell speaking."

"Eva." It was Megumi in reception, sounding as bubbly as usual. "There's someone asking for you downstairs—Brett Kline."

I sat there for a long minute, letting that sink into my fevered brain. I forwarded the alert digest to Gideon's e-mail so he'd know that I knew. Then I said, "I'll be right down."

I saw Brett in the lobby the minute I pushed through the security turnstiles. He wore black jeans and a Six-Ninths T-shirt. Sunglasses hid his eyes, but the spiky hair with its bleached tips was eye-catching, as was his body. Brett was tall and muscular, more muscular than Gideon, who was powerful without any bulk.

Brett's hands came out of his pockets when he saw me coming, his posture straightening. "Hey. Look at you."

I glanced down at my cap-sleeved dress with its flattering ruching and acknowledged that he'd never seen me dressed up. "I'm surprised you're still in town."

More surprised that he'd looked me up, but I didn't say that. I was glad he had, because I'd been worried about him.

"We sold out our Jones Beach show over the weekend, then played the Meadowlands last night. I skipped out on the guys because I wanted to see you before we head south. I searched for you online, found out where you worked, and came up."

Good old Google, I thought miserably. "I'm so stoked that everything's working out for you now. Do you have time to grab lunch?"

"Yes."

His answer came quickly and fervently, which set off a little warning. I was pissed, extremely hurt, and eager to retaliate against Gideon, but I didn't want to mislead Brett. Still, I couldn't resist taking him to the restaurant where Cary and I had once been photographed together, in the hopes of getting caught by the paparazzi again. It would serve Gideon right to see what it felt like.

On the cab ride over, Brett asked about Cary and wasn't surprised to learn that my best friend had moved across the country with me.

"You two were always inseparable," he said. "Except when he was getting laid. Tell him I said hi."

"Sure." I didn't mention that Cary was in the hospital, because it felt too private to share.

It wasn't until we were seated in the restaurant that Brett took off his shades, so that was the first time I got a glimpse of the shiner that encompassed the area from his right eyebrow down to his cheekbone.

"Jesus," I breathed, wincing. "I'm sorry."

He shrugged. "Makeup made it disappear on stage. And you've seen me with worse. Besides, I got a couple good hits in, didn't I?"

Remembering the bruising on Gideon's jaw and back, I nodded. "You did."

"So . . ." He paused as the waiter came by and dropped off two glasses and a chilled bottle of water. "You're dating Gideon Cross."

I wondered why that question always seemed to pop up at a time when I wasn't sure the relationship would last another minute. "We've been seeing each other."

"Is it serious?"

"Sometimes it seems that way," I said honestly. "Are you seeing anyone?"

"Not now."

We took some time to read the menu and place our orders. The restaurant was busy and noisy, the background music barely heard over the hum of conversation and clatter of plates from the nearby kitchen. We looked across the table at each other, sizing each other up. I felt the thrum of attraction between us. When he wet his lips with the tip of his tongue, I knew he was aware of it, too.

"Why did you write 'Golden'?" I asked suddenly, unable to hold back my curiosity a moment longer. I'd been playing it off as nothing big with both Gideon and Cary, but it was driving me crazy.

Brett sat back in his chair. "Because I think about you a lot. I can't stop thinking about you actually."

"I don't understand why."

"We had it going on for six months, Eva. That's the longest I've ever been with someone."

"But we weren't *with* each other," I argued. My voice lowered. "Aside from sexually."

His mouth thinned. "I understand what I was to you, but that doesn't mean I didn't get hurt."

I stared at him for a long minute, my heart beating too quickly in my chest. "I feel like I'm stoned or something. The way I remember it, we'd hook up after shows, then you'd go about your business. And if I wasn't there to put out, you'd grab someone else."

He leaned forward. "Bullshit. I tried getting you to hang out. I was always asking you to stick around."

I took a couple of quick, deep breaths to calm myself down. I could hardly believe that now, almost four years too late, Brett Kline was talking to me like I'd once wanted him to. We were out in public together, having a meal, almost like a date. It was messing with my head, which was already confused and scattered because of Gideon.

"I had the biggest crush on you, Brett. I wrote your name with little hearts around it like a lovesick teenager. I wanted desperately to be your girlfriend."

"Are you kidding me?" He reached out and caught my hand. "What the fuck happened, then?"

I looked down at where he was absently twirling the ring Gideon had given me. "Remember when we went to the pool hall?"

"Yeah. How could I forget that?" He bit his lower lip, clearly recalling how I'd fucked his brains out in the back of his car, determined to be the best lay he'd ever had so he wouldn't bother with other girls. "I thought we were getting to the point where we'd start seeing each other outside the bar, but you ditched me the minute we got inside."

"I went to the bathroom," I said quietly, remembering the pain and embarrassment as if the incident had just happened, "and when I came out you and Darrin were at the change machine getting quarters for the tables. Your back was to me so you didn't see me. I heard you guys talking . . . and laughing."

I pulled in a deep breath and tugged my hand away from him.

To his credit, Brett shifted in obvious embarrassment. "I can't remember exactly what was said, but . . . Shit, Eva. I was twenty-one years old. The band was just starting to get popular. The chicks were everywhere."

"I know," I said dryly. "I was one of them."

"I'd been with you a few times by then. Bringing you along to the pool hall made a statement to the guys that things were picking up between us." He rubbed at his brow in a very familiar gesture. "I didn't have the balls to own up to how I was feeling about you. I made it about the sex, but that wasn't true."

I lifted my glass and drank, forcing down the lump in my throat.

His hand dropped onto the armrest. "So I screwed it up with my big mouth. That's why you bailed that night. That's why you never went anywhere with me again."

"I was desperate, Brett," I admitted, "but I didn't want to show it."

The waiter brought our food. I wondered why I'd ordered anything—I was too unsettled to eat.

Brett started cutting into his steak, attacking it really. Suddenly, he set his knife and fork down. "I blew it back then, but now everyone knows what was going on in my head at the time. 'Golden' is our biggest single. It's what got us signed with Vidal."

The idea of closure made me smile. "It's a beautiful song, and your voice sounds amazing when you sing it. I'm really glad you came up and saw me again before you head out. It means a lot to me that we talked through this."

"What if I don't want to just head out and move on?" He took a deep breath and released it in a rush. "You've been my muse the last few years, Eva. Because of you, I've written the best material the band's ever had."

"That's very flattering," I began.

"We sizzled together. Still do. I know you feel it. The way you kissed me the other night . . ."

"That was a mistake." My hands clenched beneath the table. I couldn't deal with more drama. I couldn't go through another night like Friday. "And you need to think about the fact that Gideon controls your label. You don't want any friction there."

"Fuck it. What's he going to do?" His fingertips drummed onto the table. "I want another shot with you."

I shook my head and reached for my purse. "That's impossible. Even if I didn't have a boyfriend, I'm not the right girl for your lifestyle, Brett. I'm too high-maintenance."

"I remember," he said roughly. "God, do I remember."

I flushed. "That's not what I meant."

"And that's not all I want. I can be here for you. Look at me now—the band's on the road, but you and I are together. I can make time. I want to."

"It's not that easy." I pulled cash out of my wallet and dropped it on the table. "You don't know me. You have no idea what it would mean to have a relationship with me, how much work it would take."

"Try me," he challenged.

"I'm needy and clingy and insanely jealous. I'd drive you crazy within a week."

"You've always driven me crazy. I like it." His smile faded. "Stop running, Eva. Give me a chance."

I met his gaze and held it. "I'm in love with Gideon."

His brows rose. Even battered, his face was breathtaking. "I don't believe you."

"I'm sorry. I have to go." I pushed to my feet and moved to pass him.

He caught my elbow. "Eva—"

"Please don't make a scene," I whispered, regretting my impetuous decision to eat at a popular place.

"You didn't eat."

"I can't. I need to leave."

"Fine. But I'm not giving up." He released me. "I make mistakes, but I learn from them."

I bent over and said firmly, "There's no chance. None."

Brett stabbed his fork into a slice of his steak. "Prove it."

THE Bentley was waiting at the curb when I stepped out of the restaurant. Angus climbed out and opened the rear door for me.

"How did you know where I was?" I asked, unsettled by his unexpected appearance.

His answer was to smile kindly and touch the brim of his chauffeur's hat.

"This is creepy, Angus," I complained as I slid into the backseat.

"I don't disagree, Miss Tramell. I'm just doing my job."

I texted Cary on the ride back to the Crossfire: Had lunch with Brett. He wants another chance w/me.

Cary replied, When it rains it pours . . .

Whole day = royally fucked, I typed. I want a do-over.

My phone rang. It was Cary.

"Baby girl," he drawled. "I want to sympathize, I do, but the love triangle thing is just too delicious. The determined rock star and the possessive billionaire. *Rawr.*"

"Oh God. Hanging up now."

"See you tonight?"

"Yes. Please don't make me regret it." I hung up to the sound of his laughter, secretly thrilled to hear him sounding so happy. Trey's visit must have worked wonders.

Angus dropped me off at the curb in front of the Crossfire, and I hurried out of the heat into the cool lobby. I managed to catch an open elevator just before the doors closed. There were a half dozen other people in the car with me, forming two groups that chatted among themselves. I stood in the front corner and tried to put my personal life out of my mind. I couldn't deal with it at work.

"Hey, we passed our floor," the girl next to me said.

I looked at the needle over the door.

The guy nearest the control panel stabbed repeatedly at all the numbers, but none of them lit up . . . except for the one for the top floor. "The buttons aren't working."

My pulse quickened.

"Use the emergency phone," one of the other girls said.

The car raced up and the butterflies in my stomach got worse with every floor we passed. The elevator finally came to a gliding stop at the top and the doors opened.

232 · SYLVIA DAY

Gideon stood on the threshold, his face a gorgeous impassive mask. His eyes were brilliantly blue . . . and cold as ice. The sight of him took my breath away.

No one in the car said a word. I didn't move, praying the doors would hurry up and close. Gideon reached in, grabbed my elbow, and hauled me out. I struggled, too furious to want anything to do with him. The doors closed behind me and he let me go.

"Your behavior today has been appalling," he growled.

"*My* behavior? What about yours?"

I crossed over to the call buttons and hit the down button. It wouldn't stay lit.

"I'm talking to you, Eva."

I glanced at the security doors to Cross Industries and was relieved to see that the redheaded receptionist was away from her station.

"Really?" I faced him, hating that I could still find him so irresistibly attractive when he was being so ugly. "Funny how that doesn't lead to me actually learning anything—like about you going out with Corinne last night."

"You shouldn't be snooping online about me," he bit out. "You're deliberately trying to find something to get upset about."

"So your actions aren't the problem?" I shot back, feeling the pressure of tears at the back of my throat. "Just my finding out about them is?"

His arms crossed. "You need to trust me, Eva."

"You're making that impossible! Why didn't you tell me that you were going out to dinner with Corinne?"

"Because I knew you wouldn't like it."

"But you did it anyway." And that hurt. After all we'd talked about over the weekend . . . after he'd said that he understood how I felt . . .

"And you went out with Brett Kline knowing *I* wouldn't like it."

"What did I tell you? You're setting the precedent for how I handle my exes."

"Tit for tat? What a remarkable show of maturity."

I stumbled back from him. There was none of the Gideon I knew in the man facing me. It felt as if the man I loved had disappeared and the man standing in front of me was a total stranger in Gideon's body.

"You're making me hate you," I whispered. "Stop it."

Something passed briefly over Gideon's face, but it was gone before I could identify it. I let his body language do the talking for him. He stood far from me, with his shoulders stiff and his jaw tight.

My heart bled and my gaze dropped. "I can't be around you right now. Let me go."

Gideon moved to the other bank of elevators and pushed the call button. With his back to me and his attention on the indicator arrow, he said, "Angus will pick you up every morning. Wait for him. And I prefer that you eat lunch at your desk. It's best if you're not running around right now."

"Why not?"

"I have a lot of things on my plate at the moment—"

"Like dinner with Corinne?"

"—and I can't be worrying about you," he went on, ignoring my interruption. "I don't think I'm asking too much."

Something was wrong.

"Gideon, why won't you talk to me?" I reached out and touched his shoulder, only to have him jerk away as if I'd burned him. More than anything else, his rejection of my touch wounded me deeply. "Tell me what's going on. If there's a problem—"

"The problem is that I don't know where the hell you are half the time!" he snapped, turning to scowl at me as the elevator doors opened. "Your roommate is in the hospital. Your dad is coming to visit. Just . . . focus on that."

I stepped into the elevator with burning eyes. Aside from pulling me out of the elevator when it first arrived, Gideon hadn't touched me. He hadn't run his fingertips down my cheek or made any attempt to kiss me. And he made no mention of wanting to see me later, skipping right over the rest of the day to tell me about Angus waiting for me in the morning.

I'd never been so confused. I couldn't figure out what was happening, why there was suddenly this huge gulf between us, why Gideon was so tense and angry, why he didn't seem to care that I'd had lunch with Brett.

Why he didn't seem to care about anything at all.

The doors started to close. *Trust me, Eva.*

Had he breathed those words in the second before the doors shut? Or did I just wish that he had?

THE moment I walked into Cary's private room, he knew I was running on fumes. I'd endured a tough Krav Maga session with Parker, then stopped by the apartment only long enough to shower and eat a tasteless instant-ramen meal. The shock of the salt and carbs to my system after a day without food was more than enough to exhaust me past the point of no return.

"You look like shit," he said, muting the television.

"Look who's talking," I shot back, feeling too raw to take any criticism.

"I got hit with a baseball bat. What's your excuse?"

I arranged the pillow and scratchy blanket on my cot, then told him about my day from beginning to end.

"And I haven't heard from Gideon since," I finished wearily. "Even Brett got in touch with me after lunch. He left an envelope at the security desk with his phone number in it."

He'd also included the cash I left at the restaurant.

"Are you going to call him?" Cary asked.

"I don't want to think about Brett!" I sprawled on my back on the cot and shoved my hands through my hair. "I want to know what's wrong with Gideon. He's had a total personality transplant in the last thirty-six hours!"

"Maybe it's this."

I lifted my head off the pillow and saw him pointing at something on his bedside table. Rolling to my feet, I checked it out—a local gay periodical.

"Trey brought that over today," he said.

Cary's picture capped a front-page piece covering his attack—including speculation that the assault might have been a hate crime. His living situation with me and my romantic entanglement with Gideon Cross were mentioned, for no other reason, it seemed, than for a salacious punch.

"It's on their website, too," he added quietly. "I figure someone at the agency gossiped, and it spread and turned into someone's political crap. Honestly, I'm having a hard time imagining Cross giving a shit—"

"About your sexual orientation? He doesn't. He's not like that."

"But his PR people might feel differently. Could be why he wants to keep you under the radar. And if he's worried that someone might go after you to get to me, that explains why he wants to keep you tucked away and off the streets."

"Why wouldn't he tell me that?" I set the paper down. "Why is he being such a prick? Everything was so wonderful while we were gone. *He* was wonderful. I thought we'd turned a corner. I kept thinking he wasn't anything like the man I'd first met, and now he's worse. There's this . . . I don't know. He's a million miles away from me now. I don't understand it."

"I'm not the guy to ask, Eva." Cary grabbed my hand and squeezed. "He's the one with the answers."

"You're right." I went to my purse and pulled out my phone. "I'll be back in a bit."

I went to the little enclosed balcony off the visitors' waiting area and called Gideon. The phone rang and rang, eventually going to voice mail. I tried his home number instead. After the third ring, Gideon answered.

"Cross," he said curtly.

"Hi."

There was silence for the length of a heartbeat, then, "Hang on."

I heard a door open. The sound on the phone changed—he'd stepped away from wherever he'd been.

"Is everything all right?" he asked.

"No." I rubbed at my tired eyes. "I miss you."

He sighed. "I . . . I can't talk now, Eva."

"Why not? I don't understand why you're acting so cold to me. Did I do something wrong?" I heard murmuring and realized he'd muffled the receiver to talk to someone else. A horrible feeling of betrayal tightened my chest, making it hard to breathe. "Gideon. Who's at your place with you?"

"I have to go."

"Tell me who's there with you!"

"Angus will be at the hospital at seven. Get some sleep, angel." The line went dead.

I lowered my hand and stared at my phone, as if it could somehow reveal to me what the fuck had just happened.

I made it back to Cary's room, felt weighted down and miserable as I pushed open the door.

Cary took one look at me and sighed. "You look like your puppy just died, baby girl."

The dam broke. I started sobbing.

14

I HARDLY SLEPT all night. I tossed and turned, drifting in and out of consciousness. The frequent nurse visits to check on Cary also woke me. His brain scans and lab reports were looking good and there was nothing absolutely definitive to worry about, but I hadn't been there for him when he'd first gotten hurt. I felt like I needed to be there for him now, sleep or no sleep.

Just before six, I gave up and got out of bed.

Grabbing my tablet and wireless keyboard, I headed down to the cafeteria for coffee. I pulled up a chair at one of the tables and prepared to write a letter to Gideon. In the short amounts of time I'd managed to pin him down the last couple of days, I hadn't been able to get my thoughts across to him. Writing it all out would have to be the way it got done. Maintaining steady, open communication was the only way we were going to survive as a couple.

I sipped my coffee and began typing, starting with my thanks for the beautiful weekend away and how much it meant to me. I told him how I thought our relationship had taken a massive leap forward during the trip, which only made the week's backslide harder to bear—

"Eva. What a pleasant surprise!"

Turning my head, I found Dr. Terrence Lucas standing behind me holding a disposable coffee cup like the one I'd filled for myself. He was dressed for work in slacks and tie with a white lab coat.

"Hi," I greeted him, hoping I hid my wariness.

"Mind if I join you?" he asked, rounding me.

"Not at all."

I watched him take the seat beside me, and I refreshed my memory of his appearance. His hair was pure white, without a hint of gray, but his handsome face was unlined. His eyes were an unusual shade of green and they were keen with intelligence. His smile was both reassuring and charming. I suspected he was popular with his patients—and their mothers.

"There has to be some special reason," he began, "for you to be in the hospital long before visiting hours."

"My roommate's here." I didn't volunteer any more information, but he guessed.

"So Gideon Cross threw his money around and made arrangements for you." He shook his head and took a sip of his coffee. "And you're grateful. But what will it cost you?"

I sat back, offended on Gideon's behalf that his generosity was reduced to having an ulterior motive. "Why do you two dislike each other so much?"

His eyes lost their softness. "He hurt someone very close to me."

"Your wife. He told me." I could tell that startled him. "But that wasn't the beginning, was it? That was a result."

"You know what he did, and you're still with him?" Lucas set his elbows on the table. "He's doing the same thing to you. You look exhausted and depressed. That's part of the game to him, you know. He's an expert at worshipping a woman as if he needs her to breathe. Then suddenly he can't bear the sight of her."

The statement was a painfully accurate description of my present reality with Gideon. My pulse quickened.

His gaze slid to my throat, then back to my face. His mouth curved in a mocking, knowing smile. "You've experienced what I'm talking about. He's going to continue to play with you until you rely on his mood to gauge your own. Then he'll get bored and dump you."

"What happened between you?" I asked again, knowing that was key.

"Gideon Cross is a narcissistic sociopath," he went on as if I hadn't spoken. "I believe he's a misogynist. He uses his money to seduce women, then despises them for being shallow enough to find his wealth attractive. He uses sex to control, and you never know what sort of mood you'll find him in. That's part of the rush—when you're always steeling yourself for the worst, you psych yourself up for a surge of relief when he's at his best."

"You don't know him," I said smoothly, refusing to take the bait. "And neither does your wife."

"Neither do you." He sat back and drank his coffee, appearing as unruffled as I tried to be. "No one does. He's a master manipulator and liar. Don't underestimate him. He's a twisted, dangerous man capable of just about anything."

"The fact that you won't explain his grudge against you makes me think you're at fault."

"You shouldn't make assumptions. There are some things I'm not at liberty to discuss."

242 · SYLVIA DAY

"That's convenient."

He sighed. "I'm not your adversary, Eva, and Cross doesn't need anyone to fight his battles. You don't have to believe me. Frankly, I'm so bitter *I* wouldn't believe me if I were in your place. But you're a beautiful, smart young lady."

I hadn't been lately, but it was my responsibility to fix that. Or walk.

"If you take a step back," he continued, "and look at what he's doing to you, how you're feeling about yourself since you've been with him, and whether you're truly fulfilled by your relationship, you'll come to your own conclusions."

Something beeped and he pulled his smartphone out of his coat pocket. "Ah, my latest patient has just entered the world."

He pushed to his feet and looked down at me, setting his hand on my shoulder. "You'll be the one who gets away. I'm glad."

I watched him walk briskly out of the cafeteria and collapsed into the seat back the moment he disappeared from view, deflating from exhaustion and confusion. My gaze moved to the sleeping screen of my tablet. I didn't have the energy to finish my letter.

I packed up and went to get ready for Angus's arrival.

"You up for Chinese?"

I looked up from the layout of the blueberry coffee ad on my desk into the warm brown eyes of my boss. I realized it was Wednesday, our usual day to go eat with Steven.

For a second, I considered bowing out and eating at my desk because I wanted to make Gideon happy. But just as quickly, I knew I'd resent him if I did. I was still trying to build a new life in New York, which included making friends and having plans that existed outside the life I shared with him.

"Always up for Chinese," I said. My very first meal with Mark and Steven had been Chinese takeout here in the office, on a night when we'd worked well past closing and Steven had stopped by to feed us.

Mark and I headed out at noon, and I refused to feel guilty about something I enjoyed so much. Steven was waiting for us at the restaurant, seated at a round table with a lacquered lazy Susan in the middle.

"Hey, you." He greeted me with a big bear hug, then pulled a chair out for me. He studied me as we both sat down. "You look tired."

I guessed I must really look like shit, since everyone kept telling me that. "It's been a rough week so far."

The waitress came by and Steven ordered a dim sum appetizer and the same dishes we'd shared for that first late-evening meal— kung pao chicken and broccoli beef. When we were alone again, Steven said, "I didn't know your roommate was gay. Did you tell us that?"

"He's bi, actually." I realized Steven, or someone he knew, must have seen the same newspaper Cary had showed me. "I don't think it came up."

"How's he feeling?" Mark asked, looking genuinely concerned.

"Better. He might be coming home today." Which was something that had been weighing on me all morning, since Gideon hadn't called to tell me definitively one way or the other.

"Let us know if you need any help," Steven said, all traces of levity gone. "We're here for you."

"Thank you. It wasn't a hate crime," I clarified. "I don't know where the reporter got that. I used to respect journalists. Now, so few of them do their homework, and fewer still can write objectively."

"I'm sure it's tough living in the media spotlight." Steven squeezed my hand on the table. He was a gregarious, playful fellow, but beneath that fun exterior was a solid man with a kind heart. "But then you have to kinda expect it when you're juggling rock stars and billionaires."

"Steven," Mark scolded, frowning.

"Ugh." My nose wrinkled. "Shawna told you."

"Of course she did," Steven said. "Least she can do after not inviting me along to the concert. But don't worry. She's not a gossip. She won't be telling anyone else."

I nodded, having no anxiety about that; Shawna was good people. But it was still embarrassing having my boss know I'd kissed one man while dating another.

"Not that it would be a bad thing for Cross to get a taste of his own medicine," Steven muttered.

I frowned, confused. Then I caught Mark's sympathetic gaze.

I realized the gay newspaper wasn't the only news they'd seen. They must have seen the photos of Gideon and Corinne, too. I felt my face flush with humiliation.

"He'll get a taste," I muttered. "If I have to cram it down his throat."

Steven's brows shot up, and then he laughed and patted my hand. "Get him, girl."

I'D barely returned to my desk when my work phone rang.

"Mark Garrity's office, Eva—"

"Why is it so damn difficult for you to follow orders?" Gideon asked harshly.

I just sat there, staring at the collage of photos he'd given me, pictures of us looking connected and in love.

REFLECTED IN YOU · 245

"Eva?"

"What do you want from me, Gideon?" I asked quietly.

There was a moment of silence, then he exhaled. "Cary will be moved to your apartment this afternoon under the supervision of his doctor and a private nurse. He should be there when you get home."

"Thank you." Another stretch of quiet filled the line between us, but he didn't hang up. Finally, I queried, "Are we done?"

The question had a double meaning. I wondered if he caught that or even cared.

"Angus will give you a ride home."

My grip tightened on the phone. "Good-bye, Gideon."

I hung up and got back to work.

I checked on Cary the minute I got home. His bed had been moved aside and propped vertically against the wall to make room for a hospital bed that he could adjust at will. He was asleep when I came in, his nurse sitting in a new recliner and reading an e-book. It was the same nurse I'd seen the first night in the hospital, the pretty and exotic-looking one who had trouble taking her eyes off Gideon.

I wondered when he'd spoken to her—if he'd done it himself or sent someone else to do it—and whether she'd agreed for the money or for Gideon or both.

The fact that I was too tired to care one way or another said a lot about my own disconnection. Maybe there were people out there whose love could survive anything, but mine was fragile. It needed to be nurtured in order to thrive and grow.

I took a long, hot shower, then crawled into bed. I pulled my tablet onto my lap and tried to continue my letter to Gideon. I wanted to express my thoughts and reservations in a mature and co-gent way. I wanted to make it easy for him to understand my reactions to some of the things he did and said, so he could see things from my point of view.

In the end, I didn't have the energy.

I'm not elaborating any more, I wrote instead, *because if I keep going, I'll beg. And if you don't know me well enough to know that you're hurting me, a letter isn't going to fix our problems.*

I'm desperate for you. I'm miserable without you. I think about the weekend, and the hours we spent together, and I can't think of anything I wouldn't do to have you like that again. Instead, you're spending time with HER, while I'm alone on my fourth night without you.

Even knowing you've been with her, I want to crawl on my knees for you and beg for scraps. A touch. A kiss. One tender word. You've made me that weak.

I hate myself like this. I hate that I need you this much. I hate that I'm so obsessed with you.

I hate that I love you.

Eva

I attached it to an e-mail with the subject line *My thoughts— uncensored* and hit send.

"Don't *be afraid.*"

I woke to those three words and utter darkness. The mattress dipped as Gideon sat beside me, leaning over me with his arms bracketing my body and the blankets between us, a cocoon and barrier that allowed my mind to wake without fear. The delicious and unmistakable fragrance of his soap and shampoo mixed with the scent of his skin, soothing me along with his voice.

"*Angel.*" He took my mouth, his lips slanting over mine.

I touched his chest with my fingers, feeling bare skin. He

groaned and stood, bending over me so his mouth stayed connected to mine while he yanked the blankets off and away.

Then he was settling over me, his body nude and hot to the touch. His ardent mouth moved down my throat, his hands pushing up my camisole so he could get to my breasts. His lips surrounded my nipple and he suckled, his weight supported by one forearm on the mattress, his other hand pushing between my legs.

He cupped my sex, his fingertip gliding over the satin along the seam of my cleft. His tongue flickered over my nipple, making it hard and tight, his teeth sinking lightly into the taut flesh.

"Gideon!" Tears slid in rivulets down my temples, the protective numbness I'd felt earlier falling away, leaving me exposed. I'd been withering without him, the world around me losing its vibrancy, my body hurting from its separation from his. Having him with me . . . touching me . . . was like rain in a drought. My soul unfurled for him, opening wide to soak him in.

I loved him so much.

His hair tickled my skin as his open mouth slid over my cleavage, his chest expanding as he breathed me in, nuzzling and wallowing in my scent. He captured the tip of my other breast with hard, deep suction. The pleasure shot through me, echoing in the clenching of my sex against his teasing fingertip.

He moved down my torso, licking and nibbling a path across my stomach, the breadth of his shoulders forcing my legs wider until his hot breath gusted over my slick cleft. His nose pressed against the wet satin, stroking me. He inhaled with a groan.

"*Eva.* I've been starved for you."

With impatient fingers, Gideon shoved the crotch of my panties aside and his mouth was on me. He held me open with his thumbs, his tongue lashing over my throbbing clit. My back arched with a cry, all my senses painfully acute without the benefit of sight. Tilting his head, he thrust into the quivering opening of my sex, fucking rhythmically, teasing me with shallow plunges.

"Oh God!" I writhed with the pleasure, my core clenching and releasing with the first tingles of orgasm.

I came in a violent rush, sweat misting my skin, my lungs burning as I fought for breath. His lips were around my trembling opening, sucking, his tongue delving. He was eating me with an intensity I was helpless against. The flesh between my legs was so swollen and sensitive, so vulnerable to his ravenous hunger. I was climaxing again within moments, my nails scouring the sheets.

My eyes were opened and blinded by darkness when he ripped my underwear off me and crawled over me. I felt the wide crest of his cock notch into my cleft, and then he lunged, driving deep into me with an animalistic growl. I cried out, shocked by his aggression, turned on by it.

Gideon reared up, resting back on his heels, my thighs splayed over his. He gripped my hips, elevating them, tilting me to the angle he wanted. He rolled his hips, stirring his cock inside me, pulling me onto him until I gasped in pain at how deep he was. The lips of my sex clung to the very base of his penis, spread wide to encompass the thick root. I had all of him, every inch, crammed too full and loving it. I'd been empty for days, so lonely I ached.

He groaned my name and came, spurting hot and thick, the creamy heat spreading upward along his length because there was no room inside me. He shuddered violently, dripping sweat onto my skin, flooding me. "For you, Eva," he gasped. "Every drop."

Pulling out abruptly, he flipped me over onto my belly and yanked my hips up. I gripped my headboard, my damp face pressed into my pillow. I waited for him to push into me and shivered when

I felt his breath against my buttocks. Then I jerked violently at the feel of him licking along the seam. He rimmed me with the tip of his tongue, stimulating the puckered opening to my rear.

A broken sound escaped me. *I don't do anal play, Eva.*

The tight ring of muscle flexed as I remembered his words, helplessly responding to the delicate flutters. There was nothing in our bed but us. Nothing could touch us when we were touching each other.

Gideon squeezed both of my cheeks in his hands, grounding me in the moment. I was open and parted for him in every way, completely exposed to his lush dark kiss.

"Oh!" I tensed all over. His tongue was inside me, thrusting. My entire body began to quake from the feeling, my toes curling, my lungs heaving as he possessed me without shame or reservation. *"Ah . . . God."*

I lifted into his mouth, giving myself to him. The affinity between us was brutal and raw, nearly unbearable. I felt seared by his desire, my skin feverish, my chest shaking with sobs I couldn't hold back.

He reached beneath me, pressed the flat of his fingers against my aching clit and rubbing, massaging. His tongue was driving me insane. The orgasm brewing inside me was spurred by the knowledge that there were no longer any boundaries for him with my body. He would do anything he desired—possess it, use it, pleasure it. Burying my face in my pillow, I screamed as I came, the ecstasy so vicious my legs gave out and I melted into the mattress.

Gideon slid over my back, his knee pushing my legs wide, his perspiration-slick body blanketing mine. He mounted me, pushing his cock inside me, his fingers linking with mine and pinning my hands to the bed. I was soaked with him and he rocked against me, sliding in and out.

"I'm desperate for you," he said hoarsely. "I'm miserable without you."

I tensed. "Don't mock me."

"I need you as much." He nuzzled into my hair, fucking me slow and easy. "I'm just as obsessed. Why can't you trust me?"

I squeezed my eyes shut, hot tears leaking out. "I don't understand you. You're tearing me apart."

He turned his head and his teeth sank into the top of my shoulder. A pained growl rumbled through his chest and I felt him coming, his cock jerking as it pumped me full of scorching semen.

His jaw relaxed, releasing me. He panted, his hips still churning. "Your letter gutted me."

"You won't talk to me . . . you won't listen . . ."

"I can't." He groaned, his arms tightening around mine so that I was completely at his mercy. "I just . . . It has to be this way."

"I can't live like this, Gideon."

"I'm hurting, too, Eva. It's killing me, too. Can't you see that?"

"No." I cried, my pillow growing wet beneath my cheek.

"Then stop overthinking and *feel it*! Feel *me*."

The night passed in a blur. I punished him with greedy hands and teeth, my nails raking over sweat-slick skin and muscle until he hissed in pleasured pain.

His lust was frantic and insatiable, his need tinged with a desperation that frightened me because it felt hopeless. It felt like good-bye.

"Need your love," he whispered against my skin. "Need you."

He touched me everywhere. He was constantly inside me, with his cock or his fingers or his tongue.

My nipples burned, made raw by his sucking. My sex throbbed and felt bruised from his wild, hard drives. My skin was chafed from the stubble that prickled over his jaw. My jaw ached from sucking his thick cock. My last memory was of him spooned behind me, his arm banded around my waist as he filled me from behind, both of us sore and exhausted and unable to stop.

"Don't let go," I begged, after I'd sworn I wouldn't.

When I woke to my alarm, he was gone.

15

I STOPPED BY Cary's room before I left for work Thursday morning. I cracked the door open and peeked in. When I saw he was sleeping, I started to back out.

"Hey," he murmured, blinking at me.

"Hey." I entered. "How are you feeling?"

"I'm glad to be home." He rubbed at the corners of his eyes. "Everything all right?"

"Yeah . . . I just wanted to check on you before I head to work. I'll be home around eight. I'll grab dinner on the way back, so expect a text around seven to see what you're hungry—" I interrupted myself with a yawn.

"What kind of vitamins does Cross take?"

"Huh?"

"I'm never *not* horny, and even I can't pile-drive all night like that. I kept thinking, 'He's got to be done now.' Then he'd start up again."

I flushed and shifted on my feet.

He howled with laughter. "It's dark in here, but I know you're blushing."

"You should've put your headphones on," I mumbled.

"Don't stress about it. It was good to find out my equipment still works. I hadn't had a chubby since before the attack."

"Eww . . . Gross, Cary." I started backing out of the room. "My dad comes in tonight. Technically tomorrow. His flight lands at five."

"You picking him up?"

"Of course."

His smile faded. "You're going to kill yourself at this rate. You haven't gotten any sleep all week."

"I'll catch up. See ya."

"Hey," he called after me. "Does last night mean you and Cross are okay again?"

I leaned into the doorjamb with a sigh. "Something's wrong, and he won't talk to me about it. I wrote him a letter basically puking out all my insecurities and neuroses."

"*Never* put stuff like that in writing, baby girl."

"Yeah, well . . . all it got me was fucked half to death with no better idea of what the problem is. He said it has to be this way. I don't even know what that means."

He nodded.

"You act like you get it," I said.

"I think I get the sex."

That sent a chill down my spine. "Get-it-out-of-your-system sex?"

"It's possible," he agreed softly.

I closed my eyes and let the confirmation slide through me. Then I straightened. "I gotta run. Catch you later."

THE thing about nightmares was that you couldn't prepare for them. They sneaked up on you when you were most vulnerable, wrecking havoc and mayhem when you were totally defenseless.

And they didn't always happen while you were sleeping.

I sat in an agonized daze as Mark and Mr. Waters went over the fine points of the Kingsman Vodka ads, achingly aware of Gideon sitting at the head of the table in a black suit with white shirt and tie.

He was pointedly ignoring me, had been from the moment I walked into the Cross Industries conference room aside from a cursory handshake when Mr. Waters introduced us. That brief touch of his skin against mine had sent a charge of awareness through me, my body immediately recognizing his as the one that had pleasured it all night. Gideon hadn't seemed to register the contact at all, his gaze trained above my head as he'd said, "Miss Tramell."

The contrast to the last time we'd been in the room was profound. Then, he hadn't been able to keep his eyes off me. His focus had been searing and blatant, and when we'd left the room he'd told me that he wanted to fuck me and would dispense with anything that got in the way of his doing so.

This time, he stood abruptly when the meeting was concluded, shook the hands of Mark and Mr. Waters, and strode out the door with only a short, inscrutable glance at me. His two directors scurried after him, both attractive brunettes.

Mark shot me a questioning look across the table. I shook my head.

I made it back to my desk. I worked industriously for the rest of the day. During my lunch break, I stayed in and looked up things to do with my dad. I decided on three possibilities—the Empire State Building, the Statue of Liberty, and a Broadway play, with the trip to the Statue of Liberty reserved for if he *really* had a desire to go. Otherwise, I figured we could skip the ferry and just check her out from the shore. His time in the city was short, and I didn't want to overload it with a bunch of running around.

On my last break of the day, I called Gideon's office.

"Hi, Scott," I greeted his secretary. "Is it possible for me to talk to your boss real quick?"

"Hold on a minute and I'll see."

I half-expected to have my call rejected, but a couple of minutes later I was put through.

"Yes, Eva?"

I took the length of a heartbeat to savor the sound of his voice. "I'm sorry to bother you. This is probably a stupid question, considering, but . . . are you coming to dinner tomorrow to meet my father?"

"I'll be there," he said gruffly.

"Are you bringing Ireland?" I was surprised there wasn't a tremor in my voice, considering the overwhelming relief I felt.

There was a pause. Then, "Yes."

"Okay."

"I have a late meeting tonight, so I'll have to meet you at Dr. Petersen's. Angus will drive you over. I'll grab a cab."

"All right." I sagged into my seat, feeling a spark of hope. Continuing therapy and meeting my dad could only be seen as positive signs. Gideon and I were struggling. But he hadn't given up yet. "I'll see you then."

ANGUS dropped me off at Dr. Petersen's office at a quarter to six. I went inside and Dr. Petersen waved at me through his open office door, rising from his seat behind his desk to shake my hand.

"How are you, Eva?"

"I've been better."

His gaze swept over my face. "You look tired."

"So everyone keeps telling me," I said dryly.

He looked over my shoulder. "Where's Gideon?"

"He had a late meeting, so he's coming separately."

"All right." He gestured at the sofa. "This is a nice opportunity for us to talk alone. Is there anything in particular you'd like to discuss before he arrives?"

I settled on the seat and spilled my guts, telling Dr. Petersen about the amazing trip to the Outer Banks and then the bizarre, inexplicable week we'd had since. "I just don't get it. I feel like he's in trouble, but I can't get him to open up at all. He's completely cut me off emotionally. Honestly, I'm beginning to get whiplash. I'm also worried that his change in behavior is because of Corinne. Every time we've hit one of these walls, it's because of her."

I looked at my fingers, which were twisted around each other. They reminded me of my mother's habit of twisting handkerchiefs, and I forced my hands to relax. "It almost seems like she's got some kind of hold on him and he can't break free of it, no matter how he feels about me."

Dr. Petersen looked up from his typing, studying me. "Did he tell you that he wasn't going to make his appointment on Tuesday?"

"No." The news hit me hard. "He didn't say anything."

"He didn't tell me, either. I wouldn't say that's typical behavior for him, would you?"

I shook my head.

Dr. Petersen crossed his hands in his lap. "At times, one or both of you will backtrack a bit. That's to be expected considering the nature of your relationship—you're not just working on you as a couple, but also as individuals so you can be a couple."

"I can't deal with this, though." I took a deep breath. "I can't do this yo-yo thing. It's driving me insane. The letter I sent him . . . It was awful. All true, but awful. We've had some really beautiful moments together. He's said some—"

I had to stop a minute, and when I continued, my voice was hoarse. "He's said some w-wonderful things to me. I don't want to lose those memories in a bunch of ugly ones. I keep debating whether I should quit while I'm ahead, but I'm hanging in here because I promised him—and myself—that I wouldn't run anymore. That I was going to dig my feet in and fight for this."

"That's something you're working on?"

"Yes. Yes, it is. And it's not easy. Because some of the things he does . . . I react in ways I've learned to avoid. For my own sanity! At some point you have to say you gave it your best shot and it didn't work out. Right?"

Dr. Petersen's head tilted to the side. "And if you don't, what's the worst that could happen?"

"You're asking me?"

"Yes. Worst-case scenario."

"Well . . ." I splayed my fingers on my thighs. "He keeps drifting away from me, which makes me cling harder and lose all sense of self-worth. And we end up with him going back to life as he knew it and me going back to therapy trying to get my head on straight again."

He continued to look at me, and something about his patient watchfulness prodded me to keep talking.

"I'm afraid that he won't cut me loose when it's time and that I won't know better. That I'll keep hanging on to the sinking ship and go down with it. I just wish I could trust that he'd end it, if it comes to that."

"Do you think that needs to happen?"

"I don't know. Maybe." I pulled my gaze away from the clock on the wall. "But considering it's nearly seven and he stood us both up tonight, it seems likely."

It was crazy to me that I *wasn't* surprised to find the Bentley waiting outside my apartment at quarter to five in the morning. The driver who climbed out from behind the wheel when I stepped outside wasn't familiar to me. He was much younger than Angus; early thirties was my guess. He looked Latino, with rich caramel-hued skin, and dark hair and eyes.

"Thanks," I told him, when he rounded the front of the vehicle, "but I'll just grab a cab."

Hearing that, the night doorman to my building stepped out to the street to flag one down for me.

"Mr. Cross said I'm to take you to La Guardia," the driver said.

"You can tell Mr. Cross that I won't be requiring his transportation services now or in the future." I moved toward the cab the doorman had hailed, but stopped and turned around. "And tell him to go fuck himself, too."

I slid into the cab and settled back as it pulled away.

I'll admit to some bias when I say my father stands out in a crowd, but that didn't make it less true.

As he exited the security area, Victor Reyes commanded attention. He was six feet tall, fit and well built, and had the commanding presence of a man who wore a badge. His gaze raked the immediate area around him, always a cop even when he wasn't on duty. He had a duffel bag slung over his shoulder and wore blue jeans with a black button-down shirt. His hair was dark and wavy, his eyes stormy and gray like mine. He was seriously hot in a brooding, dangerous, bad-boy sort of way, and I tried to picture him alongside my mother's fragile, haughty beauty. I'd never seen them together, not even in pictures, and I really wanted to. If only just once.

"Daddy!" I yelled, waving.

His face lit up when he saw me, and a wide smile curved his mouth.

"There's my girl." He picked me up in a hug that had my feet dangling above the floor. "I've missed you like crazy."

I started crying. I couldn't help it. Being with him again was the last emotional straw.

"Hey." He rocked me. "What's with the tears?"

I wrapped my arms tighter around his neck, so grateful to have him with me, knowing all the other troubles in my life would fade into the background while he was around.

"I missed you like crazy, too," I said, sniffling.

We took a cab back to my place. On the ride over, my dad asked me the same sort of investigative questions about Cary's attack as the detectives had asked Cary in the hospital. I tried to keep him distracted with that discussion when we pulled up outside my building, but it didn't do any good.

My dad's eagle eyes took in the modern glass overhang attached to the brick façade of the building. He stared at the doorman, Paul, who touched the brim of his hat and opened the door for us. He studied the front desk and concierge, and rocked back on his heels as we waited for the elevator.

He didn't say anything and kept his poker face on, but I knew he was thinking about how much my digs must cost in a city like New York. When I showed him into my apartment, his sweeping gaze took in the size of the place. The massive windows had a stunning view of the city, and the flat-screen television mounted on the wall was just one of the many top-of-the-line electronics on display.

He knew I couldn't afford the place on my own. He knew my mother's husband was providing for me in ways he would never be able to. And I wondered if he thought about my mother, and how what she needed was also beyond his means.

"The security here is really tight," I told him by way of explanation. "It's impossible to get past the front desk if you're not on the list and a resident can't be reached to vouch for you."

My dad exhaled in a rush. "That's good."

"Yeah. I don't think Mom could sleep at night otherwise."

That made some of the tension leave his shoulders.

"Let me show you to your room." I led him down the hallway to the guest room suite. It had its own bathroom and mini-bar with fridge. I saw him noting those things before he dropped his duffel on the king-size bed. "Are you tired?"

He looked at me. "I know you are. And you have to work today, don't you? Why don't we nap for a bit before you have to get up?"

I stifled a yawn and nodded, knowing I could use the couple of hours of shut-eye. "Sounds good."

"Wake me when you're up," he said, rolling his shoulders back. "I'll make the coffee while you're getting ready."

"Awesome." My voice came husky with suppressed tears. Gideon almost always had coffee waiting for me on days when he'd spent the night, because he got up before me. I missed that little ritual of ours.

Somehow, I'd have to learn to live without it.

Pushing up onto my tiptoes, I kissed my dad's cheek. "I'm so glad you're here, Daddy."

I closed my eyes and clung tightly when he hugged me.

I stepped out of the small market with my bags of grocery ingredients for dinner and frowned at finding Angus idling at the curb. I'd refused a ride in the morning and again when I'd left the Crossfire, and he was still following and shadowing. It was ridiculous. I couldn't help but wonder if Gideon didn't want me as a girlfriend anymore, but his neurotic lust for my body meant that he didn't want anyone else to have me—namely Brett.

As I walked home, I entertained thoughts of having Brett over for dinner instead, imagining Angus having to make that call to Gideon when Brett came strolling up to my place. It was just a quick vengeful fantasy, since I wouldn't lead Brett on that way and he was in Florida anyway, but it did the trick. My step lightened and when I entered my apartment, I was in my first really good mood in days.

I dumped all the dinner stuff off in the kitchen, then went to find my dad. He was hanging out in Cary's room playing a video game. Cary worked a nunchuk one-handed, since his other hand was in a cast.

"Woo!" my dad shouted. "Spanked."

"You should be ashamed of yourself," Cary shot back, "taking advantage of an invalid."

"I'm crying a river here."

Cary looked at me in the doorway and winked. I loved him so much in that moment I couldn't stop myself from crossing over to him and pressing a kiss to his bruised forehead.

"Thank you," I whispered.

"Thank me with dinner. I'm starving."

I straightened. "I got the goods to make enchiladas."

My dad looked at me, smiling, knowing I'd need his help. "Yeah?"

"When you're ready," I told him. "I'm going to grab a shower."

Forty-five minutes later, my dad and I were in the kitchen rolling cheese and store-bought rotisserie chicken—my little cheat to save time—into lard-soaked white corn tortillas. In the living room, the CD changer slipped in the next disk and Van Morrison's soulful voice piped through the surround sound speakers.

"Oh yeah," my dad said, reaching for my hand and tugging me away from the counter. "Hum-de-rum, hum-de-rum, moondance," he sang in his deep baritone, twirling me.

I laughed, delighted.

Using the back of his hand against my spine to keep his greasy fingers off me, he swept me into a dance around the island, both of us singing the song and laughing. We were making our second revolution when I noticed the two people standing at the breakfast bar.

My smile fled and I stumbled, forcing my dad to catch me.

"You got two left feet?" he teased, his eyes only on me.

"Eva's a wonderful dancer," Gideon interjected, his face arrested in that implacable mask I detested.

My dad turned, his smile fading, too.

Gideon rounded the bar and entered the kitchen. He'd dressed for the occasion in jeans and a Yankees T-shirt. It was a suitably casual choice and a conversation starter, since my dad was a die-hard Padres fan.

"I hadn't realized she was such a good singer, as well. Gideon Cross," he introduced himself, holding out his hand.

"Victor Reyes." My dad waved his shiny fingers. "I'm a bit messy."

"I don't mind."

Shrugging, my dad took his hand and sized him up.

I tossed the dish towel to the guys and made my way over to Ireland, who was positively glowing. Her blue eyes were bright, her cheeks flushed with pleasure.

"I'm so glad you could make it," I said, hugging her carefully. "You look gorgeous!"

"So do you!"

It was a fib, but I appreciated it anyway. I hadn't done anything to my face or hair after my shower, because I knew my dad wouldn't care and I hadn't expected Gideon to show up. After all, the last time I'd heard from him had been when he'd said he would meet me at Dr. Petersen's office.

She looked over at the counter where I'd dumped everything. "Can I help?"

"Sure. Just don't count calories in your head—it'll explode." I introduced her to my dad, who was much warmer to her than he was to Gideon, and then I led her to the sink, where she washed up.

In short order, I had her helping to roll the last few enchiladas, while my dad put the already chilled Dos Equis Gideon had brought into the fridge. I didn't even bother to wonder how Gideon knew I was serving Mexican food for dinner. I only wondered why he'd invest the time to find out when it was very clear he had other things to do—like ditch his appointments.

My dad went to his room to wash up. Gideon came up behind me and put his hands on my waist, his lips brushing over my temple. "Eva."

I tensed against the nearly irresistible urge to lean into him. "Don't," I whispered. "I'd rather we didn't pretend."

His breath left him in a rush that ruffled my hair. His fingers tightened on my hips, kneading for a moment. Then I felt his phone vibrate and he released me, backing away to look at the screen.

"Excuse me," he said gruffly, leaving the kitchen before answering.

Ireland sidled over and whispered, "Thank you. I know you made him bring me along."

I managed a smile for her. "Nobody can make Gideon do anything he doesn't want to."

"You could." She tossed her head, throwing her sleek waist-length black hair over her shoulder. "You didn't see him watching you dance with your dad. His eyes got all shiny. I thought he was going to cry. And on the way up here, in the elevator, he tried to play it off, but I could totally tell he was nervous."

I stared down at the can of enchilada sauce in my hands, feeling my heart break a little more.

"You're mad at him, aren't you?" Ireland asked.

I cleared my throat. "Some people are just better off as friends."

"But you said you love him."

"That's not always enough." I turned around to reach the can opener and found Gideon standing at the other end of the island, staring at me. I froze.

A muscle in his jaw twitched before he unclenched it. "Would you like a beer?" he asked gruffly.

I nodded. I could've used a shot, too. Maybe a few.

"Want a glass?"

"No."

He looked at Ireland. "You thirsty? There's soda, water, milk."

"How about one of those beers?" she shot back, flashing a winsome smile.

"Try again," he said wryly.

I watched Ireland, noting how she sparkled when Gideon focused on her. I couldn't believe he didn't see how she loved him. Maybe right now it was based on superficial things, but it was there and it would grow with a little encouragement. I hoped he'd work on that.

When Gideon handed me the chilled beer, his fingers brushed mine. He held on for a minute, looking into my eyes. I knew he was thinking about the other night.

It seemed like a dream now, as if his visit never really happened. I could almost believe that I'd made it up in a desperate delusion, so hungry for his touch and his love that I couldn't go another minute without giving my mind relief from the madness of wanting and craving. If it weren't for the lingering soreness deep inside me, I wouldn't know what was real and what was nothing but false hope.

I pulled the beer out of his grasp and turned away. I didn't want to say we were done and over, but it was certain now that we needed a break from each other. Gideon needed to figure out what he was doing, what he was looking for, and whether I had any meaningful place in his life. Because this roller-coaster ride we were on was going to break me, and I couldn't let that happen. I wouldn't.

"Can I help with anything?" he asked.

I answered without looking at him, because doing so was too painful. "Can you see if we can get Cary out here? He's got a wheel-chair."

"All right."

He left the room, and I could suddenly breathe deeply again.

Ireland hurried over. "What happened to Cary?"

"I'll tell you about it while we set the table."

I was surprised I could eat. I think I was too fascinated by the silent showdown between my dad and Gideon to notice that I was stuffing food into my mouth. At one end of the table, Cary was charming Ireland into peals of laughter that kept making me smile. At the other end, my dad sat at the head of the table, with Gideon on his left and me on his right.

They were talking. The conversation had opened with baseball, as I'd expected, then migrated into golf. On the surface, both men seemed relaxed, but the air around them was highly charged. I noticed that Gideon wasn't wearing his expensive watch. He'd planned carefully to appear as "normal" as possible.

But nothing Gideon did on the outside could change who he was on the inside. It was impossible to hide what he was—a dominant male, a captain of industry, a man of privilege. It was in every gesture he made, every word he spoke, every look he gave.

So he and my father were in the position of struggling to find who would be the alpha, and I suspected *I* hung in the balance. As if anyone were in control of my life but me.

Still, I understood that my father had only really been allowed to *be* a dad in the last four years, and he wasn't ready to give it up. Gideon, however, was jockeying for a position I was no longer prepared to give him.

But he was wearing the ring I'd given him. I tried not to read anything into it, but I wanted to hope. I wanted to believe.

We'd all finished the main course and I was pushing to my feet to clear the table for dessert when the intercom buzzed. I answered.

"Eva? NYPD detectives Graves and Michna are here," the gal at the front desk said.

I glanced at Cary, wondering if the detectives had found out who'd attacked him. I gave the go-ahead for them to come up and hurried back to the dining table.

Cary looked at me with raised brows, curious.

"It's the detectives," I explained. "Maybe they have news."

My dad's focus immediately shifted. Honed. "I'll let them in."

Ireland helped me clear up. We'd just dumped the cups into the sink when the doorbell rang. I wiped my hands with a dish towel and went out to the living room.

The two detectives who entered weren't the ones I expected, because they weren't the ones who'd questioned Cary at the hospital on Monday.

Gideon appeared out of the hallway, shoving his phone into his pocket.

I wondered who'd been calling him all night.

"Eva Tramell," the female detective said, stepping deeper into my apartment. She was a thin woman with a severe face and sharply intelligent blue eyes, which were her best feature. Her hair was brown and curly, her face clean of makeup. She wore slacks over dark flats, a poplin shirt, and a lightweight jacket that didn't hide the badge and gun clipped to her belt. "I'm Detective Shelley Graves of the NYPD. This is my partner, Detective Richard Michna. We're sorry to disturb you on a Friday night."

Michna was older, taller, and portly. His hair was graying at the temples and receding at the top, but he had a strong face and dark eyes that raked the room while Graves focused on me.

"Hello," I greeted them.

My father shut the door, and something about the way he moved or carried himself caught Michna's attention. "You on the job?"

"In California," my dad confirmed. "I'm visiting Eva, my daughter. What's this about?"

"We'd just like to ask you a few questions, Miss Tramell," Graves said. She looked at Gideon. "And you, too, Mr. Cross."

"Does this have something to do with the attack on Cary?" I asked.

She glanced at him. "Why don't we sit down."

We all moved into the living room, but only Ireland and I ended up taking a seat. Everyone else remained on their feet, with my dad pushing Cary's wheelchair.

"Nice place you've got here," Michna said.

"Thank you." I looked at Cary, wondering what the hell was going on.

"How long are you in town?" the detective asked my dad.

"Just for the weekend."

Graves smiled at me. "You go out to California a lot to see your dad?"

"I just moved from there a couple months ago."

"I went to Disneyland once when I was a kid," she said. "That was a while ago, obviously. I've been meaning to get back out there."

I frowned, not understanding why we were making small talk.

"We just need to ask you a couple of questions," Michna said, pulling a notepad out of the interior pocket of his jacket. "We don't want to hold you up any longer than we have to."

Graves nodded, her eyes still on me. "Can you tell us if you're familiar with a man named Nathan Barker, Miss Tramell?"

The room spun. Cary cursed and pushed unsteadily to his feet, taking the few steps to reach the seat beside me. He caught up my hand.

"Miss Tramell?" Graves took a seat on the other end of the sectional.

"He's her former stepbrother," Cary snapped. "What's this about?"

"When's the last time you saw Barker?" Michna asked.

In a courtroom . . . I tried to swallow, but my mouth was dry as sawdust. "Eight years ago," I said hoarsely.

"Did you know he was here in New York?"

Oh God. I shook my head violently.

"Where's this going?" my dad asked.

I looked helplessly at Cary, then at Gideon. My dad didn't know about Nathan. I didn't want him to know.

Cary squeezed my hand. Gideon wouldn't even look at me.

"Mr. Cross," Graves said. "What about you?"

"What about me?"

"Do you know Nathan Barker?"

My eyes pleaded with Gideon not to say anything in front of my dad, but he never once glanced my way.

"You wouldn't be asking that question," he answered, "if you didn't already know the answer."

My stomach dropped. A violent shiver moved through me. Still, Gideon wouldn't look at me. My brain was trying to process what was happening . . . what it meant . . . what was going on . . .

"Is there a point to these questions?" my father asked.

The blood was roaring in my ears. My heart was pounding with something like terror. The mere thought of Nathan being so close was enough to send me into a panic. I was panting. The room was swimming before my eyes. I thought I might pass out.

Graves was watching me like a hawk. "Can you just tell us where you were yesterday, Miss Tramell?"

"Where I was?" I repeated. "Yesterday?"

"Don't answer that," my dad ordered. "This interview isn't going any further until we know what this is about."

Michna nodded, as if he'd expected the interruption. "Nathan Barker was found dead this morning."

16

As soon as Detective Michna finished his sentence, my dad cut the questioning off. "We're done here," he said grimly. "If you have any further questions, you can make an appointment for my daughter to come in with counsel."

"How about you, Mr. Cross?" Michna's gaze moved to Gideon. "Would you mind telling us where you were yesterday?"

Gideon moved from his position behind the couch. "Why don't we talk while I show you out?"

I stared at him, but he still wouldn't look at me.

What else didn't he want me to know? How much was he hiding from me?

Ireland's fingers threaded with mine. Cary sat on one side of me and Ireland on the other, while the man I loved stood several feet away and hadn't glanced at me in almost half an hour. I felt like a cold rock had settled in my gut.

The detectives took down my phone numbers, then left with Gideon. I watched the three of them walk out, saw my dad eyeing Gideon with a hard speculative look.

"Maybe he was buying you an engagement ring," Ireland whispered. "And he doesn't want to blow the surprise."

I squeezed her hand for being sweet and thinking so highly of her brother. I hoped he never let her down or disillusioned her. The way *I* was now disillusioned. Gideon and I were nothing—we had nothing together—if he couldn't be honest with me.

Why hadn't he told me about Nathan?

Releasing Cary and Ireland, I stood and went into the kitchen. My dad followed me.

"Want to fill me in with what's going on?" he asked.

"I have no idea. This is all news to me."

He leaned his hip into the counter and studied me. "What's the history with you and Nathan Barker? You heard his name and looked like you were going to pass out."

I started rinsing off the dishes and loading the dishwasher. "He was a bully, Dad. That's all. He didn't like that his dad remarried, and he especially didn't like that his new stepmom already had a kid."

"Why would Gideon have anything to do with him?"

"That's a really good question." As I gripped the edge of the sink, I bowed my head and closed my eyes. That was what had driven the wedge between me and Gideon—*Nathan*. I knew it.

"Eva?" My dad's hands settled on my shoulders and kneaded into the hard, aching muscles. "Are you okay?"

"I-I'm tired. I haven't been sleeping well." I shut off the water and left the rest of the dishes where they were. I went to the cupboard where we kept our vitamins and over-the-counter medicines and took out two nighttime painkillers. I wanted a deep, dreamless sleep. I needed it, so I could wake up in a condition to figure out what I needed to do.

I looked at my dad. "Can you take care of Ireland until Gideon gets back?"

"Of course." He kissed my forehead. "We'll talk in the morning."

Ireland found me before I could find her. "Are you okay?" she asked, stepping into the kitchen.

"I'm going to lie down, if you don't mind. I know that's rude."

"No, it's okay."

"Really, I'm sorry." I pulled her close for a hug. "We'll do this again. Maybe a girls' day? Hit the spa or go shopping?"

"Sure. Call me?"

"I will." I let her go and passed through the living room to get to the hallway.

The front door opened and Gideon walked in. Our gazes met and held. I could read nothing in his. I looked away, went to my room, and locked the door.

I was up at nine the next morning, feeling groggy and grumpy but no longer overwhelmingly tired. I knew I needed to call Stanton and my mom, but I needed caffeine first.

I washed my face, brushed my teeth, and shuffled out to the living room. I was almost to the kitchen—the source of the luscious smell of coffee—when the doorbell rang. My heart skipped a beat. I couldn't help the instinctive reaction I had to thoughts of Gideon, who was one of the three people on the list to get past the front desk.

But when I opened the door, it was my mother. I hoped I didn't look too disappointed, but I don't think she noticed anyway. She swept right past me in a seafoam green dress that looked painted on, and she pulled it off as very few women could, somehow making the outfit sexy and elegant and age-appropriate. Of course, she looked young enough to be my sister.

She raked a glance over my comfortable SDSU sweatpants and camisole before saying, "Eva. My God. You have no idea—"

"Nathan's dead." I shut the door and glanced nervously down the hallway at the guest bedroom, praying that my dad was still functioning on West Coast time and sleeping.

"Oh." She turned around and faced me, and I got my first good look at her. Her mouth was thinned with worry, her blue eyes haunted. "Have the police come by already? They only just left us."

"They were here last night." I headed into the kitchen and straight to the coffeemaker.

"Why didn't you call us? We should have been with you. You should've had *a lawyer* with you, at the very least."

"It was a real quick visit, Mom. Want some?" I held up the carafe.

"No, thank you. You shouldn't drink so much of that stuff. It's not good for you."

I put the carafe back and opened the fridge.

"Dear God, Eva," my mother muttered, watching me. "Do you realize how many calories are in half-and-half?"

I set a bottle of water in front of her and moved back to lighten my coffee. "They were here for about thirty minutes and then left. They didn't get anything out of me beyond Nathan being my former stepbrother and that I haven't seen him in eight years."

"Thank God you didn't say more." She twisted open her water.

I grabbed my mug. "Let's move to my sitting room."

"What? Why? You never sit in there."

She was right, but using it would help prevent a surprise run-in between my parents.

"But *you* like it," I pointed out. We entered through my bedroom and I shut the door behind us, breathing a sigh of relief.

"I do like it," my mother said, turning to take it all in.

Of course she liked it; she'd decorated it. I liked it, too, but didn't really have a use for it. I'd thought about turning it into an adjoining bedroom for Gideon, but everything could be changing now. He'd pulled away from me, hidden Nathan and a dinner with Corinne from me. I wanted an explanation, and depending on what that was, we were going to either recommit to moving forward or take the painful steps to move away from each other.

My mom settled gracefully on the chaise, her gaze coming to rest on me. "You'll have to be very careful with the police, Eva. If they want to talk to you again, let Richard know so he can have his lawyers present."

"Why? I don't understand why I should worry about what I say or don't say. I haven't done anything wrong. I didn't even know he was in town." I watched her gaze skitter away from mine, and my tone firmed. "What's going on, Mom?"

She took a drink before speaking. "Nathan showed up in Richard's office last week. He wanted two and a half million dollars."

There was a sudden roaring in my ears. *"What?"*

"He wanted money," she said stiffly. "A lot of it."

"Why the hell would he think he'd get any?"

"He has—*had*—photos, Eva." Her lower lip began to quiver. "And video. Of you."

"Oh my God." I set my coffee aside with shaking hands and bent over, putting my head between my knees. "Oh God, I'm going to be sick."

And Gideon had seen Nathan—he'd confessed as much when he answered the detectives' questions. If he'd seen the pictures . . . been disgusted by them . . . it would explain why he cut me off. Why he'd been so tormented when he came to my bed. He might still want me, but he might not be able to live with the images now filling his head.

It has to be this way, he'd said.

A horrible sound escaped me. I couldn't even begin to imagine what Nathan might have captured. I didn't want to.

No wonder Gideon couldn't stand to look at me. When he'd made love to me the last time, it had been in utter darkness, where he could hear me and smell me and feel me—but not see me.

I stifled a scream of pain by biting my forearm.

"Baby, no!" My mother sank to her knees in front of me, urging me gently off the chair and onto the floor where she could rock me. "Shh. It's over. He's dead."

I curled into her lap, sobbing, realizing it truly was over—I'd lost Gideon. He would hate himself for turning away from me, but I understood why he might not be able to stop himself. If looking at me now reminded him of his own brutal past, how could he stand it? How could I?

My mother's hand stroked over my hair. I felt her crying, too. "Shh," she hushed me, her voice shaking. "Shh, baby. I've got you. I'll take care of you."

Eventually there were no more tears left to cry. I was empty, but with that emptiness came new clarity. I couldn't change what had happened, but I could do what was necessary to make sure that no one I loved suffered for it.

I sat up and wiped at my eyes.

"You shouldn't do that," my mother scolded. "Rubbing at your eyes like that will give you wrinkles."

For some reason, I found her concern for my future crow's-feet hysterical. I tried to hold it in, but a snorted laugh broke free.

"Eva Lauren!"

I thought her indignation was funny, too. I laughed some more, and once I started, I couldn't stop. I laughed until my sides hurt and I fell over.

"Oh, stop it!" She shoved at my shoulder. "It's not funny."

I laughed until I managed to squeeze out a few more tears.

"Eva, really!" But she was starting to smile.

I laughed until I wasn't laughing so much as sobbing again, dry and silent. I heard my mother giggling, and that somehow blended perfectly with my wracking pain. I couldn't explain it, but as horrible and hopeless as I felt, my mother's presence—complete with all her little quirks and admonitions that drove me insane—was just what I needed.

With my hands on my cramping stomach, I took a deep cleansing breath. "Did he arrange it?" I asked softly.

Her smiled faded. "Who? Richard? Arrange what? The money? *Oh . . .*"

I waited.

"No!" she protested. "He wouldn't. His mind doesn't work that way."

"Okay. I just had to know." I couldn't see Stanton ordering a hit, either. But Gideon . . .

I knew from his nightmares that his desire for vengeance was colored by violence. And I'd seen him fight Brett. The memory was seared in my mind. Gideon was capable, and with his history—

I took a deep breath, then blew it out. "How much do the police know?"

"Everything." Her eyes were soft and wet with guilt. "The seal on Nathan's records was broken when he died."

278 · SYLVIA DAY

"And how did he die?"

"They didn't say."

"I suppose it's not important. We have a motive." I ran my hand through my hair. "It probably doesn't matter that we didn't personally have the opportunity. Your time is accounted for, isn't it? And Stanton's?"

"Yes. And yours, too?"

"Yes." But I didn't know about Gideon's. Not that it mattered. No one would expect men like Gideon and Stanton to get their hands dirty cleaning up a mess like Nathan.

We had more than one motive—the blackmail and revenge for what he'd done to me—and means, and means gave us the opportunity.

I brushed my hair again and splashed water on my face, all the while thinking of how I was going to get my mom out of my apartment undetected. When I found her digging through the closet in my bedroom—concerned as always about my style and appearance—I knew what to do.

"Remember that skirt I picked up at Macy's?" I asked her. "The green one?"

"Oh, yes. Very pretty."

"I haven't been able to wear it, because I can't think of anything I have to go with it. Can you help me find something?"

"Eva," she said, exasperated. "You should've established a personal style by now—and it shouldn't be sweats!"

"Help me out, Mom. I'll be right back." I took my coffee mug with me to have a purpose for leaving her. "Don't go anywhere."

"Where would I go?" she replied, her voice muffled because she'd stepped deeper into my walk-in closet.

I did a quick check of the living room and kitchen. My dad was nowhere to be seen and his bedroom door was closed, as was Cary's. I hurried back into my room.

"How's this?" she asked, holding up a champagne-hued silk blouse. The combination was gorgeous and classy.

"I love it! You rock! Thank you. But I'm sure you have to go now, right? I don't want to hold you up."

My mom frowned at me. "I'm not in a hurry."

"What about Stanton? This has got to be weighing on his mind. And it's a Saturday—he always reserves his weekends for you. He needs to have the time with you."

And God, did I feel awful for his stress. Stanton had spent a great deal of his time and money on issues pertaining to me and Nathan over the four years he'd been married to my mother. It was too much to ask of anyone, but he'd come through for us. For the rest of my life, I would owe him for loving my mother so much.

"This is weighing on your mind, too," she argued. "I want to be here for you, Eva. I want to support you."

My throat tightened, understanding that she was trying to make amends for what had happened to me because she was unable to forgive herself. "It's okay," I said hoarsely. "I'll be okay. And honestly, I'd feel terrible keeping you away from Stanton after all he's done for us. You're his reward, his little piece of heaven at the end of an endless workweek."

Her lips curved in an enchanting smile. "What a lovely thing to say."

Yes, I'd thought so, too, the times Gideon had said similar things to me.

It seemed impossible that only a week before, we'd been at the beach house, madly in love and taking firm, sure steps forward in our relationship.

But now that relationship was broken, and now I knew why. I was angry and hurt that Gideon had kept something as monumental as Nathan being in New York hidden from me. I was furious that he hadn't talked to me about what he was thinking and feeling. But I understood, too. He was a man who'd avoided talking about anything personal for years and years, and we hadn't been together long enough for that lifetime habit to change. I couldn't blame him for being who he was, just as I couldn't blame him for deciding that he couldn't live with what I was.

With a sigh, I went to my mom and hugged her. "Having you here . . . it's what I needed, Mama. Crying and laughing and just sitting with you. Nothing could be more perfect than that. Thank you."

"Really?" She hugged me tightly, feeling so small and delicate in my arms, even though we were the same size and her heels made her taller. "I thought you were going crazy."

I pulled back and smiled. "I think I did for a little bit, but you brought me back. And Stanton is a good man. I'm grateful for all he's done for us. Please tell him I said so."

Linking my arm with hers, I grabbed her clutch from my bed and led her to the front door. She hugged me again, her hands stroking up and down my back. "Call me tonight and tomorrow. I want to make sure you're doing okay."

"All right."

She studied me. "And let's plan on a spa day next week. If the doctor doesn't approve of Cary going, we'll have the technicians come here. I think we could all use a little pampering and polish right now."

"That's a really nice way of saying I look like shit." We were both rough around the edges, although she hid it much better than I did.

Nathan was still hanging over us like a dark cloud, still capable of ruining lives and destroying our peace. But we'd pretend that we were better off than we were. That was just the way we did things. "But you're right—it'll be good for us and it'll make Cary feel a whole lot better, even if he can only get a mani and pedi."

"I'll make the arrangements. I can't wait!" My mother flashed her signature megawatt smile—

—which is what my dad was hit with when I opened the front door. He stood on the threshold with Cary's keys in his hand, having been caught just about to slide one into the lock. He was dressed in running shorts and athletic shoes, his sweat-soaked shirt tossed carelessly over his shoulder. Still breathing a little quickly and glistening with sweat over tanned skin and rippling muscles, Victor Reyes was one hot hunk of a man.

And he was staring at my mom in a way that was totally indecent.

Tearing my gaze away from my seriously smokin' dad to look at my glamorous mother, I was shocked to see her looking at my father the same way he was looking at her.

Of all the times to realize my parents were in love with each other. Well, I'd suspected my dad was heartbroken over my mom, but I thought she'd been embarrassed about him, as if he were a big mistake and error in judgment in her past.

"Monica." My dad's voice was lower and deeper than I'd ever heard it, and more obviously flavored with an accent.

"Victor." My mom was breathless. "What are you doing here?"

One of his brows rose. "Visiting our daughter."

"And now Mom has to go," I prodded, torn between the novelty of seeing my parents together and a loyalty to Stanton, who was exactly what my mother needed. "I'll call you later, Mom."

My dad didn't move for a moment, his gaze sliding down the length of my mom from head to toe, then gliding back up again. Then he took a deep breath and stepped aside.

My mom stepped out into the hallway and turned toward the elevator, and then at the last minute she turned back. She placed her palm over my dad's heart and lifted onto her tiptoes, kissing one of his cheeks and then the other.

"Good-bye," she breathed.

I watched her walk unsteadily to the elevator and push the button, her back to us. My dad didn't look away until the car doors closed behind her.

He exhaled in a rush and came into my apartment.

I shut the door. "How is it that I didn't know you two are crazy in love with each other?"

The look in his eyes was painful to witness. The raw agony was like an open wound. "Because it doesn't mean anything."

"I don't believe that. Love means everything."

"It doesn't conquer all like they say." He snorted. "Can you see your mother being a cop's wife?"

I winced.

"Right," he said dryly, wiping his forehead with his shirt. "Sometimes love isn't enough. And if it's not enough, what good is it?"

The bitterness I heard in his words was something I knew very well myself. I passed him and went into the kitchen.

My dad followed me. "Are you in love with Gideon Cross?"

"Isn't it obvious?"

"Is he in love with you?"

Because I just didn't have the energy, I dumped my mug in the sink and pulled out new ones for me and my dad. "I don't know. I know he wants me, and sometimes he needs me. I think he'd do anything he could for me if I asked, because I've gotten under his skin a bit."

But he couldn't tell me that he loved me. He wouldn't tell me about his past. And he couldn't, apparently, live with the evidence of *my* past.

"You've got a good head on your shoulders."

I pulled coffee beans out of the freezer to make a fresh pot. "That's seriously debatable, Dad."

"You're honest with yourself. That's a good trait to have." He gave me a tight smile when I looked over my shoulder at him. "I used your tablet earlier to check my e-mail. It was on the coffee table. I hope you don't mind."

I shook my head. "Help yourself."

"I surfed the Internet while I was on there. Wanted to see what popped up about Cross."

My heart sank a little. "You don't like him."

"I'm withholding judgment." My dad's voice faded as he moved into the living room, then strengthened again as he returned with my tablet in hand.

As I ground the beans, he flipped open the tablet's protective case and started tapping at the screen.

"I had a hard time getting a bead on him last night. I just wanted a little more information. I found some pictures of the two of you together that looked promising." His gaze was on the screen. "Then I found something else."

He turned the tablet around to face me. "Can you explain this to me? Is this another sister of his?"

Leaving the ground coffee to sit, I moved closer, my eyes on the article my dad had found on Page Six. The picture was of Gideon and Corinne at some sort of cocktail party. He had his arm around her waist, and their body language was familiar and intimate. He was very close to her, his lips nearly touching her temple. She had a drink in her hand and was laughing.

I picked up the tablet and read the caption: *Gideon Cross, CEO of Cross Industries, and Corinne Giroux at the Kingsman Vodka publicity mixer.*

My fingers shook as I scrolled to the top of the page and read the brief article, searching for more information. I went numb when I saw the mixer had been Thursday, from six to nine, at one of Gideon's properties—one I knew all too well. He'd fucked me there, just as he'd fucked dozens of women there.

Gideon had stood me up for our appointment with Dr. Petersen to take Corinne to his fuck-pad hotel.

That was what he'd wanted to tell the detectives that he didn't want me to hear: His alibi was an evening—maybe the whole night—spent with another woman.

Setting the tablet down with more care than necessary, I released the breath I'd been holding. "That's not his sister."

"I didn't think so."

I looked at him. "Could you do me a favor and finish making the coffee? I have a call to make."

"Sure. Then I'm going to grab a shower." He reached over and set his hand on top of mine. "Let's go out and erase this whole morning. Sound good?"

"Sounds perfect."

I grabbed the phone off its base and went back to my bedroom. I hit the speed dial for Gideon's cell and waited for him to pick up. Three rings later, he did.

"Cross," he said, although his screen would've told him it was me. "I really can't talk right now."

"Then just listen. I'll time myself. One minute. One goddamn minute of your time. Can you give me that?"

"I really—"

"Did Nathan come to you with photos of me?"

"This isn't—"

"Did he?" I snapped.

"Yes," he bit out.

"Did you look at them?"

There was a long pause, then, "Yes."

I exhaled. "Okay. I think you're a total asshole for letting me go to Dr. Petersen's office when you knew you weren't coming because you were going out with another woman instead. That's just serious douche bag territory, Gideon. And worse, it was a Kingsman event, too, which should've had *some* sentimental value to you, considering that's how—"

There was the abrupt scraping noise of a chair being shoved back. I rushed on, desperate to say what needed to be said before he hung up.

"I think you're a coward for not coming right out and saying we're over, especially before you started fucking around with someone else."

"Eva. Goddamn it."

"But I want you to know that even though the way you've handled this is fucking *wrong* and you've broken my heart into millions of tiny pieces and I've lost all respect for you, I don't blame you for how you feel after seeing those pictures of me. I get it."

"Stop." His voice was little more than a whisper, making me wonder if Corinne was with him even now.

"I don't want you to blame yourself, okay? After what you and I have been through—not that I know what you've been through because you never told me—but anyway . . ." I sighed and winced at how shaky it came out. Worse, when I opened my mouth again, my words were watery with tears. "Don't blame yourself. I don't. I just want you to know that."

"Christ," he breathed. "Please stop, Eva."

"I'm done. I hope you find—" My hand clenched in my lap. "Never mind. Good-bye."

I hung up and dropped the phone on my bed. I stripped off my clothes on the way to the shower and set the ring Gideon had given me on the counter. I turned the water on as hot as I could stand it and sank numbly to the floor of the stall.

I had nothing left.

17

For the rest of Saturday and Sunday, my dad and I bounced all over the city. I made sure he did the food thing, taking him to Junior's for cheesecake, Gray's Papaya for hot dogs, and John's for pizza, which we took back to the apartment to share with Cary. We went up to the top of the Empire State Building, which also satisfied the Statue of Liberty requirement as far as my dad was concerned. We enjoyed a matinee show on Broadway. We walked to Times Square, which was hot and crowded and smelled awful but had some interesting—and a few half-naked—street performers. I snapped pictures with my phone and sent them to Cary for a laugh.

My dad was impressed with the emergency responder presence in the city and liked seeing the police officers on horseback as much as I did. We took a ride around Central Park in a horse-drawn carriage and braved the subway together. I took him to Rockefeller

Center and Macy's and the Crossfire, which he admitted was an impressive building more than capable of holding its own among other impressive buildings. But through it all, we were just hanging out. Mostly walking and talking and simply being together.

I finally learned how he'd met my mom. Her sleek little sports car had gotten a flat tire and she'd ended up at the auto shop where he was working. Their story reminded me of the old Billy Joel hit "Uptown Girl," and I told him so. My dad laughed and said it was one of his favorite songs. He said he could still see her sliding out from behind the wheel of her expensive little toy car and rocking his world. She was the most beautiful thing he'd seen before or since . . . until I came along.

"Do you resent her, Daddy?"

"I used to." He put his arm around my shoulders. "I'm never going to forgive her for not giving you my last name when you were born. But I'm not mad about the money thing anymore. I'd never be able to make her happy in the long run, and she knew herself enough to know that."

I nodded, feeling sorry for all of us.

"And really"—he sighed and rested his cheek against the top of my head for a moment—"as much as I wish I could give you all the things her husbands can, I'm just glad you're getting them. I'm not too proud to appreciate that your life is better because of her choices. And I'm not upset with my lot. I've got a good life that makes me happy and a daughter who makes me so damn proud. I consider my-self a rich man because there's nothing in this world I want that I don't already have."

I stopped walking and hugged him. "I love you, Daddy. I'm so happy you're here."

His arms came around me, and I thought I just might be all right eventually. Both my mom and my dad were living fulfilling lives without the one they loved.

I could do it, too.

I fell into a depression after my dad left. The next few days crawled by. Every day I told myself I wasn't waiting on some sort of contact from Gideon, but when I crawled into bed at night, I cried myself to sleep because another day had ended without a word from him.

The people around me worried. Steven and Mark were overly solicitous at lunch on Wednesday. We went to the Mexican restaurant where Shawna worked, and the three of them tried so hard to make me laugh and enjoy myself. I did, because I loved spending time with all three of them and hated the concern I saw in their eyes, but there was a hole inside me that nothing could fill and a niggling worry about the investigation into Nathan's death.

My mom called me every day, asking if the police had contacted me again—they hadn't—and filling me in if the police had contacted her or Stanton that day.

I worried that they were circling around Stanton, but I had to believe that because my stepfather was obviously innocent, there was nothing for them to find. Still . . . I wondered if they would end up finding anything. It was obviously a homicide or they wouldn't be investigating. With Nathan being new to the city, who did he know who'd want to kill him?

In the back of my mind, I couldn't help but think that Gideon had arranged it. That made it harder for me to get over him, because there was a part of me—the little girl I'd once been—who'd wanted Nathan dead for a long time. Who'd wanted him to hurt like he'd hurt me for years. I'd lost my innocence to him, as well as my virginity. I'd lost my self-esteem and self-respect. And in the end, I'd lost a child in an agonizing miscarriage when I was no more than a child myself.

I got through every day one minute at a time. I forced myself to go to Parker for Krav Maga, to watch TV, to smile and laugh when it was appropriate—most especially around Cary—and to get up every morning and face a new day. I tried to ignore how dead I felt inside. Nothing was vivid to me beyond the pain that throbbed through me like a constant dull ache. I lost weight and slept a lot without feeling rested.

On Thursday, Day Six After Gideon: Round Two, I left a message with Dr. Petersen's receptionist letting her know that Gideon and I wouldn't be coming to our sessions anymore. That evening, I had Clancy swing by Gideon's apartment building, and I left the ring he'd given me and the key to his apartment in a sealed envelope with the front desk. I didn't leave a note because I'd said everything I had to say.

On Friday, one of the other junior account managers got an assistant, and Mark asked if I'd help the new hire get settled. His name was Will and I liked him right away. He had dark hair that was curly but worn short. He had long sideburns and wore square-framed glasses that were very flattering on him. He drank soda instead of coffee and was still dating his high school sweetheart.

I spent much of the morning showing him around the offices.

"You like it here," he said.

"I love it here." I smiled.

Will smiled back. "I'm glad. I wasn't sure at first. You didn't seem all that enthusiastic, even when you were saying good stuff."

"My bad. I'm going through a tough breakup." I tried to shrug it off. "It's hard for me to get excited about anything right now, even things I'm crazy about. This job being one of them."

"I'm sorry about the breakup," he said, his dark eyes warm with sympathy.

"Yeah. Me, too."

Cary was looking and feeling better by Saturday. His ribs were still bandaged and his arm was going to be in a cast for a while, but he was walking around on his own and didn't need the nurse anymore.

My mom brought a beauty team over to our apartment—six women in white lab coats who appropriated my living room. Cary was in heaven. He had no qualms whatsoever about enjoying spa day. My mom looked tired, which wasn't like her at all. I knew she was worried about Stanton. And she was maybe spending time thinking about my dad, too. It seemed impossible to me that she wouldn't, after seeing him for the first time in nearly twenty-five years. His longing for her had been hot and alive to me; I couldn't imagine what it must have felt like to her.

As for me, it was just great to be around two people who loved me and knew me well enough not to bring up Gideon or give me a hard time for being a bummer to hang around with. My mom brought me a box of my favorite Knipschildt truffles, which I savored slowly. It was the one indulgence she never scolded me about. Even she agreed that a woman had a right to chocolate.

"What are you going to have done?" Cary asked me, looking at me with a bunch of black goop smeared all over his face. He was getting his hair trimmed in its usual sexily floppy style, and his toenails were being trimmed and filed into perfect rounded squares.

I licked the chocolate off my fingers and considered my answer. The last time we'd had a spa date, I'd just agreed to have an affair with Gideon. He and I were going on our first date, and I knew we'd be having sex. I'd chosen a package designed for seduction, making my skin soft and fragrant with scents purported to have aphrodisiac properties.

Everything was different now. In a way, I had a second chance to do things over. The investigation into Nathan's death was a concern for us all, but the fact that he was gone from my life forever liberated me in a way I hadn't realized I'd needed. Somewhere in the back of my mind, the fear must have been lurking there. It was always a possibility that I could see him again as long as he was alive. Now I was free.

I also had a new chance to embrace my New York life in a way I hadn't before. I was accountable to no one. I could go anywhere with anyone. *I* could *be* anyone. Who was the Eva Tramell who lived in Manhattan and had her dream job at an advertising agency? I didn't know yet. Up until now, I'd been the San Diego transplant who got swept into the orbit of an enigmatic and incredibly powerful man. *That* Eva was on Day Eight After Gideon: Round Two curled in a corner licking her wounds and would be for a long time. Maybe forever, because I couldn't imagine that I'd ever fall in love again like I had with Gideon. For better or worse, he was my soul mate. The other half of me. In many ways, he was my reflection.

"Eva?" Cary prodded, studying me.

"I want everything done," I said decisively. "I want a new haircut. Something short and flirty and chic. I want my nails painted fire engine red—fingers and toes. I want to be a new Eva."

Cary's brows rose. "Nails, yes. Hair, maybe. You shouldn't make sweeping decisions when you're fucked up over a guy. They come back to haunt you."

My chin lifted. "I'm doing it, Cary Taylor. You can either help or just shut up and watch."

"Eva!" My mother practically squealed. "You're going to look amazing! I know just the thing to do with your hair. You'll *love* it!"

Cary's lips twitched. "All righty, then, baby girl. Let's see what New Eva looks like."

NEW Eva turned out to be a modern, slightly edgy sexpot. My once long, straight blond hair was now shoulder length and cut in long layers, with platinum highlights sprinkled throughout and framing my face. I'd had my makeup done, too, to see what sort of look I should pair with my new hairdo, and I learned that smoky gray for my eyes was the way to go, along with soft pink lip gloss.

In the end, I hadn't gone with red for my nails and chose chocolate instead. I really liked it. For now, anyway. I was willing to admit I might be going through a phase.

"Okay, I take it back," Cary said, whistling. "Clearly you wear breakups well."

"See?" my mother crowed, grinning. "I told you! Now you look like an urban sophisticate."

"Is that what you call it?" I studied my reflection, amazed at the transformation. I appeared a bit older. Definitely more polished. Certainly sexier. It boosted my spirits to see someone else looking back at me besides the hollow-eyed young woman I'd been seeing for nearly two weeks now. Somehow, my thinner face and sad eyes paired well with the bolder style.

My mom insisted we go out for dinner since we all looked so good. She called Stanton and told him to get ready for a night out, and I could tell from her end of the conversation that she was delighting him with her girlish excitement. She left it to him to pick the place and make the arrangements, then continued with my makeover by picking a little black dress out of my closet. As I slipped it on, she held up one of my ivory cocktail dresses.

"Go for it," I told her, finding it amusing and pretty amazing that my mother could pull off wearing the clothes of someone nearly twenty years younger.

When we were set, she went to Cary's room and helped him get ready.

I watched from the doorway as my mother fussed over him, talking the whole time in that way she had that didn't require reciprocal conversation. Cary stood there with a sweet smile on his face, his eyes following her around the room with something like joy.

Her hands brushed over his broad shoulders, smoothing the pressed linen of his dress shirt, and then she expertly knotted his tie and stepped back to take in her handiwork. The sleeve on his casted arm was unbuttoned and rolled up, and his face still had yellow and purple bruising, but nothing could detract from the overall effect of Cary Taylor dressed for a casually elegant night out.

My mother's smile lit up the room. "Stunning, Cary. Simply stunning."

"Thank you."

Stepping forward, she kissed him on the cheek. "Almost as beautiful on the outside as you are on the inside."

I watched him blink and look at me, his green eyes filled with confusion. I leaned into the doorjamb and said, "Some of us can see right through you, Cary Taylor. Those gorgeous looks don't fool us. We know you've got that big beautiful heart inside you."

"Come on!" my mom said, grabbing both of our hands and pulling us out of the room.

When we made it down to the lobby level, we found Stanton's limousine waiting. My stepfather climbed out of the back and wrapped his arms around my mom, pressing a gentle kiss to her cheek because he knew she wouldn't want to mess up her lipstick. Stanton was an attractive man, with snow white hair and denim blue eyes. His face bore some traces of his years, but he was still a very attractive man, one who stayed fit and active.

"Eva!" He hugged me, too, and kissed my cheek. "You look ravishing."

I smiled, not quite sure whether being "ravishing" meant I looked like I was going to ravish someone or was waiting to be ravished.

Stanton shook Cary's hand and gave him a gentle slap to the shoulder. "It's good to see you back on your feet, young man. You gave us all a scare."

"Thank you. For everything."

"No thanks necessary," Stanton said, waving it off. "Ever."

My mom took a deep breath, then let it out. Her eyes were bright as she watched Stanton. She caught me looking at her and smiled, and it was a peaceful smile.

We ended up at a private club with a big band and two excellent singers—one male and one female. They switched frequently throughout the evening, providing the perfect accompaniment to a candlelit meal served in a high-backed velvet booth right out of a classic Manhattan society photo. I couldn't help but be charmed.

Between dinner and dessert, Cary asked me to dance. We'd taken formal dance classes together, at my mother's insistence, but we had to take it easy with Cary's injuries. We basically just swayed in place, enjoying the contentment that came from ending a happy day with a good meal shared with loved ones.

"Look at them," Cary said, watching Stanton expertly lead my mom around the dance floor. "He's crazy about her."

"Yes. And she's good for him. They give each other what they need."

He looked down at me. "You thinking about your dad?"

"A little." I reached up and ran my fingers through his hair, thinking of longer and darker strands that felt like thick silk. "I never really thought of myself as romantic. I mean, I like romance and grand gestures and that tipsy feeling you get when you're crushing hard on someone. But the whole Prince Charming fantasy and marrying the love of your life wasn't my thing."

"You and me, baby girl, we're too jaded. We just want mindblowing sex with someone who knows we're fucked up and accepts it."

My mouth twisted wryly. "Somewhere along the way, I deluded myself into thinking Gideon and I could have it all. That being in love was all we needed. I guess because I never really thought I'd ever fall in love like that, and there's the whole myth that when you do, you're supposed to live happily ever after."

Cary pressed his lips to my brow. "I'm sorry, Eva. I know you're hurting. I wish I could fix it."

"I don't know why it never occurred to me to just find someone I can be happy with."

"Too bad we don't want to bang each other. We'd be perfect."

I laughed and leaned my cheek against his heart.

When the song ended, we pulled apart and started toward our table. I felt fingers circle my wrist and turned my head—

I found myself looking into the eyes of Christopher Vidal Jr., Gideon's half brother.

"I'd like to have the next dance," he said, his mouth curved in a boyish grin. There was no sign of the malicious man I'd witnessed on a secret video Cary had captured during a garden party at the Vidal residence.

Cary stepped forward, looking at me for cues.

My first instinct was to refuse Christopher, and then I looked around. "Are you here alone?"

"Does it matter?" He tugged me into his arms. "You're the one I want to dance with. I've got her," he said to Cary, sweeping me off.

We'd first met just like this, with him asking me to dance. I'd been on my first date with Gideon, and things had already begun falling apart at that point.

"You look fantastic, Eva. I love your hair."

I managed a tight smile. "Thank you."

"Relax," he said. "You're so stiff. I won't bite."

"Sorry. Just want to be sure I don't offend whoever you're here with."

"Just my parents and the manager of a singer who'd like to sign with Vidal Records."

"Ah." My smile widened into one more genuine. That was just what I was hoping to hear.

As we danced, I kept searching the room. I saw it as a sign when the song ended and Elizabeth Vidal stood, catching my eye. She excused herself from her table and I excused myself from Christopher, who protested.

"I have to freshen up," I told him.

"All right. But I insist on buying you a drink when you come back."

I took off after his mother, debating whether I should just come out and tell Christopher I thought he was a total asswipe of epic proportions. I didn't know if Magdalene had told him about the video, and if she hadn't, I figured there was probably a good reason why.

I waited for Elizabeth just outside the bathroom. When she reappeared, she spotted me hanging out in the hallway and smiled. Gideon's mother was a beautiful woman, with long straight black hair and the same amazing blue eyes as her son and Ireland. Just looking at her made my heart hurt. I missed Gideon so much. It was an hourly battle with myself not to contact him and take whatever I could get.

"Eva." She greeted me with air kisses for each of my cheeks.

"Christopher said it was you. I didn't recognize you at first. You look so different with your hair like that. I think it's lovely."

"Thanks. I need to talk to you. Privately."

"Oh?" She frowned. "Is something wrong? Is it Gideon?"

"Come on." I gestured deeper down the hallway, toward the emergency exit.

"What's this about?"

Once we were away from the bathrooms, I told her. "Remember when Gideon was a child and he told you he'd been abused or violated?"

Her face paled. "He told you about that?"

"No. But I've witnessed his nightmares. His horrible, ugly, vicious nightmares where he begs for mercy." My voice was low but throbbed with anger. It was all I could do to keep my hands to myself as she stood there looking both embarrassed and militant. "It was your job to protect and support him!"

Her chin went up. "You don't know—"

"You're not to blame for what happened before you knew." I got in her face, felt satisfaction when she took a step back. "But anything that happened after he told you is entirely your fault."

"Fuck you," she spat at me. "You have no idea what you're talking about. How dare you come up to me like this and say these things to me when you're clueless!"

"Yeah, I dare. Your son is seriously damaged by what happened to him, and your refusal to believe him made it a million times worse."

"You think I would tolerate the abuse of my own child?" Her face was flushed with anger and her eyes too bright. "I had Gideon examined by two separate pediatricians to look for . . . trauma. I did everything I could be expected to do."

"Except believe him. Which is what you should've done as his mother."

"I'm Christopher's mother, too, and he was there. He swears nothing happened. Who was I supposed to believe when there was no proof? No one could find anything to support Gideon's claims."

"He shouldn't have had to provide proof. He was a child!" The anger I felt was vibrating through me. My fists were clenched against the urge to hit her. Not just for what Gideon had lost, but for what we'd lost together. "You were supposed to take his side no matter what."

"Gideon was a troubled boy, struggling through therapy over his father's death, and desperate for attention. You don't know what he was like then."

"I know what he's like now. He's broken and hurting and doesn't think he's worth loving. And you helped make him that way."

"Go to hell." She stormed off.

"I'm already there," I shouted after her. "And so is your son."

I spent all day Sunday being Old Eva.

Trey had the day off and took Cary out for brunch and a movie. I was pleased to see them together, thrilled that they were both trying. Cary hadn't invited over any of the people who called his cell, and I wondered if he was rethinking his friendships. I suspected many were of the fair-weather variety—great fun but no substance.

Having the entire apartment to myself, I slept too much, ate crappy food, and never bothered to change out of my pajamas. I cried over Gideon in the privacy of my room, staring at the collage of photos that used to be on my desk at work. I missed the weight of his ring on my finger and the sound of his voice. I missed the feel of his hands and lips on me and the tenderly possessive way he took care of me.

When Monday came around, I left the apartment as New Eva. With smoky eyes, pink lips, and my new bouncy layered cut, I felt like I could pretend to be someone else for the day. Someone who wasn't heartbroken and lost and angry.

I saw the Bentley when I stepped outside, but Angus didn't bother to exit the car, knowing I wouldn't accept a ride. It puzzled me that Gideon would have him wasting his time hanging around, just in case I might have him drive me somewhere. It didn't make any sense unless Gideon was feeling guilty. I hated guilt, hated that it afflicted so many of the people in my life. I wish they'd just drop it and move on. Like I was trying to do.

The morning at Waters Field & Leaman went by swiftly, because I had Will, the new assistant, to help out as well as my regular work to do. I was glad that he wasn't afraid to ask lots of questions, because he kept me too busy to count the seconds, minutes, and hours since the last time I'd seen Gideon.

"You look good, Eva," Mark said when I first joined him in his office. "Are you doing all right?"

"Not really. But I'll get there."

He leaned forward, setting his elbows on his desk. "Steven and I broke up once, about a year and a half into our relationship. We'd had a rough couple weeks and decided it'd be easier to let it go. It was fucking awful," he said vehemently. "I hated every minute of it. Getting up every morning was a monumental feat and he was in the same shape. So anyway . . . if you need anything . . . "

"Thank you. The best thing you can do for me right now is keep me busy. I just don't want any time to think about anything but work."

"I can do that."

When lunch came around, Will and I grabbed Megumi and we headed to a nearby pizza place. Megumi filled me in on her growing relationship with her blind date, and Will told us about his adventures at Ikea as he and his girlfriend worked on filling their loft apartment with do-it-yourself furniture. I was glad I had my spa day to talk about.

"We're heading to the Hamptons this weekend," Megumi said as we returned to the Crossfire. "My guy's grandparents have a place out there. How cool is that?"

"Very." I passed through the turnstiles beside her. "I'm jealous you'll be able to get away from the heat."

"I know, right?"

"Better than furniture assembly," Will muttered, following a group of people onto one of the elevators. "I can't wait 'til we're done."

The doors started to close, and then they slid open again. Gideon stepped into the car after us. The familiar, palpable energy that always coursed between us hit me hard. Awareness rippled down my spine and flared outward, sending goose bumps racing across my skin. The hair on my nape prickled.

Megumi glanced at me, and I shook my head. I knew better than to look directly at him. I couldn't be sure I wouldn't do something rash or desperate. I craved him so deeply, and it had been too long since he'd held me. I used to have the right to touch him, to reach for his hand, to lean into him, to sift my fingers through his hair. It was a horrible ache inside me that I wasn't allowed to do those things anymore. I had to bite my lip to stifle a moan of agony at being this close to him again.

I kept my head down, but I *felt* Gideon's eyes on me. I continued talking to my co-workers, forcing myself to focus on the discussion of furniture and the compromises necessary for cohabiting with someone of the opposite sex.

As the car continued its ascent and frequent stops, the number of people in the car dwindled. I was acutely attuned to where Gideon was, aware that he never took elevators this crowded, suspecting and hoping and praying that he'd just wanted to see me, be with me, even if it was only in this terribly impersonal way.

When we arrived on the twentieth floor, I took a deep breath and prepared to step out, hating the inevitable separation from the one thing in the world that made me feel truly alive.

The doors opened.

"Wait."

My eyes closed. I was stopped by the softly rasped command. I knew I should keep going as if I hadn't heard him. I knew it was just going to hurt so much worse if I gave him any more of myself, even a minute more of my life. But how could I possibly resist? I'd never been able to when it came to Gideon.

I stepped aside so that my co-workers could exit. Will frowned when I didn't follow, confused, but Megumi tugged him out. The doors closed.

I moved into the corner, my heart pounding. Gideon waited on the opposite side, radiating expectation and demand. As we climbed to the top floor, my body responded to his near-tangible need. My breasts swelled and became heavy; my sex grew slick and swollen. I was greedy for him. Needful. My breathing quickened.

He hadn't even touched me and I was nearly panting with desire.

The elevator glided to a stop. Gideon pulled the key out of his pocket and plugged it into the panel, suspending the car. Then he came to me.

There were only inches between us. I kept my head bowed and stared at his gleaming oxfords. I heard his breathing, deep and quick like mine. I smelled the subtly masculine scent of his skin, and my pulse leaped.

"Turn around, Eva."

A shiver moved through me at the familiar and beloved authoritative tone. Closing my eyes, I turned, then gasped as he immediately pressed against my back, flattening me to the wall of the car. His fingers linked with mine, holding my hands up by my shoulders.

"You're so beautiful," he breathed, nuzzling into my hair. "It hurts to look at you."

"Gideon. What are you doing?"

I felt his hunger pouring off him, enveloping me. His powerful frame was hard and hot, and vibrating with tension. He was aroused, his thick cock a firm pressure I couldn't stop myself from grinding into. I wanted him. I wanted him inside me. Filling me. Completing me. I'd been so empty without him.

He took a deep shuddering breath. His fingers flexed restlessly between mine, as if he wanted to touch me elsewhere but restrained himself.

I felt the ring I'd given him digging into my flesh. I turned my head to look at it and tensed when I saw it, confused and agonized.

"Why?" I whispered. "What do you want from me? An orgasm? You want to fuck me, Gideon? Is that it? Blow your load inside me?"

His breath hissed out at having those crude words thrown back in his face. "Don't."

"Don't call it what it is?" I closed my eyes. "Fine. Just do it. But don't put that ring on and act like this is something it's not."

"I never take it off. I won't. *Ever.*" His right hand released mine and he reached into his pocket. I watched as he slid the ring he'd given me back onto my finger, and then he lifted my hand to his mouth. He kissed it, then pressed his lips—quick, hard, angry—to my temple.

"Wait," he snapped.

Then he was gone. The car began its descent. My right hand curled into a fist and I backed away from the wall, breathing hard.

Wait. For what?

18

W<small>HEN I EXITED</small> the elevator on the twentieth floor, I was dry-eyed and determined. Megumi buzzed me through the security doors and pushed to her feet. "Is everything all right?"

I stopped by her desk. "I have no fucking clue. That man is a total head trip."

Her brows rose. "Keep me posted."

"I should just write a book," I muttered, resuming my walk back to my cubicle and wondering why in hell everyone was so interested in my dating life.

When I got to my desk, I dropped my purse in the drawer and sat down to call Cary.

"Hey," I said, when he answered. "If you get bored—"

"If?" He snorted.

"Remember that folder of information you compiled on Gideon? Can you make me one of those on Dr. Terrence Lucas?"

"Okay. Do I know this guy?"

"No. He's a pediatrician."

There was a pause, then, "Are you pregnant?"

"No! Jeez. And if I were, I'd need an obstetrician."

"Whew. All right. Spell his name for me."

I gave Cary what he needed, then looked up Dr. Lucas's office and made an appointment to see him. "I won't need to fill out any new-patient paperwork," I told the receptionist. "I just want a quick consult."

After that, I called Vidal Records and left a message for Christopher to call me.

When Mark came back from lunch, I went over and knocked on his open door. "Hey. I need to ask for an hour in the morning for an appointment. Is it all right if I come in at ten and stay 'til six?"

"Ten to five is fine, Eva." He looked at me carefully. "Everything okay?"

"Getting better every day."

"Good." He smiled. "I'm really glad to hear that."

We dived back into work, but thoughts of Gideon weighed heavily on my mind. I kept staring at my ring, remembering what he had said when he'd first given it to me: *The Xs are me holding on to you.*

Wait. For him? For him to come back to me? Why? I couldn't understand why he'd cut me off the way he had, then expected me to take him back. Especially with Corinne in the picture.

I spent the rest of the afternoon going over the last few weeks in my mind, recalling conversations I'd had with Gideon, things he'd said or done, searching for answers. When I left the Crossfire at the end of the day, I saw the Bentley waiting out front and waved at Angus, who smiled back. I had issues with his boss, but Angus wasn't to blame for them.

It was hot and muggy outside. Miserable. I went to the Duane Reade around the corner for a bottle of cold water to drink on the walk home and a bag of mini chocolates to enjoy once I got through my Krav Maga class. When I left the drugstore, Angus was waiting just outside the door at the curb, shadowing me. As I turned the corner back toward the Crossfire to start the trip home, I saw Gideon step out to the street with Corinne. His hand was at the small of her back, leading her toward a sleek black Mercedes sedan I recognized as one of his. She was smiling. His expression was inscrutable.

Horrified, I couldn't move or look away. I stood there in the middle of the crowded sidewalk, my stomach twisting with grief and anger and a terrible, awful feeling of betrayal.

He looked up and saw me, freezing in place just as I had. The Latino driver I'd met the day my father arrived opened the back door and Corinne disappeared into the car. Gideon remained where he was, his gaze locked with mine.

There was no way he missed me lifting my hand and flipping him the bird.

Abruptly, I was struck by a thought.

I turned my back to Gideon and moved off to the side, digging into my purse for my phone. When I found it, I speed-dialed my mom, and when she answered, I said, "That day we went out to lunch with Megumi, you freaked out on the walk back to the Crossfire. You saw him, didn't you? Nathan. You saw Nathan at the Crossfire."

"Yes," she admitted. "That's why Richard decided it would be best to just pay him what he wanted. Nathan said he'd stay away from you as long as he had the money to leave the country. Why do you ask?"

"It didn't hit me until just now that Nathan was the reason why you reacted the way you did." I faced forward again and started walking quickly toward home. The Mercedes was gone, but my temper was rising. "I have to go, Mom. I'll call you later."

"Is everything all right?" she asked anxiously.

"Not yet, but I'm working on it."

"I'm here for you, if you need me."

I sighed. "I know. I'm okay. I love you."

When I got home, Cary was sitting on the couch with his laptop on his thighs and his bare feet on the coffee table.

"Hey," he called, his gaze still on his screen.

I dumped my stuff and kicked off my shoes. "You know what?"

He looked up at me from beneath a lock of hair that had fallen over his eyes. "What?"

"I thought Gideon took a hike because of Nathan. Everything was fine and then it wasn't, and shortly after that the police were telling us about Nathan. I figured one thing was linked to the other."

"Makes sense." He frowned. "I guess."

"But Nathan was at the Crossfire the Monday before you were attacked. I know he was there to see Gideon. I *know* it. Nathan wouldn't go there to see me. Not a place like that with all the security and people I know around."

He sat back. "Okay. So what does that mean?"

"It means Gideon was fine after Nathan." I threw up my hands. "He was fine that whole week. He was more than fine that weekend we took off together. He was fine Monday morning after we got back. Then—*bam*—he lost his fucking mind and went crazy on me Monday night."

"I'm following."

"So what happened on Monday?"

Cary's brows rose. "You're asking me?"

"Grr." I grabbed my hair in my hands. "I'm asking the fucking universe. God. Anyone. What the hell happened to my boyfriend?"

"I thought we agreed you need to ask him."

"I get two answers from him: *Trust me* and *wait*. He gave my ring back today." I showed him my hand. "And he's still wearing the one I gave him. Do you have any idea how confusing that is? They're not just rings, they're promises. They're symbols of ownership and commitment. Why would he still wear his? Why is it so important to him that I wear mine? Does he seriously expect me to wait while he screws Corinne out of his system?"

"Is that what you think he's doing? Really?"

Closing my eyes, I let my head fall back. "No. And I can't decide if that makes me naïve or willfully delusional."

"Does this Dr. Lucas guy have anything to do with this?"

"No." I straightened and joined him on the couch. "Did you find anything?"

"Kind of hard, baby girl, when I don't know what I'm looking for."

"It's just a hunch." I looked at his screen. "What's that?"

"A transcript of an interview with Brett that was done yesterday on a Florida radio station."

"Oh? What are you reading that for?"

"I was listening to 'Golden' and decided to run a search on it, and this came up."

I tried reading, but my angle was bad. "What's it say?"

"He was asked if there's really an Eva out there and he said yes, there is, and he recently reconnected with her and hopes to make it work out a second time."

"What? No way!"

"Yes way." Cary grinned. "So you've got your rebound man lined up if Cross doesn't get his shit together."

I pushed to my feet. "Whatever. I'm hungry. Want something?"

"If your appetite's back, that's a good sign."

"Everything's coming back," I told him. "With a vengeance."

I was waiting at the curb for Angus the next morning. He pulled up and Paul, the doorman for my apartment building, opened the back door for me.

"Good morning, Angus," I greeted him.

"Good morning, Miss Tramell." His gaze met mine in the rearview mirror, and he smiled.

As he started to pull away, I leaned forward between the two front seats. "Do you know where Corinne Giroux lives?"

He glanced at me. "Yes."

I sat back. "That's where I want to go."

CORINNE lived around the corner from Gideon. I was certain that wasn't a coincidence.

I checked in with the front desk and waited twenty minutes before I was given permission to go up to the tenth floor. I rang the bell to her apartment and the door swung open to reveal a flushed and disheveled Corinne in a floor-length black silk robe. She was seriously gorgeous, with her silky black hair and eyes like aquamarines, and she moved with a lithe grace I admired. I'd armored up in my favorite gray sleeveless dress and was very glad I had. She made me feel downright homely.

"Eva," she said breathlessly. "What a surprise."

"I'm sorry to barge in uninvited. I just need to ask you something real quick."

"Oh?" She kept the door partially closed and leaned into the jamb.

"Can I come in?" I asked tightly.

"Uh." She glanced over her shoulder. "It's best if you didn't."

"It doesn't bother me if you have company and I promise, this won't take but a minute."

"Eva." She licked her lips. "How do I say this . . . ?"

My hands were shaking and my stomach was a quivering mess, my brain taunting me with images of Gideon standing naked behind her, their early-morning fuck interrupted by the ex-girlfriend who wouldn't get a clue. I knew how well he liked sex in the morning.

But then I knew him well, period. Knew him enough to say, "Cut the shit, Corinne."

Her eyes widened.

My mouth curved derisively. "Gideon's in love with me. He's not fucking around with you."

She recovered quickly. "He's not fucking around with you, either. I would know, since he's spending all of his free time with me."

Fine. We'd talk about this in the hallway. "I know him. I don't always understand him, but that's a different story. I know he would've told you upfront that you and he weren't going anywhere, because he wouldn't want to lead you on. He hurt you before; he won't do it again."

"This is all very fascinating. Does he know you're here?"

"No, but you'll tell him. And that's fine. I just want to know what you were doing at the Crossfire that day you came out looking as freshly fucked as you do now."

Her smile was razor sharp. "What do you *think* I was doing?"

"Not Gideon," I said decisively, even though I was silently praying that I wasn't making a total idiot out of myself. "You saw me, didn't you? From the lobby, you had a direct view across the street and you saw me coming. Gideon told you at the Waldorf dinner that I was the jealous type. Did you have a nooner with someone from one of the other offices? Or did you muss yourself up before you stepped outside?"

I saw the answer on her face. It was lightning quick, there and gone, but I saw it.

"Both of those suggestions are absurd," she said.

I nodded, savoring a moment of profound relief and satisfaction. "Listen. You're never going to have him the way you want. And I know how that hurts. I've been living it the past two weeks. I'm sorry for you, I really am."

"Fuck you and your pity," she snapped. "Save it for yourself. I'm the one he's spending time with."

"And there's your saving grace, Corinne. If you're paying attention, you know he's hurting right now. Be his friend." I headed back to the elevators and called over my shoulder, "Have a nice day."

She slammed her door shut behind me.

When I got back to the Bentley, I told Angus to take me to Dr. Terrence Lucas's office. He paused in the act of closing the door and stared down at me. "Gideon will be very angry, Eva."

I nodded, understanding the warning. "I'll deal with it when the time comes."

The building that housed Dr. Lucas's private practice was unassuming, but his offices were warm and inviting. The waiting room was paneled in dark wood and the walls covered in a mixture of pictures of infants and children. Parenting magazines covered the tables and were neatly stored in racks, while the dedicated play area was tidy and supervised.

I signed in and took a seat, but I'd barely sat when I was called back by the nurse. I was taken to Dr. Lucas's office, not an exam room, and he rose from his chair when I entered, rounding the desk quickly.

"Eva." He held out his hand and I shook it. "You didn't have to make an appointment."

I managed a smile. "I didn't know how else to reach you."

"Have a seat."

I sat, but he remained standing, choosing to lean back against the desk and grip the edge with both hands. It was a power position, and I wondered why he felt the need to use it with me.

"What can I do for you?" he asked. He had a calm, confident air and a wide, open smile. With his good looks and affable manner, I was sure any mother would have confidence in his skill and integrity.

"Gideon Cross was a patient of yours, wasn't he?"

His face closed instantly and he straightened. "I'm not at liberty to discuss my patients."

"When you gave me that 'not at liberty to discuss' line at the hospital, I didn't put it together, and I should have." My fingertips drummed into the armrest. "You lied to his mother. Why?"

He returned to the other side of his desk, putting the furniture between us. "Did he tell you that?"

"No. I'm figuring this out as I go. Hypothetically speaking, why would you lie about the results of an exam?"

"I wouldn't. You need to leave."

"Oh, come on." I sat back and crossed my legs. "I expect more from you. Where are the assertions that Gideon is a soulless monster bent on corrupting the women of the world?"

"I've done my due diligence and warned you." His gaze was hard, his lip curled in a sneer. He wasn't quite so handsome anymore. "If you continue to throw your life away, there's nothing I can do about it."

"I'm going to figure it out. I just needed to see your face. I had to know if I was right."

"You're not. Cross was never a patient of mine."

"Semantics—his mother consulted you. And while you go about your days seething over the fact that your wife fell in love with him, think about what you did to a small child who needed help." My voice took on an edge as anger surged. I couldn't think about what had happened to Gideon without wanting to do serious violence to anyone who contributed to his pain.

I uncrossed my legs and stood. "What happened between him and your wife happened between two consenting adults. What happened to him as a child was a crime and how you contributed to that is a travesty."

"Get out."

"My pleasure." I yanked the door open and nearly ran into Gideon, who'd been leaning against the wall just outside the office. His hand encircled my upper arm, but his gaze was on Dr. Lucas, icy with fury and hatred.

"Stay away from her," he said harshly.

Lucas's smile was filled with malice. "She came to me."

Gideon's returning smile made me shiver. "You see her coming, I suggest you run in the opposite direction."

"Funny. That's the advice I gave her in regard to you."

I flipped the good doctor the bird.

Snorting, Gideon caught my hand and pulled me back down the hall. "What is it with you and giving people the finger?"

"What? It's a classic."

"You can't just barge in here!" the receptionist snapped as we passed the counter.

He glanced at her. "You can cancel that call to security, we're leaving."

We exited out to the corridor. "Did Angus tattle on me?" I muttered, trying to pry my arm free.

"No. Stop wriggling. All the cars have GPS tracking."

"You're a nut job. You know that?"

He stabbed the elevator button and glared at me. "I am? What about you? You're all over the place. My mother. Corinne. Goddamned Lucas. What the fuck are you doing, Eva?"

"It's none of your business." I lifted my chin. "We broke up, remember?"

His jaw tightened. He stood there in his suit, looking so polished and urbane, while radiating a wild, feverish energy. The contrast between what I saw when I looked at him and what I felt goaded my hunger. I loved that I got to have the man inside the suit. Every delicious, untameable inch of him.

The car arrived and we stepped inside. Excitement sizzled through me. He'd come after me. That made me so hot. He shoved an elevator key into the control panel and I groaned.

"Is there anything you don't own in New York?"

He was on me in an instant, one hand in my hair and the other on my ass, his mouth on mine in a violent kiss. He wasted no time, his tongue thrusting between my lips, plunging deep and hard.

I moaned and gripped his waist, pushing onto my tiptoes to deepen the contact.

His teeth sank into my lower lip with enough force to hurt. "You think you can say a few words and end us? There is no end, Eva."

He flattened me into the side of the car. I was pinned by six feet, two inches of violently aroused male.

"I miss you," I whispered, grabbing his ass and urging him harder against me.

Gideon groaned. "Angel."

He was kissing me: deep, shamelessly desperate kisses that made my toes curl in my pumps.

"What are you doing?" he breathed. "You're going around, stirring up everything."

"I've got time on my hands," I shot back, just as breathless, "since I dumped my asshat boyfriend."

He growled, fiercely passionate, his hand in my hair pulling so tightly it pained me.

"You can't make this up with a kiss or a fuck, Gideon. Not this time." It was so hard to let him go; nearly impossible after the weeks I'd been denied the right and opportunity to touch him. I needed him.

His forehead pressed to mine. "You have to trust me."

I put my hands on his chest and shoved him back. He let me, his gaze searching my face.

"Not when you don't talk to me." I reached over, pulled the key from the control panel, and held it out to him. The car began its descent. "You put me through hell. On purpose. Made me suffer. And there's no end in sight. I don't know what the fuck you're doing, ace, but this Dr. Jekyll and Mr. Hyde shit ain't cutting it with me."

His hand went into his pocket, his movements leisurely and controlled, which was when he was at his most dangerous. "You're completely unmanageable."

"When I've got clothes on. Get used to it." The car doors opened and I stepped out. His hand went to the small of my back, and a shiver moved through me. That innocuous touch, through layers of material, had been inciting lust in me from the very first. "You put your hand on Corinne's back like this again, and I'm breaking your fingers."

"You know I don't want anyone else," he murmured. "I can't. I'm consumed with wanting you."

Both the Bentley and the Mercedes were waiting at the curb. The sky had darkened while I'd been inside, as if it were brooding along with the man beside me. There was a weighted expectation in the air, an early sign of a gathering summer storm.

I stopped beneath the entrance overhang and looked at Gideon. "Make them ride together. You and I need to talk."

"That was the plan."

Angus touched the brim of his hat and slid behind the wheel. The other driver walked up to Gideon and handed him a set of keys.

"Miss Tramell," he said, by way of greeting.

"Eva, this is Raúl."

"We meet again," I said. "Did you pass on my message last time?"

Gideon's fingers flexed against my back. "He did."

I beamed. "Thank you, Raúl."

Raúl went around to the front passenger side of the Bentley, while Gideon escorted me to the Mercedes and opened the door for me. I felt a little thrill as he got behind the wheel and adjusted the seat to accommodate his long legs. He started the engine and merged into traffic, expertly and confidently navigating the powerful car through the craziness of New York city streets.

"Watching you drive makes me want you," I told him, noting how his easy grip on the wheel tightened.

"Christ." He glanced at me. "You have a transportation fetish."

"I have a Gideon fetish." My voice lowered. "It's been weeks."

"And I hate every second of it. This is torment for me, Eva. I can't focus. I can't sleep. I lose my temper at the slightest irritants. I'm in hell without you."

I never wanted him to suffer, but I'd be lying if I said it didn't make my own misery better knowing he was missing me as much as I was missing him.

I twisted in my seat to face him. "Why are you doing this to us?"

"I had an opportunity and I took it." His jaw firmed. "This separation is the price. It won't last forever. I need you to be patient."

I shook my head. "No, Gideon. I can't. Not anymore."

"You're *not* leaving me. I won't let you."

"I've already left. Don't you see that? I'm living my life and you're not in it."

"I'm in it every way I can be right now."

"By having Angus following me around? Come on. That's not a relationship." I leaned my cheek against the seat. "Not one I want anyway."

"Eva." He exhaled harshly. "My silence is the lesser of two evils. I feel like whether I explain or not, I'll drive you away, but explaining carries the greatest risk. You think you want to know, but if I tell you, you'll regret it. Trust me when I say there are some aspects of me you don't want to see."

"You have to give me something to work with." I set my hand on his thigh and felt the muscle bunch, then twitch in response to my touch. "I've got nothing right now. I'm empty."

He set his hand over mine. "You trust me. Despite what you see to the contrary, you've come to trust in what you know. That's huge, Eva. For both of us. For us, period."

"There is no us."

"Stop saying that."

"You wanted my blind trust and you have it, but that's all I can give you. You've shared so little of yourself and I've lived with it because I had you. And now I don't—"

"You have me," he protested.

"Not the way I need you." I lifted one shoulder in an awkward shrug. "You've given me your body and I've been greedy with it, because that's the only way you're really open to me. And now I don't have that, and when I look at what I do have, it's just promises. It's not enough for me. In the absence of you, all I have is a pile of things you won't tell me."

He stared straight ahead, his profile rigid. I pulled my hand out from under his and twisted the other way, giving him my back while I looked out the window at the teeming city.

"If I lose you, Eva," he said hoarsely, "I have nothing. Everything I've done is so I don't lose you."

"I need more." I rested my forehead against the glass. "If I can't have you on the outside, I need to have you on the inside, but you've never let me in."

We drove in silence, crawling along through the morning traffic. A fat drop of rain hit the windshield, followed by another.

"After my dad died," he said softly, "I had a hard time dealing with the changes. I remember that people liked him, liked being around him. He was making everyone rich, right? And then suddenly the world flipped on its head and everyone hated him. My mother, who'd been so happy all the time, was crying nonstop. And she and my dad were fighting every day. That's what I remember most—the constant yelling and screaming."

I looked at him, studying his stony profile, but I didn't say anything, afraid to lose the moment.

"She remarried right away. We moved out of the city. She got pregnant. I never knew when I'd run across someone my dad had fucked over, and I took a lot of shit for it from other kids. From their parents. Teachers. It was big news. To this day, people still talk about my dad and what he did. I was so angry. At everyone. I had tantrums all the time. I broke things."

He stopped at a light, breathing heavily. "After Christopher came along, I got worse, and when he was five, he imitated me, pitching a fit at dinner and shoving his plate across the table and onto the floor. My mom was pregnant with Ireland then, and she and Vidal decided it was time to put me into therapy."

Tears slid down my face at the picture he painted of the child he'd once been—scared and hurting and feeling like an outsider in his mom's new life.

"They came out to the house—the shrink and a doctoral candidate she was supervising. It started out all right. They both were nice, attractive, patient. But soon the shrink was spending most of the time counseling my mother, who was having a difficult pregnancy in addition to two young boys who were out of control. I was left alone with him more and more frequently."

Gideon pulled over and put the car into park. His hands gripped the wheel with white-knuckled force, his throat working. The steady patter of rain softened, leaving us alone with our painful truths.

"You don't have to tell me any more," I whispered, unbuckling my seat belt and reaching out to him. I touched his face with fingertips damp with my tears.

His nostrils flared on a sharply indrawn breath. "He made me come. Every goddamned time, he wouldn't stop until I came, so he could say I liked it."

I kicked off my shoes and pulled his hand away from the wheel so I could straddle his lap and hold him. His grip on me was excruciatingly tight, but I didn't complain. We were on an insanely busy street, with endless cars rumbling past on one side and a crush of pedestrians on the other, but neither of us cared. He was shaking violently, as if he were sobbing uncontrollably, but he made no sound and shed no tears.

The sky cried for him, the rain coming down hard and angry, steaming off the ground.

Holding his head in my hands, I pressed my wet face to his. "Hush, baby. I understand. I know how that feels, the way they gloat afterward. And the shame and confusion and guilt you felt. It's not your fault. You didn't want it. You didn't enjoy it."

"I let him touch me at first," he whispered. "He said it was my age . . . hormones . . . I needed to masturbate and I'd be calmer. Less angry all the time. He touched me, said he'd show me how to do it right. That I was doing it wrong—"

"Gideon, no." I pulled back to look at him, imagining in my mind how it would develop from that point on, all the things that would have been said to make it seem like Gideon was the instigator in his own rape. "You were a child in the hands of an adult who knew all the right buttons to push. They want to make it our fault so they have no culpability in their crime, but it's not true."

His eyes were huge and dark in his pale face. I pressed my lips gently to his, tasting my tears. "I love you. And I believe you. And none of this was your fault."

Gideon's hands were in my hair, holding me in place as he ravaged my mouth with desperate kisses. "Don't leave me."

"Leave you? I'm going to marry you."

He inhaled sharply. Then he pulled me closer, his hands careless and rough as they slid over me.

Impatient rapping against the window made me jerk in surprise. A cop in rain gear and safety vest looked at us through the untinted front window, scowling at us from beneath the brim of her hat. "You've got thirty seconds to move on or I'll cite you both for public indecency."

Embarrassed, my face flaming, I climbed back into my seat, sprawling in an ungraceful tumble. Gideon waited until I had my seat belt on, then put the car in drive. He tapped his brow in a salute to the officer, and pulled back out into traffic.

Reaching for my hand, he lifted it to his lips and kissed my fingertips. "I love you."

322 · SYLVIA DAY

I froze, my heart pounding.

Linking our fingers together, he set them on his thigh. The windshield wipers slid from side to side, their rhythmic tempo mocking the racing of my pulse.

Swallowing hard, I whispered, "Say that again."

He slowed at a light. Turning his head, Gideon looked at me. He looked weary, as if all his usual pulsing energy had been expended and he was running on fumes. But his eyes were warm and bright, the curve of his mouth loving and hopeful. "I love you. Still not the right word, but I know you want to hear it."

"I need to hear it," I agreed softly.

"As long as you understand the difference." The light changed and he drove on. "People get over love. They can live without it, they can move on. Love can be lost and found again. But that won't happen for me. I won't survive you, Eva."

My breath caught at the look on his face when he glanced at me.

"I'm obsessed with you, angel. Addicted to you. You're everything I've ever wanted or needed, everything I've ever dreamed of. You're *everything*. I live and breathe you. For you."

I placed my other hand over our joined ones. "There's so much out there for you. You just don't know it yet."

"I don't need anything else. I get out of bed every morning and face the world because you're in it." He turned the corner and pulled up in front of the Crossfire behind the Bentley. He killed the engine, released his seat belt, and took a deep breath. "Because of you, the world makes sense to me in a way it didn't before. I have a place now, with you."

Suddenly I understood why he'd worked so hard, why he was so insanely successful at such a young age. He'd been driven to find his place in the world, to be more than an outsider.

His fingertips brushed across my cheek. I'd missed that touch so much, my heart bled at feeling it again.

"When are you coming back to me?" I asked softly.

"As soon as I can." Leaning forward, he pressed his lips to mine. "Wait."

19

WHEN I GOT to my desk, I found a voice mail from Christopher. I debated for a moment whether I should continue to pursue the truth. Christopher wasn't a man I wanted to invite any deeper into my life.

But I was haunted by the look that had been on Gideon's face when he told me about his past, and the sound of his voice, so hoarse with remembered shame and agony.

I felt his pain like my own.

In the end, there was no other choice. I returned Christopher's call and asked him out to lunch.

"Lunch with a beautiful woman?" There was a smile in his voice. "Absolutely."

"Any time you have free this week would be great."

"How about today?" he suggested. "I occasionally get a craving for that deli you took me to."

"Works for me. Noon?"

We set the time and I hung up just as Will stopped by my cubicle. He gave me puppy-dog eyes and said, "Help."

I managed a smile. "Sure."

The two hours flew by. When noon rolled around, I went downstairs and found Christopher waiting in the lobby. His auburn hair was a wild mess of short, loose waves and his grayish-green eyes sparkled. Wearing black slacks and a white dress shirt rolled up at the sleeves, he looked confident and attractive. He greeted me with his boyish grin, and it struck me then—I couldn't ask him about what he'd said to his mother long ago. He'd been a child himself, living in a dysfunctional home.

"I'm stoked you called me," he said. "But I have to admit, I'm curious about why. I'm wondering if it has anything to do with Gideon getting back together with Corinne."

That hurt. Terribly. I had to suck in a deep breath, then release my tension with it. I knew better. I had no doubts. But I was honest enough to admit that I wanted ownership of Gideon. I wanted to claim him, possess him, have everyone know that he was *mine*.

"Why do you hate him so much?" I asked, preceding him through the revolving doors. Thunder rumbled in the distance, but the hot, driving rain had ceased, leaving the streets awash in dirty water.

He joined me on the sidewalk and set his hand at the small of my back. It sent a shiver of revulsion through me. "Why? You want to exchange notes?"

"Sure. Why not?"

By the time lunch was over, I'd gotten a pretty good idea of what fueled Christopher's hatred. All he cared about was the man he saw in the mirror. Gideon was more handsome, richer, more powerful, more confident . . . just *more*. And Christopher was obviously being eaten alive by jealousy. His memories of Gideon were colored by the belief that Gideon had received all the attention as a child. Which might have been true, considering how troubled he was. Worse, the sibling rivalry had crossed over into their professional lives when Cross Industries acquired a majority share of Vidal Records. I made a mental note to ask Gideon why he'd done that.

We stopped outside the Crossfire to part ways. A taxi racing through a huge puddle sent a plume of foaming water right at me. Swearing under my breath, I dodged the spray and almost stumbled into Christopher.

"I'd like to take you out sometime, Eva. Dinner, perhaps?"

"I'll get in touch," I hedged. "My roommate's really sick right now and I need to be around for him as much as possible."

"You've got my number." He smiled and kissed the back of my hand, a gesture I'm sure he thought was charming. "And I'll keep in touch."

I made my way through the Crossfire's revolving doors and headed for the turnstiles.

One of the black-suited security guards at the desk stopped me. "Miss Tramell." He smiled. "Could you come with me, please?"

Curious, I followed him to the security office where I'd originally gotten my employee badge when I was hired. He opened the door for me, and Gideon was waiting inside.

Leaning back against the desk with his arms crossed, he looked beautiful and fuckable and wryly amused. The door shut behind me and he sighed, shaking his head.

"Are there other people in my life you plan on harassing on my behalf?" he asked.

"Are you spying on me again?"

"Keeping a protective eye on you."

I arched a brow at him. "And how do you know if I harassed him or not?"

His faint smile widened. "Because I know you."

"Well, I didn't harass him. Really. I didn't," I argued when he shot me a look of disbelief. "I was going to, but then I didn't. And why are we in this room?"

"Are you on some kind of crusade, angel?"

We were talking around each other, and I wasn't sure why. And I didn't care, because something else struck me as more significant.

"Do you realize that your reaction to my lunch with Christopher is very calm? And so is my reaction to you spending time with Corinne? We're both reacting totally different from the way we would have just a month ago."

He was different. He smiled, and there was something unique about that warm curving of his lips. "We trust each other, Eva. It feels good, doesn't it?"

"Trusting you doesn't mean I'm any less baffled by what's going on between us. Why are we hiding in this office?"

"Plausible deniability." Gideon straightened and came to me. Cupping my face in his hands, he tilted my head back and kissed me sweetly. "I love you."

"You're getting good at saying that."

He ran his fingers through my new bangs. "Remember that night, when you had your nightmare and I was out late? You wondered where I was."

"I still wonder."

"I was at the hotel, clearing out that room. My fuck pad, as you called it. Explaining that while you were puking your guts out didn't seem to be the appropriate time."

My breath left me in a rush. It was a relief to know where he'd been. An even bigger relief to know that the fuck pad was no more.

His gaze was soft as he looked at me. "I'd completely forgotten about it until it came up with Dr. Petersen. We both know I'll never use it again. My girl prefers modes of transportation to beds."

He smiled and walked out. I stared after him.

The security guard filled the open doorway and I shoved aside my roiling thoughts to examine later, when I had the time to really grasp where they were leading me.

ON the walk home, I picked up a bottle of sparkling apple juice in lieu of champagne. I saw the Bentley every now and then, following along, ever ready to pull over and pick me up. It used to irritate me, because the lingering connection it represented deepened my confusion over my breakup with Gideon. Now, the sight of it made me smile.

Dr. Petersen had been right. Abstinence and some space had cleared my head. Somehow, the distance between me and Gideon had made us stronger, made us appreciate each other more and take less for granted. I loved him more now than I ever had, and I felt that way while I was planning on a night just hanging out with my roommate, having no idea where Gideon was or who he might be with. It didn't matter. I knew I was in his thoughts, in his heart.

My phone rang and I pulled it out of my purse. Seeing my mother's name on the screen, I answered with, "Hi, Mom."

"I don't understand what they're looking for!" she complained, sounding angry and tearful. "They won't leave Richard alone. They went to his offices today and took copies of the security tapes."

"The detectives?"

"Yes. They're relentless. What do they want?"

I turned the corner to reach my street. "To catch a killer. They probably just want to see Nathan coming and going. Check the timing or something."

"That's ridiculous!"

"Yeah, it's also just a guess. Don't worry. There's nothing to find because Stanton's innocent. Everything will be okay."

"He's been so good about this, Eva," she said softly. "He's so good to me."

I sighed, hearing the pleading note in her voice. "I know, Mom. I get it. Dad gets it. You're where you should be. No one's judging you. We're all good."

It took me until I reached my front door to calm her down, during which time I wondered what the detectives would see if they pulled the Crossfire security tapes, too. The history of my relationship with Gideon could be chronicled through the times I'd been in the Cross Industries vestibule with him. He'd first propositioned me there, bluntly stating his desire. He'd pinned me to the wall there, right after I'd agreed to date him exclusively. And he'd rejected my touch that horrible day when he had first started pulling away from me. The detectives would see it all if they looked back far enough, those private and personal moments in time.

"Call me if you need me," I said as I dropped my bag and purse off at the breakfast bar. "I'll be home all night."

We hung up, and I noticed an unfamiliar trench coat slung over one of the bar stools. I shouted out to Cary, "Honey, I'm home!"

I put the bottle of apple juice in the fridge and headed down the hallway to my bedroom for a shower. I was on the threshold of my room when Cary's door opened and Tatiana came out. My eyes widened at the sight of her naughty nurse costume, complete with exposed garters and fishnets.

"Hey, honey," she said, looking smug. She was astonishingly tall in her heels, towering over me. A successful model, Tatiana Cherlin had the kind of face and body that could stop traffic. "Take care of him for me."

Blinking, I watched the leggy blonde disappear into the living room. I heard the front door shut a short time later.

Cary appeared in his doorway, looking mussed and flushed and wearing only his boxer briefs. He leaned into the doorway with a lazy, satisfied grin. "Hey."

"Hey, yourself. Looks like you had a good day."

"Hell yeah."

That made me smile. "No judgment here, but I assumed you and Tatiana were done."

"I never thought we got started." He ran a hand through his hair, ruffling it. "Then she showed up today all worried and apologetic. She's been in Prague and didn't hear about me until this morning. She rushed over wearing that, like she read my perverted mind."

I leaned into my doorway, too. "Guess she knows you."

"Guess she does." He shrugged. "We'll see how it goes. She knows Trey's in my life and I hope to keep him there. Trey, though . . . I know he won't like it."

I felt for both men. It was going to take a lot of compromising for their relationship to work out. "How about we forget about our significant others for a night and have an action movie marathon? I brought some nonalcoholic champagne home."

His brows rose. "Where's the fun in that?"

"Can't mix your meds with booze, you know," I said dryly.

"No Krav Maga for you tonight?"

"I'll make it up tomorrow. I feel like chilling with you. I want to sprawl on the couch, and eat pizza with chopsticks and Chinese food with my fingers."

"You're a rebel, baby girl." He grinned. "And you've got yourself a date."

PARKER hit the mat with a grunt and I shouted, thrilled with my own success.

"Yes," I said with a fist pump. Learning to toss a guy as heavy as Parker was no small feat. Finding the right balance to gain the leverage I needed had taken me longer than it probably should have because I'd had such a hard time concentrating over the last couple of weeks.

There was no balance in my life when my relationship with Gideon was skewed.

Laughing, Parker reached out to me for a hand up. I gripped his forearm and tugged him to his feet.

"Good. Very good," he praised. "You're firing on all cylinders tonight."

"Thanks. Wanna try it again?"

"Take a ten-minute break and hydrate," he said. "I need to talk to Jeremy before he takes off."

Jeremy was one of Parker's co-instructors, a giant of a man that the students had to work their way up to. Right then, I couldn't imagine ever being able to fend off an assailant of his size, but I'd seen some really petite women in the class do it.

I grabbed my towel and my water and headed toward the aluminum bleachers lined up against the wall. My steps faltered when I saw one of the detectives who'd come to my apartment. Detective Shelley Graves wasn't dressed for work, though. She wore a sports top and matching pants with athletic shoes, and her dark, curly hair was pulled back in a ponytail.

Since she was just entering the building and the door happened to be next to the bleachers, I found myself walking toward her. I forced myself to look nonchalant when I felt anything but.

"Miss Tramell," she greeted me. "Fancy running into you here. Have you been working with Parker long?"

"About a month. It's good to see you, Detective."

"No, it's not." Her mouth twisted wryly. "At least you don't think so. Yet. Maybe you still won't when we're done chatting."

I frowned, confused by that tangle of words. Still, one thing was clear. "I can't speak to you without my attorney present."

She spread her arms wide. "I'm off-duty. But anyway, you don't have to say anything. I'll do all the talking."

Graves gestured toward the bleachers, and I reluctantly took a seat. I had damn good reason to be wary.

"How about we move a little higher?" She climbed to the top, and I stood and followed.

Once we were settled, she set her forearms on her knees and looked at the students below. "It's different here at night. I usually catch the day sessions. I told myself that on the off chance I happened to run into you off-duty someday, I'd talk to you. I figured the odds of that were nil. And lo and behold, here you are. It must be a sign."

I wasn't buying the additional explanation. "You don't strike me as the type to believe in signs."

"You've got me there, but I'll make an exception in this case." Her lips pursed for a moment, as if she were thinking hard about something. Then she looked at me. "I think your boyfriend killed Nathan Barker."

I stiffened, my breath catching audibly.

"I'll never be able to prove it," she said grimly. "He's too smart.

Too thorough. The whole thing was precisely premeditated. The moment Gideon Cross came to the decision to kill Nathan Barker, he had his ducks in a row."

I couldn't decide if I should stay or go—what the ramifications would be of either decision. And in that moment of indecisiveness, she kept talking.

"I believe it started the Monday after your roommate was attacked. When we searched the hotel room where Barker's body was discovered, we found photos. A lot of photos of you, but the ones I'm talking about were of your roommate."

"Cary?"

"If I were to present this to the ADA for an arrest warrant, I would say that Nathan Barker attacked Cary Taylor as a way to intimidate and threaten Gideon Cross. My guess is that Cross wasn't conceding to Barker's blackmail demands."

My hands twisted in my towel. I couldn't stand the thought of Cary suffering what he had because of me.

Graves looked at me, her gaze sharp and flat. Cop's eyes. My dad had them, too. "At that point, I think Cross perceived you to be in mortal danger. And you know what? He was right. I've seen the evidence we collected from Barker's room—photos, detailed notes of your daily schedule, news clippings . . . even some of your garbage. Usually when we find that sort of thing, it's too late."

"Nathan was watching me?" Just the thought sent a violent shiver through me.

"He was stalking you. The blackmail demands he made on your stepfather and Cross were just an escalation of that. I think Cross was getting too close to you, and Barker felt threatened by your relationship. I believe he hoped Cross would step away if he knew about your past."

I held the towel to my mouth, in case I became as sick as I felt.

"So here's how I think it went down." Graves tapped her finger-tips together, her attention seemingly on the strenuous drills below. "Cross cut you off, started seeing an old flame. That served two purposes—it made Barker relax, and it wiped out Cross's motive. Why would he kill a man over a woman he'd dumped? He set that up pretty well—he didn't tell you. You strengthened the lie with your honest reactions."

Her foot started tapping along with her fingers, her slim body radiating restless energy. "Cross doesn't hire out the job. That would be stupid. He doesn't want the money trail or a hit man who could rat him out. Besides, this is personal. *You're* personal. He wants the threat gone without a doubt. He sets up a last-minute party at one of his properties for some vodka company of his. Now he's got a rock-solid alibi. Even the press is there to snap pictures. And he knows precisely where you are and that your alibi is rock-solid, too."

My fingers clenched in the towel. *My God* . . .

The sounds of bodies hitting the mat, the hum of instructions being given, and the triumphant shouts of students all faded into a steady buzzing in my ears. There was a flurry of activity happening right in front of me and my brain couldn't process it. I had a sense of retreating down an endless tunnel, my reality shrinking to a tiny black point.

Opening her bottle of water, Graves drank deeply, then wiped her mouth with the back of her hand. "I'll admit, the party tripped me up a bit. How do you break an alibi like that? I had to go back to the hotel three times before I learned there was a fire in the kitchen that night. Nothing major, but the entire hotel was evacuated for close to an hour. All the guests were milling on the sidewalk. Cross was in and out of the hotel doing whatever an owner would do under those circumstances. I talked to a half dozen employees who saw him or talked to him around then, but none of them could pinpoint times for me. All agreed it was chaotic. Who could keep track of one guy in that mess?"

I felt myself shaking my head, as if she'd been directing the question at me.

She rolled her shoulders back. "I timed the walk from the service entrance—where Cross was seen talking to the FDNY—to Barker's hotel a couple blocks over. Fifteen minutes each way. Barker was taken out by a single stab wound to the chest. Right in the heart. Would've taken no more than a minute. No defensive wounds and he was found just inside the door. My guess? He opened the door to Cross and it was over before he could blink. And get this . . . *That* hotel is owned by a subsidiary of Cross Industries. And the security cameras in the building just happened to be down for an upgrade that's been in the works for several months."

"Coincidence," I said hoarsely. My heart was pounding. In a distant part of my brain, I registered that there were a dozen people just a few feet away, going about their lives without a clue that another human being in the room was dealing with a catastrophic event.

"Sure. Why not?" Graves shrugged, but her eyes gave her away. She *knew*. She couldn't prove it, but she knew. "So here's the thing: I could keep digging and spending time on this case while there are others on my desk. But what's the point? Cross isn't a danger to the public. My partner will tell you it's never okay to take the law into your own hands. And for the most part, I'm on the same page. But Nathan Barker was going to kill you. Maybe not next week. Maybe not next year. But someday."

She stood and brushed off her pants, picked up her water and towel, and ignored the fact that I was sobbing uncontrollably.

Gideon . . . I pressed the towel to my face, overwhelmed.

"I burned my notes," she went on. "My partner agrees we've hit a dead end. No one gives a shit that Nathan Barker isn't breathing

REFLECTED IN YOU · 337

our air anymore. Even his father told me he considered his son dead years ago."

I looked up at her, blinking to clear the haze of tears from my eyes. "I don't know what to say."

"You broke up with him on the Saturday after we interrupted your dinner, didn't you?" She nodded when I did. "He was in the station then, giving a statement. He stepped out of the room, but I could see him through the window in the door. The only time I've seen pain like that is when I'm notifying next of kin. To be honest, that's why I'm telling you this now—so you can go back to him."

"Thank you." I'd never put as much feeling into those two words as I did then.

Shaking her head, she started to walk back down the stairs, then stopped and turned, looking up at me. "I'm not the one you should be thanking."

SOMEHOW, I ended up at Gideon's apartment.

I don't remember leaving Parker's studio or telling Clancy where to take me. I don't remember checking in with the front desk or riding the elevator up. When I found myself in the private foyer facing Gideon's door, I had to stop a moment, unsure of how I'd gotten from the bleachers to that point.

I rang the bell and waited. When no one answered, I sank to the floor and leaned back against the door.

Gideon found me there. The elevator doors opened and he stepped out, stopping abruptly when he saw me. He was dressed in workout clothes and his hair was still damp with sweat. He'd never looked more wonderful.

He was staring at me, unmoving, so I explained, "I don't have a key anymore."

I didn't get up because I wasn't sure my legs would support me.

He crouched. "Eva? What's wrong?"

"I ran into Detective Graves tonight." I swallowed past the knot in my throat. "They're dropping the case."

His chest expanded on a deep breath.

With that sound, I *knew*.

Dark desolation shadowed Gideon's beautiful eyes. He knew that I knew. The truth hung heavy in the air between us, a near-tangible thing.

I'd kill for you, give up everything I own for you . . . but I won't give you up.

Gideon fell to his knees on the cold, hard marble. His head bowed. Waiting.

I shifted, mirroring his kneeling pose. I lifted his chin. Touched his face with my hands and my lips. My gratitude for his gift whispered over his skin: *Thank you . . . thank you . . . thank you.*

He caught me to him, his arms banded tight around me. His face pressed into my throat. "Where do we go from here?"

I held him. "Wherever this takes us. Together."

GIDEON AND EVA'S STORY CONTINUES

IN THE POWERFULLY SENSUAL

THIRD NOVEL IN THE CROSSFIRE SERIES

ENTWINED
WITH YOU

Now available from Berkley Books!